The Good Fortune of Miss Robbins

The Good Fortune of Miss Robbins

MELANIE DICKERSON

BETHANYHOUSE
a division of Baker Publishing Group
Minneapolis, Minnesota

Published by Bethany House Publishers
Minneapolis, Minnesota
BethanyHouse.com

Bethany House Publishers is a division of
Baker Publishing Group, Grand Rapids, Michigan

Printed in the United States of America

Library of Congress Cataloging-in-Publication Data
Names: Dickerson, Melanie, author
Title: The Good Fortune of Miss Robbins / Melanie Dickerson.
Description: Minneapolis, Minnesota: Bethany House, a division of Baker Publishing Group, 2026.
Identifiers: LCCN 2025026531 | ISBN 9780764245220 paperback | ISBN 9780764246074 casebound | ISBN 9781493452477 ebook
Subjects: LCGFT: Fiction | Christian fiction | Romance fiction | Novels
Classification: LCC PS3604.I2253 G66 2026 | DDC 813/.6—dc23/eng/20250626
LC record available at https://lccn.loc.gov/2025026531

Scripture quotations are from the King James Version of the Bible.

This book is a work of fiction. Names, characters, places, and incidents are the product of the author's imagination or are used fictitiously. Any resemblance to actual events, locales, or persons, living or dead, is coincidental.

Cover design by Design Source Creative Services, Dan Thornberg

Image of couple holding hands by Lee Avison / Trevillion Images

The author is represented by the literary agency of Gardner Literary Agency.

Baker Publishing Group publications use paper produced from sustainable forestry practices and postconsumer waste whenever possible.

26 27 28 29 30 31 32 7 6 5 4 3 2

To Aaron.

I have found the one my heart loves.

Part One

One

March 1814
Bedfordshire, England

Charlotte! A letter came for you!" Hattie Jacobs emerged from the back entrance of Mrs. Southey's School for Young Ladies, waving something over her head.

I'd advertised months ago and received one reply from a Mrs. Merryweather, asking for letters of reference, which I'd supplied. Could the lady be writing to offer me a position?

I met Hattie in the middle of the garden and took the folded paper from her. It was the same address! In Berkshire, a Mrs. Merryweather of Lowndesbury House. It did not go unnoticed, either, that this letter had been franked by a peer of the realm.

"Well? Open it!" Hattie said.

I was already unfolding the paper. I skipped the initial polite greeting and read silently.

If Miss Charlotte Robbins remains unattached, we would like to offer the position of governess to her, with the salary of forty pounds per annum, for two young charges: seven-year-old twins, a boy and a girl. If this is agreeable, please respond . . .

"My father sent my nurse Addy away when I was at school, dismissed her with a yearly allowance that was hardly enough money to buy food, with nothing left over for lodging. Therefore she had to live with and care for her sister, who had consumption. And she soon became ill herself. She died of the same malady as her sister."

"I am so sorry."

"As soon as I discovered what manner of life she was living, I sent money and made certain she had the best care, but of course, she never recovered."

"That was very kind of you. I am sure she knew how much you cared for her and she was comforted by that," I said.

"No more than she deserved, as she is my example of a good mother. But perhaps it is thoughtless of me to speak of such a thing with you. You are an orphan and never knew your mother, I suppose."

"I don't remember my mother, nor any of my family, except for the haziest memory of her lying sick. But I don't mind hearing about yours."

He gave me a look so warm and compassionate that it quite took my breath away.

We were quiet for a minute. Then, in a more businesslike tone, he said, "I did want to reiterate that I appreciated your assistance after the accident, even if Mr. and Miss Skidmore did not take the time to thank you. You were of great help."

"Of course, my lord. It was no trouble."

"And I would like to receive a report from you of the children's progress every Friday afternoon. If there are any books or materials you need for their instruction, you can give me your list at that time."

"Yes, sir."

"And if you wish them to take some of their lessons out of doors, you may. Children need fresh air and sunshine."

"Thank you, sir. I agree."

"And you found the post office all right?"

"Yes, sir."

I whooped and threw my hands in the air, clutching the letter.

"You have a position? Who is your employer? When do you start?" Hattie leaned her curly blond head closer.

I held the letter out so she could see it. She read aloud.

"'If this is agreeable, please respond with a date when we might expect you at Lowndesbury House at the address on this letter. And do not bring too many possessions, as your quarters will be small and modest, but adequate. The last governess brought so many things there was not enough room to stow them. Respectfully, Mrs. Kathleen Merryweather, housekeeper to the Earl of Brookhaven.'"

Hattie gasped and grabbed my arm. "You are the new governess for the Earl of Brookhaven's siblings." Her eyes were wide, her mouth forming an O.

"What? Is that bad?"

"Yes!" Hattie looked positively stricken. "I told you my cousin's friend worked as the governess there, for the earl's half-brother and sister. The earl pays a handsome salary, to be sure, but she was dismissed after only two weeks."

"Maybe she did something wrong."

"I forget the particulars, but it was a very small, piddling thing—not enough to dismiss someone for. She said he was horrid, scowling all the time, and never spoke a kind word to her. I would be terrified." Hattie clapped a hand over her mouth, then said, "Forgive me. I don't mean to frighten you."

"I'm not frightened. I've never met an earl. It should be interesting, at the very least."

"I should have known you would say something of that sort, Charlotte." Hattie shook her head. "You're not afraid of anything."

I started to protest and say that I *was* afraid of a great many things. Presently, I was afraid of getting stuck at Mrs. Southey's school for the rest of my life. But that wouldn't have been very kind to say, since Hattie had no other ambition than to teach here. Hattie and I were the same age, and she was like a beloved sister to me, but sometimes I felt as if she'd been born old.

I looked at my letter again, then clutched it to my chest. I was finally going out into the world. Adventure awaited me, I just knew it.

Inside, Hattie retrieved her box of newspaper gossip columns that she'd collected. She found two that contained gossip about the Earl of Brookhaven.

The young earl had once been engaged to be married, but his fiancée ran off with a marquess. His mother and father, according to the newspapers, had had numerous paramours.

When his wife died, the older earl married a much younger woman, who died giving birth to twins, then the earl passed away a year later, and the only son of his first wife became the new Earl of Brookhaven and inherited the house, the title, and the guardianship of the twins.

The young earl was also said to be quite handsome.

Fascinating people and places were in my future. And the most cherished dream of all—that I would fall in love, marry, and have a real family—drove me forward. Now that I was leaving this place, with its limited number of people and lack of exciting things to see or do, I'd finally have a chance to experience something new and different.

I went inside, wrote my letter to Mrs. Merryweather accepting the position, and walked a half mile and into the village to post it. Then I began the process of saying goodbye to everyone I knew.

Mrs. Southey gave me an intense look. "You have a place here if you decide to return. I can always use a good teacher."

"Thank you, Mrs. Southey."

She stroked my cheek with the back of her soft, wrinkled hand—as much affection as one could ever hope for from her. "Don't forget to write."

"I won't."

When I'd bid farewell to my pupils, a few of the younger ones cried, which made me cry and feel a bit guilty for leaving them—

especially for being happy about leaving. Then I said goodbye to Hattie and Susan, another fellow teacher and schoolmate, who'd also stayed on to teach.

"You won't forget us, will you?" Hattie dabbed at her eyes with a handkerchief.

"Of course not. How could I forget my family?" I touched Hattie's cheek with the back of my hand, the way Mrs. Southey did.

"We are your family," Susan said in her no-nonsense way. "We shall welcome a visit from you when you are able."

"Thank you, Susan." I appreciated the warm—for Susan—sentiment, but I sincerely hoped I would not be coming back. After I married, I would send for Hattie and Susan to come and visit *me.*

How that would happen to a governess, I did not know, but anything seemed possible now that I had a position.

I'd pictured myself setting out in a fine carriage on a warm, sunny day, the light shining around me as all the pupils and teachers from Mrs. Southey's School for Young Ladies waved to me. Instead, it was before dawn and quite dark when I stepped into the empty mail coach to start my journey. Only Hattie was there, and she clutched my hand tightly while saying, "I'll pray for your safe journey. Write me every detail as soon as you arrive."

Sweet Hattie. She preferred reading the gossip columns to almost anything else, but she had no longing for adventure. She did have a big, warm, childlike heart, and I loved her at least as much as I could love a blood sister. The people at Mrs. Southey's School for Young Ladies were the only family I'd ever known, and I felt a stab of fear that no one would ever love me again.

But as the sun began spreading light over the road, I drew in a deep breath of crisp spring air. Spring was surely the best time of the year—for Mrs. Southey's garden, for the wildflowers on the roadside, and for a new life.

I was five-and-twenty, and I'd never seen anything beyond the village of Milford in Bedfordshire.

Visions of ocean vistas, rides in carriages through London, castles and palaces, hills and lakes floated through my mind. I imagined the world as a wondrous place with rivers, waterfalls, and flowering trees, magnificent sunsets and vast rolling hills, and cliffs overlooking crashing waves of the vast blue sea.

I knew, of course, that most of England probably looked very much like the tame, ordered countryside around Milford, the village and the school that had been my home since I was five years old. But with all my heart, I wanted to see for myself all the places and things I'd only read about in books.

Other passengers entered the carriage at various stops on the road, and I had new people to observe. A rosy-cheeked woman with a chicken in a basket on her lap. A man wearing a top hat and a ragged coat. A blond lady wearing a smart bonnet with a pink ribbon and silk flowers.

Now I was a woman of the world, with a purpose and a position awaiting me at my destination. But I also felt small, a girl traveling alone, an orphan, acquainted with very few people outside of Mrs. Southey's School for Young Ladies.

For most of the trip, I watched out the window, my eyes wide so I could catch as many sights—forests, lakes, streams, hills, horses, and carriages—as possible. A person never knew when they might catch a glimpse of their future. And I could hardly wait to see the Earl of Brookhaven's manor, Lowndesbury House.

I had to change coaches two hours after sunrise, where I was crammed inside a carriage that smelled worse—much worse—than the woman's chicken in a basket. A man seated across from me held a handkerchief to his nose the whole time, but I was blessed to be seated next to a window and could hold my face into the springtime air filled with flowers and sunshine.

We stopped at an inn for my final change. I took the opportunity to tidy my hair before boarding a hired curricle that would take me the last few miles. I climbed onto the seat, clutching my smaller bag while thinking of my other one, which had been stowed.

The driver was not a talkative man and sat hunched over, staring straight ahead every time I looked over at him, which was not often, as I was taken with the countryside. So green and lush! These were fortunate sheep grazing in such abundant grass, a small stream running through the middle of their pasture. I even saw a lamb jump up and kick its hind feet in the air, and my heart mimicked it.

I drew in deep, long draughts of the Berkshire air, squinting at the trees in the distance. And then I saw it on a hill a mile away, all sprawling gray stone, so magnificent, with towers that reminded me of the Milford church's bell tower, though this house was far larger and grander than the Milford church, or any other building I'd ever laid eyes on. It looked as if it had been built at least a century or two ago, which made it all the more exciting. Three towers rose above the rest of the house, and stone crenellations encircled the perimeter of the rooflines.

Lowndesbury House.

It was like a medieval castle from a storybook.

Oh, please let me explore every nook and cranny in the house. And let me find a secret room or two and a hidden staircase, please, Lord.

I wanted to know everything, everyone who had ever lived there, the entire history of it. If only I could explore it for the rest of my life.

Well, that was a silly thought. But if I happened to marry the earl's steward, perhaps I would.

There were a few positions at the earl's manor house that would be suitable for me as possible husbands, and they were the earl's steward, the butler, and possibly even the chef, gamekeeper, or the head gardener, if they were more genteel than the average of their set.

In the time leading up to this journey, I'd imagined an entire novel in my head of meeting Lord Brookhaven's steward, exchanging glances with him, then conversations when I chanced to meet him in a corridor or at mealtimes. And then when the earl held a ball at Lowndesbury House, the steward would find me outside in the garden, listening to the music, and ask me to dance. I'd finally be able to use my dancing skills with an eligible man! We would dance in the garden all night, and then, the next day, he would beg me to marry him.

Sometimes, instead of the steward, it would be the gamekeeper. Sometimes it was even the son of a baron or viscount who had his own wealth and would whisk me away to the Continent until society had forgotten that I was just a lowly orphan and governess, and we would return to England and host lovely parties, and the kindest and best women of society would become my dearest friends.

I shouldn't imagine myself marrying so high, for that might make it more difficult for my friends at Mrs. Southey's school to feel comfortable visiting me. But I supposed there was no harm in dreaming about it. I dreamed about many things when I was lonely and pondering how many children in the world had families who loved them, mothers and fathers, grandparents, aunts and uncles who cared about them, while I had no one. And when I found myself ruminating on such gloomy thoughts, I would start making up stories in which I was the heroine. Some of these fanciful stories were short, but many of them were long and intricate, and always ended with me marrying a man who adored me and living happily ever after.

Now I was far from Milford, on my own, traveling to the largest and most elaborate grand home that I'd ever seen by far, and I would be meeting an earl, a peer of the realm, and teaching his two half-siblings.

It was as if one of my made-up stories was coming true.

Two

Hattie's newspapers said the young Lord Brookhaven was quite handsome. Now I could be the judge of that, as well as of his severity, which didn't frighten me as much as it might some, since I seemed to attract severe people. Like the old Lord Hampton, who was the patron of Milford's church and treated me almost as a granddaughter, and the senior teacher at Mrs. Southey's school, who most of the other teachers were afraid of, but who made me her friend and left me her life savings—ten pounds—when she died. It seemed that they were drawn by the fact that I wasn't frightened by them.

But it's not that I wasn't afraid of anything, as Hattie had said. I was frightened of the same things as anyone else. But I befriended ill-tempered people because I wanted to discover why they were so unhappy.

As the curricle went around the side of the main building and came to a halt at the servants' entrance, I blinked to dispel a light-headed feeling. I probably should have eaten more of my bread and cheese that I'd brought with me.

As soon as the curricle halted, I hurried to step down. A servant boy emerged from the house and helped the driver retrieve my stowed luggage. Then the driver was on his way again, the gravel crunching under the wheels and horse plodding forward.

The servant boy stared at me, holding my bag with both hands, his eyes questioning.

"I'm Charlotte Robbins, the new governess." I smiled at him.

He said nothing.

"What's your name?"

"John."

A woman emerged from the house.

"You're finally here. Come, come." She stood in the doorway, her face scrunching as she looked at me. "John." She motioned to the boy.

I followed the woman, John practically running behind me, as she moved quickly through the dimly lit hallways.

The walls and floors were made of stone, and I imagined I was in a castle, headed to my room in the tallest turret. When we started up some narrow, winding stairs, I imagined a princess, flanked in front and behind by guards, being led up this same staircase two hundred years ago, taken to the very top to be locked away until her father paid her ransom.

We did indeed keep climbing until I was sure we were on the top floor. We walked down the hallway to the last door, where Mrs. Merryweather stopped, rattled her keys, and unlocked it.

"This will be your room. I am sure you will find it sufficient." She handed me the key.

There was a narrow bed, two slatted wooden chairs, and a washstand with a pitcher and basin. I liked the small window that let in some light. The room was not so different from the room I shared with Hattie at Mrs. Southey's school.

John scuttled past us, placed my bag against the wall, then slipped out.

"You could probably do with a hot meal, but I thought you might like to make a brief appearance with the children in the schoolroom first. Lord Brookhaven has been giving them lessons since the last governess was dismissed." She scrunched her face again, which I realized was her way of frowning.

"I should very much like to meet the children."

I interpreted the new look that came over her wrinkled face as one of grudging approval, but it quickly vanished. "The master allows the governess to call them by their given names, Annabelle and Samuel."

What else might I have been expected to call them? Then I reminded myself, when they grew older their position in society would be far above mine. But they were still children, and I was their governess.

I set my smaller bag on the bed and followed Mrs. Merryweather back along the hall and down more stairs in a different part of the house, trying to remember each turn so I could get back. But I got distracted by the views out of the windows—long vistas of sheep grazing among wildflowers, gently rolling hills, a few large oak trees. It was so lovely! But it made me forget to count the last turn. Or was it two turns?

One more hall and Mrs. Merryweather paused in a doorway, staring at me as I caught up. Then, with me peering around her shoulder, she turned to my young pupils. They were seated at a table, their little faces looking curiously at us.

"Children, this is your new governess, Miss Robbins. Greet her properly." The housekeeper gave them a stern look.

"How do you do, Miss Robbins?" they replied in unison.

"Very well, I thank you." I smiled at them. "May I ask what you're working on?" I moved into the room to see.

"William wants us to read this book before he gets home." The little girl, Annabelle, looked up with big, doleful eyes.

It was jarring to hear her using the earl's given name. But then, he was her brother.

"Have you ever been a governess before?" Samuel asked, one corner of his mouth quirked up.

"That is an impertinent question." Mrs. Merryweather's frown was back.

Samuel gave her a blank stare.

I'd have to earn the respect of this one. Annabelle, on the other hand, had a slightly timid look of interest.

"Miss Robbins," Mrs. Merryweather said, "I can take you back to your room if you go right now. I have other duties to attend to."

"If I stay a little while, can the children show me the way to my room?"

"Certainly not." Her expression soured. "But when their nurse-maid Hannah returns, she can escort you." Mrs. Merryweather darted away before I could say anything.

"How do you like the housekeeper?" Samuel gave a sly grin.

I tried to think how to answer. I settled for just raising my eye-brows at him. "Do you find your reading interesting? Would you prefer if I read to you?"

"Oh, yes, please!" Annabelle said.

I could see Annabelle was on page fifteen, while Samuel was on page three. I sat next to Samuel in one of the little chairs and slid his book between us.

"I shall start at the beginning, if that's all right."

Annabelle nodded and turned her book to the first page.

I began to read aloud. When I noticed Samuel fidgeting, I stopped. "How long have you been in the schoolroom?"

"Since this morning," Samuel said.

It was nearly five in the afternoon.

"It's a sunny day. If I read quickly, we should have time for a short walk before the evening meal. Will that suit?"

Samuel's eyes lit up. Annabelle smiled and nodded.

I read the rest of the book quickly. It was quite dry and dull for a child to have to listen to. If they made children's schoolbooks more appropriate to a child's mind and interests, children might behave better and learn more. It wasn't the first time I'd thought such a thing, nor was it the first time I vowed to write a book myself.

I'd finished the little book just as Hannah entered the room.

The children jumped up and went to fetch their outer clothing.

"I'm Charlotte Robbins, the new governess." I smiled at Hannah.

The nursemaid must have been around my age. She looked me in the eyes and dropped a quick curtsy. "Hannah," she said.

"Pleased to meet you, Hannah. I promised the children I'd take them for a short walk. Is there a garden for walking?"

"Yes, miss, but the master doesn't allow the young ones near the road." Her mouth looked pinched.

"Very well. We won't be long, and we won't go near the road."

I helped the children with their sturdier shoes, then they led me to the back door and out into the fresh air and sunshine. They ran as fast as they could through the garden, playing hide-and-seek and blindman's buff and generally chasing each other around.

Although I was enjoying the formal garden, I longed to explore the park nearby, with its less formal, more wild appearance, the trees and bushes growing randomly instead of in strict rows according to some human plan.

I walked, stopping to examine a pretty flower or a particularly lovely corner of the garden, until I got dizzy and had to stop and blink.

"Come!" a voice called out.

I turned to see the nursemaid standing in the back doorway, motioning to the children. They came running while she glared at me. "You kept them out too long. They'll be late for their supper."

"Forgive me." I started to say something about feeling half-starved myself, but she continued to stare coldly at me.

The children were pink-cheeked and bright-eyed. It made my heart lift to see the wan look gone from their faces.

A servant was descending some stairs, which I presumed led to the kitchen, from the savory smell that wafted from that direction.

"I shall make my way to the kitchen," I said to Hannah.

She didn't look back at me, and only said, "Just as you please."

Mrs. Southey had warned me that the servants would shun me and refuse to be friendly, but I'd hoped that was an exaggeration. Perhaps it wasn't.

My position as governess granted me a higher status as well as a higher salary than the servants, and though I was considered too low to socialize with the family, the servants wouldn't socialize with me either. They would resent me for my higher salary and status, and they would assume I, with my education, would consider them beneath me.

Downstairs, the kitchen servants were bustling about, and the chef was barking orders while stirring a steaming pot. I tried to catch someone's eye, but everyone seemed too busy to notice me. I approached a young red-faced woman kneading bread dough as if she was angry with it.

"Pardon me, but I'm the new governess, Miss Robbins, and I was wondering if I might have a small—"

"Bessie!" the chef shouted.

The shout was so loud I jumped and knocked over a tin of salt or sugar, which spilled all over the table on which the woman was working.

"Oh!" She looked at me, tears starting to leak from the corners of her eyes.

"Please forgive me. Let me help." I righted the tin of salt, but the woman held up her hand.

"No. I have it."

"What are you doing in here?" The chef, a large man with wiry hair, had turned from the stove. His and every other pair of eyes in the room were on me.

"Forgive me, I—"

His voice was deep and hard-edged. "You can have your dinner when the family is served. Come back then. Meantime, there's some bread over there." He pointed to a basket on the counter.

"Thank you." My cheeks were burning, and my stomach felt sick.

The chef began talking to Bessie, the girl who had come running when her name was called. The rest of the women went back to what they were doing, mumbling or shaking their heads.

I snatched a roll from the basket and hurried out of the kitchen.

Such an embarrassing first meeting with the servants—and I felt I could rule out the chef as a potential husband.

I trudged up the stairs, woefully aware that I didn't know the way to my bedroom. I did manage to find the schoolroom. From outside the doorway, I heard Hannah instructing the children to wash their hands and scolding them for getting their shoes muddy.

Hannah was obviously busy, so I kept going, thinking I could surely find my way back to my room alone. I turned one corner and then another. I went up some stairs, but it was clearly not the right way, so I went back down again. I finally gave up even trying to find my way and just wandered around, looking into open doors at dimly lit rooms of dark wood and furnishings, windows covered by heavy red drapes, and many more closed doors. I was thoroughly lost, but I kept going down hallways and up and down stairs.

Near tears, I sat on the stairs and ate my roll. That made me feel less dizzy and sick, so I got up, took a deep breath, and said a whispered prayer that consisted solely of "Lord God, please help me." I continued up the staircase until I was at the very top, then I climbed out onto the roof.

Nighttime was fast approaching, with shadows stretching across the green lawn below. A boy with a stick was minding the small group of sheep that were no doubt meant to keep the grass cropped short. A man was leading a horse toward a stable. In the distance I could see a small village where I should be able to post my letters to Mrs. Southey's school.

As I stared across the expanse below, a weight seemed to settle on my shoulders. How I missed my friends and my home! I was so far away and didn't know when I'd see them again.

This was a wretched beginning. I'd imagined seeing wondrous sights, meeting interesting people, and exploring this old house like it was an exotic historical artifact with secrets waiting for me to discover. Instead, I felt small and alone. Anything that might be wondrous or worth discovering seemed out of my reach. I was bothersome to the servants trying to do their work, and I was the governess whom no one wanted to know.

Had I made a terrible mistake in coming here, in leaving all my friends and the school where I felt safe? Would I prove true the old saying, "The harvest always looks greater in another man's field"?

Tiny lights became visible in the windows of the houses in the village beyond the trees, and a single tear dribbled down my cheek. I stepped closer to the edge of the roof and stumbled over a broken branch, making a noise.

A shadow moved at the other end of the tower roof.

"Who's there?" a deep voice said.

Three

I flicked the tear off my cheek with my finger and turned toward the voice.

"Miss Robbins," I answered, taking a deep breath in an effort to push back my tears.

The shadowy figure moved closer but stopped thirty feet away. He was dressed like a gentleman, though his cravat had been untied and hung loose in front. I couldn't see his features clearly, but I could make out that he was quite tall.

"I don't know any Miss Robbins." His voice was gruff.

"I'm the new governess."

He stood facing me, and since the sun was going down behind him, I couldn't see his eyes. However, the waning light was illuminating my face. I felt as if I were being scrutinized. Strangely, it didn't bother me.

After a long pause, he mumbled, "Mrs. Merryweather handles the hiring of the governesses."

Could he be Lord Brookhaven? Of course he was. Who else would he be? I curtsied, my heart in my throat at meeting the earl and lord of Lowndesbury House, especially in such a manner.

I waited for him to speak again. He turned back toward the crenellations and looked out over the edge. "How do you like the view?"

"It is impressive, my lord."

"Impressive? That is an unspecific word. How else might you describe it?"

I was as surprised at him starting such a conversation with me as I was determined not to show it. He'd asked for my opinion, and truthfully, I was delighted to share it.

"It is lovely and puts one in mind of a master painter's interpretation of the most picturesque countryside, with the large trees and grassy lawn. I can hardly imagine anything more ideally bucolic."

"Hmm. That is a tolerable description, I suppose, but only just." He stood staring out over the side of the tower for several moments before saying, "Tell me something of you."

"About myself?"

"As I said."

A moment of fear stole my breath. What would an earl want to know about me? Why would he even ask? But I didn't sense anything sinister in his manner.

"I grew up at Mrs. Southey's School for Young Ladies in Milford, Bedfordshire. I then became a teacher there. There isn't much else to tell." There was actually a great deal more, but I couldn't imagine he would want to hear it.

"Do you have family? Siblings?" His tone was demanding, but no more than would be expected of an earl, I supposed.

"My parents died when I was five years old and provided enough to put me up at Mrs. Southey's school. I have no other family."

"Hmm."

He continued to stare out over the side of the great country estate below as it grew quite dark. Even though I'd eaten my roll, my stomach rumbled. I prayed he couldn't hear it.

How did one politely excuse oneself from an earl who was also one's employer?

"It is the English way to send children away from home and family to fend for themselves at a school." His voice sounded slightly bitter.

I suddenly wanted to say something that would comfort him.

"For me, it was not so bad. Mrs. Southey and the other teachers were mostly good people, and I was well cared for."

"'Well cared for.' That is a relative way of speaking. What does it mean? That you had food and clothing? Was the food nourishing, or simply adequate to keep body and soul together? Did you have the affection that children crave from a family who loves them? No, for children aren't thought to deserve or even need such a thing."

I'd never heard anyone speak this way. And to hear an earl say it made my breath catch in my throat.

"Perhaps you will tell me that polite society doesn't talk of such things, that it is ill-bred to speak of a child's feelings and the needs of their soul."

"Not at all, my lord, for I think it perfectly right and sensible to consider the feelings of others, especially of children, since they have no power in society and therefore are more vulnerable."

He turned and stared hard at me now, his eyes catching the bit of orange sunset from the sky. "What else do you think?"

"A great many things, I assure you." I smiled.

"A smile. Thank you for that."

It seemed an odd thing to thank me for.

He turned once more toward the scene below and we stood in silence as I marveled at an earl having such a conversation with the governess. And yet it also felt perfectly natural.

He broke the silence. "Do you see that tree over there?"

I moved even closer to him and to the edge to see that he pointed to a large, gnarled old oak tree standing by itself between the wooded park and the grassy lawn.

"Yes." I stole a peek at his face, which I could now see was young and handsome, with a strong jaw, high cheekbones, and dark eyebrows.

"When I was six years old, I was trying to fly a kite. My nurse had the day off, and my mother was having a garden party with some other ladies, who were all sitting at tables that had been set up on the lawn. I was running with the kite, holding onto the string, looking behind me as it was starting to take flight. When I finally turned around, I ran straight into that tree. The whole right side of my face was cut and scraped."

"Oh my. Were you all right?"

"Only bloody and bruised. But do you know what my mother did?"

I shook my head, but he was still staring down at the tree.

"She hauled me into the house by my arm, screaming, 'How could you embarrass me so in front of my friends?' She called me a stubborn little clodpate and told the servants not to let me outside for the rest of the day. And do you know, I felt guilty for embarrassing her. I was a small child, bleeding and hurt, feeling responsible for my mother's embarrassment."

"I'm so sorry." No mother should treat her child so, but it seemed improper to speak against his mother.

"Most of my friends at school had similar stories to tell. It made us stronger—'made of sterner stuff,' do you not think? It is the English way." There was a cynical, bitter edge to his voice.

My chest squeezed at his pain. Perhaps it should feel strange that he was telling me all this. Indeed, I was surprised, but it also felt a great honor that he would share this with me.

"You must think me mad. But what is so mad about expressing something real?"

His deep voice pierced my heart. But it wasn't just his voice; it was the words. How many times had I thought the same thing when I sat in Mrs. Southey's drawing room with her guests, or when I was in someone else's home, or even just meeting someone on the street, and all they wanted to speak of was the weather, the condition of the roads, or the price of muslin and lace? I wanted to speak of my dreams, my thoughts and feelings and opinions, my longing for family and for someone who loved me more than anything else in the world.

"There is nothing wrong with it." My breath was coming fast.

He stared at me again. We stood for long moments in silence, just sharing the air and the night's muted sounds.

"You seem to be a woman who has many real thoughts, Miss Robbins. In fact, I asked you what else you thought and you said 'a great many things.' Tell me some of them."

"I came here because I wanted to see more of the world. I'd never been outside of my small country school and the little village of Milford. I was content there, but . . . I wasn't. But that doesn't make sense, I suppose."

"It makes sense. Go on."

I couldn't tell him I'd hoped to find someone to marry, that I longed for love and a family of my own, so I said, "I wanted to see and experience things I'd only read about in books, and since I am a teacher and I was blessed with a good education, I advertised for a governess position."

"And you don't feel slighted by both nature and Providence for not having the means to travel and go to London and the great cities of the Continent?"

"Most people in this world don't have the means for such luxuries, my lord." I smiled, hoping he wouldn't be offended at my insinuation that he was more fortunate than most people.

"But you wish you did."

"Yes, of course, but I'd make myself very unhappy if I dwelt upon such things."

For a few moments he said nothing, then, "What is your age?"

"Five-and-twenty."

"You are young to be so wise, but I suppose your wisdom is due to your hardships in life."

I opened my mouth but wasn't sure what to say.

"It is our misfortunes that either make us wise or make us evil, but I shall not oppress you . . ." He drew in a quick, audible breath and then let it out slowly. "Have you met your charges, Samuel and Annabelle?"

"Only just. They are very bright, sweet children. You must be so proud of them."

"Yes, well, I trust they are in good hands with you, Miss Robbins." He almost mumbled the words, his voice much quieter than before.

Again he let the silence stretch out. He rubbed his jaw and cleared his throat. "These spring evenings are still quite cold. You will catch a chill. Go, now."

Even though his words sounded like a command, there was something so forlorn about him, this earl who was also very much a man, and I had no experience with either.

"Are you sure you're all right?" I suddenly couldn't bear to leave him alone. "I think you should come inside as well."

Would he be angry that I would say something so impertinent to him? Would he dismiss me before I'd even begun my duties as governess?

"Your name is Miss Robbins?"

Though it was quite dark now, I could feel his eyes boring into me.

"Charlotte Robbins of Mrs. Southey's School."

"I'm not quite ready to leave this roof, Miss Charlotte Robbins. You should go along and get your supper. It's getting late." He went back to staring out at the nighttime countryside. A peacock called out in the distance, a hoarse, mournful cry.

There was something about the tone of his voice and his manner, the way he leaned out over the edge, that gave me a sense of urgency.

"I should very much like to go and get my supper, as I've hardly eaten anything all day, but I'm afraid I don't know how to get to either the kitchen or my room from here." I allowed a light, amused note into my voice. "I was wandering around lost, which was how I came to be here."

My plight would no doubt annoy him. A lord and master was not expected to show a servant how to get around, leading her about the house.

After a moment, he said, "I suppose I can't have you fainting on the stairs."

I'd expected to hear anger or sarcasm in his voice, but there was neither.

"Come."

He was all business now as he passed right by me and started down the steep stairs.

I did my best to follow, but I got a bit dizzy after the first step. How embarrassing if I should swoon and fall on top of him! I took slow, deliberate steps, holding on to the rail and concentrating on breathing.

When I reached the landing, he was watching me. Without a word, he turned and led me down hallways and more stairs until we were at the kitchen. He went in and told the chef something, then left, glancing in my direction as he went.

The chef had one of the servants lead me into the servants' dining hall, then bring me several courses of food. I felt as though I was eating like a queen, and I more than made up for the meals I'd missed earlier in the day.

When I was finished, a servant showed me the way to my room.

The next day was Saturday. Every week I was to have Saturday afternoon and the entirety of Sunday as my time off.

I spent the morning with Samuel and Annabelle, reading to them and asking them questions to see where they were in their studies, how much they knew of arithmetic, reading, and writing. They were obviously bright children. Samuel tried to pretend to know less than he did, while Annabelle was eager to please and thrived on words of approval. I loved them both already. It was impossible not to, as they were in my charge and as impressionable as wet clay. I so wanted to do my best for them, and I kept thinking how very much like me they were, hungry for love and attention.

But they had someone I did not have, and that was their brother, Lord Brookhaven. I could tell by a few remarks from the children that they adored him, and he also must care for them. But the earl had a lot of other things on his mind than fulfilling a needed role in the children's lives.

After we finished our half-day of lessons, I dismissed them to their nurse's care, then I quickly wrote a letter to Hattie and set off to town to post it. It was a one-mile walk to the village, and I was grateful the day was warm and only slightly overcast.

But as I walked, some darker clouds began moving in. I quickened my step. I was no longer a schoolgirl, nor was I a carefree teacher at a school and village where everyone knew and accepted my ways, so I hurried to post my letter and return to Lowndesbury House before I was drenched.

I was enjoying the different scenery around me, the rolling hills grander than what I was used to in Milford, and the variety of wildflowers, some of which I'd never seen before. Even the trees were a bit different here.

Judging that the rain was still at least a half hour away, I stepped off the road to pick a few of the pink and purple wildflowers, my new favorites. I hoped I could find someone at Lowndesbury House who might tell me their names, although I wasn't sure that was likely, since no one over the age of seven was at all inclined to speak to me.

No matter. Perhaps I would ask Lord Brookhaven.

I laughed out loud at the thought. I looked around, but the road was deserted except for me. As I picked out the flowers with the brightest colors, the sound of horses' hooves beating fast approached from behind.

I stepped a bit farther off the road. Soon the noise grew quite loud, and a carriage pulled by two runaway horses came careening around the bend and off the road in my direction. The driver was missing.

My heart started pounding. The horses seemed to see me and corrected themselves, causing the carriage to swerve back onto the road. When it did, one of the wheels broke, sending the carriage teetering toward the shallow ditch.

I held my breath as the carriage seemed to take forever to decide if it would right itself or fall. But the momentum was too much, and it fell onto its side, bringing the horses to a rather abrupt halt ten feet from where I stood.

Someone inside the carriage was screaming.

I dropped my flowers and ran toward them.

The door swung up and open, as the doorway was now facing the sky. A man climbed out, heaving himself onto the side of the carriage, while the screaming continued from inside.

The man was hatless, with gray hair out of place and a wound at his hairline that was bleeding down the side of his face. He grimaced darkly.

The sound of more hooves drew nearer, then I saw it was a single rider galloping toward us.

Lord Brookhaven.

Four

Lord Brookhaven pulled on the reins, stopping the horse just short of the overturned carriage. "Is anyone hurt?" he said as he dismounted.

The gray-haired man was holding a handkerchief to his temple, slowing the flow of blood. "I don't think my daughter is injured, just hysterical."

The woman had stopped screaming, but she must have heard her father, because she cried out, "I am injured! I'm bleeding, and I can't get out!" Then she started half-sobbing, half-wailing.

As I made my way to the carriage, the man addressed Lord Brookhaven. "Did you see our driver?"

"I saw him jump into the ditch. He appeared to be well enough."

"That's what I get for hiring an inexperienced . . ." His words trailed off.

I stepped forward and hoisted my skirt while I lifted my foot, then climbed onto the carriage. I leaned my head over the open doorway.

The young woman looked to be around my own age. Her hair was falling down from its pins, and tears made streaks through the dust on her cheeks.

"Can you climb up?" I asked her. She was tall enough to reach the opening.

"Climb? No. How can I climb?" Her voice was high and hysterical.

"It's all right. Don't worry." I made my voice as soft and soothing as I could. "Do you have any broken bones?"

"I . . . I don't know." She let out another sob.

She was standing, and I quickly determined that she was mostly uninjured.

"I can't get out," she wailed. "And my hand is bleeding."

She held up her hand, but there was only a small amount of blood, the wound appearing to be only a scratch.

I lifted my head with the intention of asking the men to assist her, but they were already approaching.

Lord Brookhaven took my elbow without speaking and helped me down. Then he took my place on the side of the carriage, while the woman's father positioned himself on the other side. Lying on their stomachs, they both reached in and pulled her up, while she cried out, "Oh no! That won't—Take care not to—I can't get my—oh! My hair."

A few strands of her hair had caught on something, and Lord Brookhaven freed them with one hand while holding her wrist in his other hand.

When she was out, she lay on the side of the carriage with outstretched arms. It put me in mind of a painting I'd once seen of a sailor splayed out on the beach who'd been washed ashore, nearly drowned.

Her father nudged her arm. "Millicent, you must get up. Come, come."

The man dragged her by her arm, and when her legs slid over the side, she screamed.

He and Lord Brookhaven took her by her elbows until her feet touched the ground.

"Oh." She let out a loud breath and started trying to pin her hair back up. "What a ridiculous, wretched business this is," she was saying, still crying. "Who ever heard of a carriage overturning." Then she suddenly cried out again. "Oh! Oh, merciful—!" She was staring as a drop of blood dripped from the back of her hand.

A moment later, her eyes started to close and she stumbled to the side.

Her father caught her and lowered her the rest of the way onto the ground, mumbling something I didn't quite catch. Was he thinking what I was thinking? That it was a wonder she'd swooned at the relatively small amount of blood on her hand but hadn't seemed to notice the much greater amount of blood running down her father's face?

I'd never swooned at the sight of blood, but I had once chased a fox away from a baby rabbit. The little thing was sitting in the bushes, very still except for its fast breathing. I tried to shoo it back to its mother and even nudged it with my foot. When I did, it moved slightly and made a terrible little sound. That was when I saw the blood on its badly mangled back foot, and my vision started going black. I had to step away, hang my head, and take deep breaths to keep from fainting. So I shouldn't judge this young woman for nearly swooning after such a terrifying event as a carriage accident.

The young woman—he'd called her Millicent—was moaning, her eyes closed. Poor thing. I dug my handkerchief out of the reticule that dangled from my wrist and knelt beside her.

I gently took the woman's injured hand and helped her sit up. "It's just a small cut. Nothing to worry about," I told her. "I'll wrap it so you don't have to see it." I did just that with one of my best handkerchiefs and tied the ends together. "There. Does it feel better?"

"Yes. Thank you." She stared at me as though seeing me for the first time. "I am Millicent Skidmore of Shropshire."

"Charlotte Robbins. I'm the new governess for Lord Brookhaven's wards."

Her smile faltered when I said the word *governess*, but she recovered quickly and whispered, "Lord Brookhaven? The Earl of Brookhaven?"

"Yes." The earl was talking with Mr. Skidmore, and they were far enough away that they couldn't hear our whispered conversation.

"And he lives nearby?" she asked.

"His estate is just beyond those trees."

"An earl. Oh my." She held her hand to her throat and stared hard at Lord Brookhaven, her eyes fairly dancing. "He is very good to stop and offer his assistance." Her attention turned to the broken, overturned carriage and she sighed. "We were traveling to the seaside to visit relatives and take the sea air, but now . . ."

Mr. Skidmore took a step toward us. "Lord Brookhaven has graciously agreed to stow our carriage on his estate until we return, and we will hire a coach to take us the rest of the way."

Miss Millicent Skidmore smiled at Lord Brookhaven as she rose. "You are very kind to go to so much trouble for us."

He did not smile back. "It is no trouble." Lord Brookhaven then looked directly at me. "You will be all right while I go to the village to inquire about a coach and driver." He said it as a statement rather than a question.

"Yes, of course. I will stay with them."

With a curt nod, he remounted his horse and rode away.

Mr. Skidmore talked of the weather and the roads and their incompetent driver, whom he assumed had done something to cause the horses to bolt. The horses were surprisingly unharmed by the accident, as they had come untethered from the carriage when it overturned. They stood grazing only a few feet away, still harnessed to each other.

After Lord Brookhaven left to hire them a carriage, the Skidmores began to ask about him. They obviously considered themselves superior to me, but they weren't above asking me if Lord Brookhaven was very wealthy and if he had a wife or was engaged to be married. I answered them as simply as I could, telling them I hardly knew anything about his private affairs and that I'd only arrived at the estate the day before.

Lord Brookhaven soon returned, a hired coach distantly behind him. "What did you wish to do about your driver?" He inclined his head toward the road behind them.

A young man was walking toward us, his hat in his hands, head down.

"There you are," Mr. Skidmore said. "What do you have to say, leaping off the seat to save yourself?"

"It weren't my fault, sir. The horses, they got spooked and took off running. They pulled the reins clean out of my hands. I tried to leap on the left one's back to grab the reins and stop him, but I couldn't hang on and ended up in the ditch."

"A likely story," Mr. Skidmore grumbled. "You're to go back to your duties in the stable. I'll not place my life into your hands again."

"Yes, sir." He lowered his head even more. "How'll I get home, if you don't mind, sir?"

Mr. Skidmore mumbled, "I ought to . . ." but the rest of his words never reached my ears as he handed the former driver some coins. I wondered if he'd have been that gracious if Lord Brookhaven had not been standing there.

The hired coach arrived. The Skidmores thanked Lord Brookhaven again and stepped inside, and soon they were rolling away down the road.

"Well, Miss Charlotte Robbins?" Lord Brookhaven was staring down at me. By the scowl on his face, one might have thought he was angry.

"Yes, sir?"

"Shall we return to Lowndesbury House?"

"I must post a letter in town first."

"Why didn't you say so? I could have posted the letter for you."

"It is no trouble. I like to walk. Besides, you were occupied with more pressing matters."

"That was not so pressing as to prevent me from posting your letter." Again, his voice was gruff. "Give me the letter and I shall frank it and put it in tomorrow's post."

"That is very kind of you, sir, but if it is all right, I shall take it myself, so it will get there a day earlier." When he just stared at me,

I continued, "I don't want my friends to worry about me any longer than they must."

"Very well." He turned, nudged his horse into a run, and was gone.

It was strange. I probably should have been afraid to speak so boldly to him. Then again, I might get back to Lowndesbury House to find he had dismissed me, just as he'd done to Hattie's cousin's friend. Great titled men could be very changeable, or so I'd heard, which made it that much more surprising to find the Earl of Brookhaven so . . . human.

By the time I'd arrived back at Lowndesbury House, the storm clouds had passed without delivering any rain, and the tall trees were casting deep shadows over the lane. Even the birds were quiet. The night was warm, and I let my shawl fall off my shoulders, draped over my arms and around my waist. How lovely to feel the cool air on the back of one's neck.

As I walked, I remembered the conversation I'd had with Mrs. Merryweather on my way out, when I'd caught a glimpse of a thin, stooped-over man with white hair disappearing into one of the rooms.

"That man is Mr. Hayes, Lord Brookhaven's estate steward," Mrs. Merryweather had informed me, *"and the room he just went into is the earl's private study. You are not to go in there."*

I'd been hoping the steward might become my first suitor, and if he was suitable, my husband. But obviously Mr. Hayes was too old.

Even though I was only a governess, I did have standards.

Perhaps the head gardener would be a genteel sort of man—genteel for a gardener—or perhaps I could catch the eye of the earl's solicitor, or maybe even the rector or vicar of the parish church. A clergyman should make a good husband, I imagined, and if he was not from too grand a family, he might deign to marry a governess.

When I reached Lowndesbury House, I was reluctant to lose

the last bit of twilight. I walked to the garden, but its perfect paths and rows of well-manicured bushes displayed a rigid, off-putting formality. I decided to go beyond the garden, and I found the large tree that Lord Brookhaven had collided with when he was a boy.

Even though it had been dark and his voice had held a certain gruffness, almost anger, he'd seemed so vulnerable when he was telling me that story. I'd felt similarly toward our rector in Milford when I was thirteen years old. When he stood in front of the congregation and spoke of feelings of guilt, joy, and condemnation for his own sins, as well as gratitude for God's mercy and grace, my heart had seemed to swell out of my chest.

No one else ever spoke of feelings—especially not men, of whom there were none in my life, unless you counted the man who made repairs around the school, or the farmer who greeted me a few times a year when I passed him on the way to the village. No one besides Hattie and a few of the other teachers at Mrs. Southey's school ever spoke of how certain past events had made them feel. But it was as if I needed that depth of conversation, longed for it with a yearning that took my breath away now, remembering how Lord Brookhaven had spoken to me the night before.

It was almost improper, unseemly for an employer to open up to his employee in that manner. But why? Why should it be unseemly to speak of emotions, to express sadness or pain? For I'd sensed a fierce pain inside him. I'd actually *felt* his pain.

I could well commiserate with the pain of the absence of loving parents. I felt it every time I saw a child with their mother or a father smiling fondly at his daughter, whether she was ten years old or twenty or thirty. It was an affectionate gaze I was never to know.

Although Lord Brookhaven had not known much affection from his mother, I suspected his relationship with his father was no better. Though I knew little of the former Lord Brookhaven, titled gentlemen were not known for their kindness and affection toward their children.

Lord God, please let me marry someone who will love me, a good man who will not refuse to speak of feelings and will not berate me for my—

"Miss Robbins."

I sucked in a loud breath and turned to find Lord Brookhaven fifteen feet away.

Five

I didn't mean to startle you."

"Not at all." I pressed a hand to my heart.

"I wanted to apologize for my manner last evening. I was morose, thinking of regrets, of things better left in the past." He stopped and faced me, his hands clasped behind his back. And though it was nearly as late as it had been when we'd spoken on the roof, there was enough light that I could see his expression. His gaze was steady and his features calm. "You will forgive me if I made you uncomfortable."

"I was not uncomfortable." I wanted to say that it was the best, most honest conversation I'd ever had with a man, but that would probably make *him* uncomfortable.

We stood in silence for a moment, listening to a lone bird singing in a nearby tree. He broke in by saying, "Thank you for stopping to assist the lady and gentleman who overturned in their carriage. It was very good of you."

"I like to be of service to others when I can."

"You were not afraid to assist in spite of the blood and hysterics, and I was impressed by your composure. Most ladies would have swooned at the sight of blood, or at least would have been afraid to involve themselves."

"Perhaps that is because society expects ladies to swoon and be afraid."

He raised his brows. "But you do not concern yourself with what society expects, Miss Robbins?"

"I care about propriety, but not enough to do things that don't seem sensible, or when common decency demands something other than what society expects."

He smiled, his eyes brightening. "What do they teach at that school of yours?"

"Forgive me if I'm being improper."

"Do you think you're being improper?"

"No, only honest."

"I like honesty. There is very little of it these days, as society makes cowards out of men and women alike."

"Cowards?"

"No one wants to be accused of being different, of holding a different viewpoint or doing something other than what's expected of them."

I nodded, hoping he would go on.

"For example, it is expected that I shall be a cold, unfeeling sort of man, just like my father and mother were, that I shall ignore the people who do the most for me, who care about me and treat me well." A bitter tone entered his voice as he stared past me for a moment. "It is expected that I shall marry a woman from a prominent family and refuse to love her. Nor am I expected to love my own children, but to disdain them until they are seventeen or eighteen years old, then suddenly treat them like slight acquaintances who should know everything about life without anyone ever having taught them. Ah." He closed his eyes and turned slightly away from me, running a hand through his hair and causing it to stick up in several places.

"I understand." I held my breath, longing to know more, feeling as if he was expressing just what I had felt many times before, even though our places in life were worlds apart.

He sighed, still staring off into the trees.

Finally, he continued. "Forgive me. It is not my way to talk so much. My nursemaid died a month ago, and I suppose . . . she was the closest thing to a mother I had, the most virtuous, purehearted human being I have ever known, and yet I am expected to feel indifferent to her because she was a servant. It is ironic, is it not, Miss Robbins?"

"I am very sorry. It must be very hard to lose someone who meant so much to you."

His jaw hardened, and a muscle in his cheek twitched.

I quickly went on. "I have never had a servant, but I think we should love the people who love us. God commands that we love everyone, but if someone sacrifices of themselves, generously giving for our good, I believe we should love them most especially, servant or not. But as for grief, I think our society must be very different from the society of the Bible, as people wailed and threw ashes on their heads, sitting in sackcloth whenever someone they loved died. And yet we are expected not to shed a single tear."

The way his expression changed as he listened to my words, as if he were truly reacting to what I was saying with understanding and agreement, made my heart lift. Wouldn't Susan shake her head at me and Hattie's eyes widen in shock if they heard me conversing with Lord Brookhaven as if I were his equal?

"Perhaps we simply do not love to the extent that they did," he said, eyeing me.

"Or perhaps we are just expected not to show it. We always must be so dignified and proper, though I do not know who decided that the show of emotion was undignified."

"Perhaps we shall start a new movement, to show emotion and not care who sees. Would you be able to support such a stance, Miss Robbins?"

"I would like that very much. However, to scream and wail anywhere and at any time, becoming violent whenever one is angry, would make for a rather chaotic society. There must be moderation, I think. But I would like to see more authenticity."

A tiny smile graced his lips.

"The challenge is how to preserve authenticity in emotion while remaining considerate of the feelings of others. No one wants to be around someone who cannot control themselves."

His grin grew bigger, with a rakish, one-sided quirk. "You have thought this through before today, Miss Robbins."

"I have." I allowed myself to smile back.

We stood in silence again. He stared everywhere around us except at me. I, on the other hand, allowed myself to look at him, imagining I was describing Lord Brookhaven in a letter to my friends. *He is tall and wears his clothes well, though he's no fop. His dark hair and heavy black eyebrows enhance the melancholy look about his eyes, as if he is wiser and sadder than other young men. He has blue eyes and a Roman nose, with a masculine jawline and chin, a heavy forehead and rectangular face. He could almost be said to have perfect features if it were not for his slightly overlapping teeth and the ironic way he has of smiling and talking out of only one side of his mouth. But I consider him handsome, more handsome than any other man I ever saw.*

I might be partial to him because he was my employer and because of the friendly way he spoke to me, but I could not attribute it solely to that. Some women preferred men who were thin and boyish, with blond hair and delicate features, but those characteristics did not appeal to me. I also was unwilling to overlook a large age difference, as some women were wont to do, marrying someone old enough to be their grandfather. I could possibly overlook some things if he was a good man—character was more important than anything else, of course—but I hoped the man I married would be young like me.

Why was I thinking about this? Lord Brookhaven was so far above my station as to probably not even see me as a woman, and I likewise could not see him as an eligible man.

He broke the silence.

"In future, allow me to frank your letters. Place them in the mail tray with the rest. Mrs. Merryweather will show you. That is all. You will forgive me for interrupting your walk." Lord Brookhaven went toward the house, not looking back, and I watched him go.

I thought meeting an earl would be interesting, but he was so much more than I'd imagined. Not a dandy, nor a thoughtless man-child bent on destroying himself with drink and gambling. Though he might be a bit arrogant, he did have reason to be, and yet I did not find him off-putting. In short, he was not like any of the stories I'd heard about titled young men.

It was only too bad he wasn't the vicar, steward, or head gardener. I smiled to myself, then followed a safe distance behind.

On Sunday, I walked to church with the rest of the servants, though no one spoke to or walked with me.

Mrs. Merryweather went ahead of everyone else, her head high in the air, while the rest of the female servants followed in clusters of two or three, talking and giggling quietly. The only other servant I'd spoken to, Hannah, talked to two other girls, covering her mouth with her hand as she did so. Her audience alternately gasped or laughed, until Mrs. Merryweather turned and said sharply, "Quiet. It is the Lord's Day, not a festival."

"Yes, ma'am," they murmured. When Mrs. Merryweather was no longer looking at them, they grinned at one another.

The walk was quiet, except for the birds overhead, and I did my best to enjoy the spring weather, but there were no flowers on the roadside here.

The church was not much bigger than the one in Milford, but the large square tower and the crenellations across the top, as well as the grayish stone, made it resemble Lowndesbury House.

A thrill went through me to imagine all the people who had come and gone, been married and buried, experienced spiritual epiphanies, and brought their babies to be christened there. And

Lord Brookhaven's family likely had always been the patrons of this parish, and as such, were in charge of hand-picking the clergy.

As I entered the church, I glanced around but did not see Lord Brookhaven. Everyone was a stranger. I thought I saw a woman who looked like Mrs. Southey, but when she turned to the side, I wondered that I ever thought such a thing. After seeing the same few dozen faces since I was five years old, it was a bit like becoming a child again to be confronted with only unfamiliar faces.

And then, all at once, everyone in the church seemed to turn and stare at me.

Where should I sit? What should I do? If I sat in someone else's seat, I'd be embarrassed when they came and asked me to move. I tried not to look so obviously self-conscious and out of place. At home, the students and teachers from Mrs. Southey's school had their own rows of seats at the back.

Behind me, the servants began climbing the stairs to the balcony. Of course. The servants would naturally sit in the least desirable place. I started to follow them up when Mrs. Merryweather placed a hand on my arm.

"Come," she said.

We sat on the outside end of a pew near the front of the church.

Moments later, Lord Brookhaven entered with Samuel and Annabelle. They sat at the other end of the same pew, next to the center aisle, and I realized Mrs. Merryweather and I were sitting in the family pew of the Earl of Brookhaven.

Another reason for the other servants to hate the governess. I was sitting in the place of the family of the earl. Or, more accurately, I was seated with his housekeeper on his family seat.

I forced myself not to stare at him, but out of the corner of my eye, I saw him glance at the children, who sat beside him. When he did, his gaze then went straight to me.

I quickly focused my eyes forward, on the large vase of flowers at the front of the church, which was impressive for its variety of colors. But I was so nervous, all I saw was the colors. After a few moments of careful breathing, I began to notice that some of the flowers were familiar, while several more were new to me. What a great variety of flora there was in the world. God created so many different types of people and flowers and animals.

As grateful as I was for Mrs. Merryweather allowing me to sit with her, I would have been more grateful if she'd talked to me to pass the time.

Samuel and Annabelle also noticed me. I gave them a very discreet little wave and smiled. They waved back, but then faced forward, as all children are instructed to do in church.

Finally, the rector came forward and began the Sunday morning services. He was rather young, not hideous, but . . . he had a wedding band on his finger.

So not only was the steward not a possibility, but the rector also was not. My choices were dwindling. But this was not a thing to be dwelling on in church. I scolded myself and pushed my thoughts back onto the words the rector was speaking.

It was not so different from the service at home in Milford, although with more Scripture reading and fewer long rants about the virtues and vices—mostly vices—of mankind. When it was over, Mrs. Merryweather said, "Come."

We walked together all the way back to Lowndesbury House. I was thankful, at first, not to have to walk by myself, but she barely said two words to me the entire way. She also surprised me with how briskly she was able to walk at her age. I suppose it was due to her small and wiry frame and years of hurrying up and down corridors and stairs at Lowndesbury House.

I was able to keep up with Mrs. Merryweather, but only just. Although I loved a good long walk, and I tried to take my exercise every day even in the rain and snow, I spent the largest part of my days studying, teaching, sitting, and standing. I was out of breath when we arrived back home.

It was my day off, so I took my midday meal in my room and

wrote letters to Susan, Mrs. Southey, a few of my fellow teachers, and even some of my students who'd begged me to write to them.

Hours later, I stood up to stretch. Then I took my letters to the tray for outgoing mail, which would be franked with Lord Brookhaven's seal.

I felt a bit guilty for allowing him to save me from paying the postage. Why did poor people have to pay to post their letters but because I was employed by an earl, I could send my letters free of charge? I would have taken the letters to post and paid for them myself if he hadn't asked me directly to let him frank them. And even now, seeing the unusually large stack of letters I was posting, it seemed egregious.

I forced away the guilt. After all, I could always take the money I would have spent on postage and put it in the donation box for the poor.

I'd grown quite restless, sitting so long and writing so many letters, and I set out on a walk. Unfortunately, the sun was already sinking low, so even though I'd wanted to explore the lanes around Lowndesbury House, I headed into the garden instead.

The air was cool and damp, as it had rained earlier, but I was wearing my sturdiest shoes and would simply take care not to slip in the mud. I kept to the stone-lined walkways until I grew tired of the sameness and moved into the wilder part of the park.

I was examining a clump of delightful red-capped mushrooms when I smelled pipe smoke, then heard someone clearing his throat. I turned to find Lord Brookhaven standing beside a tree, gazing up at its branches and holding a pipe in his right hand.

I was disturbing his solitary evening. I shouldn't have been wandering around the earl's private park. I turned to leave.

"There is a goshawk's nest up in this tree, and if you're very quiet, you can hear the nestlings chirping when the mother bird is near."

I glanced around, but there was no one else. He must be talking to me.

Six

I see you've found some red-capped mushrooms," he said, noticing what I had been examining. "Those are poisonous, you know, so don't eat them."

"I've never seen any like them before, and the only mushrooms I've ever picked to eat are chanterelles and penny buns, and only in autumn. How do you know they are poisonous?"

"The red caps and the little white spots. My nurse taught me to identify mushrooms. I have a book of illustrations and information about mushrooms in my library if you'd like to borrow it." He put the pipe between his lips and puffed once, twice.

"Thank you." I actually had very little interest in mushrooms, but I didn't want to offend him after he so generously offered. I'd never thought lords would wish to loan out books to servants, but perhaps it was because I was the governess and therefore had more education.

"Did you have a specific focus of study at Mrs. Southey's? I believe that's the school you mentioned."

"Yes. I did extra studies in literature, and that is the subject I taught."

"You must feel as if you're wasting your education with such young pupils as Samuel and Annabelle. They're only seven years old, after all." He drew on his pipe again.

"I have taught young children their age before, and it has its own rewards. I am quite content to teach your siblings. They are very bright and clever children."

"You do not think it beneath you to teach them?"

"No, of course not."

He frowned and folded his arms across his chest, again gazing up at the nest. "So you taught literature. I suppose you taught Shakespeare, Burns, and Wordsworth."

"Among others." I couldn't help smiling at his wry way of mentioning such great authors.

"Tell me your opinions. Who do you like best and least? Be honest—and be controversial, if at all possible."

I couldn't help the smile of delight I felt spreading across my face. "Well, I adore Wordsworth and Burns, but I don't care at all for Milton. So dull and sanctimonious."

"Brava, Miss Robbins!" He was truly smiling now, even showing his teeth. "A true and honest—and controversial—opinion. Thank you for that."

What would he say next?

"And you?" I asked. "What literary greats do you enjoy most and least?"

"I'm afraid I never developed an appreciation for Shakespeare. So self-important, even in his comedies. And Jonathan Swift is an absolute bore. What say you, Miss Robbins?"

"I'm afraid I cannot agree with you on Shakespeare—"

His brows went up. He almost looked . . . *delighted* that I would disagree with him.

"—but Swift, yes, he is quite dull. But you haven't said which authors you admire."

"So I haven't." He cleared his throat again. "Although I generally prefer prose to poetry, when I am in the mood for verse, I like Thomas Gray. But I rather think English writers' best novel-writing days are ahead of them, as I've read one or two recently by living authors that were very entertaining."

"May I ask which novels these were?"

"*Sense and Sensibility* and another, *Pride and Prejudice*, by the same anonymous author."

"I must read them as soon as I am able."

"I shall lend them to you."

"Thank you, my lord. That is very generous."

"Read them quickly, for I'd like to hear what you think."

He'd been asking me what I thought since our first meeting, so it seemed almost natural now.

He eyed me with a penetrating gaze from beneath heavy black brows. Again, I should have felt intimidated, but somehow I didn't. Somehow I understood that he was a man with normal human feelings, perhaps due to the familiar way he'd been speaking to me, or perhaps due to the state in which I'd seen him on the first evening, when we'd both been standing on the roof and he'd been so melancholy I'd worried about leaving him alone. The thing that was different about him was that he was *expressing* his feelings—and expressing them to me.

"It is the way of the Englishman—and Englishwoman—to send their children to an institution, and you were no exception to that, Miss Robbins. Tell me of your experiences at Mrs. Southey's school. You seemed to want me to think that you had good experiences there, but you were also mistreated, I suppose? And the teachers, the cruel ones, beat you and punished you for even minor infractions, breaking your spirit and making you feel as if you must feel guilty twenty-four hours of every day in order to make amends and eke your way into heaven?"

"No, not at all."

"And the food was rancid and barely edible, much less palatable."

"No, it's not true."

"You are smiling. My words amuse you. Why? Tell me." He suddenly looked rather severe.

"Forgive me, sir. I meant no offense."

"Explain."

It had grown so dark that I could barely make out his expression, but I thought he looked rather sullen.

"I'm sorry, but I did not have that kind of experience. My teachers were kind—most of them—and I had one or two friends at all times, from an early age, whose situations were similar to mine, and we enjoyed each other's company. There were bullies, from time to time, who made life difficult. Was your school as cruel as you describe?" My heart constricted at the thought.

He puffed on his pipe while I talked, then blew out a long cloud of smoke and said, "I'm glad your experience of school was relatively good. As for me, let us just say that I got in a lot of fights, and I lost most of them. Then a gamekeeper, a wise old man, taught me better fighting skills, such as how to hold one's fist and strike in a manner to cause the greatest impact. But you don't want to hear about that."

"I am sorry you got in so many fights." My spirit was heavy as I thought of him being forced to physically defend himself.

"Yes, well, I daresay after I learned, I won them all and the other boys decided not to fight me—not as often, anyway." He took another draw on his pipe. "I was given good food, had adequate heat in winter, and I learned to defend myself—an essential skill, wouldn't you say?"

"Indeed."

"And you were not taught to fear God and tremble in terror that your sins would find you out?"

"I was taught to fear God, of course," I replied, "but I like to read the Bible for myself, and I consider that fear to be more of a reverence, as Scripture also says that love drives out fear, and we are to love God with all our heart, soul, mind, and strength."

"Well said, Miss Robbins. You read the Bible for yourself, do you, and use your own sense to understand it?"

"I have always believed that Scripture is true and helpful, and I like to draw my own conclusions about what it means." I lifted my chin, daring him to say that I should allow the clergy to explain the Bible to me.

"Good. I respect that. Since you have no family, Miss Robbins, tell me of your friends."

"My friends, sir?" What could he possibly wish to know about my friends?

"Do you exchange gifts on holidays? Do you employ one another's help to snare an eligible man's attentions? Or do you simply talk of the weather and the state of the roads?"

"We do exchange gifts on holidays. My closest friends are Hattie and Susan, and the three of us share many of our deepest hopes and feelings. We have never assisted one another in 'snaring an eligible man's attentions,' as you say, but we certainly talk of more than the weather and the state of the roads."

He opened his mouth as if to speak, but I pretended not to notice and continued. "And you, Lord Brookhaven? What of your friends? Do you speak of more than the weather?"

"Tit for tat, eh?" He gave a wry almost-smile. "I suppose it is a bit different with men, but yes, I have one or two trusted friends with whom I speak of more than the weather." He took a quick draw on his pipe. "My aunt, Lady Derringer, who was my father's sister, is a widow and a good friend. Does that surprise you? She and my uncle, who died two years ago, were closer to me than my own parents. They were unable to have children of their own."

No wonder the earl had looked so distraught on the roof that first night. He'd lost his uncle and the woman who had been like a mother to him in a relatively short period of time.

"Have you ever lost anyone close to you, Miss Robbins?"

"In truth, I have not, sir." Was it worse to lose someone close to you? Or to never have anyone close? But I refrained from asking.

He stared pensively into the dark trees, smoking his pipe.

"When I was fifteen years old," I said, remembering, "I spent the summer with a family who lived near the school. I had thought the daughters, who were about my age, were my good friends, but things were not as I'd perceived them, and it was a very long summer for me."

Lord Brookhaven was looking at me now.

"I thought I would be welcomed into a cheerful home, where I could see what life as a family was like, but I soon realized there was something unsettling about that family. My friends, Rebecca and Christina Mead, resented their brother George's attentions toward me. I neither desired nor encouraged his attentions, but that didn't seem to matter. And his mother hated me as well, forcing me to do more than my share of the work around the house, work that her daughters had been accustomed to performing. I spent the whole summer afraid of the brother and feeling hated by the sisters."

I shivered and pulled my shawl up to my neck and held it closed over my chest. "It was a terrible experience, as bad as you might have expected me to have at a boarding school, and I was quite glad to get back to Mrs. Southey's school." I let out a deep breath, wondering why I told him that.

"That does sound like a very bad experience. But I am glad you escaped that brother. There are many evil men in this world who prey on women, I'm afraid. But I have made you melancholy, forcing you to speak of the past. I have a tendency to dwell on the past, one of my many faults. Forgive me, Miss Robbins."

"There is nothing to forgive. I am well."

He stood there holding his pipe and staring quite soberly at me. "And you have no family? None at all?"

"When I was eighteen, Mrs. Southey allowed me to read all the documents that had been brought with me when I came to her. There was some information about my parents and grandparents, who were all deceased, and a letter from my father's solicitor saying he would be sending an annual sum for my upkeep at the school, with the balance being paid to me on my eighteenth birthday. I received twenty-five pounds, all that was left of the amount my parents had entrusted to the solicitor. And as far as he knew, I had no other family."

"What was this solicitor's name?"

"I remember it was Graham . . . perhaps Gilbert Graham? No, Garrett Graham." Why did he want to know that?

He smoked a while longer, then said, "It is cold. We should go inside before Mrs. Merryweather sends out a search party for you."

With that, we started back toward the house in silence.

William's heart burned within him. He walked toward the house with Miss Charlotte Robbins beside him as he dwelt on the many emotions he'd experienced while listening to her. Never had he felt anything like this for any of the society darlings that he met in London. Miss Robbins was all truth and justice, courageous yet kind and compassionate and good. Other young ladies he knew were tepid, jaundiced in their opinions, self-centered and conceited, and never talked about their true feelings and concerns.

He knew his feelings were a bit extreme, but he wanted to protect her, shield her from the world. He didn't care that she was only a lowly governess, a poor orphan. Find him the richest duke's daughter and she wouldn't be half—nay, one-fifth—the lady Miss Charlotte Robbins was.

How unfair was life. But he, the Earl of Brookhaven, could easily raise Miss Charlotte Robbins's level in society. He could give her the life she'd only dreamed of. Samuel and Annabelle had their own inheritance from both their mother's and Father's estate. They would be taken care of. But Charlotte Robbins had nothing and no family.

He would give her the happiness that had been denied her all her life. Why not? She was a pure soul, and many impure souls had everything this world could offer. Besides, just thinking of seeing her thriving and happy, experiencing things she'd always wished to experience, gave him such a burst of joy that he wasn't sure he'd be able to think of anything else until he could see it come to pass.

But he was getting ahead of himself. She might not want for herself what he wanted for her. She deserved to be able to choose.

He felt something new and different when he was in Miss Robbins's presence. There were times it had completely driven his melancholy away, and wise or unwise, he knew he would not stop until he'd made sure Miss Robbins was truly happy.

He'd missed opportunities to do something good in the past—spoiled, selfish, only son of an earl that he was—but he would not let this one pass him by. He would not be like his father.

Seven

I frequently encountered Lord Brookhaven when I was on a walk. Often he was also taking a walk, but sometimes he was returning from a ride. Other times it seemed he must be deliberately seeking me out, although I knew that was unlikely. I'd sometimes been called pretty by my friends, and Mrs. Southey said my manners were very pleasing, but I was not prideful enough to think an earl would be interested in me as more than a mild amusement for when he had no one else with whom to converse.

Indeed, who else did he have for intelligent conversation? I suppose there was his steward, who was obviously a man of letters, but also was very old and dull, as far as I could ascertain. Mrs. Merryweather was not a talkative woman, and I could imagine the conversations they had were quite brief. The butler, Mr. Mims, I wasn't sure about, but the rector was probably Lord Brookhaven's friend, as was usually the case with the rector and his patron. But I'd never seen the earl in conversation with either of them. In fact, he didn't seem to be a particularly agreeable or friendly person in general, which made it even more astounding that he conversed so congenially with me.

Today as I rounded a bend in the garden path, I encountered Lord Brookhaven as I often did. He was staring down at the ground while smoking his pipe.

"Miss Robbins. Come here and see this little hedgehog."

I stepped closer. A little spiny animal was rooting around in the leaves two feet from the toe of Lord Brookhaven's boot.

"He is very darling."

"I had one as a pet when I was a boy."

"Did you?"

"It lived quite well in the little house I made for it for a year and a half. But when I went off to school, someone released it outside and I never saw it again."

"That is very sad."

"Did you ever have a pet, Miss Robbins?"

"No, sir. Pets weren't allowed at Mrs. Southey's school."

"And would you have liked to have a pet?"

"I should think so. It seems as if any child would enjoy having a pet."

"Yes, which is why I've decided to get one for Samuel and Annabelle. What do you think?"

"It's a splendid idea."

"I was thinking a small dog, one for each of them. Or should I only get one dog and let them share in taking care of it? Which would be best?"

"I don't know. Either idea should work just fine."

"I see you are smiling. You like the idea of a pet, then?"

"Yes, sir. I think the children will enjoy taking care of a pet."

"And you shall enjoy having the dogs around?"

"Well, yes, I believe so." I couldn't help smiling. He looked so pleased. And I did feel a lift in my heart as I imagined what it would be like having a pet around.

"What kind of dog should it be?" Lord Brookhaven looked thoughtful. "Perhaps a long-haired dog, soft and eager to be petted and played with? Or a big animal, a mastiff or Great Dane that will watch over the children when they play."

"That is for you to decide, as their guardian, whether or not you want them to have a smaller, more manageable pet or a watchdog."

"You are correct, Miss Robbins. I wanted a pet for them, not a canine guardian. Quite right." He thoughtfully puffed on his pipe. "There is another reason I was hoping to see you this evening. I wanted to tell you that I'm having a small house party, and I would like you to join the rest of the guests."

"Me, sir?"

"Yes, you. Your conversation will be far more interesting than anyone else's. My aunt, Lady Derringer, will be helping to host it. She will arrive soon and will oversee everything, including the making of a few dresses for you. The dressmaker of Lady Derringer's choosing will take your measurements."

I was at a loss for how to reply. It was so irregular. Wasn't it? To invite one's governess to a house party, and to provide clothing for her? Certainly the governess was sometimes allowed to attend a ball, especially if it was a large ball given by her employer, but a small house party?

"Sir, I'm certain I can have little in common with your guests at such a party. I am only the governess."

"What of it? You are an intelligent woman, are you not? You are a morally upright, free young woman, capable of conversation and dancing. And you will enjoy meeting Lady Derringer. I believe the two of you will get along quite well."

"I would not belong—"

"You shall belong as well as anyone." His brows lowered and his eyes were piercing. "No one will dare question my wish for you to be there."

He stared past me. Finally, he said, "I intend that you will enjoy yourself. I do not have parties often, but . . ."

Leaves rustled in a bush nearby and a dog trotted toward us, followed by a man with a rifle under his arm.

"Thompson." Lord Brookhaven nodded at the man.

"My lord."

"Fine evening for a walk. Finding any pheasant?"

"Some."

"Miss Robbins, this is Thompson. He's the gamekeeper for the estate and the best shot in the county. Thompson, this is Miss Robbins, the new governess."

"Pleased, miss." He tipped the brim of his hat to me, but he hardly glanced in my direction.

I remembered the gamekeeper was on my mental list of possible eligible matches. I felt my cheeks grow warm and was glad the sun had gone down.

Thompson made to walk past us, as his dog had walked on and was sniffing at the base of a tree closer to Lowndesbury House.

"We should be going in," Lord Brookhaven said, sweeping his hand forward, indicating that I should follow Mr. Thompson. "It's nearly dark."

I stepped forward, glad my list was only in my head. But now that I had seen the gamekeeper, I could cross him off. He didn't appear to be married, but he was so gruff and unkempt, so uninterested in me, that I couldn't imagine ever getting acquainted with him, much less wanting to marry him. Besides, he was more than twice my age.

I felt a small sinking of disappointment. But that feeling faded immediately, as I was buoyed by how Lord Brookhaven had just invited me to his house party.

How strange it was. The gamekeeper was much nearer my station, but it was Lord Brookhaven who conversed with me as if I were his equal. And it was Lord Brookhaven whose company I longed for, whose face and voice had become dear to me. Perhaps that was simply the schoolgirl in me. Having never known the company of gentlemen, of course I would form the type of attachment to Lord Brookhaven that a schoolgirl would naturally feel for a headmaster, or for her first employer.

And Lord Brookhaven was ever so handsome. His face was the height of masculinity, to my mind, and revealed a sort of restrained tension, as in someone who was at war with himself.

But it wasn't his face that I liked most about Lord Brookhaven. It was that he talked to me. He saw me, actually looked me in the eye and didn't ignore me, and we discussed real experiences and real feelings. He actually seemed to care about my opinion, and I even felt as though he admired me.

It was silly, I know. But I loved our conversations. They fed something inside me that had been asleep before I met him and now would remain awake for the rest of my life.

We walked silently back to the house, Mr. Thompson quickly outpacing us as he headed around the great house to what was probably the gamekeeper's cottage somewhere behind it.

When we reached the house, Lord Brookhaven started tapping the tobacco out of his pipe. "Good evening, Miss Robbins." It was his way of dismissing me.

"Good evening, sir." I turned on my heel and went inside.

After taking my supper in my room, I sat at the tiny desk where I wrote my letters. I was alone, so I went through the list in my head. I thought of them in alphabetical order so I could better remember them.

Butler
Chef
Estate Steward
Gamekeeper
Head Gardener
Land Steward
Rector
Solicitor
Vicar

I'd added the land steward after Mrs. Merryweather had indicated that there was both an estate steward and a land steward. But I could mentally cross off *Chef*, *Estate Steward*, *Rector*, and now *Gamekeeper*. There were still five more people on the list.

I thought about my prospects very often when I was alone. But now my mind was immersed in the conversation I'd just had with Lord Brookhaven. I tried to remember every word spoken, each of his expressions, what he was wearing, and his movements and mannerisms. I'd never thought about it before, but a pipe was perhaps the most masculine thing in the world, the look and smell of it.

I hoped my husband, whoever he turned out to be, liked to smoke a pipe.

"I hurt my finger." Annabelle held up her finger to show a very tiny scratch.

I made a face of compassion and clicked my tongue against my teeth. By now I was accustomed to Annabelle's wounds. Every day, it seemed, she had a new bruise or scrape, sometimes invisible, that required some measure of doctoring. I figured it was her way of getting attention, while Samuel's way was to say and do something slightly mischievous. Compared to other governess stories I'd heard, it was more endearing than annoying.

"Your poor finger," I said, looking at it quite gravely. "Shall I find a bandage for it?"

Annabelle nodded.

I had started keeping a stash of bandages in my desk. I soon had the finger wrapped and tied.

"There. All better?"

Annabelle nodded again.

Samuel laid his head on his child-sized desk. "That scratch is so tiny. Don't be such a baby, Annabelle."

"I'm not being a baby." Annabelle scrunched her face at her brother.

I couldn't help smiling inwardly. They bickered back and forth, but I'd also seen Annabelle put her head on Samuel's shoulder while he patted her arm. They only did it when they thought no one else was looking, and five minutes later they'd be bickering again. But I hadn't seen any evidence of cruelty or menace from them, and though I'd had little experience observing siblings, I'd heard stories from the other girls I'd grown up with at school. Annabelle and Samuel made me hope I had twins someday, a boy and a girl.

I sat between them so they wouldn't start teasing each other and got them started on our lesson for the day.

Two hours later, Lord Brookhaven appeared in the doorway to the schoolroom holding a ball of fur with two dark eyes and a little tongue sticking out. One of the footmen stood just behind him with a second wriggling puppy.

"I have a surprise for you." Lord Brookhaven was genuinely smiling, which made my stomach flip.

"Ohhh!" Annabelle cried out.

"Is one of them mine?" Samuel said, and both children ran toward their older brother.

Lessons were obviously over for the day.

Lord Brookhaven knelt on the floor with the two puppies as the children oohed and aahed over the furry pets.

"This one is a Pomeranian, for Annabelle," he said, pointing to the ball of light brown fluff. "And the other"—which Samuel was already petting—"is a cocker spaniel for Samuel."

The children were holding the puppies, which were licking their faces and making them giggle. When the puppies wagged their tails, their whole bodies wriggled.

"You must share them with Miss Robbins," Lord Brookhaven said, sneaking a look at me.

"Oh, Miss Robbins, come see how soft she is," Annabelle gushed.

I knelt beside her and touched the little ball of liveliness. "Indeed, she is very soft."

I had tears in my eyes, I didn't know why. Perhaps because the dogs were so full of life and joy and innocence. But it was more the sight of a man like Lord Brookhaven doing something just to make the children happy, children I had come to love.

His face was split in a grin as he watched the chaos, the puppies yipping and yapping in high-pitched playfulness.

Mrs. Merryweather came rushing in. "What in the name of . . ." She stopped and stared, then walked away, mumbling, "Lord bless me."

"You'll have to name them," Lord Brookhaven said. "What do you think?"

"Maizie," Annabelle called out, just as the ball of fur licked her in the mouth, making her squeal.

"I think she likes her name," Lord Brookhaven said. "Maizie it is."

"I'm naming my puppy Ernest," Samuel said.

"Maizie and Ernest. Those are splendid names." Lord Brookhaven winked at me, smiling widely. "What do you think, Miss Robbins?"

"I think they're wonderful." I laughed even as I wiped away a tear. How sentimental I was!

We played on the floor with the dogs until Hannah came and took the children for their midday meal, and a new maid, who'd been hired to help care for the dogs, came and took the canines away.

Lord Brookhaven and I were left alone in the schoolroom.

"Thank you," I said. "You have made the children very happy."

"Are you sure you should be thanking me? I'm not certain you will be able to get them to do any schoolwork at all now."

"Well, they will be happy, at least."

"And you, Miss Robbins? Are you happy?"

I opened my mouth but then shut it. I didn't know how to answer.

"Never mind. I saw how pleased you were for the children. You are a generous soul, Miss Robbins."

He looked at me quite intently, and the longer he gazed at me, the harder it was to hold back the threatening tears. What was wrong with me?

"Well," he said gently, "you may go and take your rest. Your duties are complete for today. Good day, Miss Robbins."

The next day, the children had just finished their lessons and gone with the nurse. I was putting away our books when a handsome middle-aged lady appeared in the doorway.

"Miss Robbins? Forgive me for my lack of manners." She stepped toward me.

Lord Brookhaven came into the room right behind her. "Lady Derringer, this is Miss Charlotte Robbins. Miss Robbins, this is my aunt, Lady Derringer."

We exchanged polite greetings. She was so elegant, both in her dress and her manners, but not in an off-putting way. She possessed an easy grace and an utter lack of haughtiness in her demeaner.

"I have spoken to the dressmaker," Lady Derringer said, "and I like what she has planned."

I got the feeling she was studying me as we talked about the dresses that were being made for me, discussing colors and styles and fabrics. She was certainly thinking of what would look best with my complexion and eye color, but there was more to her scrutiny than just choosing the most flattering clothes. I felt as if she was trying to decipher my character.

"Well, if you're going to talk only about muslins and lace and pink embroidery—" Lord Brookhaven said, taking a step toward the door.

"There, there," Lady Derringer said, more in irritation than placating. "I am done with that. Besides, we have a lot to do before your guests arrive." She turned to me. "Miss Robbins, it was lovely meeting you. I hope you will enjoy the party, and I shall enjoy getting better acquainted with you in the coming weeks."

They were gone, and I was left with two impressions. One, that Lady Derringer was as genuine and unpretentious as her nephew, and two, that Lord Brookhaven had been nervous for her to meet me.

Eight

It had rained the evening before, but I was determined to take my morning walk, as the sun was peeking out from behind the clouds, and the grass and flowers were sure to be sparkling with water droplets.

Spring was so lovely for my first year at Lowndesbury House, with the blooming daffodils and freesia, wood violets and hyacinths. The weather was not the best, with frequent rains and blustery days, yet it was rare that I missed my walk, for I always felt a bit forlorn when I couldn't take a walk.

I pulled my shawl more tightly around my shoulders, as the air was damp and there was a cool breeze that seemed to cut right through my skirts, but I fully expected to see Lord Brookhaven.

I wasn't inclined to think overmuch about why Lord Brookhaven talked with me so often; I just wanted to enjoy it. We'd become even more familiar with each other, as he frequently smiled, and he even laughed on occasion. My heart quickened whenever I saw him, and I ruminated, throughout my days of teaching Annabelle and Samuel, about the many things I would like to tell him. I also replayed our past conversations, sometimes over and over, as it was such a pleasant way to pass the time.

My talks with Lord Brookhaven were the extent of my friendly conversing with other adults, besides writing my letters to Hattie and Susan and anyone else from school who wrote me back. No one else at Lowndesbury House ever spoke more than a word or two to me. I couldn't really be angry with them. They weren't used to governesses staying long, and I honestly understood their resentment of me. The scullery maids, rising before dawn and doing all of the most laborious work, collapsed into bed as soon as they were finished with their work, which was always after the sun went down.

Even though I was sometimes lonely, I couldn't complain, as I was allowed to freely roam the house and borrow any book I wished from the large library. And although Annabelle and Samuel were doing well academically, for they were fast learners, they were not the easiest students to teach sometimes. They were understandably reluctant to obey me and allow me to get close to them. Samuel especially had said some things about not expecting me to stay at Lowndesbury House for long. Therefore, I aimed to be patient, as I knew what it was like to not be able to trust that someone would stay in one's life forever.

As a student at Mrs. Southey's School for Young Ladies, I'd seen more teachers come and go than I could probably recall in one sitting. But even more so, I'd seen students come and go, sometimes staying for only a month or two. The school was my entire world, especially as a young child, and the loss of a fellow student and friend was painful. And yet I continued to befriend the new students who came to board at the school. Most had families that they would return to after a short time. Only the ones who had no family at all, like Hattie, Susan, and me, stayed long-term.

Rebecca Mead once said to me, "*I pity you, living year after year with such unvaried society at the school. You must have seen no more than thirty or forty people your entire life.*" She'd sneered, and her sister laughed. George Mead had merely stared at me in that predatory way of his.

I shuddered at the memory.

I was walking up the lane toward the house when a carriage came rattling up behind me. Lord Brookhaven rarely had guests. Perhaps it was his solicitor, whom I'd learned was married and thus marked him off my list.

I stepped off the lane and waited for the carriage to pass. But I heard a female voice say, "Stop! Stop the carriage!" Then a woman stuck her head out the window. "Miss Robbins? Is that you?"

"Yes, it is."

It was the young lady whose carriage had overturned the day after I arrived.

"It is I, Millicent Skidmore!" The carriage stopped, and she threw the door open. "The last time you saw me I was bleeding and had just been in that terrible accident. Come inside. We will take you to Lowndesbury House. We're on our way there now."

Mr. Skidmore extended his hand and pulled me in, then he shut the door and the carriage jolted forward.

"How lovely to see you, Miss Robbins. I told everyone about how calm Lord Brookhaven's governess was after the carriage overturned, how hysterical I was, and how you wrapped my hand and sat with me."

I smiled. "I trust you were able to have a good visit to the seaside after the shock of the accident?"

"Oh yes, I always enjoy the seaside. It is my favorite place in the world. I can never get too much of it—the sea air and the sound of the waves. But once we returned home, we were very happy to get Lord Brookhaven's invitation to join him for a house party. Do you know who the other guests will be?"

"I don't, only that it will be a small party. Oh yes, his aunt, Lady Derringer, will be here. She has just arrived."

Miss Skidmore's eyes brightened, and she glanced at her father. "I so enjoy a good party."

Her father did not smile, but he seemed agreeable to the prospect.

"I wonder if I will know anyone besides Lord Brookhaven. And you're sure you don't know who any of the guests will be, besides his aunt?"

"I do know one other guest." I allowed myself a smile as I watched their reactions. "I will be attending. Lord Brookhaven insisted on it."

"Oh." Millicent's eyes went wide. "That is so generous of him! And fortunate for me, for I will know someone."

Mr. Skidmore's brows shot up, but he made no comment.

"Lord Brookhaven must think very highly of you. But of course he does. You are a very genteel, pleasant sort of girl." She smiled as if she had just bestowed a very great compliment on me. At least she wasn't horrified at the thought of the earl inviting his governess to a house party.

"I believe I shall only be attending in the evenings," I said, "when I'm done with my duties." I trembled inside just thinking about being with all those highborn people, but it wasn't all nerves. I would be able to see what these sorts of parties were all about, something I'd always wished for. I would hear lovely music and no doubt see the most extravagant and beautiful clothes I'd ever seen. I could satisfy my curiosity about these kinds of wealthy entertainments, and if I was fortunate, I might even be able to use the dancing skills Mrs. Southey's dancing master had taught me.

"My father is a gentleman, of course," Millicent went on, "and I am not afraid of being in the company of ladies and gentlemen, but if there are lords and ladies, earls and dukes and viscounts and the like, I shall be so frightened. Oh my." She glanced again at her father. "I do believe Lady Derringer is a duchess."

I wanted to tell her that they were only people, human beings like us, but Millicent probably wouldn't appreciate such "wisdom" from a governess and might not like me saying "us" as if she and I were on the same level.

Mr. Skidmore's carriage came to a halt, and we were handed down from the carriage. As I walked away to go around to the back of the house so I could enter near the servants' stairs, I saw Lord Brookhaven exit the front door to greet his guests.

"Miss Robbins, where are you going?" he called out.

I turned to see them all staring at me from the front steps of the house.

"Sir?"

"Come and see my guests. You know them from a few weeks ago."

Mr. Skidmore explained that they had given me a ride up the lane.

Millicent, I noticed, looked frightened and said not a word.

"Miss Robbins will be attending the party, won't you, Miss Robbins?" Lord Brookhaven was eyeing Mr. and Miss Skidmore as he spoke. He seemed to be gauging their reactions.

"Yes, I'm happy I'll have a friend at the party," Millicent finally ventured to say. "Ha-have any of the other guests arrived?"

"You are the first, besides my aunt, Lady Derringer, who is to be hostess, but I'm expecting the others later today."

I saw Millicent's disappointment that he had not volunteered the names of any of the other guests, so I said, "If I may ask, who are the other guests?"

"Lord and Lady Rutledge and their daughter, Miss Rose Rutledge, as well as the Viscount Markeley, Mr. and Mrs. Allen and their son and daughter, Percy and Priscilla Allen. And tomorrow we can expect Mr. Thomas Merritt."

Millicent sounded out of breath, her voice barely above a whisper as she said, "It sounds very . . . lovely . . . many lovely guests."

"Are you acquainted with any of them?" Lord Brookhaven asked Mr. Skidmore.

"No, I don't believe so."

"I trust you will all be good friends in no time," Lord Brookhaven said briskly. "Shall we go inside?"

I caught Millicent's eye and gave her a smile. Her breath seemed to go out of her, and she smiled back. I felt rather gratified and flattered myself that she was grateful for my being there.

Mrs. Merryweather, who was hovering just behind Lord Brookhaven, stepped forward and said, "I'll show you to your rooms."

I silently turned to go back down the front steps.

"Miss Robbins," Lord Brookhaven called.

"Yes, sir?"

"You will join us for music and dancing tonight in the west drawing room."

"Yes, sir."

Three new dresses were laid out on my bed. They were all lovely, and I was so enraptured that they were mine that I could only smile at them and sigh.

Lady Derringer had chosen the material that had been sent from London. She had been present when the dressmaker, Miss Vivaldi, who'd come specially from London to make the dresses, had me try on each one just before it was finished so she could make any alterations. It was Lady Derringer who inspected each garment along with Miss Vivaldi when I tried them on, and it was also Lady Derringer who conferred with the dressmaker if something was too tight or needed other alterations.

This morning, she sent for me. I went to her own private room, where she said, "You'll need some sort of jewelry. You may borrow my brooch to wear with the blue dress and my amber cross with the other two. They are appropriate for a young unmarried lady, and they will look lovely on you." She smiled as she handed me the two pieces.

"They are beautiful. Thank you so very much. You are very generous."

"Not at all. I'm happy to share them with you."

I went back to my room. She was being so kind to me, but she probably only did these things to keep her nephew from embarrassment. She probably guessed that I'd never owned any jewelry. And after all, it was strange for an earl to invite the governess, to have her among his superior guests, although I hadn't seen any indication that she objected to him inviting me.

The brooch and necklace were simple but appropriate, and they would provide me some adornment so that I wouldn't look quite so poor. I didn't wish to embarrass Lord Brookhaven any more than she did.

I started to don the dress that was my favorite for this first night. It was a white muslin with lovely pink and lilac embroidered flowers and vines. It was the prettiest dress I'd ever seen, and I could hardly wait for Lord Brookhaven to see me in it.

That was a silly thought. As if Lord Brookhaven would be interested in seeing me in a lovely dress. But if only to myself, I couldn't deny that I longed to see admiration in his eyes. My heart skipped a beat just thinking about it.

I couldn't forget Mrs. Merryweather's frowns when she'd escorted Miss Vivaldi to one of the spare bedrooms so she could take my measurements. Mrs. Merryweather disapproved. Was it the fact that an earl and his duchess aunt had dresses made for his governess? No doubt it was that and more. She obviously disapproved of Lord Brookhaven inviting me to his house party. But she had not warned me about my manners, nor had she given me any instructions. I hoped that meant that she at least trusted me to conduct myself properly.

Perhaps I should have refused to accept the dresses, but in the moment, I hadn't considered refusing. He hadn't given me the option. Besides, Lady Derringer was in charge of the dresses, would be helping to host the party, and therefore brought an air of respectability and kept Lord Brookhaven from seeming improper.

A thought struck me. Could Mrs. Merryweather believe that Lord Brookhaven was setting me up to be his paramour?

My stomach felt sick. She wouldn't think that, would she? As for Lord Brookhaven's part, it was utterly impossible. Lord Brookhaven surely knew me well enough to know that I would never agree to such a thing. Besides, he'd never once done or said anything untoward or improper to me. Also, why would he have asked Lady Derringer to help him host this party, and why invite respectable, reputable guests if he had nefarious ideas about having an illicit affair with me?

No, unless he did something to alarm me, I simply would not believe Lord Brookhaven meant anything of the kind.

Would I be shunned by his other guests? Even if they didn't think he was treating me with improper attention, they could hardly want to befriend a governess. Even Millicent might ignore me if she thought the other guests looked down on me. I wouldn't blame her if she did. She was afraid of being shunned herself, as she'd never met an earl before Lord Brookhaven, and the next two weeks would be miserable for her if she was not accepted by the other guests.

I, on the other hand, was becoming accustomed to having no one talk to me.

The only thing I worried about was . . . would Lord Brookhaven treat me the same as he always did? Or would he be embarrassed for his guests, Lord and Lady Rutledge or the Viscount Markeley, to see him talking with me? Would he stop talking with me in his friendly way?

Mrs. Merryweather had sent Daisy, one of the upstairs maids, to fix my hair. She'd done so quickly, jerking my hair to the point of pain, with an angry look on her face. Once she'd finished, I thanked her profusely.

Her expression changed to mild surprise, and she almost smiled before saying, "Very good. Now, I must see to my regular work," and rushed out of the room.

I needed to think of a way to thank her, make her a gift of some kind or help her with her work when this was over.

One last look in the mirror. I was transformed. My hair was beautiful, even though it might not be adorned as elaborately as the other ladies'. I did have the kind of hair that cooperated well, thankfully, and I added a couple of little curls to hang down on the sides. I liked the way the color of my dress brought out the pink in my cheeks. But would I look severely unsophisticated among such ladies of society? Well, if I did, I'd just think of this as a new adventure, something I could write about to Hattie, who'd begged me to tell her every interesting detail.

A knock came at my door as the servant's voice called, "Miss Robbins? Lord Brookhaven says you must come downstairs."

"I am coming!" I called back and quickly hurried out.

Hannah had been in the schoolroom when the guests all arrived and had pointed out who was who. Apparently she had seen them before.

"Are they frequent guests?" I'd asked.

"They have come two or three times in the last five years I've been employed here. Lord Brookhaven doesn't have a lot of guests and never has parties."

If Hannah were a friend, I would have said that I thought it was good that he was having a house party, good that he was not isolating himself, as he'd seemed very melancholy the first night I met him, and I didn't think a melancholy person should be always alone. But no doubt Hannah would think me impertinent for presuming to know what our master needed or what was good for him.

My heart was beating fast. When I reached the bottom of the stairs, I nearly tripped. I pressed my hand against my chest as I closed my eyes and concentrated on calming my breathing.

"What are you doing?" Mrs. Merryweather whispered loudly.

I opened my eyes to find her standing in front of me. "I—"

"Get in the drawing room. Make haste. He's asking for you."

Nine

I scurried down the hall toward the room from which I could hear voices, both male and female. When I entered, all eyes turned to me. Lord Brookhaven stood at the fireplace with two young gentlemen.

"There you are," Lady Derringer said, motioning me toward her. "Miss Robbins, you have not met Lord and Lady Rutledge, Miss Rose Rutledge, Mr. Thomas Merritt, Mr. and Mrs. Charles Allen, Mr. Percy Allen, Miss Priscilla Allen, and the Viscount Markeley. But you do know Mr. Skidmore and Miss Millicent Skidmore." Then she glanced around and said, "This is Miss Charlotte Robbins."

"How do you do?" My voice shook a little.

Most of the room just stared at me, but the one she called Mr. Thomas Merritt took a step forward, gave a slight bow, and smiled. "Very pleased to make your acquaintance, Miss Robbins."

I smiled back at him. He was reasonably handsome, but with light, sandy-colored hair and the same sandy side whiskers, eyebrows, and eyelashes. He was the opposite of Lord Brookhaven.

No one else said anything.

Millicent's gaze was more friendly than the other guests, so I sat near her and her father and observed the room while everyone went back to talking amongst themselves. Lady Derringer conversed with

Mr. and Mrs. Allen, and Miss Rose Rutledge was talking with Lord Brookhaven. No one spoke to Millicent or her father.

There were seven ladies and seven gentlemen, making up seven pairs, which of course would thrill Mr. Mims the butler and Mrs. Merryweather, as there must be an equal number of male and female dinner guests for seating purposes.

"Are you enjoying your stay at Lowndesbury House?" I asked Millicent and Mr. Skidmore.

Millicent seemed to let out a breath she'd been holding, and she gave me a trembly smile. "It's a lovely house, and I have a view of the garden from my room. Very lovely." Millicent's eyes were wide. Poor thing. She was so intimidated by these people. They were her people, not mine, as she was a gentleman's daughter, but her very fear of them was probably making them despise her. If she were to pretend confidence and bravado, they'd accept her. It was human nature. I'd seen it even in the hierarchy of the country society around Milford.

Why didn't I feel frightened by these people? I was a lowly governess, after all. Perhaps it was because I knew these lords and ladies and gentlemen would never see me as an equal, so it hardly mattered what I did or didn't do. Also, I knew myself. I was a young woman of some talents and accomplishments and intelligence. I was not exceptionally beautiful or brilliant, but I had enough confidence in myself to not feel inferior, and although I would be considered of inferior birth, that wasn't something I could control, and therefore I couldn't feel bad about it.

And perhaps most important of all, Scripture said, "God is no respecter of persons," so why should I or anyone else be? Clearly, from Scripture, it was wrong to treat people differently based on how much money or power or rank they possessed.

Millicent and I talked of the things I'd always imagined ladies talked of—our new frocks, the hope that we would be asked to dance when there would be dancing, and then I asked her if she'd like to take a walk with me in the morning.

"It will be early," I told her, "for I must at least try to teach my pupils, even though they are excited about all the company and the extra activity and their new puppies. They have not paid enough attention to their studies to learn anything the past two days."

"Oh, I love an early walk." Millicent's face brightened. "I've never been one to sleep overmuch. Shall I meet you outside in the garden?"

"Yes."

I enjoyed my solitary walks, but it would be good to walk with someone else for a change. I didn't suppose Lord Brookhaven would be wandering through the garden while he had so many guests to entertain, and I was always in need of conversation.

Soon dinner was announced. The gentlemen would escort the lady nearest their station. I couldn't help wondering which gentleman I would be paired with, since there was no one so lowly as me. There were three gentleman without a title, so it must be one of them.

I sat and waited, wishing my heart wasn't beating so hard. Lord Markeley escorted the hostess, Lady Derringer. Lord Brookhaven escorted Lady Rutledge, while Lord Rutledge escorted his daughter, Rose Rutledge. Thomas Merritt escorted Priscilla Allen, and I saw the young Percy Allen approach me.

"May I escort you to dinner, Miss Robbins?" His expression was very sober and grave.

I gave a small smile and a nod, then took his arm.

Lord Brookhaven sat at the head of the table, with Lady Rutledge seated to his right and Miss Rose Rutledge to his left. Lady Derringer sat at the opposite end, as the hostess, with Lord Markeley seated to her right and Lord Rutledge to her left.

I ended up seated at the middle of the table, in the least important place, between Mr. Percy Allen and Mr. Skidmore, who'd escorted his daughter, who sat across the table from me. Truly, I'd expected no less than to be seated in the middle, and I was too delighted to be there, and also with the deliciousness and variety of food, to think of where I was seated.

I made an effort to talk with Mr. Percy Allen, but he was not much of a conversationalist. He was probably a bit older than I was, but he seemed younger, with very little to say.

I did my best to draw him out, asking what he enjoyed. Did he like to shoot pheasants? He did. Did he enjoy reading? He did not. Did he know any languages? Only English, as he had no great interest in foreign travel. I eventually gave up and just enjoyed the rest of the meal. I had to resort to only tasting the food, as there were so many courses and dishes, and I felt like a stuffed bird above Lord Brookhaven's mantel well before the last course.

I couldn't help overhearing bits of other conversations. Nor could I ignore Miss Rose Rutledge's frequent laughter as she talked with Lord Brookhaven. He, on the other hand, sometimes looked a bit out of sorts, and more than once I caught him looking at me when I glanced his way. Another time I noticed Miss Rutledge staring at me with an unfriendly expression.

No doubt they were all wondering why the Earl of Brookhaven would invite his governess to sit at dinner with his guests.

After the final course had been served, the ladies retired to the drawing room and the men to Lord Brookhaven's study, where they would smoke and drink port. But it was past my usual bedtime, and I could scarcely keep my eyes open. I turned to Millicent and said, "Forgive me, but I must retire to bed. No one wants to see me yawning."

Millicent's eyes went wide. "I wish you wouldn't leave me."

"You'll be all right," I whispered. "Don't allow them to make you feel inferior. You have every right to be here. You were invited by the Earl of Brookhaven, after all."

"Yes." She nodded, pursing her lips. "Thank you, Miss Robbins."

"Call me Charlotte."

We parted and promised to see each other for our walk in the morning.

My morning was rather enjoyable, as Millicent and I talked of all the guests, the things we'd heard them say the evening before, and our admiration for the lovely dresses. Millicent had even been brave enough to talk with Thomas Merritt and the Viscount Markeley, who she said had been schoolfellows of Lord Brookhaven's.

"And Lord Brookhaven talked very little to Rose Rutledge. He even deigned to speak to me, as he asked me where you had gone to, and I had to tell him you went to bed. He looked none too happy, but I suppose that's how he always looks—grim and slightly angry."

I almost said that he rarely looked that way, but I didn't want her to think I was boasting about my relationship with Lord Brookhaven.

After a half hour of walking and talking, Millicent gave a small grimace and said haltingly, "Forgive me for what I'm about to say—and don't mistake me, I am very glad Lord Brookhaven included you in our party—but . . ."

"You may say it. I'll not be offended."

"Some of the ladies—Miss Rutledge in particular—were talking when Lord Brookhaven excused himself briefly of why he would invite his governess to the party. The men, particularly Mr. Thomas Merritt, defended you and said you were very pretty and very genteel, and he even suggested that Miss Rutledge was jealous. Her face turned positively red, and she said she could never be jealous of anyone who was so beneath her. But just then Lord Brookhaven entered the room, and they stopped talking. It was quite amusing how quickly they ended *that* conversation. The most amusing thing is that it does seem as if Miss Rutledge is jealous of you. Can you imagine? Is that not the most amusing thing?"

"Oh yes, quite diverting." I did my best to laugh along with her, and I forced myself not to consider why I felt a pain in my chest and a sinking in my stomach. I'd ruminate about that later, when I was alone.

"But why do you think Lord Brookhaven invited you? I am sorry, I don't mean to give offense, but you must admit it's very unusual for an earl to invite a governess."

"I am very aware of how it must seem. And I am at a loss, as much as anyone, as to how to explain it."

I wanted to say that Lord Brookhaven enjoyed my company, that he wanted me there so he could engage in intelligent conversation with me, but that did not seem to be the case last evening, when he barely spoke to me at all.

With a perplexed expression, Millicent said, "Perhaps they needed another lady to make up for a gentleman they hadn't expected."

"Yes, perhaps. And perhaps I will beg off tonight," I murmured.

"Oh, I wish you would not." Millicent grabbed my arm. "You saw how I have not a single friend in the party. Besides you," she added.

I didn't want Millicent to be unhappy and alone, with no one to talk to, but I didn't enjoy being exposed to the unkind remarks of his high-ranking guests.

"Lord Rutledge is a baron. Did you know?"

I shook my head.

"But you'd think he was a duke the way Lady Rutledge and Miss Rose Rutledge parade around with their haughty looks." She sighed again. "I think Lord Brookhaven is thinking of marrying her. That must surely be why he invited us all to his house, to have the chance to court her in a respectable way and ask for her hand."

I felt sick. Perhaps I was getting a cold or some kind of fever. At least that would be a good excuse to not return to the drawing room tonight.

Millicent stared down at her dress. "I'm glad it's not muddy. My hems are surviving our walk quite well, thankfully. I do hate cleaning my own hems, but I didn't bring a lady's maid, and I don't wish to ask . . ."

I really wasn't listening to Millicent. Instead, I was thinking that I wasn't sure I could bear to watch Lord Brookhaven courting a vain, haughty girl like Miss Rose Rutledge. He had seated Miss Rutledge next to himself at dinner. And he had talked mostly to her when we were waiting for dinner to be announced.

But surely Millicent was wrong. Why would he invite so many

people if there was only one lady he was interested in? And why invite me, for goodness' sake?

I felt quite heavy as we made our way back to the house. The sun was shining, but it was as if clouds had darkened the sky and rain was threatening to fall.

Millicent went upstairs to go back to bed. "I might as well sleep while the rest of the ladies are sleeping," she said.

I went to the schoolroom to see if the children were ready for their lessons. As I walked in, the children and Hannah were just entering from the children's bedroom, and Lord Brookhaven was standing there, leaning against a bookcase.

"There you all are," he said, pushing himself to his full height. "I have some news." He looked from me to the children. "You are to have a holiday from lessons while my guests are here. No more books. You may do as you please for two weeks."

Samuel whooped, throwing his hands in the air. "I shall ride horses and play with Ernest and get dirty and muddy!"

Hannah began to scold him, but Lord Brookhaven cut her off. "And Annabelle? What shall you do?"

"Play with Maizie and my dolls." She smiled.

"All right, then, go play. I expect to hear a report on Friday about how much you've enjoyed yourselves."

Samuel whooped again as Hannah ushered him back into their room to change into some play clothes "so that you don't spoil your good clothes and give Bessie and me a headache of work, cleaning the mud stains out of your best things."

When they were gone, Lord Brookhaven turned to me. "And what shall you do with your holiday?"

"There are many books I've found that I want to read, including the copies of *Sense and Sensibility* and *Pride and Prejudice* that you gave me, and I can catch up on my letter writing."

"And you will have no excuse to leave the party early tonight." He was staring at me with an intense look in his eyes. "It is my wish that you stay and enjoy yourself. You are enjoying yourself, are you not?"

I cast about in my mind and finally said, "I enjoyed talking with Millicent Skidmore. And I enjoyed dinner. Thank you, sir, for inviting me."

"This evening after dinner we shall have music. Or would you rather play at cards?"

"I'm not much of a card player." Then I quickly added, "But just as you please, my lord. It is your house party."

"Do you play the pianoforte? And sing?"

"I only play a little, and I don't sing. But I do enjoy hearing others play and sing."

"And you can dance."

"Yes."

"Good. Well, then, I shall expect you in the drawing this evening."

Saying thank you didn't seem the right thing. I might say what I was thinking, which was that his guests didn't want me there, and even I wondered why he was subjecting me to their contempt and ill grace, but before I could decide what to say, he was gone.

The day seemed to go by slowly, with me wondering what would happen tonight. Would Lord Brookhaven's guests be even more open with their disdain and dislike of me? Or would they gradually warm to me? One thing was certain: Lord Brookhaven was determined to have me there.

Since I had the whole day to myself, I did my own hair, which took a lot more time than I thought it would. I was not as expert at it as Daisy was, but I did well enough. I also dressed myself in the second of the new gowns and wore Lady Derringer's amber cross.

Would I feel awkward around Mr. Thomas Merritt, knowing that he had said I was pretty and genteel? Hopefully not, since he wouldn't know that Millicent had told me.

I also caught up on my letter writing, a long letter to Hattie and shorter letters to my other correspondents. As I wrote, I told Hattie as many interesting details as possible about the dinner and Lord Brookhaven's guests. I remembered how, when I was younger, I used to imagine that what Mrs. Southey had told me about my parents was not true, but that I was actually the secret daughter of a duke, and that one day, when he was released from prison—or sometimes it was when he escaped from the dungeon of his enemy, or when he'd returned from being a pirate ship captain—he would come and take me away from Mrs. Southey's school and bring me to London with him, where I would be the most sought-after girl of the *ton*.

London had always seemed like the most exciting, interesting place. I'd always longed to go there and be fashionable and go to balls and parties and concerts, even theatricals. Or to be able to attend parties, wear fashionable clothing, and dance with eligible men.

Sometimes it wasn't my father who was the rescuer in my stories. Sometimes it was a rich uncle who had thought me dead. When he discovered I was alive, he would come and take me back to France or Ireland or some other faraway place, where I would, again, be fashionable and the most sought-after dance partner at every party.

It was a fantasy that helped me through periods of loneliness. I'd never told anyone about these fantasies except Hattie, who thankfully never judged me.

Dear Hattie. So trusting and sweet. She was almost too good for this world.

Finally, it was time to venture downstairs. I found Millicent on the landing, lurking in the shadows.

"Charlotte!" she exclaimed, hurrying forward and taking my arm. "I didn't want to go down without you. Father went down an hour ago to smoke his pipe with Lord Brookhaven. Such a dirty habit, don't you think? Oh, and the rumor is that there will be dancing tonight." She whispered close to my ear, "I will be so mortified if no one asks me to dance."

"I'm sure someone will ask you." It was I who was in danger of being ignored all night. But I told myself I would refuse to care. I'd just feel thankful to be there at all, to be able to hear the music and watch the others dance. At least that was my intention. But I knew myself well enough to know that I'd be disappointed if no one asked me to dance. I might even struggle to hold back tears.

Lord God, please don't let me cry in front of these people.

I heard voices and laughter before we reached the drawing room. When Millicent and I entered, no one even noticed, and we each took a glass of lemonade from the sideboard and sat down on the sofa nearest the door. But a few minutes later, Lady Derringer broke away from Lady Rutledge and came over to say, "You both look very pretty this evening. Did you occupy yourselves pleasantly today?"

"We did," Millicent answered. "We went for a morning walk—the grounds at Lowndesbury House are beautiful—and then I confess I went back to bed."

"Sounds very pleasant. And you, Miss Robbins?"

"After our walk I caught up on some letter writing and read a book."

"Also very pleasant."

Lord Brookhaven was suddenly by Lady Derringer's side.

"These two ladies spent their time very pleasantly this morning," she told him.

"Very good." He looked at me. "Did you read any good books, Miss Robbins?"

"I read one of the books you loaned me, *Pride and Prejudice*. It was so good I couldn't stop until I finished it. I read it so quickly that I think I will have to read it again to see what I missed."

He actually smiled at this. "I thought you would enjoy it. The author—authoress, I believe—has a certain wit and liveliness one doesn't often find."

"Oh yes, I agree. And the characters were so real, it was as if I could see and hear them, as if I knew them."

His eyes danced.

"I wish I was more of a reader," Millicent said.

"I also do not read as much as I should," Lady Derringer said. "I can see you both enjoyed that novel."

"Lord Brookhaven!" Miss Rose Rutledge called from the other side of the room. "Come and settle an argument I'm having with Lord Markeley."

Lord Brookhaven's expression instantly changed, like a thundercloud descending. "Pray excuse me," he told Miss Rutledge. "Ask Mr. Merritt to settle your argument." He turned back to me. "What did you think of Lady Catherine and Mr. Collins?"

"They were both so shocking. I laughed out loud several times."

He opened his mouth to say something just as dinner was announced.

He bowed to me with a smile and went to find his dinner partner.

Again, we made our way into the dining room, but this time no one seemed to care about the rules of class and rank, as I was escorted by Thomas Merritt and Millicent was escorted by the Viscount Markeley. I could tell by her expression that she was nervous but gratified, as he was attentive, smiling and talking to her.

Mr. Thomas Merritt turned out to be a much better conversationalist than Mr. Percy Allen had been the night before. I found myself once again seated in the middle of the table, but I was opposite Mr. Merritt and beside Lord Markeley. The conversation became quite lively at one point, with Mr. Merritt and the viscount debating which was less important to a gentleman's education: studying literature or learning Greek and Latin, languages that they would never use in their lives.

"And how much of any of these subjects did you master?" I couldn't help asking, smiling to let them know I was more amused than disapproving.

"Well, now, that's a good point," Mr. Merritt said, also smiling. "I was forced to memorize several poems and even some prose, and I conjugated my share of Greek verbs, but I daresay I remember none of it now."

"You did better than me, Merritt," Lord Markeley said. "What do you think of the importance of such subjects of study, Miss Robbins?" Lord Markeley's gaze held a glint of mischief.

"Yes." Mr. Merritt focused his striking blue eyes on me. "As an educator, you must have an opinion."

"I'd venture to guess she thinks we should have been better students," Lord Markeley said. The viscount was almost as handsome as Mr. Merritt, but taller and thinner, with coarse brown hair and brown eyes.

"Truthfully, having grown up in a school for ladies, I have little experience with the education of gentlemen, but I should think their education would be better applied to the tasks they would naturally be expected to know and perform in their future adult lives, whatever that might be, and only apply themselves to literature and languages if they feel so inclined—beyond a rudimentary knowledge of each, so that they don't embarrass themselves in company."

"Ah, thank you for that, Miss Robbins," Mr. Merritt said, attempting to bow to me, even though the table was between us.

"Yes, thank you, Miss Robbins," Lord Markeley said. "The next time my mother scolds me for spending more time running away from my tutor than studying, I shall repeat your words as a great educator and authority."

"I beg you would not characterize me so." I chuckled, realizing he was mostly in jest. "I am neither a great educator nor an authority."

I glanced at the head of the table, where Lord Brookhaven was glowering down at us. Did he disapprove of how loud we were being? Lady Rutledge and Miss Rose Rutledge both looked quite unamused. I wasn't sure I'd ever seen anyone look so dour.

But then one corner of Lord Brookhaven's mouth turned up slightly. Could this change in demeanor be due to his amusement at the Rutledges' disapproval? I was delighted to think so.

The dinner was delicious, I was sure, but I hardly noticed. I was not so stuffed as I'd been the evening before either, as I was too busy talking with Mr. Merritt and Lord Markeley to eat overmuch. I even talked past the viscount to include Millicent in the conversation, which the viscount didn't seem to mind at all. In fact, he seemed rather amused and surprised by me.

My mood was quite elevated by the gentlemen's attentions. It was almost as if I was someone else. I was lively and vivacious, speaking my mind while keeping my conversation proper. I never felt . . . prettier.

I only wished it was Lord Brookhaven who was seated next to me instead of Lord Markeley, sharing my lively, pleasant mood and sometimes-clever words.

As it was, I hoped he didn't think I was shamelessly flirting with the gentlemen. The thought made my stomach sink, but I was enjoying myself so much, I decided I didn't care. Not very much, anyway.

Why did Lord Brookhaven have to escort Rose Rutledge to dinner, which meant she was sitting beside him again? Lord Brookhaven spent much of his time staring morosely down at his plate, since those on his other side, Mr. Skidmore and Mrs. Allen, seemed quite engrossed in their own conversation. Rose, having her father on the other side of her, seemed less in the mood for talking than usual.

I felt rather sorry for Lord Brookhaven, but it was his dinner party. If he wished for livelier conversation, he should stop seating Rose Rutledge beside him. In fact, Lord Brookhaven could escort anyone he wished, or he could move the place cards to wherever he wanted his guests to sit.

I grinned as I imagined him taking the place cards and moving them around just before dinner, placing me beside him in the highest place, rather than the lowest.

"What are you smiling about? Pray tell, Miss Robbins." Lord Markeley then turned to Millicent. "What do you think she is smiling about? You are her friend. Does she laugh at us when we are not nearby?"

"Oh no, I don't believe Miss Robbins would laugh at anyone." Millicent was looking quite earnest as she stared at the viscount. "She is very kind."

"Thank you, Millicent." I winked at her.

"A wink!" Lord Markeley exclaimed, looking across at Mr. Merritt. "She is winking now. A very bad sign for us, eh, Merritt?"

"Indeed it is. I'm afraid Miss Skidmore is the kind one."

I simply shook my head, allowing myself a small, mysterious smile. In the interest of not taking the gentlemen's bait, I said, "Miss Skidmore is very kind and generous. That is certainly true."

"Ahh," Lord Markeley said, nodding, and Mr. Merritt frowned knowingly, then winked at me.

It was all in good fun, but Lady Rutledge cleared her throat and growled, "High spirits—perhaps too high for the dinner table."

I glanced at Lady Derringer, terrified she would appear angry with us for being too loud. She gave me a crooked smile, as if to let me know she did not share Lady Rutledge's disapproval. Nevertheless, the conversation was much more subdued for the rest of dinner.

We all retired to the music room, the men forgoing their usual smoking and drinking, and Miss Priscilla Allen was prevailed upon to play on the pianoforte and sing a duet with her brother Percy Allen. I enjoyed hearing the music and the verses of the song. It was a pleasure I'd had at Mrs. Southey's school many times, but I'd not heard any music since I'd come to Lowndesbury House.

After two more songs, Miss Rose Rutledge took a turn. Truly, she had a very refined voice—much better than Miss Allen's, of which Miss Rutledge was surely well aware—but she only played the one song before saying, "Mother, won't you play something that will allow us to dance?"

"Of course, darling." Lady Rutledge took her place at the instrument and looked at Lord Brookhaven. "Shall I play some lively tunes for dancing?"

"Of course. Just as you like." Lord Brookhaven was the picture of an amiable host. He and the other gentlemen proceeded to move the furniture against the walls to make more room.

Lord Markeley took a step toward me at the exact moment Thomas Merritt opened his mouth as if to speak to me. But when Mr. Merritt saw Markeley, he turned immediately to Miss Priscilla Allen, while Lord Markeley asked me, "Will you do me the honor of granting me the first dance?"

"It would be my pleasure." Now, if only I didn't make a misstep and embarrass myself.

Lord Brookhaven, as I expected, asked Rose Rutledge to be his partner for the first dance. And Mr. Percy Allen asked Millicent.

When we had all taken our places, Lady Rutledge began to play and the dancing began.

Despite my nerves, my heart soared as my feet moved in time to the music and in concert with Lord Markeley. Was this really me, Charlotte Robbins, a woman of no family or wealth, dancing with a young and handsome viscount?

And yet I couldn't help wishing I was dancing with Lord Brookhaven instead.

How could he wish to dance with a coldhearted, haughty-eyed woman like Miss Rutledge? He couldn't intend to marry her, could he? My thoughts seemed jealous and even envious. That was not the kind of person I strived to be. But I would need to think about that later. Now I would enjoy my partner and the music and this dance and not clutter my mind with anything else.

Indeed, I did enjoy the way Lord Markeley kept his eyes on me, obviously enjoying the dance. I could tell that everyone else was stepping lively, almost bumping into one another, as this wasn't meant to be a ballroom. And yet it was sufficient for our fourteen people, only eight of whom were dancing.

We were moving too fast for conversation, so we spun and hopped and skipped our way around the other three couples. I could feel my cheeks growing pink with the exertion, and I don't think I could have stopped smiling if I'd wanted to.

As the song ended, Priscilla Allen cried out, then limped toward her mother. Everyone fluttered around her. Apparently she had turned her ankle. Her mother was asking her if she wanted someone to help her to her room.

"No, no, I'll just rest it." Her expression was sullen as she let out a quick breath and sat with her mother, who patted her arm.

We all wondered which of the men would have to do without a partner, until Percy Allen said, "Unless Lady Derringer wishes to dance, I'll sit out the rest."

Did the man never smile?

"My dancing days are over, I'm afraid," Lady Derringer said apologetically.

So there were only three pairs of dancers getting ready for the next song. Lady Rutledge raised her brows, waiting for her cue, while we exchanged partners. Mr. Merritt claimed me, while Lord Brookhaven asked Millicent, and Lord Markeley stood opposite Rose Rutledge.

Once again, we all whirled around the floor. I was spinning so, my swaying dress almost got caught around my ankles a time or two.

Mr. Merritt was as agreeable a partner as Lord Markeley had been, perhaps even more so, since Mr. Merritt had a slightly more mature air about him. Lord Markeley still had something of a boy's manner, though he was the same age as me, Millicent had confided. She had consulted her copy of *Debrett's Peerage* to also discover that Lord Brookhaven was six-and-twenty, and since he and Thomas Merritt were schoolfellows, he was probably also the same age.

I'd glanced at Millicent and Lord Brookhaven—how could I not?—and I found Lord Brookhaven giving Millicent his full attention, while she was looking enthralled, if a little nervous, as she gazed up at him. Truly, his was the most commanding presence in the room. Would he dance with me next? Or was that going too far, for an earl to lower himself to dance with a governess?

Again, I reminded myself to enjoy my partner, Mr. Merritt, who was undeniably handsome and agreeable.

The dance was soon over, and Mr. Merritt suggested we take some lemonade, which had been brought in after the last dance. My heart was beating fast as my eyes met Millicent's. She was obviously happy, her eyes sparkling and her cheeks rosy. But I was highly aware of Lord Brookhaven throwing back his lemonade as if it were a cup of medicine. How could even that small act be so masculine and appealing?

When Lady Rutledge signaled that she was ready to play, Mr. Merritt wasted no time in asking Rose Rutledge for the next dance. Lord Markeley approached Millicent, and I allowed myself to look toward Lord Brookhaven. I'd already danced with the other gentlemen, who had now paired themselves with the other ladies. It was Lord Brookhaven's turn to ask me, but he was speaking with the butler, Mr. Mims, in the doorway.

Would I be passed over by Lord Brookhaven and be forced to sit down for this dance? I tried not to let my face show my disappointment.

I watched as Millicent stood opposite Lord Markeley and Mr. Merritt smiled at Rose Rutledge. Lady Rutledge was frowning from her place at the pianoforte, looking impatiently toward Lord Brookhaven.

My stomach twisted as the others glanced over at Lord Brookhaven, still in quiet conversation with the butler, and then at me. I could feel my cheeks starting to burn.

Suddenly, Lord Brookhaven waved Lady Derringer over, who immediately took over the conversation with the butler, allowing Lord Brookhaven to escape.

His gaze found me, and he strode over. "May I have this dance?"

"Of course." I gave him my gloved hand. It was the first time we had ever touched, and a thrill went up my arm and across my shoulders.

He signaled to Lady Rutledge to begin, then he led me to the middle of the room as the music started to play.

Relief and joy enlivened me as I stared up at Lord Brookhaven, though I tried not to look *too* happy. No sense embarrassing myself in front of him and the rest of his guests.

Just like in my dreams, he was gazing at me with those mysterious blue eyes, and my heart was bursting out of my chest.

Dancing was for flirtation and courting and entertainment, although Lord Brookhaven had never struck me as being interested in flirting, courting, or entertainment. He would need to secure a wife at some point, but he was so serious, even melancholy, that dancing in and of itself didn't seem to be something he would engage in for pleasure.

I fancied I knew him, that I understood his nature, but from the expression on his face, I struggled to decipher his thoughts and emotions. Perhaps he was enjoying himself, though not as much as he enjoyed a good solitary ramble or deep conversation.

There was a moment during the dance that we waited for our turn to proceed between the two lines of dancers, and Lord Brookhaven had just enough time to say, "You dance very well, Miss Robbins."

His words of praise went straight to my head and I nearly made a misstep as we galloped between the other dancers, took a twirl with other partners, then came back together.

"Thank you, sir, and you as well," I said.

He wasn't smiling as the rest of the dancers were. Was he even enjoying himself?

I, on the other hand, couldn't think of anything I enjoyed as much as dancing with Lord Brookhaven in this moment. Although my fear of making a serious misstep did detract a bit from my enjoyment.

But then, halfway through the dance, he reached for my gloved hands and his fingers stroked my bare arm—unintentionally, of course. In that moment, the way he looked at me . . . no one had ever gazed at me so intensely. My arm tingled, and I seemed to be lost in those unfathomable eyes.

A moment before, I had struggled to decipher what he was thinking. Was I insane to think I now could feel his emotions, the depth of his thoughts? I could even imagine that he loved me.

I was flooded with a joy so intense it was almost painful. But maybe the pain was only from knowing that he couldn't possibly love me, and I couldn't escape this unrequited love I felt for him. It was as thrilling as it was sobering, but falling in love with him was as inevitable as my next breath.

Indeed, thinking about how much each day revolved around whether I saw him and talked with him, I'd probably been falling in love with him since that first evening when he'd related his childhood memory of running into a tree.

The music ended too soon. My heart was in my throat as he

squeezed my hand, bowed, then turned away before I could enjoy how close he was to me.

I felt bereft and overwhelmed with joy, and everything in between those two emotions, all at once. *Dear Lord, please don't let it show on my face.*

The next dance was with Lord Markeley, who seemed a bit tipsy, having brought from dinner a glass of what I presumed was a spirit with high alcohol content. He stumbled during the dance, nearly stepping on my toes, and leaned heavily on my arm while we waited our turn. I was praying we would make it through the song.

Lord Brookhaven was staring sharply at us, ignoring Miss Rutledge. When it ended, Lord Brookhaven said, almost scowling, "That's enough dancing for this evening."

Lord Markeley let out a rather loud hiccup.

"Darling," Lady Rutledge said to her daughter as she stood up and moved away from the pianoforte, "why don't you play something?"

Rose Rutledge went to the instrument and began to play and sing while everyone else found a seat.

Again, I was impressed by her talent. I'd once aspired to play well, but alas, I didn't have the patience to sit and practice for hours every day after my schoolwork was done. I soon accepted that I was destined to only play "a little."

As we listened to the music, Millicent looked happier than I'd ever seen her. I suddenly suspected that Lord Brookhaven had invited Millicent to the party specifically for me, knowing that we'd both be the outsiders of the group.

Tears stung my eyes. How good and kind he was. But why? He couldn't care for me in a romantic sense. Yet, it seemed too much for an earl to condescend with so much kindness toward his governess, a girl of no family and no fortune at all. It was too much even for Lord Brookhaven.

Trays of tea and biscuits were brought, likely with Lord Markeley in mind, to sober him up a bit. The servant who brought them glanced at me. Her face was drawn, and she had dark smudges under her eyes, and I knew it was well past her usual bedtime. She quickly left the room, and I felt a pang of pity for her before remembering that she had snubbed me the last two Sundays, giving me a pointed look of disdain before whispering to her companion behind her hand, then giggling as they rushed past me.

No doubt she would hate me even more by next Lord's Day.

I sipped my cup of tea while we listened to Miss Rutledge. When the song ended, we clapped as politely as we would have if she had not sang well and played excellently. That was the way of society. It was always polite. Until one was unfortunate enough to fall out of favor with society.

Lord Markeley was leaning back against the cushions of his chair, looking as if he might be about to fall asleep. At least he wasn't drinking any more strong spirits.

We were quiet, probably all trying to think of some safe subject of conversation, when Lord Brookhaven asked, "Would you all like to play a game of pall mall on the lawn tomorrow?"

"Oh yes!" Millicent said.

"If the weather is fair," Lord Brookhaven added, his gaze fastening on mine.

"As long as we can play competitively," Lord Markeley said.

"I agree," Mr. Merritt said. "I once hit a young lady's ball into the trees and she cried. Her mama looked as if she could murder me. The rest of the afternoon was not very pleasant."

Lord Markeley laughed, a cynical look on his face.

"Then we shall warn everyone that the game shall be played in the most cutthroat manner, and there are to be no tears." Lord Brookhaven's face was unreadable, his voice deep and even.

I had to stifle my laugh behind my hand.

"Absolutely no crying allowed." Lord Brookhaven gave me a pointed look.

"Of course." I smiled. I fancied I saw the corner of his mouth quirk upward.

"I can certainly be competitive if I must," Millicent was saying. "And I should hope I won't cry over a silly game of pall mall."

Neither of us would cry, especially now that we knew it wasn't permitted, but in truth, I was glad they made that stipulation. I could be very competitive myself.

Rose Rutledge played another song, then declared that she would let someone else play. "Miss Allen?" Rose said. "Are you well enough to come and play?"

"I don't know." She stuck her bottom lip out slightly.

"Try to stand on it," her mother said.

Lord Brookhaven and Mr. Merritt helped her stand, and she tried her weight on it.

"I think I can walk," she said. "But I should like to go up to my room now."

Everyone else decided to retire for the evening as well, and so I realized I could go too.

"Shall we go for a walk in the morning?" Millicent whispered as we parted from each other on the staircase landing.

I nodded, and as I turned to go to my room, caught Lord Brookhaven's eye.

"Good night, Miss Robbins," he said.

"Sleep well," I answered and continued up the stairs to the servants' quarters on the next floor.

Eleven

As I waited for Millicent at our meeting place, I pondered my reckless thought the night before, that I was in love with Lord Brookhaven.

Such a thing could not happen. It had only been the excitement of the moment. Not only was he an earl, and therefore far above me and out of my social sphere, but he was my employer.

The relationship would be unfair to us both. Unfair to him because it would bring him down in the eyes of his peers and possibly even cause the ruin of his family name, thereby harming Samuel and Annabelle. And it was unfair to me due to the fact that, as a poor governess with no family, I had no power. Although if he wished to marry me . . .

But peers of the realm simply did not marry servants, and I was in fact a servant, even if the other servants never considered me one of them.

And if I was right about him, Lord Brookhaven was too good a man to take advantage of a girl like me with no power, privilege, or say-so. And as far-fetched as a marriage proposal from Lord Brookhaven might seem, I could not accept even if he offered, since I could not harm Samuel and Annabelle that way.

I felt the air go out of me. Until that moment, I hadn't realized how much I'd been hoping to think of a way Lord Brookhaven might marry me.

A tear dripped from my eye. I tore off my glove and flicked the offending drop away. How foolish to cry about something that I knew could never be. Had the invitation to the house party made me think I could be like the members of society, of gentlemen, lords, and ladies born into privilege and wealth? I was not one of them. No doubt Lord Brookhaven only invited me because he needed one more female to have enough pairs for dinner and partners for dancing. I was only performing a service for my lord, serving in the capacity for which he needed me. That was all.

A stab of pain went through me. I didn't want to believe it, but I must. Otherwise my heart would be torn from my chest when I had to accept the truth, and I didn't want to humiliate myself in the process.

"Miss Robbins?"

I spun around. Lord Brookhaven was standing not ten feet away in the shadow of an oak tree.

"My lord." I rubbed my cheek, then quickly dropped my hand, lest he suspect I was wiping away tears.

"Are you well?"

"Oh yes, very well. It is a fine morning for a walk."

"A bit foggy, but otherwise fine." He was staring hard at me.

I smiled to show him that he was mistaken if he thought I'd been crying. "I very much enjoyed the evening," I said. "Dancing and the music. And the dinner was very good as well. Very pleasant."

"I am glad to hear it. I hope Lord Markeley's behavior toward you was not improper in any way. He was quite inebriated last evening."

"No, not at all. There was nothing improper."

"Good. He'd received some unwelcome news from home."

"I am very sorry for his bad news. I hope it was nothing too terrible."

"His mother's illness. But I shall allow him to tell you of it, if he wishes."

The conversation paused. I wondered what he was thinking. Had he sought me out this morning? Or was it only by chance that he encountered me here? Shamelessly, I was just happy to see him and to have this moment alone with him.

"I believe I see Miss Millicent Skidmore coming this way. I shall leave you two to your walk. But I will see you this evening."

"Yes, of course."

He was gone before Millicent had made her way to me.

"Was that Lord Brookhaven?" she whispered.

"It was."

"Did he arrange to meet you here?" She lowered her voice even more.

"No, no. I suppose he was taking his morning walk and came upon me unintentionally." I said it as though there could be no other explanation.

Millicent began chattering about the evening, about dancing with such amiable gentlemen as Lord Brookhaven, Lord Markeley, and Mr. Thomas Merritt. "Truly, I cannot believe my good fortune at being here. My cousins shall be so envious. Do you know I have three cousins, all ladies, all out at the same time? My grandmother is completely unable to single me out to help me find suitors, and even though our carriage accident was very frightening, it was rather providential in the end."

"It was, for now you are here with me." I linked my arm through hers and we started down the path toward the garden.

"Oh, yes. I do hope you will write to me when I've gone home to Shropshire. I do enjoy receiving letters, though I am not much of a letter writer, but I will write to you, I promise. Am I not a silly, selfish girl?"

"Not at all. You just don't enjoy writing letters. The fact that you write anyone at all shows unselfishness."

"You are so good, Charlotte. A true friend." She gave me a gratifying smile and squeezed my arm. "And even though Rose Rutledge has not yet condescended to have a conversation with me, she does sing and play divinely, does she not?"

"She does indeed."

"She is very accomplished, or so I've overheard from her mama and Mrs. Allen."

So we had all heard. Lady Rutledge had proclaimed all of her daughter's accomplishments loudly and often since they'd arrived. And I would never have told anyone, but I had mentally counted off each accomplishment—fluent in French, German, and Italian; skilled in painting and fancy needlework; well-read in both prose and poetry; beautiful penmanship and letter-writing skills; a thorough education in arithmetic and the sciences. And I allowed myself the prideful thought that I could match each one, all except her playing and singing abilities. But it hardly made me the kind of "catch" that Miss Rose Rutledge was considered, since she was a wealthy baron's daughter and would receive a large dowry.

I changed the subject, and we talked of the banter between us, Lord Markeley, and Mr. Merritt at the dinner table.

"I would accept a marriage proposal from either of them." Millicent sighed. "They are both so handsome. I'd been worried I'd end up married to one of my father's widower friends. They're so old." She scrunched her face and squeezed her eyes shut.

I hadn't noticed either Mr. Merritt or Lord Markeley showing any interest in her, but I hoped for her sake that one of them would. Either of them could offer her a life of great privilege and security.

I hadn't noticed Millicent mentioning anything about love, but I suspected she thought marriage was the same thing as love, that she would instantly love her husband, and that she could make her husband love her. But I'd seen too many marriages, just being a vigilant observer in church and around the village of Milford, to have noticed that there seemed to be little affection between most husbands and wives. And one of the teachers at Mrs. Southey's school had been carrying on some kind of relationship with a married man, a wealthy former tradesman who lived in Milford. Mrs. Southey dismissed her as soon as she learned of it. Such a thing could have been the ruinous end of our school, if gossip of the affair had spread.

Love. It was the thing I wanted most in the world, perhaps because I'd received so little of it. And I just couldn't bear the thought that I might never have a husband who loved me.

Even Miss Allen, with her injured ankle, came out to play pall mall.

The weather was perfect, with only a slight breeze and some clouds but no threat of rain as Miss Allen pulled names written on small pieces of paper out of Lord Markeley's hat to see who would go first. Rose Rutledge's name was chosen first, mine was next to last, and Lord Brookhaven was last.

The one-foot-tall iron hoop stood about a hundred feet away from us on the grassy lawn. Traditionally, the alley on which one played pall mall was not grassy but made of hard, bare ground, but "the grass is very short here," Lord Brookhaven said, "and so it shall serve nearly as well."

After we had started to play, Lady Derringer came strolling out.

"Come and join us," I called to her.

"We can work you in," Lord Brookhaven said. "Not everyone has taken a turn yet."

"I may not stay," she said. "I'm expecting a letter from a friend, so I shall just watch."

By the time it was my turn, Mr. Merritt had the best score. It had taken him three hits with his wooden mallet to get the ball through the iron hoop at the end of the grassy alley. No one else had done it in less than five tries.

I set my feet on either side of the ball, drew back my mallet, and hit it.

I hadn't shared the information that I'd played pall mall before. Mrs. Southey believed it was an appropriate exercise for young ladies. Therefore, the garden at Mrs. Southey's school possessed an alley and iron hoop, and all the girls who boarded at the school were gifted a mallet their first Christmas, and there were spare mallets for the other girls. I'd been playing pall mall since I was six years old.

The ball rolled straight. Lord Markeley's eyebrows rose. "It's still going."

The small amount of conversation that had been going on suddenly ceased. Someone gasped. Then my ball passed cleanly through the hoop without touching.

"Oh my!" Millicent exclaimed.

"Well done!" Mr. Merritt clapped his hands.

Miss Allen's voice trailed off as she said, "I've never seen anyone . . ."

Rose Rutledge was glaring, as was her mama.

"How did you do that?" Millicent said.

I couldn't help smiling as I turned to Lord Brookhaven. "Your turn, my lord."

"I'm not sure if there's any need for me to take a turn now."

"Don't forget what you said, that we would play in a cutthroat manner and that there were to be absolutely no tears."

His mouth fell open slightly.

Mr. Merritt guffawed and slapped his own leg. "She has you there, Brooksie!"

"Cutthroat indeed!" Lord Markeley was looking on with wide eyes and an even wider smile.

"Miss Robbins is quite right," Lord Brookhaven said. "No crying. I suppose I must take my turn now."

I was so relieved he was taking my win—and my jest—with such good grace. And now, as his gaze settled on me . . . it made my heart swell to bursting.

"It's the only way to finish the game."

"Very well, then." He stared a moment longer, his grin turning into a crooked frown.

He took his first shot, which went short and wide. After two more, his ball went through the hoop on the fourth hit.

"Well done, Brookhaven," Lord Markeley said, "but you were bested by myself, and especially by Miss Robbins." With an exaggerated bow and a smirk, he acknowledged my win.

Mr. Merritt came over and tipped his hat to me. "I hope you will not be offended when I say that I was surprised that you bested me."

"Not at all." I did my best to hide my own smirk.

"Shall we play again?" Mr. Merritt asked the group.

Everyone seemed agreeable, so Miss Allen drew names again. This time I was first. And once again, my ball went through the hoop on the first hit.

"What is happening here?"

"How, Miss Robbins?"

"Is it your mallet?"

"Something's not right here. No one is that lucky."

The latter comment was made by Miss Rose Rutledge.

"Tell us your secret, Miss Robbins." Thomas Merritt stepped toward me and leaned on his mallet. "How do you do it?"

"The secret," I said, "is that I've had a lot of practice."

Everyone was talking at once, giving their opinions, some loudly and some whispered to their neighbor.

"Well played."

I turned to see Lord Brookhaven standing near my right shoulder. He was smiling in a congratulatory way.

"Did you know about this?" Miss Rose Rutledge demanded, staring at Lord Brookhaven.

"Know about what?" he asked, his expression bland.

Lady Rutledge scowled.

"That she was born playing pall mall and couldn't miss?" Lord Markeley said.

"That she would show us all up?" Mr. Merritt added.

Lord Brookhaven took his time answering. "No, I did not know of Miss Robbins's experience with playing pall mall. If I had, it wouldn't have mattered—not to me, at least. It appears she has earned her expertise at playing the game from extensive practice."

Both Rutledge ladies continued to look disgruntled, perhaps more so because of his coming to my defense.

"It is not as though anyone has placed any wagers on the game," Lord Brookhaven continued.

"Speak for yourself," Lord Markeley muttered, exchanging a look with Mr. Merritt.

After some more grumbling, I said, "If I may? To make the game harder, my friends and I added small iron stakes to the alley. We had to hit each stake once on our way to the hoop. For example, if we put a zigzag of three stakes on the alley, we would have to hit the ball so that it touched each stake once, and then get it through the hoop. And if you like, everyone else could just get their ball through the hoop without having to touch the stakes."

"That seems fair," Rose Rutledge said.

"I will do what Miss Robbins does," Mr. Merritt said. "I will hit the stakes and take my ball through the hoop."

"I will as well," Lord Markeley said, then murmured, "though I know it is folly to play pall mall with Miss Robbins."

Lord Brookhaven sent a servant to fetch three iron stakes, then said, "Everyone may do as they wish. When it is your turn, you must announce whether you plan to hit the stakes or whether you simply wish to hit your ball through the hoop."

It was a livelier game after that. Lord Brookhaven looked as if he was enjoying it.

Out of the next three games, I won two quite easily and tied the third with Mr. Merritt. I was able to observe Lord Brookhaven's good-natured way of playing, as well as Miss Rutledge's petulance.

Mr. Merritt and Lord Markeley were quite competitive and enjoyed wagering over the outcome of each game, and Millicent seemed in awe of the liveliness of the gentlemen. And I enjoyed myself immensely.

We decided to pause our playing and have tea. As we were walking, I ended up a bit isolated from the others as we passed through the hedge. Then I saw Miss Rose Rutledge draw near, as if she'd been waiting for me. She said in a hushed voice, "I don't know what you aim to achieve from this little game, but you will not get your claws into Lord Brookhaven. He would never marry a servant."

She said the last word with a sneering twist of her lips.

I stared at her, too surprised to think of a retort.

Her face changed as she seemed to catch sight of someone, and she called out, "Lord Brookhaven."

He was rather close behind me. Had he heard what she'd said about him never marrying a servant? I couldn't tell from the impassive look on his face.

"Miss Rutledge," he said cooly, then addressed me. "Do you think Samuel and Annabelle would enjoy this game?"

"Oh yes. I wanted to ask if we could leave the alley set up as it is so that I can teach them to play." My words were a bit halting, as I was still recovering from the shock of Miss Rutledge's words. Was she truly worried that Lord Brookhaven might want to marry me? That I was scheming to make him propose marriage? There was a pain in my chest that I'd better not examine just now, right here.

He was gazing into my eyes, and the thought occurred to me that Rose Rutledge was jealous—jealous of *me* and the attention Lord Brookhaven paid to me.

It was such a strange thought, but once again, I couldn't examine my feelings just now, as I was completely captured by his gaze. There was such a serious expression on his face. What was he thinking?

The rest of the day and evening, Rose Rutledge seemed to hover around Lord Brookhaven, while his mood was quiet and his expression morose.

William paced around his room after all his guests had retired to bed.

He wished he'd never invited Rose Rutledge to his house party. How dare she speak to Charlotte Robbins that way?

But it was evidence of two things: one, that he had allowed his feelings for Charlotte to show more than he'd intended; and two, that his plan to try to get his friends to accept Charlotte Robbins into their social circle was not working as well as he might have liked. Even Merritt and Markeley were beginning to notice his attitude toward Miss Robbins was more as an admirer than employer. They'd mentioned it to him the night before.

"You know you can't marry her," Markeley had said as he and Merritt caught him in the hallway near their rooms.

"If you wish to set her up in her own place, no one will judge you, as long as you're discreet." Merritt said the words quietly.

"So you wish me to ruin her while saving my reputation?"

"Ruin her?" Markeley sneered. "She's a governess."

William thought about punching him in the face. "You must think me a selfish heathen who cares about no one but himself."

"What do you mean?" Markeley said, looking truly confused. "Miss Robbins could hardly get a better offer. She'd never have to work another day, and you'd provide well for her, I'm sure."

Again, the thought of punching him was very appealing, but William knew the man was only speaking as a selfish, privileged young gentleman of the *ton*, unused to thinking of the welfare and the feelings of others. And both Merritt's and Markeley's spiritual state was much worse than he'd imagined, that they could be so off-hand about leading an innocent woman into a life of degradation and sin.

"Send her away, then," Merritt said. "But don't throw yourself away on her. Even now you could have Miss Rose Rutledge for fifty thousand pounds. Or many other young ladies of even higher social standing."

He turned his face in the opposite direction, taking a moment to calm himself. When he was confident he could speak in a cool, collected manner, he said, "So you think her unworthy of marriage to a gentleman?"

They both stared at him for a moment. Finally, Merritt said, "That is not the issue."

Markeley added, "You're not making sense."

"The issue is not her worthiness as a wife but your worthiness as an earl. You should be marrying the daughter of an earl, or at least the daughter of someone . . ." Merritt seemed to be searching for the right word. "Someone with an old name and a fortune."

"At least one or the other," Markeley added.

He could try to explain to them that he wanted someone who was worthy due to their good character. Or he could tell them that he wanted to make certain he didn't end up married to someone like his mother—or his father. But they'd never understand. To them, marriage was similar to winning the best prize in a contest, and neither the prize nor the contest had anything to do with the person's character or temperament.

"So if it was discovered that she had an old name or a fortune . . . ?"

"Since she was a governess, she'd need both to be accepted," Merritt said.

"A large fortune, though . . . that's probably all she needs to make her respectable." Markeley raised his brows. "But there isn't much chance of that, since she's an orphan."

"You're not going to do anything impulsive, are you?" Merritt gave him a worried look. "I remember you liked to defend the weaker boys in school. It never got you anything but a bloody nose."

"Just find her a place in town," Markeley drawled. "Put her up, give her a little money, and enjoy life a little before you have to get married and produce an heir."

William's face was growing quite warm. He glared at Markeley. "That I will not do. And Miss Robbins would never . . . never let anyone treat her that way. You don't know her, obviously. She has self-respect, and she believes in right and wrong. She's not like you, not like the wealthy and privileged who take whatever they want."

"Easy, now," Merritt said. "You're 'the wealthy and privileged' too."

"Don't go getting crusty," Markeley said.

"We're just trying to advise you." Merritt leaned closer. "You were ill-used by that cunning baggage you were once engaged to. But that's all in the past. You were young; no one blames you. It's time to find an innocent young viscount's daughter, someone who will swoon at your attention."

"Or at least swoon at your houses and your money." Markeley had changed since they were schoolfellows of fourteen or fifteen. He used to have a kind heart. Now he was more or less like everyone else of his acquaintance. They both were.

A servant was coming down the hall, so they parted quickly. And now that he was alone, he thought some more about Charlotte Robbins inheriting a fortune.

Lady Derringer had yet to say anything about his inviting Miss Robbins to his house party except that she liked her. After she met her, Lady Derringer had said, "She's a very lovely young woman, intelligent, with an easy and kind way about her. It's a pity she has no fortune."

If Miss Robbins did have a fortune, she could do as she wished, go where she liked, and see all the things she'd ever wanted to see. She would have more choices and could live her life as she wished.

All her life she'd been limited to staying in her little village and teaching at the same school where she grew up, or else taking her chances on finding a position as a governess. And he knew, from all the stories he'd heard, that governesses often were preyed upon by someone at the house where they were employed, usually the master of the house, or one of the older sons. A governess had no one to protect her.

But a fortune of her own would change all of that.

Lady Derringer often asked him if she could be of service introducing him to young ladies. It seemed wise to employ his aunt's help in introducing his governess into society. And it gave him great pleasure to give Charlotte that chance to dance and enjoy herself, to see the smile on her face. When had she ever been able to have a holiday from teaching and enjoy the kind of indulgent pleasures that he and his social set took for granted every day? Extravagant dinners, long conversations, walks in the park, dancing and playing and singing?

As it turned out, she did have quite a bit of experience with playing pall mall.

He imagined Miss Robbins being sought after, befriended by people who previously would never have spoken to her. He pictured her meeting Markeley and Merritt in London. How they might fall all over themselves trying to win her attention. They might even ask to marry her if her fortune was large enough. And he would laugh when she rejected them.

Yes, he was still conceited enough to believe that she would prefer to marry him over Merritt and Markeley. They had a connection, did they not? He felt as if she knew him and he knew her, that they were similar enough in temperament and priorities that they could fall in love and live happily together. But even if she did not choose him, it would give him pleasure to see her happy.

A thought had been lurking in his mind. Was he unselfish enough to simply wish to see Miss Robbins happy, to see her free to make her own choices?

Already a plan was forming in his mind. But it would take time to implement, and he might need to ask his aunt for her help. He wasn't sure how she would react, but if anyone was willing to help him, it was her. Besides, he would need someone with discretion, and he knew no one more discreet than Lady Derringer.

His heart swelled as he saw Charlotte, in his mind's eye, smiling and full of joy. And he suddenly wanted that more than he wanted anything else.

The next day it rained, and I decided to forgo my walk. I spent the morning writing letters and talking with Millicent over a shared pot of tea in Mrs. Merryweather's alcove that she allowed me to use.

"I can't believe Rose Rutledge said that," Millicent whispered, even though the door was closed and we were alone. “She obviously feels threatened by you.” Millicent took a sip of her tea, staring at the wall behind me.

I wanted to ask her if she thought it was at all possible that Lord Brookhaven wished to marry me. But I was sure I knew the answer; she did not. If she’d thought it was possible, she would have said so.

Why was I even thinking like this? An earl didn’t marry his governess. Never ever. He might marry a tradesman’s daughter, although that was quite rare, but never a governess. No, as threatened as Rose Rutledge might feel, Millicent was right.

“Lord Markeley and Mr. Merritt were flirting with you so much during the game yesterday.” Millicent grinned at me. “Were you not flattered by their attentions?”

“They were friendly, but I didn’t consider it flirting.”

“Oh, believe me, they were flirting.”

But neither of them would marry me either. I could imagine from her expression that that was exactly what Millicent was thinking. Unless they were a first son with a fortune of their own, they’d be trying to marry an heiress, or a lady with a large dowry. It was the way things were done to ensure one did not lose one’s gentility or the approval of society and one’s relatives.

I thought about my list of marriage prospects. As much as I had enjoyed socializing with ladies and gentlemen this week, including an earl and a viscount, I knew that list represented my only real prospects for marriage.

The only remaining ones were butler, head gardener, land steward, and vicar. But I should probably cross off the butler, for I simply couldn’t imagine marrying him. He was so severe and even cruel to the lesser servants, and he allowed the chef to treat the kitchen servants very badly—and he used very foul language when he was talking under his breath and thought no one could hear him.

That meant my only remaining prospects were the head gardener, the vicar, and the steward. But as I thought about each of them, I felt tears sting the back of my eyes. How could I marry any of them when I was in love . . . with Lord Brookhaven?

Millicent was telling me everything Lord Markeley had said to her the day before. My mind had wandered but she hadn't noticed, as she spoke with an enraptured expression. She could dream of marrying the viscount. She at least had a chance with him. I, on the other hand, did not.

I sipped my tea and tried not to dwell on what I would do if the head gardener, the land steward, and the vicar were all already married or otherwise unacceptable. Would I leave Lowndesbury House and find another position elsewhere? I didn't wish to leave Samuel or Annabelle, especially since they had been abandoned so many times already. And the thought of leaving Lord Brookhaven made my chest ache.

Truly, I had set myself up for heartbreak.

I stared out the window at the falling rain and sighed. My longing for home and the familiar faces at Mrs. Southey's school seemed to be competing with my pain at leaving Lowndesbury House. But such was the life of a governess, I suppose.

Twelve

That evening, dinner was quieter than usual, and we all retired a little early.

The next day, I avoided the drawing rooms where the guests were gathered.

"They're playing cards," Millicent informed me as she retreated with me to my little alcove again. It was really Mrs. Merryweather's alcove, but she rarely ever took the time to even take her tea, so busy was she with running the household, and never in her little alcove. But it had a window looking out on the garden, and I liked to sit next to it while I sipped my tea and ruminated.

"I must tell you something I overheard yesterday evening." Millicent spoke in a low voice, even though we were obviously alone.

My heart sank a bit as I braced myself. I could tell that what she was about to say was not going to be good.

"Rose Rutledge was speaking with Miss Allen about how well you played at pall mall, and I heard her say, 'She probably had nothing else to do at that little school for orphans.'"

"Well, she's not far wrong," I said wryly, trying to sound amused as I tamped down my other emotions.

"But it's cruel of her to say it, and I only hope Lord Brookhaven doesn't marry her." She pressed her lips together as if she'd just said something very daring.

I really was grateful to have her as a friend, but I might be more grateful if Millicent shared less about the unkind things Lord Brookhaven's guests said about me.

That evening after dinner, Lord Brookhaven seemed quiet. He left the room twice and came back each time smelling like pipe smoke. He spoke little and seemed not in a good humor, reminding me of the first time I saw him on the roof the evening I came to Lowndesbury House.

I had not been sleeping very well, and when I could no longer stop myself from yawning, I excused myself. Millicent had already whispered to me that she would stay and see if they gossiped about me again.

I wanted to assure her that I cared not a whit about their gossip and didn't want to know what they might say about me, but I refrained and left to go up to bed.

"Miss Robbins."

I turned on the stairs and saw Lord Brookhaven looking at me from the landing.

"Are you well?" he asked.

"I am, but I'm tired."

He stared up at me, but it was too dark to see his expression.

"Good night, then, Miss Robbins."

"Good night, sir."

I turned to continue up the stairs, but when I glanced over my shoulder he was still standing there, gazing up at me.

The house party resumed the next day in a similar fashion. At dinner, I was seated between Mr. Thomas Merritt and Lord Markeley, both of whom were unusually quiet. Then, near the end of the meal, their eyes met over my head.

Mr. Merritt leaned down and said quietly, "It seems as though Lord Brookhaven has developed an affection for you, Miss Robbins."

My heart jolted. "Wh-what do you mean?" I could barely breathe.

"We think he may even be considering asking you to marry him."

My cheeks grew hot. Mr. Merritt's expression was one of disapproval, almost anger.

"That is right," Lord Markeley said, forcing me to turn in his direction. "And you must not allow him to ruin himself."

"I am sorry, Miss Robbins," Mr. Merritt said, drawing my attention back to him, "but you will ruin him if you do."

My thoughts were whirling. Could it be true? Could he really want to marry me? And would that truly ruin him?

"I am sure you are mistaken." I still sounded breathless.

"Perhaps," Mr. Merritt said.

They went on eating. I could see Lord Brookhaven staring in our direction. I forced myself to take a bite of my roasted potatoes. I chewed but it took me some time before I could swallow past the lump in my throat.

"You won't be doing him any favors by saying yes if he does ask you," Lord Markeley hissed near my ear. "He'll be cast out by good society, by all the best families, by his peers."

Mr. Merritt added, "If you care for him, you will refuse him."

"Remember your place," Lord Markeley said.

"What are you saying there?" Lord Brookhaven was glaring in our direction. "Merritt? Markeley?"

I was frozen in place. My vision began to grow dim. I wanted to sink through the floor.

At the same time, somewhere deep inside me, a bubble of joy was hiding in a safe place, waiting for me to examine the fact that Lord Brookhaven had made these gentlemen think that he wanted to ask me to marry him.

Lord Markeley looked nearly as frozen as I felt. But Mr. Merritt said, "We were just asking Miss Robbins if she would teach us her secrets, how to play pall mall."

Everyone was staring now.

Did I look as red-faced as I felt? Could everyone read my thoughts? I did my best to appear confident and gratified by their desire to learn to play pall mall, but I ended up just staring down at my plate. Or at least I directed my eyes at my plate. My vision was still blurred and I could attend to nothing.

Please don't look at me. Please talk of something else.

Finally, other conversations resumed, and Mr. Merritt and Lord Markeley fell silent.

I dared not glance in Millicent's direction, even though she was sitting directly across from me. I started pushing the food around with my fork, with no intention of putting it in my mouth.

Surely Mr. Merritt and Lord Markeley were mistaken. Lord Brookhaven would never ask me to marry him. How could he even fall in love with someone as lowly as I?

The strange thing was that I hadn't felt so lowly these last several weeks that I'd been at Lowndesbury House. And since the commencement of the house party, I'd felt as if I were the equal of any of the lord's guests, at least in sense and education. I'd seen how cold they often were to one another, and certainly to me. Even toward Millicent, simply because . . . well, I wasn't sure why. Was it because her father was less wealthy than they were? Or did they think there was something lacking in her manners and demeanor? Or was it simply because they didn't know her and could detect no gain from becoming her friend?

If I were wealthy, if I had inherited a fortune or possessed an old and respected family name, they'd have treated me differently. And that was the problem. They were not kind people, and therefore it was impossible for me to respect them.

Which brought me around to the problem that had been niggling at me for days: Why would Lord Brookhaven invite such people to his home for fourteen days for an intimate house party? Surely he could see what kind of people they were, that they were selfish and petty and cruel.

But seeing Lord Brookhaven next to them had made him stand out even more than he already did. He was good and he was kind. He was not like them. Had he had the same realization? And had he seen the contrast between them and me?

I was flattering myself. I was not so good. I thought all manner of unkind thoughts about the other guests. And here I was comparing myself to them, when that was clearly not a Christian thing to do.

Mr. Merritt, Lord Markeley, and Miss Rutledge must have all been mistaken about Lord Brookhaven wishing to marry me. He probably said something favorable about me, perhaps complimented me to Mr. Merritt and Lord Markeley in an unguarded moment, never imagining that they would think he wished to marry me. It was all just a misunderstanding. That was the simplest explanation, and in my experience, the simplest explanation was usually the right one.

I thought of the shame that Mr. Merritt and Lord Markeley would assign to him if he married his governess. And they were not the only ones. No doubt the entire *ton* would shun him, aghast at him marrying a lowly governess. How the mothers of young ladies hoping to marry an earl would hate him—and would hate me even more.

If he did love me and then married me, would I shame him? Could his love for me survive that kind of adversity?

I'd always dreamed of marrying for love, of being the most important person in someone's life. I'd always thought that husband would be a rector or a steward. I'd never truly believed I'd inspire love in someone who was titled, certainly not an earl. It was . . . ludicrous. And to believe that an earl could give up his social status for me, well, it wasn't believable.

The thought of being married to someone who was ashamed of me, who would grow to resent me, hate me for marrying him . . . it was perhaps worse than never being loved at all.

Young ladies wished for security, status, and position, but I also wanted a family. I wanted love. It was the only thing I could imagine that would make me feel whole and content. And if Lord Brookhaven lost his position in society and then came to resent me . . . No, I shouldn't marry him, even if he asked me.

Thirteen

The next morning, I set out early for my walk. I'd slept very little, and although Millicent might be up and willing to go for a walk with me, I was afraid of her counsel. Besides the fact that I seemed to think more clearly when I was walking—perhaps it was the fresh air—I also couldn't help hoping I'd run into Lord Brookhaven.

I'd been silently arguing with myself for several minutes, walking in the woods just west of the garden, when I heard a twig break behind me. I turned to find Lord Brookhaven standing several feet away, holding his unlit pipe.

"Lord Brookhaven." I sounded out of breath again. "Good morning."

"Good morning. People say the damp is bad for the lungs."

"I have never suffered any ill effects. From the damp, I mean." It was ridiculous how I was practically gasping for air.

The way he was staring at me made my heart thump hard against my chest.

"Are you sure you're well, Miss Robbins?"

"Yes, very well, sir."

"If I may ask, what were Mr. Merritt and Lord Markeley speaking with you about last evening?"

A lump formed in my throat.

"You seemed disturbed by their words."

"No, sir, not . . . that is, I-I don't—I don't recall everything we spoke about." It was a true statement in substance if not in spirit.

Suddenly, I was on the verge of tears. I felt the betrayers damming up behind my eyes, pushing their way forward.

Lord Brookhaven turned half away from me as he gazed out at the trees.

I concentrated on breathing deeply in and out, blinking back the offending tears. I would not cry in front of Lord Brookhaven. I would not.

"Miss Robbins, do you remember the day you arrived here at Lowndesbury House? How you found me on the roof?"

"Yes, sir."

"Do you know that I was feeling melancholy that day? More than melancholy. I was thinking of . . . well, I was thinking of my nursemaid, Addy. I'd just learned of her death a month ago. I was also thinking of my own mother, whose treatment of me was rather cold and unfeeling. I have already confessed all this to you. But you may not know that a year ago I'd had a failed engagement. The girl I loved, whom I thought loved me, ran away with a marquess, the son of a duke. Did you know that?"

"I did, sir." My breath came rushing back as I seemed to feel his pain deep inside me. How I wanted to be able to comfort him, to go to him and put my arms around him.

Foolish thought.

He cleared his throat. "Do you remember what you said to me, Miss Robbins, that evening as we stood on the roof?"

"No, sir."

"You said you thought it was perfectly right and sensible to consider the feelings of others, especially of children. You said we should consider their feelings because they are vulnerable and have no power in society. It surprised me so much that it shook me right out of that moment of pain I was in, dwelling on the past as I was."

"I admit, I thought you seemed very melancholy."

"And you told me the truth, with great kindness and openness, as you always do. Do you see, Miss Robbins? You are like a ray of sunlight to me." He was looking directly at me now, piercing me with those eyes.

For a moment, I couldn't speak for the lump in my throat. "I am so very thankful that I happened to be there with you that day. Surely God wanted me to be." I was back to sounding breathless.

"The house party will be over in three more days, and I believe the Allens are departing today."

I was afraid to speak, so I nodded.

"I trust that you have enjoyed the activities," he said.

Again, I nodded. I swallowed hard and managed to say, "Thank you for inviting me. You have been very good to me. Inordinately so."

"These kinds of parties are often the impetus of marriage proposals. Do you think any of my guests have attached themselves to each other? Do you think any marriage proposals might come from a fortnight together?"

"I don't know."

I'd seen the way Miss Rose Rutledge looked at him, her smirk, and the way her mother would get that self-satisfied, catlike expression when her gaze shifted from Lord Brookhaven to her daughter. Was he trying to tell me that he planned to ask Rose Rutledge to marry him?

I saw myself as he must see me—as Mr. Merritt and Lord Markeley saw me. I was not in the same social realm as Lord Brookhaven or Rose Rutledge. I was not someone who was able to attend fashionable parties, and the only reason I had appropriate clothing for Lord Brookhaven's house party, appropriate for mingling with his guests, was because his aunt had provided it for me, which in itself was a bit improper.

I could ruin his reputation even if there was no marriage proposal, if Miss Rutledge or some of the other guests spread the news around London and within fashionable society that Lord Brookhaven's aunt had had clothing made for his governess, and that the earl had invited her to his house party so that she might socialize with him and his peers.

I felt sick.

"You should not have invited me." The words burst forth from my mouth. I couldn't take them back, so I went on. "People will talk. They will say bad things about you. I'm not in your social class, and I should not have been invited."

A little sob escaped, and I pressed my hand over my mouth. I kept my back to him as I wiped furiously at the tears running down my face.

How mortifying! What was wrong with me? I shouldn't have said anything. I should have kept quiet.

It was all I could do to keep from sobbing aloud.

"Please do not distress yourself." Lord Brookhaven's tone was agitated. "I'm sorry if you felt compromised by . . . did anyone say anything untoward?"

I shook my head, feeling utterly miserable. Stupid, stupid girl. I never should have said anything.

"Was that what Merritt and Markeley were saying to you? I will teach them to—"

"No!" This was getting worse and worse. "They didn't say anything untoward. They have been . . . very kind to me." *Until last night.* "I'm sorry. I shouldn't have attended. It wasn't right or proper for me to accept . . . your invitation or Lady Derringer's gifts." I no longer even tried to stop the tears, but I concentrated on keeping my voice steady.

"Miss Robbins." He'd moved closer until he was bending down, his face a few feet from mine. "There was nothing improper."

"I know, but people will talk. They will say—"

"They will not. And even if they do, they will be wrong. I don't care what people say. Do you think I care about that?" He sounded angry now. There was an edge in his tone, his expression tight, his eyes wide.

He took a deep breath. He blinked slowly, and when he spoke

again, his voice was low and even. "Gossips will say what they will, but my reputation will not be easily tarnished. Men have that privilege in society, but I realize . . . Forgive me, Miss Robbins."

By the end of his speech, he sounded deflated. Defeated.

I wanted to tell him there was nothing to forgive, that I didn't consider him to have done anything wrong, but I knew my voice wouldn't hold out.

After a minute of silence, in which I was able to compose myself, I said, "I think perhaps I should find a position elsewhere."

"No. No, that is precisely what you must not do. It will cause the gossipmongers to talk more. And although I care nothing for my sake, I am thinking of you, of your reputation, Miss Robbins."

"My reputation is of no consequence." After all, I was not a member of fashionable society. It hardly mattered what they said about me. I was nobody, a poor, lowly orphan who would simply go back to Mrs. Southey's School for Young Ladies. Where I belonged. The only place I belonged.

He was quiet for so long, my thoughts wandered to Samuel and Annabelle. Perhaps it would have been better if I left his employ and went back to Mrs. Southey's, but I could not leave Samuel and Annabelle. My heart wrenched at the thought. I couldn't abandon them.

"It will not be necessary for you to find another position." He enunciated each word carefully, as though he was trying to keep control of his voice. "In fact, I want you to stay—I ask you to stay—to continue Samuel and Annabelle's education."

"Very well. I will stay, for the children."

"Forgive me, Miss Robbins." His voice sounded even, passionless. "I suppose I didn't think it through, the outcome of . . . you joining us. I . . . Forgive me for causing you distress or embarrassment."

We stood silently staring out into the garden, listening to the twitter of birds that sounded so happy that anyone listening would never have known that there was a young woman standing there who was absolutely wretched and mortified, who could only berate herself for ever thinking that an earl might ask her to marry him, for thinking that a governess should feel welcome at an earl's house party . . . for falling in love.

When I'd berated myself to the point of driving out any strong emotions, I was able to say, "There is nothing to forgive. I am sorry if I've caused you trouble or lessened anyone's enjoyment of the party."

"You did not. I was pleased to have you there. You were as welcome as anyone, and will be for the rest of the time."

"I will not be attending this evening. Please excuse me."

"I don't wish to excuse you." The edge was back in his voice.

"Forgive me, but you must excuse me."

Lord Brookhaven was quiet. I was too afraid to look at him.

The silence began to feel awkward, so I said, "I must go . . . to my room. Good day, sir."

I began walking toward the house, then I heard him call out. "Miss Robbins."

I stopped but did not turn around.

"I shall see you tonight for dinner."

I did not respond, only continued walking.

Millicent came to take tea with me and tried to talk me into coming to the next three days' festivities, even after I told her what Mr. Merritt and Lord Markeley had said.

"You must come. It will look strange if you suddenly stop showing up. Besides, who will I talk to if you are not there?"

"I'm sorry, Millicent. Truly, I am. Surely someone will talk to you. It would be too rude to just ignore you and let you sit all alone."

"I won't be alone. I'll have Father." She rolled her eyes and sighed.

We sat in morose silence, sipping our tea and nibbling on biscuits.

I sent my apologies for not coming to dinner, saying I had a headache, which was true enough. Millicent promised to tell me all about it, especially anything that was said about me. Again, I almost told her not to bother, that I didn't want to know what they were saying about me. It was too hurtful. But I knew my curiosity would overpower my fear of hearing it.

The next three days I did not even have the distraction of my lessons with Samuel and Annabelle. I did go and visit them for a while every day, to play a game with them, tell them a story, or listen to them chatter about their new puppies.

Millicent came every day to visit me for an hour or two, but as I'd expected, the other guests were much friendlier to her now that she wasn't constantly talking to me.

When it was time for everyone to depart, Millicent and I said our farewells, promising to write. She had said she was not a very enthusiastic letter writer, but I hoped I'd at least hear from her once or twice in the coming months. I would miss her. I enjoyed her friendship, and it had been good to make a new friend.

It had been inordinately stormy and rainy, so I hadn't seen or spoken to Lord Brookhaven for a few days, until he called me into his library. The last of the guests had departed two hours earlier.

He looked a bit more animated than usual, and his desk was messy with paper and ink, blotters and pens, as if he'd been writing multiple letters. His cravat was missing, and I saw a bit of dark hair sticking out above his shirt. Did he understand how attractive he was to me? He couldn't, else he wouldn't look at me so intensely. It made my knees weak.

"Are you unhappy here, Miss Robbins?"

"I have not been unhappy." *But I am in love with you and I cannot marry you, as everyone considers me to be beneath you . . .* Still, there was some joy just in being in love and being in his presence.

Lord Brookhaven's jaw was set in stone, even as a muscle in his cheek jumped. "You mentioned leaving a few days ago, but there is no reason for you to leave. My guests will not dare to gossip about you, and Lady Derringer would fix things even if they did. She has a lot of influence on society."

"I am glad to hear that, sir, for your sake."

"As I told you, you do not need to worry about me." His voice sounded like he was grumbling. Then he stuck his hand in his pocket and said, “Here is your pay, twenty pounds.” He held out the coins to me.

“That is too much.” I curled my hand against my stomach, refusing to take it.

“You must be paid.” He moved quite close to me.

“But you don’t owe me that much. We agreed on forty pounds per annum, and I’ve only worked for three months. You only owe me ten.”

“If I wish to give you twenty pounds, it is my own money. I may do with it what I like.”

He took my hand and poured the coins into my open palm. His much-larger hand was warm, and I wasn’t wearing any gloves. He stood holding my hand and my gaze.

“If you need more, you need only ask.” His voice was rough and low, but gentle. “You will not leave?”

“No. I won’t leave.”

As soon as he released me, I turned to go, as my eyes were quickly filling with tears.

I practically ran from the room.

Fourteen

There was joy at being back at my duties with Samuel and Annabelle, in teaching. The children were trusting me more and more. Annabelle had begun to hug me every afternoon when the nursemaid came to collect them after our lessons were finished. And Samuel had brought me a tiny flat piece of ivory carved in the shape of a bird that he'd found in the garden.

"What is it?" he asked.

"It probably broke off a hatpin or a brooch. It's very pretty." I handed it back to him, but he didn't take it.

"You can keep it," he said. "It will be a good marker for a book, to hold your place."

"You are right. Thank you, Samuel."

He turned a little red, but I pretended not to notice.

Although I'd seriously considered returning to Mrs. Southey's school, it felt good to have made the decision to stay.

I did long to see my friends again, to return for a visit to the only place I remembered as home. I longed to see everyone smiling and looking happy to see me again. It might blunt the pain of being treated like a leper by both the other servants and Lord Brookhaven's guests—or at least being told I wasn't good enough to marry Lord Brookhaven.

It was summer now, and in the weeks to come, Lord Brookhaven and I met as we'd done before on our walks. Things between us soon became as easy and comfortable as they'd been. We discussed many subjects, including politics, religion, and literature. Our beliefs and tastes were remarkably similar, and when we did disagree, he never tried to force his opinions on me. I always felt as if he respected me, and in fact, he became quite gentle—his voice was softer, and he had ceased to sound commanding and never made demands of me. He never treated me like a servant, but like a friend. And he seemed to go out of his way to show anyone watching that we were taking walks together but nothing more. Everything was proper and aboveboard.

I tried to tell myself it was my imagination that his manner had changed, that he no longer treated me like a servant, especially when he would look at me in a particularly intense or admiring way. My heart would beat fast and my thoughts would soar, and I'd have to scold myself later for my foolishness.

There were a few times when he would point out a stag or a fox or a bird's nest he had found, and he would lean so close that his shoulder would brush against mine. Or he'd hand me a bunch of flowers he'd picked for me and our fingers would touch. I'd think about it for hours, still able to feel my skin tingling. But always I would tell myself it meant nothing. He was lonely for a friend, and I was more than happy to be that friend.

Although, in my heart of hearts, I longed to be so much more.

Lady Derringer had gone home, but she wrote to me once a week—surprisingly friendly letters, telling me about her life in London, parties or balls or concerts she'd attended, asking me if I'd like to come to London sometime as her guest, talking of the places we would go. It seemed strange but also quite pleasant, to think the widow of a duke would wish to spend time with me, although I considered her thoughts on a future invitation to be just that—thoughts that would never come to fruition. But I enjoyed her friendship, and I would have enjoyed her letters just as much were she not a duchess or even wealthy.

I wrote letters, but I also spent a lot of time writing stories for

Samuel and Annabelle. I used these stories to teach the children new words, comprehension skills, decision-making, and problem-solving. And I dreamed of someday having them printed in book form for other children and their teachers to read and use in their lessons.

Many of the stories were about two dogs named Ernest and Maizie who had lots of adventures. Samuel and Annabelle were particularly fond of those.

One day when we were reading one of those stories, I looked up to see a servant beckoning me from the hallway. I excused myself and went to see what she wanted.

"A Mr. Sullivan is here to see you. He says he's a solicitor from London."

I couldn't imagine what business a London solicitor could have with me, but the servant led me downstairs to Lord Brookhaven's library.

Lord Brookhaven sat behind his desk, looking quite serious, his brows drawn together. A short, balding man stood when I entered the room.

"Miss Charlotte Robbins?"

"Yes."

"I am Jonah Sullivan. I was hired to find you and notify you . . . I think you will want to sit down for this."

We all sat, me rather heavily, as he pulled some papers out of his leather case. His hands shook slightly, making the papers tremble.

"Were you aware, Miss Robbins, that you had a relative, an uncle of some means, John Robert Robbins, who has died and left you fifty thousand pounds?"

An uncle? I blinked, trying to comprehend his words. Fifty thousand pounds was an enormous sum.

"Sir, my parents died when I was almost five years old. I barely remember them, and I was told that I have no other relatives."

"Yes, well, your father was estranged from his elder brother, John Robert Robbins, who was my client until his death." He stared past me, as if the wall behind me drew his interest. "It was his dying wish that you receive the whole of his fortune, which amounts to just over fifty thousand pounds."

An uncle! I longed to know more about him. How sad that he died and I could never meet him or speak to him. And now he'd left me his fortune. I could hardly take it in. Could such a thing be true?

"He was a solitary man, only engaging in business, rarely involving himself in society. He did not even belong to a gentleman's club, and he never traveled to London, which is why he had no home there."

"What of his home?"

"He instructed me to sell it and all his possessions upon his death and settle all his debts. The remainder is the fifty thousand pounds he left to you."

I'd inherited a fortune—a truly enormous fortune—from an uncle I never knew I had.

I should feel elated, but my breath had gone out of me. I couldn't seem to think with all this swirling in my head.

Mr. Sullivan was still talking, but his words seemed to float past me without catching hold.

"Miss Robbins? I said you can either return to London with me, where I will transfer the funds to you, or I will bring them personally to you in a few days and you can deposit the funds in the nearest bank. Which do you prefer?"

"I . . . I don't know."

"Would you like me to wait while you speak to someone, to ask for advice?" He gave me a smile that looked like a grimace.

"Lady Derringer is here from London," Lord Brookhaven said. "She arrived last evening. Would you like to speak to her?"

"Yes, thank you."

Lord Brookhaven said he would take me to her, and we excused ourselves from Mr. Sullivan.

I stood and half stumbled through the door.

We found Lady Derringer in the drawing room, almost as if she was waiting for us. Lord Brookhaven left us, and I began to tell her everything Mr. Sullivan had told me, pausing only while a servant brought us our tea.

"This is such a wonderful opportunity for you," Lady Derringer said. "You are a wealthy woman now."

"It seems so strange."

"You may do whatever you wish. What do you wish for? To go to London? You could let a house in town, go to all the shops, visit famous places."

"It's a bit overwhelming, isn't it?"

Lady Derringer looked amused, but then she changed her expression to one of compassion. "Forget everything I said and just think of what you would like to do if you had all the time and money in the world. Would you go to London?"

"Perhaps. I've always wished to see London."

"Very well, then, go to London. Do whatever your heart desires."

"It just feels so . . . unreal." And the question I'd actually been wondering was—now that I had a fortune, could Lord Brookhaven marry me without dire consequences? Would he want to?

Instead, I said, "Mrs. Southey told me I didn't have any family. Why did my uncle not contact me?"

"I suppose he didn't want to be known to you while your father was alive, and perhaps he didn't know your father had died. These things happen sometimes."

"Fifty thousand pounds is an enormous sum." I'd never dreamed of half so much. My stomach felt a bit sick, and I pressed my hand to my middle. "I have no idea how to proceed."

"You said you wished to go to London, did you not?"

"I do, but I don't want to abandon Samuel and Annabelle. They've been abandoned by nearly everyone else in their lives. I don't want them to feel as if I'm abandoning them as well."

Lady Derringer's expression was impossible to read, as if she was deliberately trying to hide what she was thinking. She simply stared back at me and said nothing.

"I'm not sure what to do," I said. "Will you advise me?"

"I know you don't wish to leave Samuel and Annabelle behind, so what do you think of taking them with us? Lord Brookhaven and I will accompany you to London, we'll bring the children, and we can all be in London together. You won't need to do their lessons. We can hire someone—of your choosing, if you like—and you can instruct their new governess. What do you think?"

"Lord Brookhaven wishes to do this?"

"I will need to ask him, but I am sure he would be agreeable."

I bit my lip. I'd still be abandoning the children, as I'd no longer be their governess. But perhaps if I visited them every day . . .

"And Lord Brookhaven and I can show you around London, introduce you, take you to see all the sights—the Tower of London, the beautiful churches. Would you like that?"

Her eyes were bright, and I believed that she truly did wish to do all those things with and for me.

"You are so kind." My voice choked up, and I had to stop and take a few breaths. "I would like that very much."

"Your care and concern for Samuel and Annabelle do you great credit, Miss Robbins. May I call you Charlotte?"

"Oh, yes, of course."

"Yes, I think this is all going to work out quite well." Lady Derringer gave me such a sincere smile that I couldn't help smiling back.

Her confidence seemed to give me a bit more courage, and it helped me begin to believe that I truly was an heiress, as strange and mysterious and incredibly fortunate as that was.

"You will have Lord Brookhaven and me, but you will also need an older woman who will be able to protect your reputation, a companion who will live with you and accompany you to all social events."

"You are certainly acquainted with more people than I am; I know no one in London. Is there someone you could recommend?"

"I believe I may know one or two older women who would be appropriate for such a role. You will need someone who is wise in the ways of society, who will help look out for your best interests, but mainly you simply need someone to help ensure that no one accuses you of impropriety."

I pressed my hands against my cheeks and tried to take in a deep breath as my thoughts kept going to Lord Brookhaven.

How I wanted to believe that he would be able to marry me now, but I was still a former governess—the former governess for his own siblings. Was my new fortune enough to keep the gossipmongers from looking down on him?

Lady Derringer leaned closer. "Are you well, my dear?"

"I . . . yes, I'm well. Just a bit . . . overwhelmed." I managed a smile. I was getting ahead of myself. He might not have any wish to marry me. As an earl, he could marry anyone. He was also young, handsome, and wealthy.

But I could see him socially—or, at least, it wasn't beyond the realm of possibility. We could meet and talk again, be friends, even attend the same balls, possibly.

"I'll help you with finding the best dress shops," Lady Derringer was saying. "You'll want to get a full wardrobe. And perhaps Mr. Sullivan, Lord Brookhaven, and I can help you find a suitable townhouse near his and advise you on financial matters, as well. If you wish it."

"Oh yes, thank you. But will I be able to afford to lease a house in London?"

"With fifty thousand pounds? I should think so."

My thoughts were spinning like a whirlwind, but in the center of the spinning thoughts was Lord Brookhaven.

I now had something that might make it possible to socialize with him—a large fortune.

Part Two

Fifteen

London was big, busy, noisy, and dirty—everything I'd ever been told and more.

The streets were packed with people, horses, and carriages at all hours of the day and night. There were many smells, most of them bad and came from unmentionable sources, and there was a perpetual haze of smoke, as there were so many houses and they all had cook fires. London was ugly and impressive, exciting and frightening all at once.

Lord Brookhaven, Lady Derringer, Samuel, and Annabelle accompanied me to London in Lord Brookhaven's largest carriage. The children had to leave their puppies at Lowndesbury House, which they mentioned a few times during the trip. But their excitement about going to town and traveling excited them so much that they eventually wore themselves out after a few hours of asking questions and talking of all the things they might see. I told them a story that I'd just begun to work on, and they fell asleep, Annabelle with her head on my lap and Samuel wedged between Lord Brookhaven and the side of the carriage.

When we reached London, we left the children in the care of their nursemaid, who had traveled in a separate carriage with a few other servants.

Lady Derringer made no move to exit the carriage, saying, "Mr.

Sullivan has gone ahead of us to find some houses for you to consider. Would you like to go see one?"

The house Mr. Sullivan had found for me was grand and spacious, with a beautiful, intricate staircase and marble floors, located in what seemed a very wealthy part of London. And it was only a few houses away from Lord Brookhaven's house, on the same street. Mr. Sullivan told me the terms of the lease.

Lady Derringer raised her brows. "It sounds fair. What do you think, William?"

"Hmm, yes, very fair." Lord Brookhaven wandered to the window looking out on the street.

The drawing room and dining room were spacious. There was a small sitting room as well, and enough bedrooms that I could invite Hattie and Susan and Millicent to stay at the same time.

I spoke up. "I'll take the house."

Thinking about being able to introduce Hattie into society, to give her a holiday away from teaching school and to expose her to London and parties and dancing filled me with joy. Had we not always dreamed of attending balls and parties? And now that I had inherited a fortune, the best way to become the kind of woman Lord Brookhaven could marry without being looked down upon was to join London society.

Besides, I'd enjoyed Lord Brookhaven's house party—well, everything except being treated as if I were beneath them. Would the people in Lord Brookhaven's set still treat me that way? Or would my fortune be enough for them to accept me?

I managed to push any fears away . . . most of the time.

I never imagined I'd be so fortunate as to be wealthy, but especially not without a husband. How many young ladies married so that they could be independent and secure? And here I was an heiress with my own fortune, beholden to no man. It was a heady feeling indeed.

The next two days were a whirlwind as Lady Derringer and Mr. Sullivan guided me through all the transactions, including purchasing a new carriage and horses, hiring servants, and choosing a lady of good character and reputation to be my new chaperone and companion.

We settled on a Mrs. Phyllis Drake, a widow. She was genteel and enjoyed many connections from growing up the daughter of a baron in London. Her marriage to Mr. Drake had been rather tragic, as she had no children who survived infancy, and when her husband died, he had left her virtually penniless after some disastrous financial investments. But she seemed a rather cheerful woman in spite of her unfortunate circumstances.

"This is what we must do, first and foremost," Mrs. Drake said when we were alone. "We must call on some of my old acquaintances, and we must have some new clothes made for you."

She looked at my frock as she said this. It was an old one that I wore to church in Milford on Sundays, my best dress until Lady Derringer had new dresses made for me, but I could see that it would not do for someone who now wished to be accepted by the upper classes of society.

For someone who was hoping a certain earl would ask her to marry him.

This was my secret. Did Lady Derringer suspect it? She'd given no indication that she did, although she sometimes looked back and forth between the earl and me in a way that made me think she noticed something. But I had told no one except Hattie, and only in a letter and only in a cryptic way that hopefully no one else would understand. And Mrs. Drake was in my employ, and Mrs. Southey had once told me that one should never confide in one's servants. She'd said, *"If I had to dismiss a servant for any reason, then gossiping about me and telling my secrets would be her only way of getting revenge. So it is always better to keep one's distance."*

I'd written to Hattie as soon as I got the news about the fortune, and she had promised to come to London for a visit at the end of the week. I was also hoping to write to Millicent and convince her to visit.

On our first outing to the shops, we had just stepped down from our hired carriage when a little boy approached us with his hand outstretched, palm up.

"Please, mum, can you spare a farthing?"

"Get away from her, you little beggar!" Mrs. Drake cried. She shooed him with her hands, waving at him as if she were trying to ward off a dangerous animal.

The little boy's expression barely registered the rejection as he turned and bolted away.

"I could have given him a coin," I protested to Mrs. Drake. "He was only a little child." His face was streaked with soot, and his clothing looked as if it hadn't been washed in a long time. His eyes were a bit sunken, as if he was not getting enough to eat. How much had the poor child suffered?

"He has a handler, you can be sure, Miss Robbins. You don't know this, for you have spent your whole life in the country, but thieves and beggars are aplenty in London. You'd do well to send them away immediately. Giving them money only encourages their thieving." She shook her finger and said adamantly, "Drive them away on first sight."

I wanted to say, *How could giving money to them encourage thieving? I'd think it would be just the contrary.* But Mrs. Drake was already opening the door to the nearest shop.

Perhaps she was right, that I was from the country and therefore knew nothing about how things worked in London. But I was certain I'd be thinking about that little boy for some time and feeling guilty that I hadn't given him something. After all, hadn't Jesus said, "Whatever you do for the least of these, you do for me"? I vowed to do better if I was given another opportunity to help a child begging on the streets.

We went to several dress shops, and I ordered four new dresses, feeling a lump in my throat at the price I was paying for finery and frills when there were children begging in the streets. But I didn't particularly wish for Lord Brookhaven to see me in the same dresses his aunt had paid for. I wanted him and the rest of London to see that I was an independently wealthy woman now, an heiress who could afford her own clothes—and her own place in society.

"Mrs. Drake, I will not call on anyone else today, nor possibly ever again."

After three straight days of calling on Mrs. Drake's high-society acquaintances, I declared a halt to the humiliating practice.

"But my dear Miss Robbins, why?" she said, looking aghast, with her hand over her heart.

Because most of the people we called on were either rude to me or sent their servant back to tell us that they were not home.

The only person I wanted to call on was Lord Brookhaven, and when we had called on him the day before, his servant took my card and said Lord Brookhaven wasn't at home. When I asked to see Samuel and Annabelle, the servant said they were instructed by Lord Brookhaven to allow me to visit the children any time I wished.

So I spent an hour with them, listening to them tell me what they had been doing, asking them what kind of outing they'd like to go on with me. I was even able to tell them a short story I made up about an orphan boy living on the streets and begging for coins who was adopted by a wealthy duke, and the boy never had to go hungry again.

Hannah came then to give them their midday meal, and I left, promising to take them with me to the park very soon.

"More often than not," I said to answer Mrs. Drake's question, "the people are not home, or as is often the case, are only pretending to be away from home. And when they are home, they look at me as if I am some kind of bug to be examined, or as if they are suspicious of my intentions."

"What a thing to say!" Mrs. Drake's pressed her hand to her chest and raised her brows at me.

I was beginning to wonder about Mrs. Drake. Would she really pretend she hadn't noticed the way the fashionable ladies looked at me? They always asked questions such as, "Who are your parents?" "Where is your family estate?" "How long have you been out in society?"

The answers were that my parents were of no consequence, there was no family estate, and I'd never been formally introduced into society. When I told them those things, I was met with cold stares. Although there *were* one or two mothers of younger sons who gave me a look of potential interest.

After three days of that, I was done.

When Mrs. Drake and I took our exercise, we walked past Lord Brookhaven's townhouse. He and Lady Derringer were the only people I cared to call on, but I was afraid of seeming as if I were clinging to them. Besides, I knew Lady Derringer had gone to take care of some business at her country estate just after Mrs. Drake had entered my employ and moved into my townhouse.

"My dear, if you wish to secure a husband, you must make your presence known. You cannot succeed if you don't try."

"I'm not so certain I shall marry." I said it partly to see the look of horror on her face and partly because I was too afraid I'd already put all my hope in marrying for love and there were no guarantees that that would ever come about. "After all, I could marry someone in whose character I was mistaken, and then I would live with my regret forever, since what is done cannot be undone. Or he could squander all my money. That is why I think it best that I should take advantage of this new fortune to do what I've always wanted, which is to write all the stories for children that have been floating about in my head and get them printed into books."

"Write stories for children? Whatever for?"

"Writing stories for children will give me a sense of purpose, and perhaps they will be helpful to the children who read them. Besides, writing will be an interesting way to pass time while still accomplishing something."

Mrs. Drake continued to stare with a look of bewilderment. Finally, she said, "It is a lady's responsibility to marry well. Aim high, or your aim will always disappoint you. I did not follow this advice and look where it has gotten me."

She sounded slightly bitter and despairing. But I could hardly blame her.

Still, I would not call on any more of her highborn friends. It felt demeaning. But I would call on Lord Brookhaven. I missed seeing him, even though it had only been a few days, and I couldn't imagine *he* would deliberately snub me by pretending not to be home. I might be an orphan of little consequence, but I knew he cared about me as a friend, at least. But I wouldn't throw myself at Lord Brookhaven or anyone else. I didn't have to, because I was an heiress with fifty thousand pounds.

"Lord Brookhaven, are you well?"

Mrs. Wells, the housekeeper, stared at him.

"I asked if you'd like me to show Mr. Sullivan into your library."

William had been staring at the card with Charlotte Robbins's name and address, cursing himself for being away from home when she'd called.

"Show him in."

"Yes, sir." She left the room, and he made his way across the hall and sat behind his desk.

"Lord Brookhaven." The short, balding man appeared in the doorway and made a slight bow.

He probably shouldn't have trusted Mr. Sullivan, the man who'd been his solicitor until he stole two thousand pounds from him to pay his gambling debts. Lady Derringer, the only other person who was privy to William's scheme to give Miss Charlotte Robbins a significant amount of his own fortune, had warned him that it was dangerous to take a thief like Mr. Sullivan into his confidence and trust him with this undertaking, but William had leverage with Mr. Sullivan. If he didn't want to go to prison, he had to either pay back the two thousand pounds, which William knew he could not, or do as he wished in this matter. Besides, Mr. Sullivan was a very good liar.

"Mr. Sullivan. Do you have news for me?"

"Yes, Lord Brookhaven. Miss Charlotte Robbins has taken the house, as you probably know, and she hired a companion, Mrs. Drake, a widow from London and the daughter of a baron."

"Does she suspect the money came from me?"

"No, sir. She is buying new frocks and has hired servants but otherwise has not spent much of your money."

"It is not my money. The money belongs to her now and she can do as she pleases with it."

"Yes, sir."

William saw the slight frown. It chafed Mr. Sullivan that he would give such a large sum of money to a woman who had no connection to him other than that she was once his wards' governess, but Mr. Sullivan would keep quiet about it—or else. He didn't look like the type of man who could survive prison.

William was about to dismiss him when he said, "She asked about you."

"What did she say?" He glared at him.

"She asked if you were in town and about your habits, whether you liked to take walks while you were in London, things like that. I was very vague, of course, and told her I didn't know. I do believe the woman she's hired, Mrs. Drake, is endeavoring to get her accepted to society, invited to balls and parties and such. I overheard a bit of conversation about that."

"Very well. You may go." William made sure to give him his best scowl.

Mr. Sullivan bowed and left.

He hated trusting Mr. Sullivan, but up until now, everything seemed to have gone as well as possible. He just hadn't anticipated how nervous he'd be about seeing Charlotte again, knowing that she now had the freedom to choose any man she wished. He'd never been so cowardly before. But love made cowards of the stoutest men. He must have read that somewhere.

Nervous or not, he wanted to see her. And if she needed an introduction to society—and every person did, if they weren't part of society before they inherited their fortune—then he and Lady Derringer could make that happen.

He rang for Mrs. Wells and told her he wanted to give a ball. To her credit, she didn't mention the fact that he'd never given a ball before. She simply raised her brows slightly and said, "Very good, sir, and how many guests will you invite?"

"Lady Derringer should arrive later today, and she will be helpful in making a list of guests."

They discussed plans and preparations for a few minutes. Thankfully, Mrs. Wells was familiar with the best of society, the people who normally invited him to their balls and the like, so he asked her to make up the list and then he and Lady Derringer would approve it.

"And I wish to invite Miss Charlotte Robbins." He gave her the address.

"Very good, sir."

He'd never looked forward to a ball before. It was a new feeling. But looking forward to dancing with her again was a familiar one. He only hoped she would be looking forward to dancing with him as well.

"The post has come, and there's something for you. I believe it's an invitation." Mrs. Drake's eyes were wide as she handed me the paper. It was from Lord Brookhaven.

I unfolded it while Mrs. Drake waited with pursed lips.

"It's an invitation to a ball at Lord Brookhaven's townhouse."

"Oh." Mrs. Drake clasped her hands over her chest. "This means he's home. We must call on him today."

The first few days of Mrs. Drake's employ, I would have agreed, but I'd be miserable if I continued doing everything Mrs. Drake thought I should do.

"No, not today. I shall take my exercise, perhaps walk to Hyde Park. Will you accompany me?"

Mrs. Drake raised her head, pinched her lips together, and said while staring down at the breakfast table, "I suppose I shall. You cannot very well walk to Hyde Park alone. It would be improper."

I said nothing, and she sat there sipping her tea and staring at the food, her hand hovering as she chose a tart.

I ate another scone with a healthy dollop of lemon curd—the cook I'd hired made the best scones I'd ever eaten—then went to change into my walking shoes, fetch my shawl, and tie on my bonnet.

Mrs. Drake obviously resented having to go on a long walk with me when she thought I should be calling on Lord Brookhaven. But I was already tired of the sort of machinations that seemed to be the expected way for a young lady to behave in order to secure a husband—a wealthy, sought-after husband, I should say.

I didn't intend to embarrass myself by engaging in such artifice and schemes. Besides, the only person whose good opinion I cared about was Lord Brookhaven's. Although I'd also need to secure the good opinion of the rest of society, since I didn't want Lord Brookhaven to be looked down upon for marrying me.

My heart raced every time I thought about him in that way, so I put aside that thought and just told myself it would be enough to be his friend again.

Mrs. Drake was waiting for me. She was a good chaperone and companion in that she was always available, punctual, and efficient. I would have rather she was more of a friend and less of a servant, but Mrs. Southey had warned me in a letter:

You have never had servants of your own, so I will tell you: It would be a mistake to treat your hired companion, or any of your servants, as a friend. You must not do it, otherwise they will take advantage of your good nature. You must be firm but fair in all your dealings, detached but kind.

Firm but fair, detached but kind. I'd said the words over and over like a mantra. After all, my inclination was to be friendly and warm with the people who were helping me, but Mrs. Southey was much older, wiser, and experienced than I, and she was a woman of unreproachable character.

Lord Brookhaven's townhouse was between mine and Hyde Park, and that was at the forefront of my thoughts as Mrs. Drake and I set out to take the morning air.

Sixteen

There she was. Miss Charlotte Robbins, walking down the street past William's door.

He grabbed the first jacket his hand came to and threw it on as he raced down the stairs and outside. He slowed his walk, just in case she turned to look and saw him running like a madman. But at this rate, they'd be at Hyde Park before he caught up to her.

"Miss Robbins?" William called at what he hoped was an appropriate volume.

She turned and broke into a smile. She and her companion stopped and waited for him.

His heart seemed to think he was running uphill, and his cravat was suddenly too tight around his neck. But he managed to speak. "Good day, Miss Robbins."

"Good day, Lord Brookhaven."

Her smile was so beautiful. Thankfully, they continued walking so he wasn't staring straight at her anymore.

She said, "I received the invitation you sent, for the ball at your home."

"I hope you will be able to attend."

"Yes, thank you. I was planning to send my acceptance this afternoon. And how are Samuel and Annabelle?"

"They are well. They were very happy that you came and visited them."

"I have longed to see them. Perhaps you would allow them to come on a walk to Hyde Park with me soon?"

"Yes, of course. Name the day and we shall all accompany you."

"Tomorrow, if that suits."

"Of course. Tomorrow it shall be."

"I have invited someone you know, Miss Millicent Skidmore, to visit me. If she arrives before the ball, will your invitation include her?"

"Yes, of course. I will send a revised invitation right away. Anyone you wish to bring with you is invited, in fact, if you have any other friends visiting."

"Thank you, that is very kind." She smiled as if she could see right through him, as though she knew he would do anything for her . . . as if she knew what he'd done. But she couldn't know, could she?

They continued walking toward Hyde Park while they talked—Miss Robbins, Mrs. Drake, and William. At once it was like their walks at Lowndesbury House, and not at all like that. For one thing, on their old walks they'd been alone, able to speak more intimately. Miss Robbins was now a wealthy lady, not a poor orphaned governess, and her clothing and even the tilt of her head and shoulders seemed to indicate her new status, although her face was as lovely as ever, her eyes as sparkling and blue.

He needed to say something before she realized his lovesick thoughts.

"There will be some people at the ball that you've met before."

"Oh?"

"Lord Markeley and Mr. Merritt will be attending."

Her smile faltered. He'd suspected they'd said something to her the last night she'd dined with the house party group that had caused her to refuse to attend again. Would she be able to overlook whatever they'd said, now that she had a fortune of her own? They'd got on so well, until that dinner.

"And I suppose Miss Rutledge will be there with Mr. and Mrs. Rutledge?"

"Indeed, no. They are not in London just now."

Her expression brightened when he said Miss Rutledge wouldn't be there. Did that mean she was jealous of Rose Rutledge?

Not necessarily. He knew Miss Rutledge hadn't been very kind to her. Charlotte was probably just relieved that she wouldn't have to see the person who had been so unfriendly to her.

They walked along in silence, even though there were so many things he wanted to say and ask. Had she been enjoying being able to be mistress of her own home in London? Were there places in London she'd like to visit, places he could show her? How did it feel to have her own fortune?

When she'd arrived at Lowndesbury House, she'd been so kind, so forthright and artless, so unafraid to say what she really thought. Would the fortune change her? Did she feel differently about him now?

Mrs. Drake began to talk of balls she'd attended as a young lady. It was the kind of inane chatter he'd endured many times before, the kind he could easily ignore. Charlotte merely stared straight ahead, occasionally glancing at her chaperone to nod and smile. Mrs. Drake dropped names of many important people she'd met or with whose sons she'd danced. Miss Robbins didn't speak, and he imagined she wasn't even listening, as there was frequently a faraway look on her face, and she glanced at him once or twice.

They arrived at the park where he tried to steer them away from people as much as possible. But inevitably someone recognized him. The mother of the marriageable Miss Martindale, whose father had been a close acquaintance of his father, approached them. Unfortunately, she seemed set on him noticing her daughter, as they had both called on him multiple times. Fortunately, he'd been away from home each time, and they'd invited him to dine at their home, an invitation he'd been able to decline all but once. It had been an uncomfortable evening of rather obvious insinuations and hopes.

"Lord Brookhaven," Mrs. Martindale cried out in delighted tones.

"Mrs. Martindale. You are looking well."

"Say nothing of me, although I have been rather well. You are the picture of health, I must say. And you remember my daughter, Miss Elizabeth Martindale."

"Of course. Pleased to see you again, Miss Martindale."

The young lady bridled and smirked, while her mother stared pointedly at Charlotte.

"I'd heard you might be giving a ball while you were in town, but I have never known you to give a ball." Mrs. Martindale patted his arm with her fan as if they were old friends.

He supposed he couldn't not invite her now without giving offense, even though it was in poor taste and bad manners for her to practically invite herself.

"I shall send you an invitation."

Her face lit up. "Then it is true! A ball given by the Earl of Brookhaven. Delightful, indeed."

She was deliberately excluding Miss Robbins, who looked as if she was about to walk away.

"Mrs. Martindale, this is Miss Charlotte Robbins and her companion, Mrs. Drake. Miss Robbins and Mrs. Drake, this is Mrs. Edward Martindale and her daughter, Miss Elizabeth Martindale."

Charlotte smiled and nodded politely. "Very pleased to make your acquaintance."

Mrs. Martindale stared. "And how do you know Lord Brookhaven, my dear?"

"I was in his employ at Lowndesbury House, as the governess for his brother and sister."

Mrs. Martindale actually leaned away from Charlotte and laid a hand over her chest. "The governess. Oh, I see." A look of horror came over her face, as if she were witnessing a crime being committed right in front of her.

"Miss Robbins recently inherited a large fortune from her uncle," he was quick to say.

"A fortune, did she?" Mrs. Martindale mumbled.

Charlotte's look was defiant, so Mrs. Drake rushed to intercede. "Miss Robbins had an uncle, whom she hadn't known, who left her fifty thousand pounds." She whispered the last part, as if whispering made it more genteel and appropriate to tell the exact sum.

"Oh." Mrs. Martindale raised her brows, as if Charlotte had done something to admire.

"Yes, and now I am rich enough to buy my way into society." There was a feisty smirk on Charlotte's face.

Mrs. Martindale's eyelids fluttered and she started fanning herself, frowning ferociously at Charlotte, who looked amused.

He couldn't help smiling at Charlotte's pluck and vinegar. But would that same pluck and vinegar gain her friends? Or enemies? It was too soon to tell.

After that exchange, they kept meeting more people, and he couldn't converse with Charlotte as they had at Lowndesbury House. He could feel his frustration rising with the heat in his forehead.

"Are you ready to turn back?" he asked her. It was rude of him, but if he had to talk to one more person, he might end up doing or saying something they'd all regret.

She said, "I suppose I am."

As they left the park and were walking down the street, they met a young man whose face showed recognition when he saw Mrs. Drake. Then his eye was obviously caught by Charlotte Robbins's fair face and figure.

"Mrs. Drake, it is so good to see you." He stepped forward to greet her.

"Mr. Welton, you are looking well." Mrs. Drake smiled quite broadly. She made the introductions, introducing him as Mr. Anthony Welton, the son of one of her friends. Mrs. Drake introduced Charlotte and added, "She has just let a house on Grosvenor Square."

"Miss Robbins, it is truly a pleasure to make your acquaintance." He reached for her hand, but she pretended not to notice.

William didn't trust this Anthony Welton. He had dark, shifty eyes that showed an obvious interest in Charlotte, especially after hearing she had a house on Grosvenor Square.

"Perhaps I will see you at a theatrical or a concert in town," he said. "Do you like theatricals?"

"I don't know, as I have never been to one."

"I would be glad to escort you. Will you allow me to call on you tomorrow?"

Charlotte looked uncertain, but Mrs. Drake said, "Of course you may. Here is one of Miss Robbins's cards. The direction is on the back."

The cheeky blighter pressed the card to his chest. "Thank you. I shall call on you tomorrow." He excused himself, having never once looked William directly in the eye.

They continued on their way, but he had an uncomfortable feeling. Would Charlotte welcome that man's attention? She would receive him tomorrow, even though he was a stranger to her, after only one brief introduction, after Mrs. Drake invited him. Of course, it wasn't wrong for her to do so, but it stirred up something inside William's chest that he didn't like.

Mrs. Drake started talking as if her job was to prevent even a moment of silence. The only way he could hold onto his sanity was by ignoring her—and talking over her.

"Miss Robbins, how are you settling in to life in London?" It was an inane question, but was the first thing that came to mind, and it blessedly caused Mrs. Drake to stop speaking.

"Very well, I thank you. I'm not accustomed to so many people, but I do like looking at all the beautiful homes, and Hyde Park. I enjoy the park."

"You don't find it too crowded?"

"It is a bit more crowded than your beautiful grounds at Lowndesbury House, but I never meet anyone I know, so it is rare I am forced to speak with anyone."

"Ah, I suppose I ruined your walk, then."

"No, not at all. It is very good to see you again. We are old friends, are we not?"

Her gaze locked on his. Was it his imagination, or did her voice become a bit breathless?

"Yes, indeed."

"Perhaps I will take my walk a bit earlier from now on, when fewer people will be out, as I did at Lowndesbury House."

William liked that idea.

"Although, not tomorrow. I don't want the children to have to rise too early."

"Of course. The same time tomorrow should suit them very well." After a moment's pause, he said, "I know you have never lived in London before. Is there anything that I might do to help?"

"Thank you. That is very kind. Mrs. Drake has been very helpful, as she has lived here all her life. But I did think perhaps it would be lovely if you accompanied the children and me to the Tower of London, to see the menagerie?"

"That sounds like a pleasant outing. The day after tomorrow?"

"Yes."

They were approaching his townhouse.

"Well, if there is ever anything you need, please do not hesitate to send word. I am not far from you, as you know. And you may call on me and the children any time." He felt his face grow warm. He wasn't accustomed to giving such an eager and open invitation.

"You are very kind . . . and generous." She gazed up at him in a way that made him tug at his cravat.

Where had all the air gone?

They were nearly to his front door.

"We shall be looking forward to attending the ball next week, Lord Brookhaven," Mrs. Drake said. "Thank you for your gracious—"

"I shall walk you to your door."

Mrs. Drake began falling behind. She was breathing heavily, and he realized he'd quickened his pace and was walking too fast for her. Well, it was a good way to keep her from talking.

He slowed a bit, and they soon reached Charlotte's door.

"Good day, Mrs. Drake, Miss Robbins."

"Thank you for accompanying us."

He nodded and turned to leave, just as he thought perhaps Miss Robbins had been lifting her hand to him.

He cursed himself for not taking her hand. He imagined the sensation of kissing her hand, even though the fabric of her glove would separate his lips from her skin. But it was too late now.

Mr. Anthony Welton did indeed call on me the next day.

We'd just arrived home after taking Samuel and Annabelle to the park with Lord Brookhaven. It had been a lovely outing. Lord Brookhaven had gazed deeply into my eyes, and I'd felt a bit lightheaded, like those women who swoon in novels. I was both breathless with joy and amused at my foolishness. He lingered with me at my door, but I didn't make the mistake again of assuming he might want to kiss my hand, and we parted with a slight bow on both sides.

Mr. Welton was very pleasant and attentive, complimenting me and smiling a lot. I gathered that his mother and Mrs. Drake were close friends and had been for many years. If I am honest, I enjoyed his attention. He made no attempt to disguise his interest in me, which I found refreshing. I was well aware, however, that I knew nothing of his character.

The next day Mr. Anthony Welton called again while we were away and left his card. I found that I wasn't bothered by missing him, as Lord Brookhaven and I were taking the children to see the menagerie at the Tower of London.

The children gasped and exclaimed over the animals, asking, "What is that?" and "Does it eat people?" and "Does it live in the jungle or the desert?"

Lord Brookhaven was gentle and patient, answering their many questions and explaining things in a way that was appropriate for seven-year-olds.

"How do you like the menagerie?" Lord Brookhaven asked me when the children were distracted by watching the lions being fed.

"It is fascinating to see the exotic animals, but it also makes me a bit sad to think of them caged like criminals, unable to roam as they were created to do. But the children are learning about them and enjoying them. I actually liked seeing and learning about the Tower of London more."

He paid quite as much attention to me as Mr. Welton had, but I enjoyed Lord Brookhaven's attention more, as he was serious when he gazed into my eyes, listening to my every word.

I watched as Samuel and Annabelle would let their older brother take their hand and lead them, the way they respected his instruction, and how they looked up to him. It was obvious they loved him.

Indeed, how could anyone not love him?

But the next day, I was home during calling hours.

"Miss Robbins, you are a breath of fresh air," Mr. Anthony Welton told me once he arrived.

"And how am I a breath of fresh air?" I knew he was only flirting with me, but I was curious if he would be able to come up with a plausible answer to that.

"You are not like all the other young ladies on the hunt for a husband."

"No, I suspect I am not. For one thing, at five-and-twenty, I am older than they are. And for another, I don't need a husband and therefore am not 'on the hunt,' as you say."

"Alas," he said, grasping at his chest, "you are destined to break my heart, Miss Robbins."

I only laughed at his dramatics.

He seemed to wrestle with himself over whether to be offended by my laugh, but he ended by smiling and repeating, "You are a breath of fresh air, Miss Robbins."

But all his flattery made it difficult to take him seriously.

Later that day, just before the evening meal, Mrs. Drake said, "You know, Mr. Welton will inherit a fortune if his oldest brother, who is currently sick with consumption, should be unfortunate enough to die from his illness. And if his second oldest brother drinks himself to death, which seems likely, since he is known for having to be brought home nearly every morning by the constable, so inebriated that he doesn't know his own name."

"Indeed," I said, "it is unfortunate to have the person who should be your closest friend wait for you to die."

"I did not say he was waiting for them to die." Mrs. Drake frowned in that pinched way of hers. "One cannot be blamed if one shall inherit upon the death of a relative. It is not as if Mr. Welton wants his brothers to die, but it is a fact of life that he shall inherit the family fortune should his brothers pass away."

"Well, then, let us pray for their good health so Mr. Welton doesn't lose his brothers."

Mrs. Drake looked quite angry and excused herself from the room.

Sometimes I think she didn't like me very much, and perhaps I was a little hard on her, with my forcing her to face the ridiculous aspects of society while she had little choice but to be polite to me.

Still, I had no intention of becoming Mr. Welton's consolation prize.

I was well aware that my fifty thousand pounds would go directly into my husband's pocket if I should ever marry. Mrs. Drake had told me of other men who had asked to be introduced to me, and some approached her right in front of me, hoping for an introduction.

I had to admit, there was a part of me that enjoyed this. It was a heady feeling, being sought after by gentlemen of good names from old families. But I did not trust that any of them cared for me. When they looked at me, they surely saw fifty thousand pounds, not my character, intelligence, or personality.

I made the mistake of saying so to Mrs. Drake one evening.

"Miss Robbins, how can you talk so?" She looked truly shocked.

"It is every woman's duty to marry and have children, if they can. And it is only wise to marry where there is security on both sides. You would not marry foolishly, marrying a man with no name and no fortune. Or who has no career in the military or the church, which would make him unable to provide for you and your children. And a gentleman must also marry where there is the most benefit to himself. Otherwise there will be sorrow that no amount of love can assuage."

"I understand what you are saying, and I agree to some extent, I suppose, but I don't wish to marry someone who wants me only for what money I can provide." My fortune was so new to me, why should I be eager to part with it just so a man would marry me—fortune, old name, respected family, or not?

Mrs. Drake sighed forcefully. "That is not the way to think of it. Consider what a man provides that you cannot provide for yourself—children, his good name, the respect afforded to his wife, his protection, a home . . ."

"I already have a home and a good name, and I have servants to respect me and offer protection." It was probably cruel of me to take pleasure in teasing Mrs. Drake so. But I was speaking the truth, even though I knew it was contrary to what Mrs. Drake believed.

"Miss Robbins, you are not seriously . . . I have not been speaking of that kind of . . ." She huffed out another forceful sigh.

"Forgive me, Mrs. Drake, but just as you wish for me to be wise in how I conduct myself, I also wish to be wise. I want to be loved for who I am, not for my fifty thousand pounds, and therefore I'd like to take careful stock and not marry the first man who shows an interest." I was quick to add, "Not that anyone has asked me to marry him."

"Perhaps not, but you will get your first marriage proposal soon enough." She smiled as though a marriage proposal was all my heart desired.

Indeed, I did wish to be married, but not for the reasons she'd recited. I wished to marry for love—the kind of love I'd dreamed about since I was a little girl—and the love of children and a family. None of those other things seemed worth the risks.

Seventeen

William was on his way to the jewelers on a busy street in London when he turned a corner and saw *her*.

She was with her mother, sister, and another young lady. It was the first time he'd seen Letitia since she'd broken their engagement by running away to Gretna Green with the Marquess of Wexford.

Then he realized the young lady with her was Rose Rutledge.

As he started to turn and walk the other way, both she and Rose Rutledge saw him.

"Lord Brookhaven!" Miss Rutledge's voice behind him forced a decision.

It seemed less cowardly and more gentlemanly to turn and face her, and as he could hear her footsteps hurrying toward him, he reluctantly did so. Besides, he'd only have to speak with Rose Rutledge. As bold as she was, even Letitia wouldn't be bold enough to speak to him.

"Miss Rutledge," he said, giving her a quick bow. "I did not know you were in town."

"I only just arrived yesterday. I hope you and Lady Derringer are well."

"Yes, we are well. And Lord and Lady Rutledge are well, I trust?"

"Yes, relatively. Father has trouble with gout, but it is not serious. They are gone to Bath to take the waters."

"Ah yes. Well, it is good to see you." He was about to bid her a good day and go retrieve his horse, but as he took a step away, she took a step forward.

"I heard Miss Charlotte Robbins is in town and that she has inherited a fortune."

"Yes, I heard the same."

"You were seen with her, walking in Hyde Park." She gave him a smirk, as though she was in on some secret of his.

"I accompanied Miss Robbins and Mrs. Drake on a walk, that is correct."

"I also heard you were giving a ball. I would love to be invited, but I am staying with Lady Wexford, so I understand if you do not want to ask her, and if you think it rude to send an invitation asking only me—"

"Yes, that would be rude. I'm glad you understand."

Her face fell.

"Well, it is good to see you," she said, quickly renewing her smile, "and I hope you won't hold it against me that I am staying with your former fiancée. She and I have been good friends, and our fathers—"

"I had not known you were in such close acquaintance with Miss—with Lady Wexford."

"Oh, well, I only just became acquainted with her when we were both invited to Lord and Lady Cloverdale's country house in Derbyshire. She and I became fast friends, and I—"

"I hope you have a pleasant stay in London. Forgive me, but I have an errand, and I don't wish to be late. Good day, Miss Rutledge."

"Good day. I do hope we will see each other again."

He tipped his hat to her as he walked away. Lady Wexford was still standing where Miss Rutledge had left her, looking quite petulant as she frowned, staring his way. She then flicked open the fan in her hand and started fanning herself.

Strange that he'd once thought he was in love with her.

He barely saw anything as he walked, remembering the ball where his Letitia—for they had been engaged for a month at the time—had flirted with the marquess. William had thought little of it, so sure was he that his fiancée was in love with him. She'd smiled and flicked her fan much in the same way she had just done, except she'd used it not to fan herself but to tap Lord Wexford's arm. She'd said something, then they'd both laughed.

How stupid William had felt when she ran off with the marquess a week later.

He'd worried about marrying her, but only because she was so young and innocent, only sixteen. He'd seen himself as her protector, her provider. She'd been his sweet angelic dove. He'd written her such sentimental drivel, sending her a letter every day after they were engaged. In his mind, she was completely unlike his mother.

But it had only been in his mind. When someone wealthier and with a higher-ranking title, someone who would one day be a duke, had asked her to run away with him, she'd forgotten William completely.

And here he was, imagining that Charlotte Robbins was the same sort of innocent, good kind of woman. Was he fooling himself again? How well did he truly know her?

And now he'd done something that was even more irreversible than becoming engaged—he'd given a large portion of his fortune to Miss Robbins.

Samuel and Annabelle's inheritances were safe in a trust, which would not be diminished by his giving away the fifty thousand pounds. But although he was hoping she'd fall in love with him, he now realized it would be much more painful to marry her and have her turn out to be just like his mother . . . and Letitia.

But hadn't he already seen sufficient evidence to know that Charlotte Robbins was not like them? She was the furthest thing from it. And he just wanted to see her happy, to give her the choices she'd never had before, to see her living and thriving the way she was meant to. And he still hoped, when given the choice, she would choose to marry him.

But even if she didn't, he would have to be resigned to that. There was no turning back.

Millicent was a welcome sight, even if she did arrive talking and hardly took a breath the first two hours. She shared with me her favorite shops in London, then we stayed awake most of the night, laughing and telling each other our deepest secrets.

Millicent had her heart set on Lord Markeley. I thought him rather an unlikely match for her, but I did not say so. She was my only real friend in London, and I didn't want her to hear that from me. Besides, who was I to say that the fifteen thousand pounds that her father was offering to whomever married her wasn't enough for Lord Markeley, or that he wouldn't fall in love with her? I did rather hope that someone else might distract her from Lord Markeley before she made the unhappy discovery that he was not in love with her.

I, of course, shared with her my feelings for Lord Brookhaven and the details of our walk to Hyde Park, as well as our two outings with Samuel and Annabelle. "But I am not so conceited as to think he would want to marry me," I was quick to add. "He's the Earl of Brookhaven. None of his friends will want him to marry a former governess. He'd be ashamed of me."

"Do not think anything of the kind," Millicent protested. "You have your own fortune now—a very large fortune—and surely that is more important than the fact that you were once a governess. And he has no parents to protest or force him to marry someone of higher status and with a family estate and old name. He can do as he pleases."

"Perhaps, but I would feel terrible if I were the reason my husband is looked down upon by the rest of his peers."

"That kind of scandal never affects a landed gentleman very much, especially someone who is also an earl with a large estate. Besides, think of the benefits of being married to Lord Brookhaven. He is very wealthy; you'd be a lady—the wife of an earl; you'd be the mistress of Lowndesbury House, and your children would have large inheritances and an old name. What more could you wish for?"

"I could wish for love, for my husband's respect, and for him to feel respected by his peers. I don't want to be the cause of my husband's disgrace."

One side of Millicent's mouth turned down. "I think it would be worth it. Can you truly say you would refuse him if Lord Brookhaven asked you to marry him?"

"Truthfully, I can't be sure, but I hope for his sake that he doesn't ask me, at least until I feel I am accepted by society."

"Well, I think it would be very exciting. I could say I was the dear friend of Lady Brookhaven, the wife of the Earl of Brookhaven." Millicent paraded around my bedroom where we'd been talking, holding her hand out as if offering it for a kiss, stretching her neck up, and looking down her nose.

I shook my head at her.

"Actually," I said, "I don't have to marry anyone. I have decided that if no great love finds me in the form of a handsome gentleman, then I shall write and publish stories."

"Stories?"

"Yes. I used to write stories for my friends when I was a schoolgirl. And I've written a lot of stories for Samuel and Annabelle—children's stories, and they seem to enjoy them. I believe I might be able to find a publisher for them."

"You must let me read your stories."

"Of course you may." I yawned. "But if I don't get some sleep, I'll be nodding off at Lord Brookhaven's ball."

"We can't have that," Millicent said cheerily.

We bid each other good night, and I prayed for plenty of sleep before my first London ball.

We entered the beautiful townhouse and waited in the receiving line to be greeted by Lady Derringer.

"Yes, my nephew asked me to be his hostess. One cannot have a ball without a hostess," she was saying rather loudly to the couple who had come in just before us.

"My dear Miss Robbins," Lady Derringer said, suddenly giving us her attention. "I know Mrs. Drake, of course, and have met Miss Skidmore before. It is so good to see you all again." Then, looking into my eyes, she said, "How are you, my dear?"

It was lovely to see Lady Derringer. Lord Brookhaven was standing beside her. An older couple was talking with him now, but I saw him glance at me.

We all said our pleasantries, and then Lady Derringer said to me, "I wish I were going to be in town to show you the most interesting places and keep you company, but I'm afraid I've just gotten word that my late husband's sister has died and I must return to Devonshire in the morning for the funeral."

"Oh, I am very sorry to hear of your loss. I shall pray for comfort from Providence and safe travels for you."

"Thank you, my dear." She stared into my eyes longer than expected, since there were people waiting behind me to be greeted. She made me believe that she genuinely liked me.

Lord Brookhaven was suddenly free of the couple ahead of us and stepped toward me. "Come," Lord Brookhaven said. He offered his arm to me and led us away from his aunt. "There is lemonade and whatever you fancy." He took us personally to the refreshments table. He seemed a bit nervous, the way he kept glancing at me, then away.

When we had been at Lowndesbury House, he'd seemed so confident. He'd also seemed older, somehow, never in a hurry. Tonight, I saw in his face that he was only a year or two older than I was, and I was reminded of how alone he was in the world, both of us orphans. I was glad he at least had Lady Derringer, Samuel, and Annabelle.

Then I saw Lord Markeley and Mr. Merritt standing in the doorway of the ballroom, staring quite brazenly at me. Just as I thought they might come and greet us, Lord Brookhaven excused himself and walked toward his friends.

Millicent raised her eyebrows at me as she sipped her lemonade. "They're here," she whispered.

"Just smile and keep talking."

We sipped our lemonade while Millicent whispered observations about Lord Markeley and Mr. Merritt, about their clothing and how they looked, while the three men stood talking for a few moments. Then Lord Brookhaven walked away to rejoin his aunt in greeting their guests.

We put down our cups and went to where Mrs. Drake was standing with another woman.

"Ah!" Mrs. Drake held out her hand to me. "Here they are. Mrs. Welton, this is Miss Charlotte Robbins and her friend, Miss Millicent Skidmore of Shropshire. And this is Mrs. Welton, a longtime friend of my family."

We greeted each other politely. "That is my niece there," Mrs. Welton said, "dancing with Lord Hatton."

She was a lovely girl, and there could be little doubt that her aunt was proud that she'd snagged a dance with Lord Hatton, who would be considered a great match for any woman in the room, as he was the oldest son of the Duke of Emberley.

Lord Markeley and Mr. Merritt finally approached and greeted us. Lord Markeley was closer to Millicent than to me, so I began to engage Mr. Merritt in conversation, while Millicent conversed with Lord Markeley.

I said, "I trust you have been well since I saw you last at Lowndesbury House."

"Yes, quite well, and you have been well, I hear, having inherited an unexpected fortune—from an uncle, wasn't it?"

"Yes, it was very unexpected. I should have very much liked to have known him."

"Well; he cared enough to leave you his fortune."

Only because there was no other family member to leave it to. I changed the subject. "And all is well with your family?"

"Oh yes. My sister got married, and that was a bit of a to-do. My mother is pleased, for they are settled quite near her, and she may never think of the rest of her children again."

"I am sure that cannot be true."

"You do not know my mother. Out of sight is out of mind. I believe she forgot about my existence when I was off at school. You would think her daughters were her only children."

He was smiling, as if it were a mild joke that didn't bother him, and I allowed myself to look into his eyes. He was a handsome man, and he was not without some strengths of character, but I kept remembering what he'd said to me at Lowndesbury House, about how I'd be ruining Lord Brookhaven if I married him.

He asked me for the next dance, just as I heard Lord Markeley asking Millicent.

If Lord Brookhaven had any intentions toward me, would he not have made sure to ask me for the first dance? Instead, he'd let his friend Mr. Merritt ask me.

I made my way to the dance floor, a sinking feeling in my stomach.

Blast. Thomas Merritt was dancing with Charlotte.

William felt the heat rising from his chest. Why hadn't he made sure to ask her first?

But there was plenty of evening left, and there should be many more opportunities. Still, it made him want to punch Merritt. He should know how William felt about Charlotte. He was even surprised Merritt hadn't suspected that her new fortune had come from him.

He looked across the room. There was that blackguard, Anthony Welton, watching Charlotte dance with Merritt.

It was necessary to have a hostess, but he wished his aunt had not invited certain people without asking him first. It was her way to only see the good in people. Even if he'd told her about Welton's character, his aunt was friends with Welton's grandmother and probably would have invited him anyway.

There was no more time to dwell on these matters as he began to be accosted by one person after another, asking him questions, remarking on how he'd never given a ball before, hoping it would be just the beginning of many such events, and on and on. He was introduced to young ladies who were making their debut in society, most of whom his aunt had invited. No doubt she hoped that if things did not work out with Miss Robbins, he would find one with whom to make a match. Or perhaps she simply was populating the event with the people who were most likely to spread the word around town that Miss Robbins had inherited a large fortune and therefore it should be forgotten that she had once been a penniless, orphaned governess.

But the mothers in the crowd were eyeing him. He could imagine what they were thinking: He'd already had one failed engagement, and therefore he must be eager to correct his previous blunder and leap headfirst into matrimony.

He made a mighty effort to be polite to them. It wasn't easy, especially after they cost him an opportunity to ask Miss Robbins for the next dance. Instead, he had to watch her being asked by that Anthony Welton, which caused him to stop being polite, and a miracle happened—everyone excused themselves and left him to bother someone else.

But perhaps that was due more to the scowl on his face than any miracle.

Why was that scoundrel leaning close to her? And why wasn't she shoving him off?

"William? Are you well?" Lady Derringer looked concerned.

"Of course I'm well."

"You don't look well. You look angry, and you're frightening your guests."

If only that were true. Then they might leave. "I don't care if

Anthony Welton is your friend's grandson—if he gets any closer to Miss Robbins, I will take him by the collar and throw him off the balcony."

She gave him a look that he hadn't seen since he was a young boy and had trampled her rhododendrons. "If you like the girl so much, just ask her to marry you and have it done."

"I cannot . . ." He didn't want to talk about this with her, especially not here.

"Why not? I'm sure she'll say yes."

He wasn't so sure. "She's not the kind of woman who only cares about my rank and my money." Besides, she might think he was too self-conceited, which he was, and too . . . discontented. And he wasn't sure he could change.

"You want her to fall in love with you," Lady Derringer said matter-of-factly. "Then court her. Take her for drives, escort her to concerts and theatricals, call on her every day and tell her pretty words."

Perhaps she was right. But he needed to be sure that she loved him. He'd been hurt and humiliated before. Besides, Miss Robbins would wish to marry the man with the strongest character, especially since she had fifty thousand pounds and could choose anyone, and William's temperament was often gruff, melancholy, and just plain irritable.

It would be good if he could become a better person, and quickly.

His fears made him want to wait, to truly get to know her character, to know that fortune could not change her. He'd thought he knew her when they'd walked around his gardens at Lowndesbury House, when he'd received her weekly reports about the children's progress, and he'd seen it at the house party with a few guests. She'd comported herself well.

But hadn't he also been sure about Letitia?

Lady Derringer had said he should court Miss Robbins, spend time with her and say flattering things to her—and he wanted to. But every time he thought about making his intentions known, there was a part of him that stopped him, that forced him to keep her at arm's length, and he didn't know how to conquer it. Or even if he should.

Eighteen

I danced several more dances, each time with a different gentleman. I smiled and drank lemonade and danced some more, always aware of Lord Brookhaven, who never danced at all.

Why had he given this ball? He stood near the wall, scowling, barely speaking to anyone. Meanwhile, I danced with every gentleman who asked me. It was what ladies did, and I seemed to be in demand as a dance partner, as much as any other lady in the room.

One gentleman in particular was quite attentive—Mr. Welton. He asked me to dance before many of the guests had even arrived, fetched me lemonade, and seemed always eager to whisper some bit of gossip in my ear. Later in the evening, he asked me to dance again. While we danced the second time, he flirted shamelessly, making me laugh and leaning his head quite close to mine while gazing into my eyes. It was a bit disconcerting. But mostly, it just made me feel alive and . . . pretty.

Logically, I told myself that the men who flirted and asked me to dance were only doing it because of my fifty thousand pounds, but it was something I was not accustomed to, and I'd hardly be human if I didn't enjoy it.

Lord Brookhaven appeared at my side. His face was serious, though not quite so hard and angry as it had looked for most of the night. "Do you have a partner for the last dance?"

"No."

"Would you do me the honor?"

"Of course."

The musicians were preparing to play, and Lord Brookhaven led me onto the floor. While we stood there waiting for other couples to join us, he said, "I wish to put you on your guard about Mr. Welton. He's a scoundrel of the first order and is only after the lady with the largest fortune. You'd do well to stay clear of him."

I said nothing as the music started and we moved in a round with the other couples.

But the more I thought about what he said, the angrier I felt. I'd waited all night to dance with him, and this was the only thing he said to me? How dare he suggest that Mr. Welton could only be interested in me for my fortune! Did he think that I had no merit or worth on my own?

Tears stung my eyes. It was true—no one would have danced or flirted with me if I had not inherited a fortune. I'd be shunned and ignored if not for the money, a poor orphan, nobody at all, exactly as I'd been during Lord Brookhaven's house party. It hurt even more that Lord Brookhaven had been the one to point this out.

He was probably just trying to be a good friend. He couldn't know how much it hurt, especially coming from him.

And he hadn't danced with me or talked with me all night, only now asking me to dance when he couldn't possibly ask me for a second dance. We danced in silence.

When it was over and everyone was politely applauding the musicians, Lord Brookhaven said, "I hope you are not angry with me for wishing to put you on your guard."

I wasn't angry with him for *that*, but . . . "I don't understand why you think a gentleman could not wish to know me for myself. Am I so odious that my fortune is the only thing about me that could interest a man?"

I should not be saying such things, but it was as if saying them scratched an unignorable itch.

I'd probably regret it later, though.

I could also see how my words affected him. His lips parted as a flash of pain flitted over his face. Then his jaw hardened.

"Forgive me. I meant no offense." He turned his head as if looking for a way out.

"Forgive me. I should not have . . . Thank you for putting me on my guard. I am sure you meant well." My cheeks were burning.

I didn't wait for him to reply. I hurried to where Mrs. Drake and Millicent were waiting for me.

It hurt so much that Lord Brookhaven only wished to warn me about other men, not court me or flirt with me himself. After the "triumph" of having so many dance partners, all I wanted to do was go home and have a good cry.

The ball was a disaster.

Even two days after the ball, William was berating his lack of wisdom, which had induced him to warn Miss Charlotte Robbins about scoundrels at the ball, while also wishing he'd asked her to dance sooner—and kept his mouth shut.

She'd looked so beautiful there in his house, dancing and smiling and charming everyone, including his aunt.

Lady Derringer. Perhaps she could help him. When his aunt returned, he would send her to speak to Charlotte, to find out if he'd lost all hope of winning her affections. But that was perhaps a bad idea and might make him look like a coward. Which he was.

When he watched so many men flattering her, flirting with her, and she flirting with them and welcoming their attention, he nearly lost his mind.

But then when he warned her about Mr. Welton, she said nothing at first, but he saw the tears in her eyes. And when she said he must think her odious, he realized how his words might have made her feel, that she was only worthy because of her fortune.

He should have told her that nothing could be further from the truth. It was only that these addlepated nick-ninnies couldn't see her worth. They only saw the fifty thousand pounds, and she was worth so much more than that. But she'd been undervalued her whole life. Of course she would misunderstand his intention. It was no wonder his words had come across the wrong way.

Then again, his intentions had been good, as he was afraid she hadn't known that Anthony Welton was a scoundrel. How could she know? She would have assumed that he'd only invite good people of good character to his ball.

He was staring out the window when he caught sight of Miss Robbins walking down the street with Miss Skidmore and Mrs. Drake. He only hesitated a moment, then ran to the stairs and took them two and three at a time.

He kept his distance. The weather was relatively warm, with only a few clouds and no wind, and although he preferred country walks to walks in London, it was entirely plausible that he was also going for a walk.

Suddenly, a child ran out from a side street and grabbed Mrs. Drake's arm. The child cried out, "Help! Please help me!"

William quickened his pace. This was a common way for thieves to distract their victims, while someone else jumped out at them and snatched a purse, or laid them out with a blow to the head so they could look through the man's pockets.

Mrs. Drake said something that sounded like a harsh reprimand and shook off the child's hold on her arm. While her companions stepped away from the child, Charlotte stepped closer.

As William drew near, he could see the child was dirty and its clothes were ragged. The child appeared to be crying—and she appeared to be a girl.

She was sobbing and clinging to Miss Robbins's hand when he arrived.

"My brother is hurt. Come, please!" The child's voice was high and pleading.

Mrs. Drake said, "Charlotte, no, you mustn't. It could be a trap."

Charlotte looked up at him. There was a flicker of surprise, then she said, “Lord Brookhaven. Will you come with me?”

“Yes.”

They started down the side street with the child pulling Miss Robbins’s hand, William following close behind.

They went round several corners as he made mental note of all the turns so he could find the way back. Then they came to an abandoned building. The child led Miss Robbins through a small opening. It was just big enough for him to bend down and squeeze through.

A little boy was lying on the dirty floor, his arm and face bloody and bruised. He looked to be about six years old.

“Please help him,” the little girl said.

He knelt beside the child and Miss Robbins did the same.

“What happened?” Miss Robbins asked.

“A carriage ran him over,” the little girl said.

“The wheel went clean over my arm,” the little boy said.

He reached toward the little boy’s arm.

“Don’t touch it,” he said, warding them off with his other hand.

“Is the bone through the skin?”

The boy shook his head.

“You need a doctor,” Miss Robbins said gently. “The doctor will put on a splint and then I’m sure it will be all right.”

“My physician is nearby,” William said.

Miss Robbins’s eyes met his. Had there ever been more beautiful eyes than hers? Not only were they pretty and blue, with dark delicate lashes, but there was so much compassion and concern in them. They swam with tears as she gazed up at him. He felt his throat tighten.

But he couldn’t dwell on Miss Charlotte Robbins’s teary eyes, as much as he wanted to. He needed to get this child some medical attention.

My heart seemed to melt as I gazed gratefully into Lord Brookhaven's eyes. How kind, how good he was. Mrs. Drake and Millicent had huddled together, looking horrified, but Lord Brookhaven hadn't batted an eye. He just followed the child with me.

He turned back to the little boy and said, "I can carry you to the physician, but you will need to keep your arm still. Can you do that?"

His eyes darted anxiously toward his sister.

I said, "Perhaps we could take a piece of cloth and bind his arm close to his body. I saw it done once when a girl at my school fell out of a tree and broke her arm. Mrs. Southey bound her arm to her side until we could get her inside and fetch the doctor."

I looked around at the squalor. There was a place near the wall where it looked as if they'd been building fires to keep warm. But I didn't see anything that looked like strips of cloth.

Lord Brookhaven untied his cravat, which was long and white. Then he took a penknife out of his pocket and started cutting it into narrow strips.

My eye was drawn to the bare skin at his throat, the small hollow place there, and the bit of dark hair peeking out from the top of his shirt. I quickly looked away.

He bent down with the cloth. We worked together as he passed the cloth under the little boy's back and I pulled it from my side and passed it around his arm.

"What's your name?" I asked.

"Joshua," he said in a trembly voice. His face was streaked where his tears had made tracks through the dirt on his cheeks, but his eyes were dry now. The blood on his face, which seemed to come from his hairline above his forehead, was drying. I wished I had a cloth and some water so I could clean it.

"And your sister's name?"

"Sarah."

I made sure the cloth was snug, and after a few passes, I tied the ends together.

Lord Brookhaven slid his hands underneath Joshua's body and lifted him, looking purposeful as he moved slowly and carefully. He ducked, carefully moving sideways so Joshua wouldn't bump his head or catch his feet on the narrow opening. Joshua bit his lip, but he didn't cry out.

As we moved through the narrow streets, Sarah walked beside me, chewing her fingers, while we followed Lord Brookhaven.

We turned down three or four streets before Lord Brookhaven stopped in front of a brick two-story house. "Miss Robbins, would you knock on the door?"

I knocked and the door was opened by a servant, who led us inside, where Lord Brookhaven laid Joshua on a small bed and the physician, Dr. Morton, came in and examined the boy.

"May I have some water to wash his face?" I said quietly to the servant.

"No need, mum. I shall wash him." She left and returned a few minutes later.

"If you could wait in the room across the hall," Dr. Morton said, nodding in that direction, "I shall send for you when I'm sure the bone is set."

"You won't hurt him none?" Sarah looked near to tears again.

"I shall make sure the bone heals straight and true. Now, go and wait." His manner was gentle, for which I was grateful.

While we waited, sitting on straight chairs in a small drawing room, I asked Sarah, "Were you living in that building we saw?"

"Yes, ma'am. It's just Joshua and me, but we take care of each other."

"How old are you?"

"Nine years."

"Would you and Joshua like to come and stay with me? I have an extra room with a comfortable bed. You can stay until your brother's arm heals, at least."

"And then will you send us to the poorhouse? We was there and we ran away. We don't aim to go back."

"I promise I won't send you to the poorhouse, nor anywhere else you don't want to go."

The girl said nothing. I couldn't bear to think of her and her little brother sleeping on the floor of that broken and rundown building. I could surely convince her to come and stay with me. I had so much room, and she and her brother were so young and vulnerable.

What was Lord Brookhaven thinking? Did he disapprove of my taking these orphaned children to live with me? If he did, he made no mention of it. But Mrs. Drake would disapprove, I could well imagine, and so would Millicent. Or perhaps I was wrong and their compassion and better natures would win out.

Lord Brookhaven's face was serious, but there was a gentleness too. My mind went to what he'd said to me at the ball, and I realized I'd reacted badly. He'd only been trying to be helpful, saying what any friend would have said who was trying to look out for me.

I was distracted from planning what I would say to him by the sight of his bare neck.

I'd seen many servants working in the fields or in gardens and stables with part of their chests bare, their shirts open at the neck and chest hair peeking out, but it had never seemed anything but ordinary, and I'd never felt drawn to stare at them. Lord Brookhaven, however . . .

I forced myself to think instead about how kind Lord Brookhaven had been, how gently he had treated the little injured boy. Would any of the other gentlemen I'd met so far, danced and flirted with in London, have been so kind? No, they'd probably have reacted similarly to Mrs. Drake, whose behavior—flinching away and yelling at them—reflected most people's feelings toward orphans and those who begged on the street. Where was their Christian charity? At best, it was overwhelmed by their fear. At worst, they felt none.

While we waited for the physician to finish, a servant brought tea and cakes. And with a little encouragement, Sarah began to eat.

"Can I save some for my brother?" she whispered to me. Her eyes were wide, and a few crumbs sprayed from the corners of her mouth.

"Of course, when the surgeon is finished with him."

While she was distracted by the food, I turned to Lord Brookhaven. "Thank you so much for helping me. I wouldn't have known where to take him, and you appeared just when we needed you."

Just when *I* needed him. I felt the tears crowd my eyes.

"I am glad that I came upon you when I did and was able to help."

"You must think me foolish." I said the words very quietly, hoping Sarah wouldn't hear.

"Not at all. I think you showed a compassion and courage that is very admirable."

"And you will help me bring them to my home?" I steeled myself for what he might say.

"Of course. You may rely upon me."

My heart swelled and the tears threatened to fall. I blinked desperately to hold them back.

"After all," he said with a tiny smile, "I've been carrying children around for seven years now. I am up to the task."

I could have asked him more directly if he disapproved of me bringing the children to my home, but I was certain I had my answer.

Nineteen

"Miss Robbins, you cannot expect me to say nothing about your bringing two strange children of no account and no family into your own home. They are filthy, they've been living on the streets, and they will steal from you and take advantage of you. I would not be surprised if they attack you in your bed while you sleep."

"Mrs. Drake, I will ask you to at least lower your voice if you must say such unkind things."

"Unkind things?" Mrs. Drake had a look of exasperation on her face.

Millicent stood nearby, seeming almost frightened.

"Miss Robbins, I realize you are young and have not been very much in the world, and heaven knows how you got Lord Brookhaven to go along with you, but it is well-known that these little . . . vermin run around thieving and accosting good people in the streets."

"Mrs. Drake, they are children. They are not vermin."

"Well, then, the cast-off, disorderly children no one wants."

"They need someone to look after them and provide for them. And if my parents had not been able to provide for me, I might have ended up on the street."

Mrs. Drake huffed out a breath and crossed her arms over her chest. "You are much too innocent for London, Miss Robbins. Much too innocent, but you are not prudent. Next thing we know you'll be inviting a band of gypsies to dine with us."

"Mrs. Drake."

"Forgive me." She held out her hands in a gesture of surrender. "I shall say no more. But I want you to remember that I was against this scheme from the beginning."

The only servant who seemed at all happy with my new guests was a motherly kitchen servant named Gretchen, so I elevated her to the position of nursemaid, to help with caring for the children, since the upstairs maid looked horrified when I asked her to watch them a moment while I went to order them a bath drawn.

"You may leave the young ones to me, miss," Gretchen said. "I had two of my own. They're grown now, but I remember well the days when they were the age of these ones."

"Thank you, Gretchen. Please come directly to me if you need anything or have any concerns."

"Yes, miss, I will."

It was impossible to explain, but when I thought about the children sleeping in a bed under my own roof, and when I watched them eat heartily, as if they thought the food might disappear at any moment, my heart filled with love, and I couldn't stop the smile spreading over my face and the tears stinging my eyes.

Perhaps *this* was why God had been so good to me, so good as to give me a fortune. It was so I could help these children. And perhaps I could use this situation to show Mrs. Drake and Millicent that orphaned children were not to be feared and shunned. They were human beings who needed kindness. After all, God asked us to care for the fatherless and widows in their affliction.

I couldn't help but contrast Sarah and Joshua with Samuel and Annabelle. They were similar in many ways, but Sarah and Joshua were quiet and humble, eyes wide nearly all the time, watchful and cautious. Samuel and Annabelle were also orphans, but their situation made them more confident and often a bit unruly, as they had no fear that necessities, and even kindness, would be withheld from them if they misbehaved or didn't show gratitude.

I spent some time the next day seeing how much my new wards knew. Sarah knew her letters and numbers but nothing much beyond, and Joshua had no schooling at all. I spent some time reading to them, but they were only able to pay attention for a short while. So I played a game with them. I hid some wooden blocks, which I'd sent the footman to town to buy, under three bowls I borrowed from the kitchen. Then I moved them around on the table. When Joshua tried to guess which bowl had the most blocks, I lifted the bowl and showed him he was wrong. He laughed out loud.

"Can I try?" he asked. He only had the use of one hand, as the physician had splinted his broken arm and wrapped it to twice its normal size.

"You can't, Josh. Your arm." Sarah pointed to his injured limb.

"I can do it. Turn your back. Don't look."

So Sarah and I turned our backs to him while he moved the bowls around with his one good hand.

"Now choose," he said, after prompting us to turn toward him again. "Which one has the most blocks?"

We played the game for several more minutes, with me asking them questions like, "How many blocks are under this bowl? Is that more than the other bowl, or fewer? How many more? How many fewer?" We counted blocks until they grew tired of that game, then I let them look out the window at the people passing on the street. They entered a lively discussion about the ladies and gentlemen, horses and carriages passing below.

I left them to Gretchen's care when I thought I heard a knock at the front door, and soon the servant announced Lord Brookhaven.

Mrs. Drake, Millicent, and I received him in the sitting room. A picture of him carrying Joshua flashed through my mind, his cravat missing from his neck and tied around Joshua's arm.

We exchanged the usual pleasantries, then he said, "How is the little fellow?"

"He is well. The broken arm hasn't slowed him down much, although he barely moved yesterday after we brought him home. He slept ten hours, and this morning he was much better, I think."

Lord Brookhaven smiled. His smiles were so rare, they were all the more pleasant.

"I am glad he's doing well. And glad he found such a kind and good friend in you, Miss Robbins."

Mrs. Drake made a *hmph* sound, then disguised it with a small cough into her handkerchief.

Lord Brookhaven's gaze did not stray from mine as he said, "I heard from one of my servants that some are not very happy with your inviting two homeless street children into your home."

"Well, I am very happy that I did." I smirked back at Lord Brookhaven, trying to look as though I could not have cared less what other people thought.

I was actually trying to watch, out of the corner of my eye, Mrs. Drake's reaction to my words. I needed to seem utterly confident in my decision—and indeed, I was confident that it was the right thing, and as I said, it made me very happy. But I also preferred that Mrs. Drake not quit my employ in disgust. She simply didn't understand Christian charity the way I did. At least, that's what I was telling myself.

The servant announced a new caller. "Mr. Anthony Welton."

I caught the scowl on Lord Brookhaven's face just before he changed it to a look of indifference.

When Mr. Welton saw Lord Brookhaven, his smile faltered, but only for a moment. He addressed me with a slightly exaggerated bow. "Miss Robbins, you are looking particularly well on this fine morning."

"Thank you, Mr. Welton."

"I hope you don't mind that I took the liberty of bringing you these flowers." He held out a bouquet of red roses and lilies of the valley.

"These are lovely. Thank you." I took them and held them up to my face. No one had ever given me flowers before. I drank in their beauty and fragrance even as I imagined they came from Lord Brookhaven instead of Mr. Welton.

I handed the flowers off to a servant, who went to find a vase for them, and we all sat down again.

"Lord Brookhaven, fancy seeing you here," Mr. Welton said with a cocky grin.

The Earl of Brookhaven simply stared back at him and said nothing.

Mr. Welton began talking of going for a drive in his father's barouche. "It is a very fast carriage, lightweight but substantial enough to not overturn around corners and curves. I am sure you would enjoy a little speed and the wind in your hair, Miss Robbins."

I smiled but said nothing. Perhaps it wasn't strictly appropriate for him to ask me such a question, but he was a young, handsome gentleman teasing me in a flattering way. And Lord Markeley and Mr. Merritt had talked with me and teased me at Lord Brookhaven's house party.

But then I'd discovered exactly what they thought of me—that I wasn't good enough for Lord Brookhaven to think of marrying, and the implication, of course, was that I wasn't good enough for them either.

"Lord Brookhaven," Mrs. Drake said, turning the conversation away from Mr. Welton, "your estate is in Berkshire, is that correct?"

"Yes."

"I hear it is a lovely prospect, with vast gardens and excellent paths for walking. I suppose you spend most of your time in the country?"

"Yes."

Mr. Welton pretended to stifle a yawn. "Shall we go for a walk? Miss Robbins, I know you are a great walker, and it isn't often we have such fine weather in this soggy old town."

I shook my head at him. Saying such a thing about London seemed almost irreverent.

"It is rather late in the day for a walk, I should think," Mrs. Drake said.

"A walk seems a fine idea to me," I said, pretending not to have heard Mrs. Drake's remark. "We can go to Hyde Park. Lord Brookhaven? Will you accompany us?"

Mr. Welton began to speak and drowned out whatever Lord Brookhaven was beginning to say. But Lord Brookhaven stood, and the men waited until Mrs. Drake, Millicent, and I had fetched our bonnets and parasols, and we were soon on our way.

Lord Brookhaven said not a word, but Mr. Welton talked so much that he could hardly have got a word in if he'd tried.

When we reached Lord Brookhaven's townhouse, he stopped and said, "I shall part with you here. Good day, Miss Robbins." He nodded to everyone, even Mr. Welton, and went inside.

"Hmm, the air seems less stodgy somehow." Mr. Welton glanced around and grinned.

"You are incorrigible, Mr. Welton."

"Well, I do hope I at least know how to have a good day and enjoy the company around me." He looked pointedly at me. "Especially that of such lively company as I happily find myself in today."

Was I lively? No one had ever called me that before. I suppose I was, compared to some ladies. I only hoped I hadn't offended Lord Brookhaven. I tried to remember anything improper I might have said or done. Certainly, I hadn't rejected Mr. Welton's attentions after Lord Brookhaven warned me about him, saying that he was only after my fortune. Lord Brookhaven might be right. But how was I to know that if I didn't spend time with him?

Mr. Welton was never serious the whole way to Hyde Park and back, making me laugh several times, and by the time we were home again and parted from him, I had a headache.

"You are in London, and you are an earl," Lady Derringer was saying, "and therefore you should make an appearance at this evening assembly."

William sighed. His aunt had returned from her brief trip to the country—her estate was nearby so she could come and go more easily than most—and now she was giving him advice on how to keep up his status as an eligible bachelor.

"I have every intention of attending the evening assembly."

"Well, good, for I have just seen Miss Charlotte Robbins in Trafalgar Square, and she says she will be there with her friends, Miss Millicent Skidmore and another young lady, who she said is arriving today. I believe her name was Hattie Something-or-other. And you had better not tiptoe around, for I believe that Anthony Welton may very well ask her to marry him soon."

"What makes you say that?" He imagined himself demanding a duel with that blackguard, pistols at twenty paces. Or better yet, swords—all the better to give vent to his feelings with lunging, slashing, and striking.

"He was escorting her and her friend, but it was obvious that he was after Miss Robbins."

"And she? How did she behave?" He wouldn't have asked anyone besides his aunt, but it still rankled that he asked.

"You're not still testing her, are you? Truly, William—"

"I'm not testing her. I never said I was testing her." But he wasn't certain yet if Miss Robbins cared for him. Besides, the whole point of giving her the fortune was to allow her to choose for herself what she wanted to do with her life, not to test her.

"I can hardly blame you, I suppose, after what happened with Letitia, but Miss Robbins is artless in the best possible way, and yet also clever. I do wish . . ."

He was no longer listening. Lady Derringer knew he never wished to speak of his former fiancée, that her name was not to be spoken around him.

It all came rushing back, the memories he tried so hard not to think about. What a fool he was to trust her. But at least he'd escaped, and it was that whey-faced Wexford who was married to her now.

Not only had she not loved him, but she must have hated him to treat him thus—

"William? Did you hear me?"

"No."

"I said, I fear for what she will say and feel when she discovers her fortune came from you. So why not marry her? Now that she has a fortune, no one will judge you."

"How strange that people would judge me for wishing to marry someone for herself and not her money."

"That isn't exactly what I was saying. You know how people would have talked if you'd married her when she was your governess. You know this as well as anyone."

"And why, exactly, should I care about how people would talk?"

Lady Derringer frowned at him in her scolding, older-aunt way.

"I'm going for a ride. I shall be ready when it is time." He bowed out of the room with her still frowning at him.

Twenty

An evening assembly," Hattie said, her eyes wide. "I cannot believe I am attending an evening assembly in London."

"You will probably meet the Earl of Brookhaven," Millicent said. "He is Charlotte's good friend, you know."

Hattie kept clasping and unclasping her hands in the carriage. "Are you sure my dancing is good enough for an evening assembly such as this?"

"Yes, I'm sure." I patted Hattie's hand. "Just take a deep breath and don't look at your feet. I assure you, you dance as well as most of the young ladies who will be there."

Hattie still looked frightened, but she said, "Thank you so much for loaning me your dress."

"I shall have some made for you now that you're here."

"That is too generous, Charlotte. I would say no, but I don't want you to be embarrassed by me around your new friends."

Mrs. Drake was staring out the window, fanning herself. I could guess her thoughts. She thought I should find new friends, ones of higher birth than Hattie and Millicent, as I sought the approval of this new social class. But what good was a fortune if I had to cower to others, people who were neither related to me nor to anyone I loved and therefore should have no bearing on my opinions?

We arrived at the assembly rooms at the same time as everyone else in London.

"What a line of carriages," Mrs. Drake said. "We shall sit here half the night waiting for our turn, I dare say."

But we did not wait half the night, and soon we were pressed in with the rest of the crowd who were being greeted one by one by the hostess. Then we were in the ballroom, where the musicians were already playing a lively dance tune.

All the faces around me were unfamiliar. I searched, hoping to see someone I knew.

"I shall be sitting here," Mrs. Drake said, heading to a chair against the wall, beside one of her friends. "Take every opportunity to dance," she said, "and check in with me after each one."

Hattie leaned close to me and whispered, "I shouldn't be here. Everyone looks so elegant."

Her face had gone pale, and her eyes were watery.

"No, Hattie. You have every right to be here. You are my guest, and you are safe, do you understand?"

She barely nodded, and I could see that her hands were trembling.

Three gentlemen approached, and I recognized Mr. Merritt.

We greeted each other. I introduced Mr. Merritt to Hattie, and then he introduced his two friends, Mr. Honeycutt and Mr. Treadwell. Mr. Honeycutt asked Millicent to dance, while Mr. Treadwell engaged Hattie in conversation. However, I could see from Mr. Treadwell's frozen expression and raised eyebrows that he was put off by Hattie's nervous manner. A moment later, he was excusing himself and asking the young lady standing just behind Hattie to dance, who politely declined.

I said quietly to Mr. Merritt, "Would you mind terribly asking Miss Jacobs to dance? She is nervous, and—"

"Of course." He immediately stepped forward and held his hand out to Hattie. "Miss Jacobs, would you do me the honor of dancing with me?"

Hattie placed her trembling hand on Mr. Merritt's arm and let him lead her to the dance floor.

I quickly excused myself from Mr. Treadwell before he could ask me to dance. I wasn't certain I could be civil to a man who had slighted my friend.

"Oh." I bumped right into Lord Brookhaven. "Forgive me."

"The fault was mine," he said.

"I wasn't looking where I was going, and—"

"Will you dance with me?" He held out his arm.

I laid my hand upon it, and we took our places beside Hattie and Mr. Merritt.

How I'd looked forward to dancing with Lord Brookhaven again, to make up for the last time when I'd been offended by his warning me about Mr. Welton.

His handsome face was serious as he gazed at me, bringing to mind pleasant memories from my time at Lowndesbury House.

The dance steps frequently had us spinning away from each other and switching partners for short periods, and I took the opportunity to glance at Hattie.

Her face looked frozen, but her shoulders had slowly loosened, and I even saw her smile at Mr. Merritt, who seemed to be doing a wonderful job putting her at ease. *God bless Mr. Merritt.*

When the dance brought us together again, Lord Brookhaven asked, "Is this young lady your friend from school?"

"Yes."

"I would be pleased if you would introduce me."

"Of course." I gave him a smile and wondered if there were any other earl in all of England who would ask to be introduced to a poor orphaned schoolteacher. But from my estimation, she was as good a person as anyone with a title, whether in this ballroom or outside of it.

It was not a common opinion, I was aware.

The dance ended, and Lord Brookhaven asked, "How are Joshua and Sarah?"

"Well, I thank you. They are good children, and I quite adore them. They make me think of Samuel and Annabelle. I was thinking of visiting them later this week, if that is all right."

"Yes, of course it is. They would be pleased to see you. You should bring Joshua and Sarah, if you like." His blue eyes met mine as we stopped near Mrs. Drake.

Hattie and Mr. Merritt stood nearby, so I introduced Hattie and Lord Brookhaven. He spoke with her for a moment, welcoming her to London, then asked, "Would you do me the honor of dancing with me?"

Hattie's eyes widened and her voice cracked as she said, "Yes."

I watched as Lord Brookhaven escorted her to the floor, my heart expanding in my chest as Hattie smiled at something Lord Brookhaven said.

"And now, may I have a dance with you, Miss Robbins?" Mr. Merritt was holding out his hand to me.

"Yes, you may."

I happily danced, looking nearly as much at Hattie as at Mr. Merritt. When it was over, as he was escorting me back to Mrs. Drake, I said quietly, "Thank you for being kind to my friend. It is her first time in London."

"She is a skilled partner, and I enjoyed dancing with her. But I admit, I enjoyed dancing with you even more."

What could he mean by that? Probably just a little flirtation, as when we were at Lowndesbury House, although he'd never said anything quite like that before.

"May I fetch you some lemonade?" he asked.

"Oh, um, yes, thank you."

Lord Brookhaven was looking at me at that moment, then he turned and walked away.

"There you are, Miss Robbins." Mr. Anthony Welton suddenly appeared at my side. "Will you dance with me?" He was leaning quite close and gazing into my eyes.

"Of course."

"I have been searching for you."

He was a bit too close for comfort, so I took a step away from him. "You have not met my friend Hattie." I introduced him.

After initial pleasantries, Hattie and Millicent began talking of the people they had met and of which of the ladies' dresses they thought was the most beautiful.

Mr. Welton leaned close again and said, "You are looking particularly beautiful this evening, Miss Robbins."

"I thank you."

I couldn't help enjoying his attention, even if I did think his behavior was a bit too forward.

Mr. Merritt returned with two cups of lemonade. He gave one to me and the other to Hattie as Millicent walked away to speak to an acquaintance she'd spotted on the other side of the room.

I knew Mr. Welton was waiting for me to accompany him to the dance floor, but I pretended not to notice as I sipped my lemonade.

The two men eyed each other, as they stood one on either side of me.

Mr. Welton said to Mr. Merritt, "Didn't I see you at Hyde Park yesterday? Your horse had thrown a shoe, and you were leading him home."

"No, you are mistaken." Mr. Merritt looked away from him as if to signal that the conversation was over.

"It was you. Your horse was limping, and you were wearing a green coat and black hat."

"It was someone else. I wasn't at Hyde Park yesterday. Miss Robbins, would you care to get some air?"

Before I could speak, Mr. Welton said, "She is engaged to dance the next with me."

I gave Mr. Merritt an apologetic look.

Mr. Welton said, "You will excuse us, as our dance is about to begin."

"Very well. I shall see you later in the evening, perhaps." Mr. Merritt bowed to me and to Hattie and excused himself.

I placed my cup on a tray, and Mr. Welton and I joined the dancers.

This dance was more stately than lively, and Mr. Welton barely took his eyes off me the entire time. When it was over, he squeezed my gloved hand and tucked it in the crook of his arm while he led me back to Mrs. Drake, whose smile was wide and approving.

I had to admit, my mood was quite joyful; I liked being the object of a young handsome gentleman's attentions, but I also hoped Lord Brookhaven wouldn't be angry with me for dancing so much with the man about whom he'd tried to put me on my guard.

The musicians took a short break to shuffle through their music sheets and to drink a glass from a tray brought to them by a servant.

"Miss Robbins, I—"

"Charlotte—oh, forgive me," Millicent said. "I didn't realize I was interrupting you."

"It is all right. Miss Skidmore, is it not?" Mr. Welton gave Millicent a bland smile. "And are you enjoying the evening?"

"Oh yes, very much. I always enjoy a good party."

"Then you must dance with me after I've had one more dance with Miss Robbins." He raised his eyebrows at me and held out his hand, as people were starting to line up for the next dance.

I let him lead me back to the dance floor. We didn't have long to wait before the music started.

It was probably my imagination, but it seemed people were staring at us and whispering behind their hands. Had I done something wrong? Had my hem ripped, or was it caught on my shoe? I didn't feel anything amiss, so I didn't think it was that. I almost made a misstep, so I concentrated on the dance and stopped glancing about the room.

William watched as Welton escorted Miss Robbins back onto the dance floor only moments after their first dance was over. So was this how it was? Was she now allowing the entire room to think she'd accepted some kind of proposal from Welton?

From the look on her face, she was oblivious to the implications of dancing two dances with Mr. Welton, one immediately after the other. It showed the gentleman's obvious preference for her, and it showed that she accepted his preference and that it was mutual. Surely she knew that it was nearly the same as an engagement.

What had he done in giving her this fortune? In trying to secure her happiness—and also his own—had he destroyed everything?

Did she truly prefer Welton over him?

But she probably didn't know. She couldn't know. She was completely new to the machinations of society and the ridiculous social rules that most young ladies were taught from the cradle to the ballroom.

This was his fault. He should have been quicker to ask her to dance at his ball, should have chased that damnable Welton away, should have made him to know that he would live to regret getting too close to Miss Robbins. She was too good for him, too good for . . . anyone in this room, himself included. She was innocent and kind and . . .

How could he be so foolish as to not protect her from a blackguard like Welton?

The heat was rising into his neck, creeping into his forehead. The room was suddenly too hot and stuffy. But he wouldn't go out to get some air. He would stay here and see if he would be needed to assist Miss Robbins.

When the dance was over, Mr. Welton escorted me to where Mrs. Drake was sitting with her friend, and she'd been joined by Mrs. Welton. The two women were smiling out of all proportion, it seemed to me.

"I shall fetch you and your friends some lemonade," Mr. Welton was saying, "and I may also go and see some friends. But I shall return shortly. I shall count the minutes until I see you again." He looked into my eyes, an excitement in his that wasn't usually there. Then he strode away.

Mrs. Drake was still smiling at me, which was not her normal expression, so I asked, "What is the matter?"

"Why, nothing at all. All is well, my dear."

But there was something she wasn't telling me.

Hattie was in conversation with a gentleman—I believe it was someone Lord Brookhaven had introduced her to—and Millicent was already returning to the dance floor. Her partner was Lord Markeley, so I was sure she was very happy.

Until now, I'd had gentlemen practically bumping into one another to ask me to dance, but suddenly there was no one asking me, and I stood alone, watching as the dance commenced.

I tried not to think too much about it. I couldn't expect to be asked to dance every dance. After all, there were more young ladies in want of a partner than there were gentlemen. Such a thing was not at all unusual. But I knew that something had changed, and I was almost willing to ask Mrs. Drake what it was.

Mr. Merritt was walking toward me. "Miss Robbins, am I to wish you joy?"

"Whatever do you mean?"

He looked slightly uncomfortable as he hesitated to speak.

"I know there is something amiss, but I cannot make out what it is. Will you please tell me?"

"Ah. I suppose you would be ignorant about such things. Well . . . how shall I say this?"

I was feeling quite annoyed by now, so I said, "Just tell me."

"When a young lady dances more than once with a certain gentleman, especially one consecutive dance after the other at a public assembly, it generally signifies that they are engaged to be married—or at least, it's a public declaration that they prefer each other over anyone else."

I covered my mouth with my hand. "Oh, but I am not engaged

to Mr. Welton, nor to anyone. Is that what everyone thinks? It is not true. Oh dear." I felt my face burning and started fanning myself with the little fan that hung from my wrist.

Mr. Merritt looked as if he was stifling a laugh.

"Don't you dare laugh at me. It is not amusing. You must help me. You must tell everyone that I am not engaged to Mr. Welton."

"If I were to spread such information, it might have just the opposite effect. People might believe it all the more for the protestation."

He was right. Oh, this was very bad. And Mr. Welton knew what people would think, the scoundrel. Lord Brookhaven was right about him. Did he think he could trick me into marrying him?

"Let me think." Mr. Merritt looked serious, thankfully. A moment later, his eyes widened. "I have it. Dance with me again. Then you should also dance a second time with Lord Brookhaven—I'll arrange it with him—and since you can't be engaged to three men . . ." He raised his brows at me.

"Do you think it will work?"

"Yes. Come. The dance is starting."

We joined the dancers on the floor. People were looking, whispering behind their hands again. But I supposed that was good, since I needed them to notice that I was dancing with Mr. Merritt for the second time.

Were people's lives so dull that they actually paid attention to how many times each lady danced with each gentleman?

"Thank you for this," I said to Mr. Merritt. "I hope it doesn't make trouble for you, dancing with me twice."

"Heaven forbid." He winked.

"I do appreciate you coming to my rescue."

"Well, it will help if Brookhaven joins in our scheme. I shall speak to him as soon as the dance ends."

"Thank you." I felt embarrassed at the thought of enlisting Lord Brookhaven's help. I hadn't minded letting Mr. Merritt help me, and I didn't have time to think why it was different.

Perhaps I should have been aware that to dance with a gentleman twice consecutively was nearly the same as acknowledging that you were engaged, but I honestly hadn't known. There were so many rules. How could I keep up with them all, especially when I hadn't lived among fashionable society my entire life?

The dance ended, and I made sure to smile at Mr. Merritt, who smiled back, then led me once again to where my chaperone was seated. "I shall return in a moment, or I'll send Lord Brookhaven."

I watched him go. He went straight to Lord Brookhaven and turned him aside, and they spoke for a few moments. Lord Brookhaven scowled.

My heart beat faster. Did Lord Brookhaven think less of me for having got myself in this predicament? Did he even believe what Mr. Merritt was saying?

Finally, Lord Brookhaven began making his way to me.

"Miss Robbins, would you do me the honor of dancing with me?" His manner of speaking was stilted.

"It would be my pleasure," I said, almost losing my voice entirely.

How mortifying to see how much Lord Brookhaven did not wish to dance with me. Did he think I'd manipulated him into dancing with me again? Did he blame me? Was he thinking "I told you so"? My cheeks were positively burning. Several people were staring, although I tried not to notice.

He led me onto the dance floor. We made it just as the music started.

If only I'd never come to this assembly. If only I'd stayed home and enjoyed a quiet evening with my two friends.

If only I'd never met Mr. Anthony Welton.

When the dance was over, before he could escort me off the floor, I said, "Thank you for dancing with me. It was Mr. Merritt's idea, so that people wouldn't think something about me that wasn't true. But I am truly sorry if it has caused you any embarrassment. I am terribly embarrassed myself, but I didn't know—"

"Miss Robbins, please say no more. I was glad to help. But you will remember that I did warn you about Mr. Welton."

Could he not see that I was mortified? His words could not have stung me more if he'd said, *I warned you Welton was only after your money, and yet you were foolish and thought he might care for you.*

I pressed my lips together and said nothing as he led me toward Mrs. Drake. But I was thinking, perhaps Mr. Welton did care for me. Perhaps he was trying to gather the courage, even at this moment, to ask me to marry him. At least he'd wanted everyone to think he was engaged to me. That was certainly more than I could say for Lord Brookhaven.

He bowed to me and left.

Suddenly, a young lady swooned in her chair on the other side of the ballroom. It was fortunate for me, since everyone was too busy watching the spectacle, as she had to be assisted out of the heated room and to the balcony to get some air. Everyone seemed too busy speculating about her to remember that I'd danced two times with three different gentlemen in one evening.

Millicent caught hold of my arm. "Did you see me dancing with Lord Markeley?" She was smiling quite broadly.

"I did indeed."

"He even stood talking with me through the next dance and hasn't danced with anyone else since," she whispered near my ear.

"That is very promising," I whispered back, happy to see her so happy.

Hattie was sitting beside Mrs. Drake, so Millicent and I went to ask if anything was the matter.

"Oh, no, I am well," Hattie said, but she looked a bit pale as she fanned herself.

"I saw you dancing with Lord Brookhaven," I said. "Did you enjoy yourself?"

"Yes, he was very kind."

I sat next to Hattie, hoping it would encourage her to tell me what was making her look slightly frightened. "He was kind?" I asked.

"Oh, Charlotte," she said quietly, leaning toward me, "I never imagined I'd dance with so many gentlemen and certainly never with an earl." She seemed to lose her breath and closed her eyes and swallowed hard.

"Dear Hattie, he is only a man. You mustn't be overcome by his station in society. He is only a man," I repeated quietly for her ears alone.

She still looked frightened as she met my gaze. After a few moments, she said, "Yes, you are right. Of course. For God himself is no respecter of persons." She took a deep breath, and the color began to come back into her cheeks.

"Yes, exactly. Very true indeed. And I suspect that Lord Brookhaven himself would not wish you to be in awe of him, even though he is an earl."

"He was very gracious and kind."

"Yes. Now come over here with Millicent and me where the gentlemen can see you and ask you to dance again. You are up to dancing again, are you not?"

"I believe I am." She managed a small smile.

"Good." I squeezed her arm to show my approval. "Come."

We stood together, each of us facing the crowd in order to look the more inviting.

Truly, these fashionable soirees were hardly any different from the two dances I'd attended in Milford at the White Swan Inn. There were more ladies than gentlemen at those dances—not very different from tonight's dance—but just as we did now, we all stood against the wall and watched the other dancers and hoped to be asked for the next dance.

No one asked me to dance the next one, but Mr. Merritt introduced to me to one of his acquaintances, who then asked me. And so it went the rest of the night. I was asked to dance most of the dances, Millicent danced with several gentlemen, and Hattie three more times. And at the end of the evening, for the very last dance, Mr. Welton returned to me looking flushed and smelling of brandy, his hair slightly out of place.

"Miss Robbins, there you are," he said, smiling.

"And here you are, Mr. Welton." I frowned and refrained from saying that he'd promised to return to me soon, and that had been almost two hours ago. I also didn't mention that I now understood what his dancing with me two times in succession had meant.

A gentleman, someone Lord Markeley had introduced to me earlier, was walking toward me, but his step faltered when he saw Mr. Welton talking with me. So I stepped toward him, leaving Mr. Welton with his mouth hanging open.

"Miss Robbins, would you honor me with the last dance of the evening?" the gentleman asked.

"I will." I led *him* to the dance floor. I could not remember his name, but it hardly mattered. He was an agreeable partner who didn't step on my feet, and he'd got me away from Mr. Welton.

When the dance was over, my partner thanked me and led me to Mrs. Drake. Mr. Welton was standing just beside her, an almost pouty look on his face.

When my dance partner had gone, Mr. Welton said, "Miss Robbins, I thought you knew I wanted to dance the last dance with you." The look on his face was so manipulative I nearly laughed out loud.

"You must have also known, Mr. Welton, that there were other gentlemen who wished to dance with me."

It was a bold thing to say, I know. Lord Brookhaven had been walking past us at that very moment, and I was fairly certain he heard me, for he cut his eyes our way. Perhaps I should have added that he wasn't the only gentleman after my fortune. But that would have sounded even more brazen.

"Lord Brookhaven!" I turned to him just as Mr. Welton narrowed his eyes and opened his mouth to speak. "I have so enjoyed attending this assembly and seeing you and Lady Derringer again. Do you know where I might find your aunt?"

"I believe she is just over by the door." He nodded in that direction, a very sober look on his face. Without even acknowledging Mr. Welton, he lent me his arm, and we headed that way.

I said my farewells to Lady Derringer, and she promised to call on me soon, and I told them I'd come soon to see the children and perhaps bring Joshua and Sarah.

"Oh yes, that is a wonderful idea," Lady Derringer said.

Lord Brookhaven gazed into my eyes as we bid each other a good night. "Until tomorrow," he said. Just then, he bent over my hand and kissed it.

A little wave of feeling went through me—relief that he wasn't angry with me, desire to get closer to him—but then he was gone.

As I feigned to ignore Mr. Welton, the look on his face became more and more disgruntled. But I pretended not to notice and instead chatted with Hattie and Millicent as we gathered our things and waited for Mrs. Drake to accompany us.

"Miss Robbins, may I call I on you tomorrow?" Mr. Welton said, stepping quite close.

"I am not sure I shall be home."

He looked confused, then disgruntled. "Well . . . I shall call on you very soon."

I said nothing and he sauntered away, stumbling slightly, proving how much he had been drinking.

As soon as he'd gone, Mr. Merritt appeared at my side. "I want to wish you a good evening, Miss Robbins. May I call on you tomorrow?"

"Of course."

While we waited for our carriage, one or two other gentlemen approached with the same question. Oh dear. Well, if they must all come, I suppose they might as well all come at once.

Twenty-One

The first gentleman caller to arrive the next day was Mr. Merritt. It was the usual time of day for callers, so it wasn't surprising when Lord Markeley arrived shortly thereafter. He seemed surprised to see Mr. Merritt there, who didn't give him a very warm welcome. Lord Markeley did not stay long, excusing himself after only about five minutes. Then two more gentlemen with whom I'd danced the evening before joined Mr. Merritt, Millicent, Hattie, Mrs. Drake, and me. We made small talk as a group, and indeed, the conversation was rather dull, and yet a bit tense at the same time.

Since I hadn't slept much, it took an enormous effort to force back a yawn. I drank so much tea that my hand had a slight quiver. As yet another yawn threatened, I had to clench my jaws shut to prevent the ruin of my reputation as a polite hostess.

When the two gentlemen stood to leave, Mr. Merritt moved closer, and while no one was listening, he said that he'd like to go for a ride with me.

"I'm afraid I'm not much of a rider," I said. "I never owned a horse nor learned to ride."

Without hesitation, he said, "Then I'd like to take a walk with you to Hyde Park tomorrow, if the weather is not too foul."

If I didn't know better, I'd say he was acting as if he was trying to court me.

I knew very well what he thought of me. I'd never forget what he'd said to me at the house party in Berkshire.

Unfortunately, Lord Brookhaven was right about all these men only wanting me for my fortune. I sighed heavily.

Mr. Welton was announced a moment before he entered the room. He bowed to us, then he and Mr. Merritt gave each other barely disguised looks of disgust.

Mr. Merritt had stayed longer than was typical, but he seemed in no hurry to leave now that Mr. Welton was here.

Mr. Welton seated himself as near to me as he could. Hattie looked as if she was suppressing a grin as she glanced from Mr. Welton to Mr. Merritt and then to me. Millicent just lifted her brows slightly as she met my eye.

There were long lulls in the conversation. I felt so weary, I wondered if the hours for accepting calls would never end. Finally, Mrs. Drake said, "Mr. Merritt, I wonder that your mother can spare you for so long. I hear she is in town."

I gave Mrs. Drake a look. I would have to tell her later that even though Mr. Welton was a favorite of hers, it was not acceptable to be rude to our other guests.

As Mr. Merritt was leaving, he said quietly, "Shall I see you tomorrow? For our walk?"

"Nine o'clock is when I like to have my morning walk."

"I will be here then."

Mr. Welton had a smug look on his face as he bid Mr. Merritt a good day. I was fairly certain he'd heard what we had said.

When Mr. Merritt had gone, I saw Mr. Welton wink at Mrs. Drake.

"Come, Miss Skidmore, Miss Jacobs. I have some fabric I want to consult you about, whether it will make a good afternoon dress. Miss Robbins, you stay here and keep Mr. Welton company until we return." By the smirk, I knew something was afoot.

I felt my stomach drop.

Millicent and Hattie glanced back at me as they left the room.

As soon as they were gone, Mr. Welton slid to one knee on the floor in front of me.

"Miss Robbins, I think you've been able to see what an attachment I have to you, and I believe that you have formed an attachment to me as well. In fact, my feelings for you are too strong to be restrained, and I beg you to marry me and put me out of this misery I find myself in, longing for your company every moment of every day."

The first thought that came to me was that he reminded me of a fish with its mouth open. The second was that if he longed for my company every moment, why had he left me at the dance and not returned for nearly two hours?

But I needed to be serious, for Mr. Welton was obviously very serious and needed a serious answer. Oh dear. I didn't wish to give him pain, but I had to give him an honest answer.

"Mr. Welton, I am very flattered by your sentiments and by your proposal, but I am afraid you have mistaken my friendship for something more. I am sorry, but—"

"Before you say anything else, I beg you to think it over. I can wait for an answer. I should have realized you would need more time, and I should have spent more time courting you. Is that why you are reluctant to say yes to my heartfelt proposal? I am willing to share all my worldly goods, everything with you." He grabbed my hand from my lap and squeezed it between both of his. "Please, Miss Robbins. Won't you give me a chance to make you love me?"

I pulled my hand out of his grasp as I stood, leaving him kneeling on the floor.

"Miss Robbins, do you feel nothing for the pain you are causing me? You led me to believe you felt as much affection for me as I did for you."

"No, Mr. Welton, I did not. I—"

"What of the assembly last evening? You danced with me two times, one after the other. Everyone saw your preference for me. No one will believe that you did not prefer me over every other gentleman in the room."

I started for the door.

"Wait, please. Let us not quarrel."

I did not stop until I had snatched the door open and startled when I found the servant standing there. "Lord Brookhaven is here to see you, ma'am."

And indeed, he stood just behind the servant and was looking past me and at Mr. Welton in the room behind me. And he was scowling.

William could see over Miss Robbins's shoulder that Welton was there, and he was getting up off his knees.

"Come in, Lord Brookhaven," she said, standing aside, and told the servant, "Please fetch Mrs. Drake, Miss Skidmore, and Miss Jacobs."

The servant bowed and strode away.

Mr. Welton was now standing. William hoped the man could see the warning in his eyes, for if he had accosted Miss Robbins in any way, he would regret it.

They waited for Miss Robbins to sit before taking their seats. They had to immediately return to their feet as Mrs. Drake, Millicent, and Hattie entered the room and made their polite greetings.

Mrs. Drake said, "We enjoyed seeing you at the assembly last evening, both you and Lady Derringer, Lord Brookhaven."

"Thank you." His voice was gruff, almost a grunt. He was still trying to figure out what had taken place between Welton and Miss Robbins. If he was on his knees, that probably meant a proposal, but as he did not look at all triumphant, but rather just the opposite, she must not have accepted him.

Mr. Welton said, "Yes, those assembly rooms there are tolerably spacious. The estate I am to inherit in Derbyshire has a ballroom that is nearly as large, and I shall throw many parties there."

William couldn't help saying, "It was my understanding that your aunt, who owns that estate, plans to leave it to your cousin, Mr. Fortner."

Welton barely glanced at him before replying, "She has not settled it on my cousin yet, nor do I believe she will. Fortner is a worthless sort of fellow, and I'm sure he will do something to offend our aunt. If he does, I would be next in line to inherit. She has told me so herself."

Mrs. Drake said, "What Mr. Welton says is very true. Mr. Fortner is known to frequent the gaming tables and he's . . . well, there has already been a scandal involving a young woman of questionable birth. I cannot imagine Lady Partridge, their aunt, passing over Mr. Welton in favor of Mr. Fortner, for our Mr. Welton is a much more steady, gentlemanly sort." She smirked at Miss Robbins.

What was that smirk about? He'd learned Mrs. Drake and Welton's mother were close friends, but did she stand to gain something from Miss Robbins marrying Welton? If so, what?

They all sat in silence until Mrs. Drake said, "Lord Brookhaven, it was very gracious of you to call on us." By her tone, he realized she was insinuating it was time for him to leave.

Miss Robbins sat up straighter, opening her mouth as if to speak. He beat her to it.

"I came to ask after the children, Joshua and Sarah."

"They are well. Joshua's arm seems to be healing, and they seem to get on well with their nurse. They are looking less hollow-cheeked already, I do believe. I was hoping to bring them to meet Samuel and Annabelle later this week. Would you like to see them now?"

Normally an earl would not wish to leave the company of other adults to visit children, especially children who were unrelated to him. But he said, "Yes, I would. Although I do not wish to take you away from your . . . guest." He glanced in Mr. Welton's direction.

Miss Robbins quickly stood. "I'm sure Mr. Welton doesn't mind, and I'd enjoy seeing them myself."

Mrs. Drake's wide-eyed expression quickly changed to a scowl. "Charlotte, I'm sure—"

"I have been wanting to check in on them," Miss Robbins said, striding to the door and pretending not to hear Mrs. Drake. "Hattie? Would you like to accompany us? The children have really warmed to Hattie . . ." She continued talking while they left the room, Hattie scurrying after them, looking frightened.

Miss Robbins walked close beside him and said softly, "I'm sorry for Mrs. Drake's rudeness."

"There is no need to apologize for someone else's behavior."

As they walked up the staircase in silence, he continued to wonder why Miss Robbins had been alone in the room with Mr. Welton. Propriety did not allow an unmarried gentleman and lady to be alone in a room together unless the gentleman was asking her to marry him.

"Miss Jacobs," he said, glancing back at Hattie, "I hope you are enjoying your time away from your teaching duties in Bedfordshire."

"Yes, sir, I thank you."

"You teach history and drawing, I believe."

"Yes, sir."

"Those were two of my favorite subjects," he said.

"Oh."

"I didn't know you liked to draw," Miss Robbins said, turning to look at him.

"I have not much talent for it, but I liked it . . . better than arithmetic."

They arrived at the children's room and found them playing a game of backgammon while the matronly nursemaid Gretchen sat nearby with some mending.

"Miss Robbins!" the children cried, their faces lighting up when they saw Charlotte. Her face lit up as well as she moved forward and greeted them warmly.

"Mrs. Gretchen taught us to play this game," Joshua said. "Will you play it with us?"

"First, say good afternoon to Lord Brookhaven and Miss Jacobs," she said.

Joshua and Sarah obediently greeted their visitors. William sat down with them and played backgammon, and Hattie watched, while Miss Robbins talked with Gretchen, asking about the children. Soon they were all watching the game, as he let the children get the better of him.

Sarah cried out, "I won!" Then she immediately covered her mouth as if she'd done something wrong.

"Well done," William said, smiling. "You and your brother are very clever to learn the game so quickly."

"Shall we play again?" Joshua asked.

"I need to speak with Miss Robbins for a moment, but we will play again another time. And when your arm is healed, we shall have to teach you to play pall mall. Miss Robbins is the best I've ever seen," he whispered loudly.

"Are you good at pall mall, Miss Robbins?" Sarah asked eagerly.

"I dare say I am." She winked at her. "But Miss Jacobs is as skilled as I am."

"Oh, no, I do not play pall mall as well as Miss Robbins."

"What is pall mall?" Joshua asked.

William explained, "It is a game you play on the grass—or some flat ground—and you use a wooden mallet to strike a ball." He explained the game, aware of Miss Robbins watching him, and even as he talked, he wished they could both be back at Lowndesbury House again, reliving the conversations they'd had, not having to worry that she might engage herself to marry some worthless young man.

Gretchen returned and said, "It's about time for the children's washing up and then for their supper."

We said our goodbyes to the children, and as soon as we were in the hallway, Miss Jacobs said, "I have something to attend to. It was very good to see you again, Lord Brookhaven."

"And you, Miss Jacobs."

Hattie hurried toward her bedroom, went inside, and closed the door.

"You wished to speak to me?" Miss Robbins's face was turned up to his, and he suddenly had to know.

"Miss Robbins, are you engaged to marry Mr. Welton?"

He could see the anger begin to spark in her eyes, but she remained silent.

"I am aware that I am not a relative of yours and therefore have no right to ask." He cleared his throat, turning away from her, trying to tamp down his feelings. "But as your friend, I thought you would wish to hear my advice, as it is well-meant." But one glance in her direction told him he'd said the wrong thing.

Advice. Advice? "I know that you think every gentleman who comes near me is only after my fortune. Is it so difficult to believe that he might be in love with me?"

Why had I said that? I didn't even believe that. There must be a reason for this anger. I would need to ponder that later.

"Miss Robbins, you may do as you wish, but I'm afraid—"

"Yes, I may do as I wish. I am an independent woman of means and intelligence."

His jaw hardened, and there was that little twitch in his cheek. "As your friend, I am only trying to help—"

"Then please don't insult me by saying that no gentleman could possibly wish to marry me for myself." Was I overstating my point, saying too much? I felt tears sting my eyes.

"Did I ever say such a thing?"

"No." A tear fell onto my cheek, and I quickly swiped at it with my hand.

"Miss Robbins, I am well aware that any gentleman of good sense and character might very well wish to marry you, but I am only saying that Mr. Welton is not that kind of gentleman. I only say this out of concern for you."

Tears poured from my eyes. I could only hope, in the dimly lit hallway, that he could not see them.

I swallowed, took a breath, and said, "I am not engaged to Mr. Welton. He asked, and I refused him."

Lord Brookhaven's jaw went slack. Then he nodded. After a moment's silence, he said, "Forgive me. I have been rude and impertinent. But it was out of concern for your welfare."

His words did nothing to dispel the heat and turmoil inside me.

"You are angry with me," he said. "What can I say to make it right?"

I could not tell him, as I was just beginning to realize that the real reason for my tears was my disappointment that he wasn't concerned enough about me marrying Mr. Welton to marry me himself.

I took as deep a breath as I could get into my constricted chest, then another and another. Finally, I said, "You have done nothing wrong. Forgive my incivility."

"There is nothing to forgive. We are friends, are we not? You can say whatever you wish to me, whatever you feel."

His words undid all my efforts to dispel the tears. Friends. That's all we were and all we would ever be to each other. Foolish girl. Did I really think an earl would want me—or my fifty thousand pounds?

"You were right about Mr. Welton," I said, feeling humbled. "I thank you for the warning."

"It was impertinent of me. You have deduced his true character on your own without any interference from me."

I did not answer, as I was still fighting back the tears.

"I shall endeavor not to give unsolicited advice in future. But please know . . . I speak and act only out of my desire for you to be happy, Miss Robbins."

His words were so softly spoken and sounded so sincere that I felt a physical ache inside my chest.

I turned aside and used my hand to wipe the tears that were threatening to drip from my chin. A moment later, Lord Brookhaven was handing me his handkerchief.

My stomach twisted, but I had little choice but to take the offered handkerchief and mop my face.

Thankfully, he said nothing as I endeavored to drive away the still-threatening tears and make myself presentable.

I simply would not think about how he didn't love me, didn't want to marry me, and knew that the gentleman who asked me to marry him was only interested in my fortune. No, I wouldn't think about that. I'd think about Joshua and Sarah, and about Samuel and Annabelle. If for no other reason than to not hurt them, I would not end my friendship with Lord Brookhaven.

Who was I trying to fool? *I* enjoyed his company, and I valued his opinion, or I should, especially now that I knew he only cared for me as a friend.

"I would never wish to make you unhappy," he said.

"You haven't." I wanted to tell him that I had enough gentleman callers to make me happy—that one of them, at least, would love me for myself, and he would be a gentleman of good character with his own fortune. Together we would be very happy, so Lord Brookhaven needn't worry about my happiness. He should tend to his own.

But I said none of those things. I needed to get somewhere quiet where I could think, where I'd have time to search my own heart and settle my feelings.

I turned and started down the stairs and heard him following behind me.

Thankfully, when we returned to the sitting room, Mr. Welton had gone. Visiting hours were over, as it was after six o'clock. We instead found Mrs. Drake and Millicent sitting in silence, and they did not smile when we walked in.

"How were the children?" Millicent asked, a bit of a caustic tone in her voice. No doubt she was angry that she'd been left behind, and I felt a pang of guilt.

"They are well," I said. "They were pleased to see Lord Brookhaven again."

"Mr. Welton wished to give you his regards," Mrs. Drake said with a sour expression. "Lord Brookhaven, it is so charitable of you to take an interest in the little orphan children. I'm sure when the boy's arm is recovered, Miss Robbins will find a suitable situation for them both. Perhaps you can help her."

I was in no mood to brook Mrs. Drake's impertinence, especially after I'd rebuffed Lord Brookhaven's so completely. "I have no interest in sending the children to any other 'situation.'" For I knew what she meant. She'd have me send them to someone to work for only food and a cot to sleep on, or worse yet, to a workhouse. She didn't know me at all if she thought I'd even consider such a thing.

Mrs. Drake raised her brows at me. But before she could speak, Lord Brookhaven said, "Thank you again, Miss Robbins, for allowing me to see the children. I am pleased they are so well taken care of here with you. Please don't hesitate to ask if you ever need anything."

"Thank you."

Then he took his leave and was gone.

Twenty-Two

Early the next morning, when Hattie, Millicent, and I were waiting for Mr. Merritt to arrive for our walk, Mrs. Drake still wore the same expression she'd had all last evening. So I decided to speak to her privately about the events of the previous afternoon.

"I am certain you mean well, Mrs. Drake, and I know you are partial to Mr. Welton, but please do not allow your preference for him to cause you to be rude to my other guests."

Mrs. Drake gave me a sharp look. "Of what are you speaking?"

"Of your remark to Lord Brookhaven, when you told him it was good of him to call, as if you were dismissing him."

"Well, if I was rude to Lord Brookhaven, I would think he would tell me so himself . . . *if* I was rude. Miss Robbins, I realize you have a preference for Lord Brookhaven, but let me put you on your guard. If your refusal of Mr. Welton's offer of marriage was due to your attachment to Lord Brookhaven, then let me say that he, being a titled peer of the realm and from a very old, very proud family name, will be expected to marry someone of equal high social standing. You understand my meaning, I am sure.

"Mr. Welton, on the other hand, is perfectly willing to lower himself to marry a former governess of no particular family name at all. And I assure you, between his family's inheritance and his aunt's, he is likely to be very well set up in life, and it's unlikely you may ever get such a good offer again. I only say these things out of my concern for you, Miss Robbins."

She kept her brows raised during the entire discourse, as if she were truly and disinterestedly looking out for my welfare.

My breath was coming fast, but I reminded myself that I knew my worth and therefore did not need to allow anyone to make me feel as though I was worth less than anyone else. Mrs. Drake's opinion could never change the truth.

"I understand your meaning perfectly well, Mrs. Drake, but I assure you that whether or not I ever get another offer of marriage, I will never . . . marry . . . Mr. Welton."

Mrs. Drake stared back at me, expressionless, her lips pursed in a tight line.

In the silence, I put on my bonnet and tied the strings, determined to enjoy my walk and some conversation with the usually very agreeable Mr. Merritt.

A moment later, he arrived and we began our walk.

And Mr. Merritt was very agreeable. He smiled and talked and even laughed as he, Millicent, Hattie, Mrs. Drake, and I walked to Hyde Park. But indeed, I had to take several deep breaths and force myself to set aside Mrs. Drake's words.

I did, in fact, enjoy the walk so much that I decided not to mention that the clouds looked ominous. Just as we arrived at the park, rain started to fall. We took shelter underneath a large oak tree.

Thankfully, we ladies all had our parasols. Though they would not keep us dry in a storm, they were better than nothing in this light rain, and each of us had worn a bonnet and a spencer. Mr. Merritt had his hat.

I was staring out at the rain before noticing that Mrs. Drake, Millicent, and Hattie were huddled under another tree a few feet away from Mr. Merritt and me. And Mr. Merritt was gazing into my eyes.

"Miss Robbins, you must have perceived that I have grown quite fond of you since I first met you at Lowndesbury House. And that fondness has grown into something more. You are lovely and kind and genteel, and I have quite fallen in love with you."

My stomach did a strange flip. Was Mr. Merritt truly speaking to me? Mr. Merritt, who had seemed nearly as far out of reach socially as Lord Brookhaven at the time that I met him? Mr. Merritt, who'd told me that if I married Lord Brookhaven I would ruin him? Mr. Merritt, who was confident and the very picture of a gentleman of family and fortune? Well, family, if not fortune.

And therein lay the trouble. He looked at me and no doubt saw fifty thousand pounds. He was not the oldest son, and therefore if he did not marry for money, he would be forced to make his own way as a soldier, in parliament, or in the church. And although I felt a thrill at being singled out by him, at his flattering speech, at his offer of marriage, I did not believe he loved me.

I imagined what Lord Brookhaven would say.

Merritt is a good sort of fellow, he would say in his monotone voice, *and he does not wish to lose his life of leisure. He chose well in choosing you, for you would make him a much better wife than any girl he has met so far.*

I flattered myself with the latter part of his imagined discourse, as the first part made me feel what I'd felt when I cried in front of him yesterday.

It was not a terrible offer for me, as offers went. Mr. Merritt's family had not been associated with any scandals, and he would inherit some money from his mother's side of the family.

"You are hesitating," he said, then quickly added, "I understand. But I intend to make the church my occupation, and with my family's connections, I should be able to secure a desirable situation. We shall be set up very well, you must realize, and you will have whatever your heart desires. I believe I can make you very happy, and I know you will make me the happiest man in England if you say yes."

Again, the two thoughts were at war inside me. On the one hand, it was tempting to accept someone of Mr. Merritt's good looks, manners, and family connections. He was pleasant and a good conversationalist, which was more than could be said for most gentlemen I'd met so far.

But on the other hand, I was certain his main inducement for marrying me was my fortune. Could I ever feel truly loved knowing that he never would have thought of me as a wife if my uncle hadn't died and left me fifty thousand pounds?

My head hurt.

"I need some time to think, to consider," I said. "But please know I am very aware of the compliment you have bestowed upon me by offering marriage." My voice trailed off.

He looked quite earnest as he said, "Please take all the time you need. You may think I should have taken more time to take you driving, to teach you to ride, to dance with you at parties, to go for walks, and to call on you, and perhaps you would be right. Yes, I see that now. But I see your character, Miss Robbins, and I know you are the kind of woman who would make a wonderful wife, and I was too afraid that someone else would make you an offer and I would lose you."

I nearly said, *I am not yours to lose*, but I refrained, cognizant that my rejection of his offer, even if he didn't love me, would cause him pain.

"As I said, I need some time to consider your offer, and I do thank you, Mr. Merritt, and I promise not to make you wait longer than necessary."

"Thank you, Miss Robbins, for considering my proposal, and I shall wait as patiently as I can for your answer."

Seeing his downturned face, looking as humble as I'd ever seen him—and I'd never seen him look humble before—made me feel all jumbled up inside and a bit weary.

Soon, the rain began to slow to a drizzle, and Mrs. Drake suggested we walk home before it could get any worse. Back at my townhouse, Mr. Merritt took his leave with a longing look, holding my gloved hand in his, then bent down and kissed it before turning and leaving out the front door.

As we took off our wet things in the cloakroom, Millicent cried, "He asked you to marry him, didn't he? Oh, I just knew it! You shall be Mrs. Thomas Merritt! I am so happy for you, Charlotte. What a good match it is."

Mrs. Drake looked dour indeed, and Hattie's face registered alarm.

"I have not accepted his proposal," I said.

"What? Why not?" Millicent said.

"Mr. Merritt is not in love with me."

"Two perfectly good marriage proposals, and you've refused them both?" Mrs. Drake's lip curled, and she looked away.

"I did not refuse Mr. Merritt. I told him I needed some time to think it over." Besides, she should be happy if and when I refused them both, since I'd have no need of her the moment I was married.

"Hmph." Mrs. Drake threw down her wet shawl and walked toward the staircase. "It is only fortunate for you that you . . ." Her voice became inaudible as she got farther away, but I knew exactly what she was saying.

Millicent and Hattie went with me up to my room, and we lay across my bed, each of us wrapped in a wool shawl as we waited for the tea I'd ordered.

"You should do what makes you happy," Hattie was saying.

Would Mr. Merritt make me happy? I could easily imagine him as my husband, me attending parties on his arm, and the thought of being the wife of the vicar in charge of a church parish was actually a very happy thought. I'd always imagined such a role in life to be pleasant and desirable. I could spend my time being charitable to the poor of our parish, looking after the less fortunate, receiving the respect and well-wishes of our parishioners.

Lord Brookhaven's face rose before me. What would he think of me marrying his friend? He knew Mr. Merritt better than I did. But the thought of asking Lord Brookhaven's opinion made me cringe.

"He always did single you out when we were at Lowndesbury House," Millicent said. "I thought he might be in love with you then."

"But you know what he said to me, that I would ruin Lord Brookhaven if I married him."

"You cannot hold that against him," Millicent said, sitting up. "You were a governess then, with no money, and he was only trying to look out for his friend."

And why had Mr. Merritt thought Lord Brookhaven was in love with me and on the brink of asking me to marry him? It obviously wasn't true, and that hurt more than anything.

"But it doesn't make me love Mr. Merritt, and it doesn't give me confidence in his sentiments and claims that he's in love with me. He certainly wasn't in love with me then, so how can he love me now?"

"Love is not like that," Millicent insisted. "Love comes after you're married. That's what my mother told me once. And I believe it would be true for you and Mr. Merritt." No one said anything, then Millicent went on. "But you should do what you wish. I'm not trying to tell you to marry him if you think you wouldn't be happy."

"I'm not sure if I would or wouldn't. That's why I told him I needed time to consider." I sighed.

I wanted love. I wanted it so much I was afraid I would marry someone because I could imagine myself happy with him, not because I truly was in love with him, and then later regret my decision. But then it would be too late and I would have lost my one chance at love.

Perhaps Millicent was right. One married and then love came. I believed it was true for some marriages. Others, as I'd heard, started out as love matches, but then when children and troubles arrived, the love died. I'd seen couples at church in Milford who never looked at each other, much less spoke to each other. I'd heard the stories of titled gentlemen and their wives living separately, taking lovers.

What if Mr. Merritt's feelings took the opposite turn? What if I loved him—and I would, if I married him—but he stopped loving me? How could I bear that?

The next day, I went to call on Samuel and Annabelle, and I took Joshua and Sarah with me.

They looked quite nice in their new clothes I'd bought for them. In fact, one could not have told them apart from a wealthy family's children except for the almost-imperceptible browbeaten look, a hesitant wariness.

Lord Brookhaven had already told the children to expect us, so when we arrived, Joshua and Sarah greeted Samuel and Annabelle as I had taught them. The children were very standoffish until Lord Brookhaven suggested we all go up to the playroom.

In the playroom, the boys began stacking wooden blocks and the girls each chose one of Annabelle's dolls and began making beds for them out of blankets and pillows. Lord Brookhaven and I watched over them, with Hannah nearby. They played together surprisingly well.

Lord Brookhaven and I talked of Lady Derringer and her trips back and forth to her country estate, comparing our walks in the country and to the park in town, as I wondered what he would think of . . .

"Mr. Merritt asked me to marry him," I blurted out, but quietly enough that no one else in the room could hear me.

"I see." His jaw hardened.

Was that all he was going to say? He looked away from me, straight ahead at the children playing.

"I suppose he told you, since you are friends."

"He did not."

"Well, I haven't given him an answer yet."

I could see no reaction in him. Finally, he said, "You haven't given him an answer because you haven't decided whether or not to accept him?"

"I am not in love with him, and so I suppose I will refuse him." I watched him carefully, hoping to get some insight into his thoughts, but he was stone-faced. "I thought perhaps you might have some advice for me."

"Now you are asking for my advice?"

"Yes, I am."

He turned and looked at me. Still, I couldn't read his expression.

"You should do what your heart is telling you. Is it telling you to marry Mr. Merritt?"

"No. But you know him better than I do." To provoke him to say something, I said, "I am sure Mrs. Drake thinks I should accept him. She was annoyed that I refused Mr. Welton, and she seemed disgusted that I would not accept Mr. Merritt either."

"Mrs. Drake thinks, like most people, that money and status, names and estates are the most important factors in whether a lady should marry a gentleman, and that a lady must marry and have children."

"What do you think?"

He stared hard at me for a moment, then looked away. "I think you should please yourself, and only you know what would please you."

That was no help at all. "What would please me would be to marry someone who loves me and whom I love. And I don't believe Mr. Merritt loves me, and I don't love Mr. Merritt." *I love you.*

Part of me wanted to say it.

At that moment, Annabelle suddenly put her doll down, went into the corner of the room, and burst into tears.

I ran over, reaching her before Hannah or Lord Brookhaven.

"Annabelle, what's wrong?" I knelt beside her and watched the tears stream down her face. She didn't speak, only wiped her tears with her hands, so I asked, "Did you and Sarah quarrel?" I hadn't seen them quarreling, but I could have missed something.

Annabelle shook her head.

Lord Brookhaven and Hannah stood a respectful distance away, allowing me to talk with her privately.

"What is it, then? Won't you tell me?"

She looked at me, and though she seemed calmer, a lone tear slid down her cheek. "Do you love Sarah more than me?"

"Oh, Annabelle." My chest ached at her question and what she must be feeling. She'd been abandoned by so many people in her life—everyone, in fact, except her older brother, Lord Brookhaven. "I love you very much, Annabelle. I'm so sorry I haven't visited you more often. But you mustn't think I love you any less because Sarah and Joshua have come to live with me. They had nowhere else to go. But I have an idea. Why don't we ask your brother if you may come and sleep over at my house? Would you like that? We can have breakfast together, take tea together, and you can play with Sarah and Joshua. Would you like that?"

"Can Samuel come too?"

"Of course. Absolutely." I hugged her tight, wondering if I was the most selfish, obtuse person in the world to have not realized that she would be feeling this way.

We talked it over with Lord Brookhaven and the other children and soon a plan was concocted to have Annabelle and Samuel spend the night at my house tonight, and then all the children would spend a night at Lord Brookhaven's the next night.

Hannah stayed behind to pack Samuel and Annabelle's things and would soon follow us. Then all the children, the four of them holding hands, walked the short way to my townhouse, with Lord Brookhaven and me close behind.

I wondered how mothers were able to cope, and I blessed Gretchen and Hannah and the help they were to me as the children played and made noise, needed help with various things, and occasionally quarreled. But the next day, when all the children went to spend the night at Lord Brookhaven's townhouse, it was so quiet and dull, I wondered what to do with myself.

I dreaded sitting at home and waiting for callers the next day, so I made sure to be out, showing Hattie some of the London sights that she hadn't seen, including St. Paul's Cathedral, Westminster Abbey, and the Tower of London, which I knew would be too tiring and dull an outing for the children, and it would take up all of the hours for callers. Millicent and Mrs. Drake came along as well, of course. But every time Mrs. Drake complained about missing callers, how we should go home, how her feet hurt, how handsome Mr. Welton was, what a great match he and I would make, and what a great family the Weltons were, my desire to replace her as my companion increased. In fact, I planned to ask Lady Derringer if she knew of anyone else who might be suitable for the position.

First, I should probably speak with Mrs. Drake in private, again, about the fact that I had already refused Mr. Welton and there was no instance in which I would change my mind. I didn't think it would make a difference to her, but I felt it my duty to try. Thankfully, she thought that I had refused Mr. Merritt already, for I was sure if she knew that I was still considering it, she would begin to tell me of all the ways in which Mr. Welton was Mr. Merritt's superior.

I myself had only viewed the Tower of London from a distance, but in touring it, I was caught up in its history and the beauty of its buildings. There were moments when it reminded me of Lowndesbury House so much that I felt an ache in my chest.

When the sun was about to set, it felt safe to return home, and it was quite dark when we arrived. We went in to find several calling cards. There was Mr. Welton's card, Mr. Merritt's, and three other gentlemen's cards with whom I'd danced. And there was Lord Markeley's calling card.

Millicent's face lit up when she saw it. "Do you think he will return tomorrow? Oh, I hope so. What bad luck that we were out when he called."

"I'm sorry we missed him, Millicent."

"Oh, it's all right, Charlotte. I just . . . I'm sure he will return."

But I could see how disappointed she was. I only hoped she didn't break her heart over him.

"I know!" Millicent's eyes widened. "We could have a dinner party and invite Lord Markeley, Mr. Merritt, and Lord Brookhaven. It would be just like the house party at Lowndesbury House!"

"Oh, I don't know . . ." When I saw Millicent's hurt expression, I murmured, "I'm just not sure it's a good idea for me to invite Mr. Merritt."

Mrs. Drake was doing some embroidery across the room, and I hoped she couldn't hear me. But since Millicent and Hattie knew about Mr. Merritt's proposal, I didn't have to explain myself.

When Millicent's face fell, I relented. "I suppose I could. After all, I can't avoid him forever. I'll need to give him an answer soon."

"Give Mr. Merritt an answer?" Mrs. Drake had dropped her work in her lap and was staring at me with narrowed eyes. "Did you not already refuse his proposal of marriage?"

I forced away the frown that pulled at my face. "I have not given him an answer."

"That is a bit cruel, do you not think? To keep the man waiting?"

"Perhaps. But I haven't decided whether or not to accept."

"Hmph." Then she picked up her work and mumbled what sounded like, "And what makes Mr. Merritt more worthy than Mr. Welton, pray tell?"

"Pardon me, what did you say?"

"Nothing at all." Mrs. Drake did not look up.

By the next day, Millicent had talked me into giving a dinner party and inviting Lord Markeley, Lord Brookhaven, Mr. Percy Allen, whom we'd discovered was in town, and Mr. Merritt. But as soon as I sent the invitations, Mr. Merritt called on us.

He made eye contact with me less frequently, but otherwise he was his usual self. He was handsome, there was no doubt about it, but somehow, the more I looked at him, the harder it was to imagine myself married to him. And if I was honest, when I asked myself who I did imagine myself married to, it was always Lord Brookhaven who came to mind.

Of course I knew that was never to be, and yet it was difficult to give up hope.

We'd barely said our greetings and pleasantries when Millicent said, "Did you get your invitation?"

"My . . . invitation?" Mr. Merritt asked.

"Yes, to a dinner party Charlotte is giving."

"Your invitation probably just missed you while you were on your way here. It's to be a small affair," I said, rattling on nervously. "I'm inviting four gentlemen—you, Lord Markeley, Lord Brookhaven, and Mr. Percy Allen—to even out us four ladies."

"Do you see, it's a reunion," Millicent said, "of the party at Lowndesbury House."

Suddenly, the servant announced the arrival of Lord Markeley. It seemed we would have a bit of a reunion now.

Lord Markeley entered the room with a friendly expression and bowed, but when he caught sight of Mr. Merritt, a slight scowl formed across his brow. Still, they greeted each other in a civil enough manner.

Lord Markeley sat between Millicent and me. Millicent spoke to him, asking him a question, as Mr. Merritt asked me, "Will you walk to church on Sunday?"

"Yes, I believe so. Mrs. Drake and I went last week. It is a short walk."

"May I escort you this Sunday?" Mr. Merritt asked.

As I couldn't think of a reason to say no, I said, "Yes, I thank you."

When I looked up, Lord Markeley was looking at me. "I am sorry I didn't dance with you at the assembly. Every time I tried to ask you, someone else got to you before I could."

He grinned as if it were an amusing story. I wanted to tell him to smile at Millicent, not me. I only hoped the reason he was calling was simply to tell me that he'd meant no offense in not asking me to dance. But when he kept talking to me, asking me about my walking and shopping habits, where I liked to go and when . . .

Oh dear. Lord Markeley was supposed to pay his attentions to Millicent, or at least not to anyone else. This was worse than getting two marriage proposals in one week from men with whom I wasn't in love.

I wanted to rush out of the room, make some excuse, and when I noticed Millicent looked as if she might cry, I said, "Oh my, I'm not feeling well. I shall run up to my room and fetch my smelling salts."

"Oh!" Hattie cried, jumping up. "I'll get them for you."

"No, no, I'll just get some air as well and return shortly." The gentlemen had all stood and were obviously about to offer their assistance, but I was already hurrying out the door. I practically ran up the stairs.

I didn't even own smelling salts, but I did throw open the window in my room and breathe deeply of the damp, smoky London air.

I rubbed my forehead. The tension—and the very real fear of what Millicent would feel if Lord Markeley continued to pay attention to me—was giving me a headache. *Go away, Lord Markeley, please.*

And now I'd already sent the invitation to dinner for tomorrow night. Did he think I was singling him out? But he'd see that I'd also invited Mr. Merritt, Mr. Allen, and Lord Brookhaven. Surely that would let him know that I had no real interest in him.

And then there were the sad puppy looks Mr. Merritt was giving me. Oh, what should I do?

Since I was afraid at any moment someone would come looking for me in my room, I hurried to go visit Joshua and Sarah and their guests, Samuel and Annabelle.

They were having their tea and biscuits. I hugged all four children, then sat and had a second tea with them.

It was terribly rude of me to leave my guests, but it seemed the lesser of two evils, and it cheered me to see Joshua and Sarah looking clean and happy and well-fed. Their eyes were bright and lively, so different from when I'd first met them. I didn't like to think where they'd be if I hadn't brought them home—if Lord Brookhaven hadn't helped me bring them home. And Samuel and Annabelle also looked happy, more relaxed somehow. When Annabelle met my eye, I winked, and she laughed.

I was in the middle of playing a game of checkers when Hattie came in the room.

"Here you are," she said. "Mrs. Drake sent me to look for you. Are you all right?"

"Oh yes, I'm well. Just visiting with the children."

"Go on back to your gentlemen callers," Gretchen said, shooing me away. "The children are well."

I said goodbye to the children and stopped Hattie outside in the hall.

"Have they gone yet?" I whispered.

"Lord Markeley left just before Mrs. Drake sent me to find you, but Mr. Merritt was still there."

I sighed. "Once I would have thought having more than one gentleman calling on me and making me offers of marriage was a wonderful occurrence, but it's not wonderful at all."

"Never mind. You always told me you wouldn't marry unless you were in love," Hattie said. "You needn't say yes to anyone you don't love."

"You are right." I smiled and hugged my friend. "Of course. But . . . won't Millicent be angry with me if she thinks Lord Markeley wants to marry me?"

"I think . . ." Hattie's face contorted. "I don't know. I only hope he doesn't pay you so much attention at the dinner party."

"Yes. Exactly."

By that evening, all four gentlemen had accepted my invitation to dinner. In the words of the poet Walter Scott, *Oh, what a tangled web we weave when first we practice to deceive . . .*

I'd hoped to please a friend. But what I'd done instead was attract yet another suitor in want of my fifty thousand pounds.

Twenty-Three

The next morning only Hattie accompanied me on my walk, as I got up too early for Mrs. Drake, and Millicent said she would rather catch up on some letter writing.

When we returned, I proposed that we all go shopping again. Yes, I wanted to avoid being called on, but I also wanted to buy the children some new toys and games.

Mrs. Drake was putting on her shawl and bonnet when she said with a frown, "You don't have to always be out if you don't wish to receive callers. You can just have the servants tell your callers that you're not at home. It is a very common practice."

I'd rather not ask my servants to lie, even if it was a common practice, but I only said, "I have some shopping to do. But I'm well aware that we need to return in time to ready ourselves for our dinner guests."

Indeed, I enjoyed the shopping trip and purchasing toys I thought the children would like. But every time I thought of Lord Markeley, I felt a twist in my stomach, worrying that Millicent was hurt and angry with me, and worrying that tonight would further cause her pain.

Somehow I needed to put Lord Markeley off, to convince him that I would not marry him even if he asked.

Perhaps I could find a way to tell him privately that Millicent

Skidmore had a fortune of her own, for her father had dedicated fifteen thousand pounds to go to her when she married, plus an annuity of five hundred pounds. That was no small dowry. Lord Markeley could certainly do worse. But I suspected he already knew what her dowry was. Such things were usually public knowledge so that each gentleman knew what he was getting before he proposed marriage.

After an enjoyable time shopping, we arrived home just after calling hours were over. Samuel and Annabelle had gone back to Lord Brookhaven's. "We decided the children needed a little time apart," Gretchen said with a smile when I came upstairs.

So Sarah and Joshua were alone in their room when I brought the gifts to them. When Sarah saw one of the dolls, with its real blond hair and bright blue painted eyes, she cried out and hugged it to her chest.

"My very own doll," she gasped.

"Yes, indeed."

But the moment was not to last, for Joshua whooped as loud as any banshee as he fell upon the wooden rocking horse the footman brought and set down in the middle of the playroom. He immediately climbed on and held the rein with his good hand, yelling, "Get up and go, horsey!"

I stayed as long as I could, watching them play, my heart full of joy and my eyes equally full of tears, at times, until I had to get ready for our dinner party. Somehow, after the joy I'd felt at the children's excitement, I couldn't feel any dread about the evening, though I'd lain awake the night before, trying to plan what to do.

Lord Brookhaven was the first to arrive, followed immediately by Mr. Merritt. We sat in the drawing room. The conversation felt rather forced, but when Lord Markeley arrived, he'd obviously been imbibing in spirits. His eyes were red, and he couldn't seem to stop talking.

"Miss Robbins, you're looking particularly pretty this evening," he said, stumbling over the many syllables in *particularly*.

"Miss Skidmore loaned me her ribbon, and doesn't she look fetching? I think the way the servant did her hair this evening is especially attractive."

Lord Markeley seemed reluctant to turn his head and look at Miss Skidmore, but he finally did and said, "Miss Skidmore looks wonderfully well, as always." He made a point to bow to her, and in doing so, he spilled a few drops of his drink on the floor.

Mrs. Drake rang for a servant while Lord Brookhaven threw down his handkerchief to soak up the wine.

"Come on, Markeley," Mr. Merritt muttered. "Why don't you drink some tea so you don't end up embarrassing yourself."

"Embarrassing myself?" Lord Markeley scrunched his face and let out a long hiss. "I'm not the one—" Lord Brookhaven put his arm around Lord Markeley's shoulders and guided him out the door into the hall, talking quietly in his ear.

"But I'm not the one who—" could be heard growing quieter as the two men made their way away from the other guests.

Percy Allen arrived and then there was nothing left to do but pray that Lord Brookhaven could get Lord Markeley to sober up before making their way back by the time dinner was announced.

"Allow me to congratulate you on your inheritance, Miss Robbins," Mr. Allen said, the most words I'd heard him string together at one time. "My father and mother asked me to send their good wishes for your health and happiness."

"Thank you, Mr. Allen. Are your parents well?"

"They are, I thank you."

The conversation was just that scintillating, until Millicent, Hattie, and Mr. Allen began to talk of their favorite music. Then Mr. Merritt turned to me and said quietly enough that no one else could hear, "Have you thought any more about my proposal?"

"I have thought about it, and I know it isn't fair to you, but I haven't come to a decision yet. Forgive me. I promise not to make you wait much longer."

He was quiet, staring down at the sofa cushion between us. Finally, he said, "I believe I may promise that you will be very comfortable, very content when you are my wife."

I said nothing, and he went on.

"I would treat you gently, and you would lack for nothing. I'd protect and honor you. You believe me?"

"I . . . I do believe you." But I immediately wondered if that was true.

"Dinner is ready, ma'am." The servant bowed and left the room.

No one spoke for a moment, then Mr. Merritt said, "I'll go and see if I can fetch the two errant lords."

We all smiled at his referring to the earl and the viscount as if they were children.

Less than a minute later, the three men returned, Lord Markeley looking a bit more sober, and we were able to pair up and proceed into the dining room.

I'd paired Millicent with Lord Markeley and Hattie with Mr. Allen, who was so much altered from the house party at Lowndesbury House that I wondered if his parents' presence there had caused him to be antisocial. I'd paired Mrs. Drake with Mr. Merritt, and myself with Lord Brookhaven, since his status as an earl would entitle him to the highest place at the table. But that meant that these two gentlemen were on either side of me.

The meal progressed pleasantly enough, with Millicent, Lord Markeley, and Mr. Allen telling Hattie stories of the party at Lowndesbury House. And Lord Brookhaven and Mr. Merritt talking pleasantly enough with me and Mrs. Drake. I never would have sensed any tension between the two gentlemen if not for the fact that I'd seen them speaking much more familiarly and in a much friendlier manner at Lowndesbury House.

I'd managed to sneak away just long enough to whisper to the servant pouring the wine and ask him to make certain he only gave Lord Markeley the watered-down wine I reserved for myself and Hattie. It was the only kind of wine Mrs. Southey allowed her schoolgirls and teachers to drink, so we preferred it.

I hoped it helped keep Lord Markeley from ruining our evening.

While we were being served the second course, I thought I heard a knock at the front door. But I ignored it, until half a minute later I heard shouting.

I jumped up and rushed toward the sounds of raised voices. In the hall, I felt Lord Brookhaven's hand on my shoulder.

"Allow me to go first," he said, even as he maneuvered himself between me and the man shouting at the young footman who'd answered the door.

"Them's m' rightful kin," he was shouting. "Your mistress took 'em unlawful-like. You bring 'em down here to me."

"You are trespassing, sir," Lord Brookhaven said.

"I want what's rightfully mine! I know my Joshua and Sarah are here."

"Joshua and Sarah are orphans," I said from behind Lord Brookhaven's shoulder. "You're not their father."

"That's all you know! They's my own niece and nephew, my sister's young'uns. Now hand 'em over, or I'll be fetching the constable."

"We will speak to your solicitor about it in the morning," Lord Brookhaven said.

The man spit out a curse, and that was when I smelled the alcohol on him.

"Ain't never had no solicitor. But I'll be back, mark my words." He pointed a dirty finger at me. "You ain't seen the last of me."

"And what is your name?" Lord Brookhaven asked.

"Gilbert White, and I know my rights. This is still England, and the lady of this house has my kin."

The man backed out the open door, and Lord Brookhaven shut and locked it.

I lifted my hand to my face, then noticed it was shaking and put it down again.

"Are you all right?" Lord Brookhaven asked.

"Yes."

"Have you ever seen that man before, or have the children mentioned him?"

"No, I haven't, and they have told me themselves that their parents are dead and they have no home." I crossed my arms over my chest. "I will not allow that man to take them. They are happy here. I won't allow it."

Mr. Merritt, Mr. Allen, and Lord Markeley were standing in the hall behind us, just outside the dining room. The ladies appeared to be crowded behind them.

I heard a bit of shuffling and glanced at the stairs. At the top of the landing were Sarah and Joshua, looking wide-eyed.

"I'll be back in a moment," I said to my guests, then climbed the stairs.

"Why aren't you in bed?" My hands were starting to shake even more, as if I was having a late reaction to what had transpired moments ago.

"We heard shouting," Sarah said softly.

I knelt down in front of them so I could look into their eyes. "Did you recognize that man?"

Joshua and Sarah exchanged glances but said nothing.

"He says he's your uncle. Is that true?"

They nodded. "I think he is our uncle," Sarah said quietly, "but we never saw him until our mother died. Will he bring the constable and take you to jail? Take us?"

"No. No, that will not happen. Don't worry. I will not let him take you. Your home is here with me. You are safe, do you understand?"

They nodded, but fear made their faces look pinched, the same blank-eyed, nervous expressions from when Lord Brookhaven and I found them on the street.

Gretchen hurried toward us, dressed in a quilted wrapper. "So sorry, miss. I didn't hear them get up. Come along, children."

She reached for their hands, but I gathered them in my arms and said, "All will be well. Now go to sleep and I'll talk to you in the morning. All is well." I smiled at them and let Gretchen lead them back to bed. But their resigned expressions gave me an uneasy ache in my chest.

When I turned to go back down the stairs, all four gentlemen were waiting for me outside the dining room.

We were quiet as we made our way back to our seats.

"I hope my cook doesn't leave me after I've let his dishes grow cold." I smiled at my weak jest.

No one smiled back.

Mrs. Drake let out a loud sigh and murmured, "Oh dear. Dear me."

Lord Brookhaven said, "You needn't worry or be intimidated by that man. Even if he is their uncle, which I doubt, he obviously was not taking care of them. And by the look of him, he's probably one of those thieves who roams London and forces young children to do their thievery."

Mrs. Drake pasted on a friendly look as she clicked her tongue against her teeth. "Must we talk of such things? It is a dinner party and there are young, innocent ladies present."

"I have heard of such things," I said, ignoring Mrs. Drake and addressing Lord Brookhaven, "and I believe you are right."

"I cannot hold my tongue any longer," Mrs. Drake said. "Those children are not your relatives and not your responsibility. You should give them to that man, since he wants them. It is the right thing to do." She nodded but didn't meet my eye.

"And if the children wish to go with him . . ." Mr. Merritt was saying.

I stared at him. "They do not wish to go with him. Why would they? They are safe and warm and fed here with me, and they were sleeping on the ground in an abandoned building before."

My voice faltered as I realized I hadn't asked them directly if they wanted to go with him. But I could see on their faces that they were afraid of him. Still, I would ask them outright, but it would completely break my heart if they did.

Out of the corner of my eye, I caught the look of disgust on Mrs.

Drake's face, the distress on Hattie's, and the judgment on Mr. Allen's and Lord Markeley's faces. Even Millicent looked unhappy with me. Only Lord Brookhaven looked at me with approval.

The rest of the dinner no one mentioned the children or the unwelcome visitor. Then Lord Markeley said during the last course, "This was a fine dinner, Miss Robbins, and more lively than most. It isn't often the hostess has an argument about orphans with a vagrant off the street."

He grinned, while everyone else stared down at their plates. Then his face fell and he said, "Forgive me if I gave offense."

"Not at all," I forced out, smiling back at him. "It is not a regular occurrence for any of us, I am sure."

"I do remember a time . . ." and Lord Markeley proceeded to regale them with a tale from their school days when Lord Brookhaven had defended a kitchen maid from a man who was trying to drag her away. "The man said, 'I'll teach you to send your wages to your sister and not to your own da.' And then Brookhaven grabbed him by the scruff of his neck—he was half Brookhaven's size—and tossed him out the door. Brooksie said, 'And if you come around here harassing the servants again, I'll sic the constable on you.'" Lord Markeley laughed.

Again, no one else laughed, and Lord Markeley said, "I think I've said the wrong thing again. Maybe I should just be quiet."

"Do not worry, Markeley," Mr. Merritt said, and even Lord Brookhaven gave him a lopsided smile.

"Shall we adjourn to the drawing room?" I stood and everyone else followed.

Millicent volunteered to play the pianoforte for us, and I found myself seated next to Lord Markeley.

"Forgive me," he said softly during Millicent's playing, and I cringed inwardly. She hated it when anyone talked during a performance.

"Of course," I whispered back. "All is well."

"For what I said at dinner," he continued. "If you wish to care for those two orphans, I think it's very admirable."

I stared to see if he was sincere. He was still a little drunk, but that probably made him more truthful, not less so.

"May I call on you again tomorrow, Miss Robbins? I'd like to take you on a walk. Perhaps we could have a private moment to talk."

My stomach sank.

I focused my eyes on Millicent, who glanced often in Lord Markeley's direction while she played. I smiled at her.

"Miss Robbins?" Lord Markeley whispered loudly.

"Yes, yes, of course," I said quickly. It wasn't what I wanted to say, but it silenced him.

The rest of the night was as pleasant as it could be, with me thinking of the terrible Gilbert White who threatened to return tomorrow, the "private talk" Lord Markeley wished to have, and my anger at Mr. Merritt's and Mrs. Drake's reaction to my saying I would not give up Joshua and Sarah to that man.

When everyone began to go home, Lord Brookhaven took me aside and said, "I will send one of my men—Henson, he's very stout and dependable—to guard your house. If that Gilbert White returns, Henson will not allow him to get in again."

"But what if he brings the constable?"

"He won't. But there is no need to worry even if he does. The constable in this part of London is an old friend of my father's. All will be well. And I won't let him take the children. We'll hide them at Lowndesbury House if we must."

I was so relieved, my knees went weak. "Thank you." I wanted to tell him I was grateful for his help, but my throat tightened and I couldn't speak.

He squeezed my hand before donning his hat and leaving.

Twenty-Four

The next morning, I was standing near the front door and putting on my gloves for my morning walk when I heard raised voices just outside.

I started to open the door, but something told me to wait. I heard the voice of the man from the night before, Gilbert White, and another male voice shouting back and forth about going in, staying out, taking what was his, and on and on. Then I heard a new voice, speaking in a normal tone, which was too quiet for me to make out.

"Charlotte!" Hattie was hurrying toward me, Millicent just behind her. "I saw from my window . . . that man from last night and another rough-looking fellow, and they appeared to be arguing. Then, just now, Lord Brookhaven and another man have come." Her eyes were big, and she covered her mouth after she finished speaking.

I reached for the doorknob.

"I don't know if you should—"

I opened the door. If Lord Brookhaven was outside, it should be safe. Besides, I didn't want that nefarious man to think I was frightened of him.

"I'll fetch the constable if you don't give me my kin!" Mr. White was saying, his hands balled into fists as he faced the large man who I suddenly realized was probably Henson, Lord Brookhaven's man.

Lord Brookhaven's eyes were narrowed as he and the gentleman beside him stared Mr. White down. But when he saw me at the door, Lord Brookhaven took a step, motioning for me to stay back.

I closed the door partway, watching through the crack.

"Who are you to keep me children from me?" Mr. White was saying. "I'll fetch the constable, I will!"

"I am the constable." The man with Lord Brookhaven scowled. "William Thomas Beckwith the third, and I'm the constable for Grosvenor Square. So if you don't mind, sir, I'll ask you to stop disturbing the peace of this house and go home."

"I see how it be." Mr. White raised his voice again. "The rich man and the constable are stopping me from taking what's mine. But I know my rights. And I'll be back. You will see me again, and next time I'll talk to the lady what stole my children. Dividing families and taking poor folkses' children. Is that what you rich people do now? I have my rights, same as the rich."

He walked away a few feet, then turned around and pointed a finger straight at me. "I won't go quiet, y' hear? I'll be back for my kin."

The three men were between me and him, so I wasn't in any real danger, but my heart beat fast.

"Sorry about that, miss." Henson took off his hat and nodded toward me. "I wouldn't have let him get through the door."

Lord Brookhaven looked at me with a concerned expression.

"Come inside, please, gentlemen."

Lord Brookhaven said something to Henson, who moved away, then he and the constable came in.

I ordered a larger breakfast, and we all went into the breakfast room. I usually ate something small—a scone or fruit tart—before my walk, and then a bigger breakfast afterward, but I wasn't sure I would even take a walk this morning.

Lord Brookhaven made all the introductions, and Mr. Beckwith, the constable, greeted everyone politely.

"Do you know this man, Gilbert White?" I asked Mr. Beckwith. "Do you think he could have been using the children for thievery?"

"He is a known pickpocket and petty thief, so I suspect he was."

It was all I needed to know to quell the guilt I'd been feeling. I of all people knew the pain of having no family, no relatives of any kind. Or at least I'd thought I had no relatives, until my uncle died. I would have loved to have met him and to have felt some kind of connection to him. Why would I ever want to keep anyone from their relatives?

I didn't want to deny Joshua and Sarah a relationship with their uncle. But if this man was a thief and was using them . . . I was more determined than ever to keep them from him. But the fact that he found them useful would also make him more determined to take them back.

"What did you call your uncle?" I asked Sarah while Joshua was playing with the toy soldiers I'd bought him.

"Uncle Gil," Sarah said quietly.

"Did he take care of you and give you a place to sleep?"

She stared at me blankly for a moment, then said, "We slept in the old building you saw. He slept there too sometimes."

"What did you do when Uncle Gil was around?"

Sarah looked like she might cry.

"You don't have to tell me if you don't want to." It was enough for me that he didn't even provide them a safe or warm place to sleep and didn't stay with them every night to protect them.

"I don't think you would like me anymore if I told you." A tear slipped down her cheek.

"Of course I would like you." I squeezed her arm and looked into her eyes. "There is nothing you could say to make me not like you. Besides, if your uncle made you do something bad, that is his fault, not yours. He's a grown-up, and grown-ups are supposed to take care of children, not ask them to do bad things."

"He sometimes made us steal food."

I nodded to show her it was all right and to encourage her to go on.

"He tried to make me steal from gentlemen's pockets, but I was too scared."

"I'm proud of you for telling me. And you don't need to worry about him anymore, do you understand? I will protect you."

She nodded but she didn't look completely reassured. She bit her lip and went back to playing with her doll.

The next morning, I got ready to go on my walk as usual. Lord Markeley had not come to have his private talk, and I was greatly relieved.

Mrs. Drake and Hattie came with me, but Millicent stayed home. She wasn't as much of a walker as I was, but she'd seemed distant lately. I hoped I was imagining it.

I nodded to Henson on my way out. He was watching the front door, and I knew Lord Brookhaven had sent a second man to watch the back and to go and fetch help should Henson need it.

Lord Brookhaven's townhouse was not very far from mine, and I could see him up ahead, as if he were waiting for me. He greeted us and fell in with our group.

"You are very kind to accompany us, Lord Brookhaven," I said. "But you must allow me to pay your men who have been guarding my house. It is not as if I can't pay them."

"Whatever do you mean, Miss Robbins?" He gave me a sly, side-eyed look.

"You know very well what I mean," I said.

"I care about Joshua and Sarah, just as you do. I want to offer them some protection while the need seems pressing. Once we are sure Mr. White is no longer trying to take the children, I will allow you to dismiss my men back to me."

I wasn't sure if I should be annoyed at his high-handed way of taking charge of guarding my house and the children, or if I should just politely thank him for his care. He immediately changed the subject and asked Hattie what she liked and disliked most about London, so I wrestled with my thoughts in silence.

Lord Brookhaven was more gregarious than usual, especially with Hattie, and I was grateful. She'd often said she felt out of place as we socialized in London, but Lord Brookhaven was helping me to prove the point that only unkind people would ever want her to think she was less important than someone who was wealthier and more fashionable.

And the way Mrs. Drake smirked and bridled when she saw one of her old friends on the street made me want to roll my eyes. She might as well have said, *Look at me. I am walking in the company of the Earl of Brookhaven. Don't you think better of me now?*

I almost felt sorry for Lord Brookhaven. How could he ever know if someone cared for him because of himself, or because of his title? How many times had he felt used by people who only pretended to like him for who he truly was?

As we neared the park, Mr. Merritt was leaning against the big oak at the entrance. His expression changed when he saw Lord Brookhaven with us.

The two gentlemen bowed to each other—rather stiffly, I thought—and we all exchanged small talk about the weather and the state of the roads.

"I shall leave you ladies in the capable hands of Mr. Merritt," Lord Brookhaven said. He bowed and turned to leave.

I wanted to call him back, to tell him I'd rather have his company than Mr. Merritt's, but of course I could not. I watched him go and somehow felt it was my fault Mr. Merritt was here.

Well, of course it was my fault. I still hadn't given him an answer on whether or not I would marry him.

I would tell him today. It was not helping anyone for me to wait.

We walked through the park more slowly than I would have liked. If I were a man I could have walked at a very quick pace, but I was a woman so I had to have my chaperone, and she could not go at the pace I could.

This inheritance had taught me, however, that life was not as easy for either gentlemen or ladies as I'd once thought. They might not have to take up an occupation as I had, but there were so many rules and expectations, so many mistakes they could make that would doom them to being looked down upon for the rest of their lives.

At least if I married a clergyman, as Mr. Merritt planned to become, I would have a purpose, as my duty would be to care for my husband's parishioners. But deep in my heart, I knew I wasn't in love with Mr. Merritt. And after what he'd said at our dinner party about my caring for Joshua and Sarah, I knew I couldn't marry him.

Perhaps moving to London had not been the best idea. If I'd bought a small country estate with my fifty thousand pounds, I could have walked my own gardens and grounds alone and uninhibited any time I liked. It would have been like being at Lowndesbury House, when I wandered the lovely grounds and was happy.

Except that I would have missed having Lord Brookhaven as my companion.

No, it would not have been the same at all. But still, it was something to think about. Perhaps a small country estate near Milford and Mrs. Southey's school. At least there I'd be close to Hattie, Susan, and Mrs. Southey.

"It looks as if we're alone for the moment," Mr. Merritt said, and I saw that Mrs. Drake and Hattie had wandered a few feet away and were watching some children playing a game of blindman's buff with their nursemaids. "It gives me an opportunity to ask if you have thought any more about my offer to love and admire you for the rest of our lives."

I gazed into his face, half expecting him to be smiling in jest. But his expression was sober.

My stomach flipped at what I was about to say. "Forgive me, Mr. Merritt, for you know I have great respect for you and I enjoy your company. We have been good friends. But I'm sorry that I cannot marry you. I'm sorry," I repeated, my stomach twisting into knots.

"And may I ask why you cannot marry me, a gentleman of good character and family and prospects?"

"You are a very good match for any young lady," I said quickly, pausing our walk. "You are handsome and your manners are impeccable. But I'm afraid I cannot marry you because . . . well, I don't believe you love me the way I wish to be loved, and I . . . please forgive me."

If only I could think of something better to say! I hated the resentful expression, the way his lips pressed together and he avoided looking me in the eye, his brows drawn together in a scowl.

"I daresay you would have said yes if I hadn't warned you not to ruin Lord Brookhaven by marrying him when you were his governess."

"Perhaps I might have," I said quietly.

"Then why do you let that come between us? Things have changed. The circumstances are different now."

My circumstances were different. His were unchanged. But why should I point out that he only wished to marry me because of these changed circumstances? He knew it as well as I did. Why should I defend myself?

"You will forgive me," I said. "I wish you all the happiness in the world. May you find love with the woman who will make you truly happy."

"I wanted that woman to be you." He turned away from me, picking the bark off a small birch tree beside us.

My chest ached, and I wondered if I'd done the right thing. Had I just thrown away my best chance at happiness? But something told me that it was all right. Mr. Merritt would forget me, and I would find true and lasting love. *Father God, please let it be so.*

My mind was in a fog. I wasn't sure how we'd ended up deciding to leave the park and start back home, but we hadn't gone far when Mr. Merritt said, "Forgive me, but I shall leave you here. Good day." He nodded to each of us, not meeting my gaze, then turned and strode away.

We did not converse very much as we walked. No doubt Mrs. Drake and Hattie could both surmise what had taken place between Mr. Merritt and me, and I said nothing, as I was in no mood to listen to Mrs. Drake's barely disguised criticisms.

Meanwhile, my thoughts were turning to anger. It certainly wasn't very chivalrous of Mr. Merritt to be offended at my refusal. How could he expect me to believe that he was in love with me in so short a time after he'd said I wasn't good enough for his friend, or that anything less than true love would induce me to marry him when all he had to offer was his name?

I was in a right rotten mood.

We were not far from home when a man stepped out of a side street directly in front of us. It was Gilbert White.

Twenty-Five

Gilbert White's leering smile showed black, rotting teeth. He lunged, making Hattie and Mrs. Drake cry out and step back. But I stood my ground. How dare he think he could intimidate us?

"You will excuse us," I said. "We need to pass."

"You had better watch yourself, missy." He pointed his finger a few inches from my face. "If you want me to stay out of your way, you can give me my kin or pay up."

"Get out of our way." I concentrated on not looking the least bit afraid. He couldn't see my heart beating hard and fast, after all.

I took Hattie's arm and steered her around the man, but he sidestepped to block us.

"Your money or my kin," he said. "I'll take a hundred and fifty quid, and you'll never see me again."

"I will not bribe you to leave me alone, but I will tell the constable. He will arrest you for harassing ladies on the street." I gave him the meanest glare I could conjure.

"You give me that money." He snarled like an animal and lunged at me again.

I stepped away, and he stumbled. His foot slipped off the raised sidewalk and he fell face-first on the road.

Hattie screamed, and Mrs. Drake cried, "Run, girls!"

I was pleased with how fast Mrs. Drake was able to move when so motivated. She held onto Hattie's arm, and I kept to the rear and glanced back to watch Mr. White lift himself out of the muck of the street. He scowled and yelled in our direction. I couldn't make out his words, and he did not follow us.

After changing clothes and freshening our hair after our walk, we had just got settled in the parlor when our first caller was announced—Lord Markeley.

Millicent's gaze went to the doorway while mine went to her. *Dear God, please don't let Lord Markeley ruin my friendship with Millicent.*

Lord Markeley looked directly at me, bowed with a flourish, and came and sat to my right. He made small talk and said charming things to Mrs. Drake, Hattie, and Millicent. But his words were so similar to each of them, complimenting them on their dress and their smiles, that they sounded rather meaningless. Then he turned to me and said in a more intimate tone, "You are looking particularly beautiful today, Miss Robbins. I would that this were a ball and that I was dancing every dance with you."

Because of his low tone, I wasn't sure if the others heard what he said, but in my desperation, I laughed. "What pretty words you have for us all today, Lord Markeley," I said brightly.

"Yes, and it hasn't been a very pretty day so far," Mrs. Drake said, a peevish note in her voice.

"What do you mean?" Lord Markeley turned toward Mrs. Drake. It was all the encouragement she needed.

"As they say, no good deed goes unpunished, and Miss Robbins's *'good deed'* of taking in those two street urchins continues to cause no end of trouble for us all. This morning we were taking a nice walk in the park with Mr. Merritt and Lord Brookhaven—although Lord Brookhaven left us when we reached the park. And unfortunately Mr. Merritt left us too, before we got to our street, which is more

Miss Robbins's fault than any failing of Mr. Merritt's, but we shall say no more on that subject."

I was fairly certain that Mrs. Drake would, on the contrary, say much more on that subject, but hopefully she would spare Lord Markeley.

"And then that horrid man who interrupted our dinner party the other night jumped out at us, blocking our way. And he told Miss Robbins that if she gave him a hundred and fifty pounds sterling she'd never see him again, so I hope Miss Robbins won't be so stubborn as to hold out. Personally, I think she should give him back the children, but it isn't for me to say, so I don't say a thing, one way or another."

So help me, if I didn't find someone to replace Mrs. Drake, I'd die trying.

"Miss Robbins, is this true?" Lord Markeley turned back to me. "Were you accosted again this morning?"

"I'm afraid so, but he was not able to lay a hand on me, so all is well."

"No, all is not well," Mrs. Drake said. "That filthy man will be after us again, I dare say, the next time we try to walk down the street, unless the constable arrests him and puts him in prison where he belongs."

"Perhaps you should give him the money," Lord Markeley said. "It is not so very much, and your safety is certainly worth that, and much more."

"Perhaps, but I object on principle. It would be as if I were buying the children for a hundred and fifty pounds. Besides, if I give him money, he will only return for more. No, he shall get nothing from me."

"What is to prevent him from coming here again and disturbing our peace as he did the night of your lovely dinner party?" Mrs. Drake exclaimed.

"He cannot do that again, for Lord Brookhaven has his men watching the house. They will not allow it."

"Lord Brookhaven has sent men, has he?" Lord Markeley said.

"They are large men, not the kind to back down or be taken advantage of."

"Oh." Lord Markeley nodded but looked away as he mumbled, "That is good."

After ten minutes, I thought Lord Markeley would go, but instead he stayed half an hour longer and seemed reluctant to leave even then. Oh dear. I dreaded what it meant.

Indeed, Lord Markeley called the next two days, then asked if I would accompany him to an afternoon theatrical at Covent Garden. "And Mrs. Drake may come along, of course."

It would be unseemly if she didn't, but I didn't wish to go with him. I cast about desperately in my mind for an excuse. "I really shouldn't leave my guests," I said, speaking whatever came to mind. "They have come to London to visit me and for me to show them . . . places."

For a moment, I thought Lord Markeley would invite them to come too, but he opened his mouth and then closed it. "I understand," he said. But his face was quite downcast. "May we take a walk, then?"

"Of course." I didn't have the heart to say no when I could see I'd disappointed him so much about going to Covent Garden.

We ladies gathered our walking things—gloves, bonnets, and shawls—and Lord Markeley escorted us down the street, but the opposite way from the park, which meant we would avoid walking past Lord Brookhaven's house.

We walked slowly. Lord Markeley had placed himself between me and Millicent, and Millicent asked him about his horse and his estate in Wiltshire.

"Ah yes, I left Marauder at Benton Downs. He had a bit of a problem with his leg, but my stable master knows everything about horses. He'll have him running about in no time at all. I'm surprised you remembered my horse." He gave Millicent the slightest smile, but it made her face light up.

"Oh, I remember."

An uncomfortable look crossed Lord Markeley's face, and he started to look away from her.

"Millicent brought her favorite horse back with her from Shropshire, and she went for a ride just yesterday," I said quickly. "I'm no rider at all, myself, so the servant had to go with her, but Millicent is a keen rider and great horsewoman."

"Is that so?" Lord Markeley smiled and nodded at Millicent but immediately turned back to me. "And why, pray tell, are you no rider, Miss Robbins? If it's lack of opportunity, I can bring over one of my horses for you and teach you until you are as comfortable on a horse as you could wish to be."

It was not the response I'd been hoping for. He was supposed to talk to Millicent, to realize he had more in common with her than with me, and to offer to go riding with her.

"I have no real interest in riding. Horses frighten me, and as long as I can walk and ride in a carriage, I see no need to learn to ride."

He laughed. "Ah, Miss Robbins. If only all ladies were as open and honest as you are." And then he winked at me.

Dear Lord, how I hated a winking man.

"Oh, look," Hattie cried. "Someone is giving away kittens."

We made our way to a woman on the sidewalk with a basket. Inside was a mother cat and four kittens. She immediately started telling us she was "looking for a good home for the lot of 'em. My mistress won't allow me to keep them, but the mama cat is as good at catching mice as any cat I've seen."

There weren't any mice at my townhouse, I didn't think, but I wouldn't have minded having a friendly cat who would sit with me when I was knitting or reading in the evenings. The idea of a soft, purring cat was quite appealing, but as Hattie, Millicent, and Mrs. Drake began exclaiming over the kittens and petting them and picking them up, Lord Markeley drew me back with a hand on my arm.

"Miss Robbins," he said in a whisper, "do tell me now if I have any chance at winning your heart. I would do anything to make you love me the way I love you."

"I am sorry, but I . . . No. Forgive me. I do not love you."

Of course I didn't love him. He drank too much, and he hadn't thought me nearly good enough until I'd inherited fifty thousand pounds. But even more importantly, Millicent obviously liked him, and he must realize that.

But when his face fell and he looked genuinely crushed, I did feel a pang of guilt stab my chest. I didn't wish to give anyone pain. Still, I was glad to be able to tell him the truth and get it over with.

Millicent turned just then and looked from Lord Markeley to me. Her jaw hardened, as if she were clenching her teeth, and she turned away again.

Soon we said goodbye to the cats and their owner and started home.

The walk back seemed to take a long time, even though we walked much faster on the return. Millicent stared straight ahead, her lips pursed.

All the while Lord Markeley looked slightly sheepish one minute, slightly angry the next. Thankfully, he took his leave of us at the front door and was gone.

Calling hours were nearly over. I glanced at Millicent but said nothing. I was working on a piece of embroidery with wildflowers that reminded me of the grounds around Lowndesbury House. It usually lifted my spirits to work on it, with its blue and violet and pink and yellow threads, but today . . . I kept thinking of Lord Markeley's facial expressions, and of Millicent's, and how obvious it had been that the viscount had asked me to marry him and I had rejected him.

I wondered if it were possible to advertise that I was no longer able to receive marriage proposals, as I had decided to give the fifty thousand pounds to the poor. Wouldn't Mrs. Drake have an apoplectic fit at that? I was tempted to announce it to the whole room.

I was becoming a rather perverse person. Had the fifty thousand pounds turned me into someone I never wished to be?

At first, I'd enjoyed all the attention. I could do anything I wanted, and it was thrilling to have the freedom and independence to rent my own house, to bring my friends to visit me, and to go shopping and buy new things. But along with what I'd gained, I'd also lost things, such as my relationships with Mr. Merritt and Lord Markeley. Now that I'd rejected their marriage proposals, I knew things between us would never be the same. And nothing felt the same between Lord Brookhaven and me, either. I missed our conversations, our easy banter, and the way he seemed to understand me. And even though he didn't seem to want to marry me, I just wanted to be near him, to hear his thoughts and opinions . . . and to see his dear face.

I was near tears. I kept my head down, thankful to have my embroidery in my lap so no one would see my face.

How happy I'd been to inherit such a fortune! I must surely be the most fortunate girl in all of England. Or so I'd thought. I could marry whomever I pleased. I remembered thinking that if Lord Brookhaven was in love with me, now he could marry me.

But was that true? I might have a fortune, but I was still an orphan with no family name of importance, and he was still an earl. The fact that he'd made very little effort to spend time with me, and that he'd stood aside and allowed his friends to ask me to marry them, made it seem as though he couldn't love me, or else he would have asked me already.

A tear dripped from my eye to the fabric. I took a deep breath and quietly released it, breathing in and out and telling myself, *I'll give away the money.*

Well, I wouldn't give it all away. I needed something to live on. But there were so many children, like Sarah and Joshua, who lived on the streets and struggled to fend for themselves in a harsh world. I could help them if I just applied a fraction of my fortune toward

. . . an orphanage, maybe. A place with kind caregivers like Gretchen who would nurture and care for them in a loving way. After all, didn't Scripture say that taking care of orphans and widows in their distress was the very definition of Christianity?

I was lost in my thoughts when the servant announced a visitor. "Lady Derringer."

I quickly swiped at my face with my hand, lest there be remnants of my tears, and set my embroidery aside.

"I just wanted to call on you, my dear," she said, looking at me, "for I will be leaving London and returning to the country again soon."

"I am sorry to hear it," I said.

"Why thank you, my dear. I shall miss all of you ladies." She glanced around the room, but her eyes settled on me again. "Might you come over tomorrow and have a private chat with me? My nephew will be away, and I have something I wish to tell you."

"Of course." I was surprised, especially since she made it clear she only wished for me to come.

"Is eleven o'clock all right?"

"Yes."

Twenty-Six

Lady Derringer met me in the hallway the next morning at eleven. She led me into a small sitting room on the ground floor and said, "Thank you for coming. Lord Brookhaven will be returning soon. I wanted to see you and ask . . . how are you?"

"I am very well, thank you."

"Has that horrid man Gilbert White bothered you any more after he accosted you on the street?"

"No, thankfully. We haven't seen him."

"That is good." She sighed, giving me a compassionate look. "It cannot be very easy coming into so much money and having no close relatives to help you navigate the difficulties of society and the fortune-hunting men, if you will forgive me for saying that."

I smiled, relieved that she was talking about something I actually wanted to talk about. "You are right. It hasn't been easy."

"That is why I asked you here, to offer my help. I have been remiss, and I realize that now and ask for your forgiveness. If there is anything you need, if you need to ask my advice—oh, I know, no one wants to be told what to do or how to think—but if you do feel the need to ask, I am very happy to help if I can."

"I have thought a few times that I'd like to ask your advice, but I didn't want to impose on your time."

"No, my dear! Do not think you are imposing on me. I am your friend, I hope, and I want you to feel you can trust me to be discreet, to keep what you tell me in confidence, and to give you the best advice I can."

I assured her I trusted her discretion and her sincerity. "It has been difficult, as I feel I am losing so many friends. Mr. Merritt and Lord Markeley have both asked to marry me."

"And you refused them?"

"I did. But I am afraid my friendship with them is now at an end, and it makes me sad. There was also Mr. Welton. I felt as if he only wanted my fortune, ultimately. But I want to marry for love."

"And you shall." She clasped my wrist and smiled, leaning close.

"But in the meantime, I think what will make me happy is to do something good and meaningful with the fortune. That is, I think I should like to open an orphanage for children who have nowhere to go, who need shelter and food and someone to care for them."

"What a wonderful thought." Lady Derringer's lips parted, and she stared at me, wide-eyed.

"Why should I live in luxury when there are innocent children starving on the streets of London? Joshua and Sarah are such precious children. I can't bear to think that there are others like them who are cold and hungry and in danger from evil men who want to use them."

"Of course." Lady Derringer had a faraway look in her eyes. "I believe I may know some ladies who would want to help you in this endeavor, who are more compassionate than most." She raised her brows. "You should speak to Lord Brookhaven about this as well. I believe he would want to help. I imagine he would have some excellent ideas about such a scheme. He has a good head for organization and the structure of such things. Yes, I think this will work out very well."

She smiled at me as if she were very happy from some secret that I knew nothing about.

We sipped our tea and discussed various aspects of my plan,

which was in its infancy but about which I had not been able to stop thinking since the day before.

"I spoke with Sarah and Joshua about their life on the streets. They wish to assist me in finding the children who need our help. They know of some, of course."

"Yes, I would think so."

"I will have to hire some men to help me keep the children safe, for as I have discovered, there are those who will not appreciate me taking their young workers whom they've been using to steal. Did you know they even use children to wade into the Thames and pick up whatever they can find from the bottom, as there are quite a few valuables and coins that can be found that way? But the children often are cut or otherwise injured by broken glass and metal, for there are all manner of discarded things in the mud at the bottom."

Too late, I realized this was not the kind of conversation ladies would normally engage in, but Lady Derringer put down her teacup and said, "How dreadful for those poor children! Yes, it is a cruel, harsh world for orphans in London. We must do what we can, and you are so good, Miss Robbins, for most young ladies who had just inherited a fortune would never trouble themselves about such a thing."

"I think it is mostly because I am an orphan myself, and I realize how fortunate I was to grow up in a good school rather than on the street. And that is why I wish for this orphanage to be a school, a place where they can learn and be happy, where they never have to know desperation. They can learn skills and knowledge and have a productive, happy life."

"It will be costly," Lady Derringer said, "but it is not impossible."

"Anything is possible, if God so wills it." It was something I'd heard an elderly lady in Milford say, and it had stuck with me.

"Yes, indeed. Faith and Providence are what we need for this venture."

We discussed it a bit more, then Lady Derringer said, "I shall send you a list of names of wealthy ladies I believe might wish to be involved, and when I am back in town, I shall introduce you to them. But I'll also give the list to William, in case he might be able to introduce you to some of them."

"That would be lovely, thank you."

I walked home with a lightness of heart and step. Perhaps this fortune was not only for my benefit, but also for the benefit of others.

The next morning, a visitor was announced just after nine thirty. Regular calling hours were from ten to six, so I wondered who would call at such an unfashionable hour.

The housekeeper looked ill at ease. "It is your solicitor, Mr. Sullivan, but he has a woman with him."

"Did they say what this is about?"

"Mr. Sullivan only said it was a matter of business that was quite pressing."

"Very well. Show them into the sitting room."

Mr. Sullivan stood when I walked into the room, and the young woman stood as well. Her eyes darted around, and her brown hair was held down with a frayed straw hat. She smelled of woodsmoke, her skin had the hue of someone who labored outdoors, and her mouth had a defiant tilt.

"Thank you for seeing us, Miss Robbins," Mr. Sullivan said.

"Please sit down." I nodded to the young woman.

"Miss Robbins, this is Mrs. Abigail Robbins Newman. She is the natural born daughter of your uncle, Mr. John Robert Robbins of Yorkshire, and it seems as though the fortune you inherited . . ." Mr. Sullivan paused to take out his handkerchief and wipe his face before continuing. "It seems Mrs. Newman is the rightful heir, and she is here to declare that the fortune is rightfully hers."

My mind seemed to go blank.

"I have looked into it, I assure you," Mr. Sullivan was saying.

My mind seemed too sluggish to form any rational thoughts. It all seemed a bit strange. Even Mr. Sullivan's manner was strange.

"I would not have troubled you with this otherwise. This young woman is the legitimate daughter of your uncle. It is true, she was estranged from her father, but it was her own doing and not his. We had been searching for her, but she led him to believe that she had died. Now, due to the circumstances, Mrs. Newman will not require you to pay back what you have already spent of the fifty thousand pounds, but you must release what is left of it immediately. I am very sorry, Miss Robbins, but a judge will be more sympathetic to a daughter than a niece, and I am quite sure that if you try to take this to court, you will not only lose the fortune, but you will be forced to pay back every penny that you have already spent."

I should have known this was all too good to be true. I should have known.

What had I done, accepting a fortune that wasn't rightfully mine?

"I have children," the woman said. "My husband broke his leg and can't work."

Mr. Sullivan said, "Her father didn't approve of the marriage. That was the reason for the estrangement and why she allowed her father to think she was dead. But her claim to the fortune is legitimate. She is the daughter, and you are only the niece. I hope you understand, Miss Robbins."

"I've got children to feed," the woman insisted.

Was this young woman my cousin, my own uncle's daughter? I at once wanted to know her and wanted to believe she had a bit more civility than she seemed at this moment to possess. The expression on her face was a combination of resentment and defiance. With her rosy cheeks and nose, she also had the appearance of someone who'd had too much to drink already this morning. But I might be wrong about that, and I didn't want to falsely accuse her.

"I want to do the right thing," I said, still feeling a bit numb.

"Yes, of course, Miss Robbins, and it is the right thing to do to hand over the money to its rightful owner. You understand. You will be all right. You can go back to the school where you taught, or Lord Brookhaven might give you your old position as governess."

I felt sick. "I-I will need some time."

"Some time? Why, we can go to the bank right now. The sooner the better, for Mrs. Newman's sake and the sake of her young children. You don't want to keep a fortune that is not rightfully yours, Miss Robbins."

"I need a day or two. I will need to notify my staff and . . . and my guests, and we must remove our possessions . . ."

"If you must. But I shall return tomorrow morning to accompany you and Mrs. Newman to the bank to make the transfer. I pray you will not force Mrs. Newman to wait longer than that. And in the meantime, the less said about the matter, the better. You do not wish to look as if you are trying to keep a fortune that is not lawfully yours."

Mr. Sullivan stood up, and Mrs. Newman stood with him.

"It was very good to meet you, Mrs. Newman." I held out my hand to her. She placed hers limply in mine. "I hope that, as relatives, we might become friends as well."

The woman's smirk faltered. She stared back at me as though bewildered.

"Thank you for understanding and being civil in this matter," Mr. Sullivan was saying, hustling Mrs. Newman toward the door. "I will call again tomorrow."

I let the servant lead them out.

I sank down on the sofa. What was to become of all my plans now? And most importantly, what was to become of Sarah and Joshua?

I had to tell my servants as soon as possible so that they could try to make arrangements for another position. I hated that I could not even give them a few months' wages to help, since it might take them a while to find a new position. And I must tell Millicent and Hattie so they could make travel arrangements.

The worst part was, a decision had to be made about Joshua and Sarah. I couldn't just send them back onto the streets for the likes of that Gilbert White to prey upon. But I also didn't think

Mrs. Southey would allow me to bring them to her school. With my salary, I couldn't afford to pay for their room and board, and I didn't think Mrs. Southey was charity-minded enough to take on the expense herself. Besides, Joshua would be out of place in a school for young ladies.

Lady Derringer kept coming to mind. She'd seemed so full of wisdom yesterday, so interested in helping me with the orphanage.

Before I might change my mind, I put on my shawl and walked out the door, praying silently that Lady Derringer would still be at Lord Brookhaven's.

Twenty-Seven

So you see the predicament I'm in. Sarah and Joshua must have somewhere to go, and I must return the fortune to my uncle's daughter. It is all right, of course. I shall be all right. I am only unclear as to what to do for Joshua and Sarah."

If I were not so horrified and still a bit numb, I would have cried at the words I'd just spoken to Lady Derringer and Lord Brookhaven, for both of them were at home, and they both received me in Lord Brookhaven's drawing room.

The situation was humiliating. No doubt I would groan enough over it when I was back in Milford, just a poor spinster schoolteacher, remembering the weeks I'd spent in London as a wealthy heiress.

A pity I hadn't accepted one of the marriage proposals I'd so quickly rejected. It was a joke I repeated to myself. The irony was quite amusing—or would be, if I could feel anything.

But why was Lord Brookhaven looking as if all the blood had drained from his face? Was he so appalled that I should lose my fortune and be penniless once again?

"Yes, we must think what to do." Lady Derringer herself seemed quite alarmed as she stared pointedly at her nephew.

"That blackguard." Lord Brookhaven's voice was low but vicious.

"Who?" I asked.

I could see the muscles twitching in his jawline. But he remained silent.

"It wasn't my uncle's fault. He was trying to find his daughter," I said. "But according to Mr. Sullivan, she intentionally misled him to believe that she was dead."

"That woman is not the rightful heir," Lord Brookhaven said.

"But Mr. Sullivan said he investigated her claims and that she is—"

"She is not the daughter of your uncle."

"How do you know that?"

Lord Brookhaven spoke slowly but steadily. "I know it because you have no uncle."

"What do you mean? John Robert Robbins was my uncle."

"No."

Lady Derringer raised her brows at Lord Brookhaven, but he ignored her and looked me in the eye.

"You cannot give that woman your fortune because she isn't your uncle's daughter. And she isn't your uncle's daughter because your uncle never existed. I invented him. The fifty thousand pounds . . . actually came from me."

I studied Lord Brookhaven. Had he gone mad?

"What about Mr. Sullivan? What—?"

"Mr. Sullivan was acting on my behalf when he gave you the money. But now he is only trying to take advantage of your good nature to get the fifty thousand pounds for himself. He may give the woman a small fee, but . . . I never should have trusted him for this task."

"I don't understand. The money came from you? You gave me fifty thousand pounds?"

"I did."

"But . . ." It made no sense. "Why?"

He looked at his aunt. "Now you can say you told me so."

I stood up. I was confused, but I was angry too. "Were you making sport of me? Playing a game with my life?

"Never. I never . . ." Lord Brookhaven said. "Let me explain."

I wanted to hear his explanation, to understand how this made any sense, but at the same time, I could feel the flood of tears starting to sting my eyes. I turned and hurried from the room.

As I entered the hall, Lord Brookhaven caught me by the arm.

I kept my back to him while I wiped my face. I said, "Explain."

"I wanted . . . I wanted you to know what it was like to have a fortune of your own. I wanted you to be able to choose for yourself, to enjoy having the wherewithal to experience life in society. You had so few choices in life, and I wanted to give you that."

"But why? Was this some kind of . . . twisted entertainment? To see what I would do? To see what would happen?"

"No, not at all. I—"

"And why, pray tell? What would you have done if I had accepted Mr. Welton's marriage proposal, or Mr. Merritt's? Would you have sent Mr. Sullivan to me with a woman you had hired and told me that the rightful heir had just shown up? So that you could demand the fortune be returned to you and see if my fiancé would marry me anyway? Was that the plan?"

"No, of course not."

"There is no 'of course not,' for I never would have believed you capable of deceiving me with a fake uncle and a fake inheritance."

"The money was yours. You could do whatever you wished with it. I never planned to take it back. You weren't supposed to ever find out it came from me."

"I see."

I did not see.

"So you just gave me a fortune for no reason. You created a grand, elaborate scheme to give away a huge sum of money, and for what reason? I cannot imagine. How would you explain it? How?"

I was nearly hysterical, and I knew it was unbecoming, which was why I kept my face turned partially away from him and didn't look him in the eye. But he stepped in front of me.

"I am sorry if this has hurt you, but—"

"No, you are not allowed to say 'if this has hurt you.' You have no right." I was sobbing now. I felt embarrassed, but more than that, I felt manipulated and deceived.

He just stood there like a fish that had been caught and dragged onto dry land.

I pointed my finger at his face, not caring how rude it was. "I will return the fortune to you, every farthing. I am no one's plaything."

I stomped out the front door and walked home as fast as I could, my thoughts going every possible direction, feeling as if nothing made sense. Nothing. But now I knew that the large inheritance that I'd had such difficulty believing was real . . . wasn't. And my hope of making a love match felt impossible now. And worst of all, I'd promised to keep Joshua and Sarah safe, and I could no longer keep that promise.

I couldn't possibly keep Lord Brookhaven's fifty thousand pounds. Why had he given me that fortune, why? At his own expense and the expense of his own heirs? He'd shown so little interest in me that I'd given up hope of him asking me to marry him.

That's not true. I knew deep down that was, in part, why I had rejected Mr. Welton, Mr. Merritt, and Lord Markeley. I'd been hoping that Lord Brookhaven might love me. I'd flirted and danced with other men, but he was the one I was thinking of.

And now I couldn't stand the thought of seeing him again.

Finally, I reached my own door—although it wouldn't be my door for much longer. I stepped inside and raced up the stairs to my room to cry in peace.

Over and over in my head came the words, *No one will love me now.* And, *What will become of Joshua and Sarah, after I promised to give them a home?*

This was an unmitigated disaster. What had he been thinking, giving her that fortune?

William paced back and forth in the drawing room, Lady Derringer looking on.

"I know you don't want to hear this, but I did tell you something like this would happen."

The only thing saving Lady Derringer's life right now was that she looked distraught, because if she'd looked snide or triumphant . . .

"Not helpful," he said.

Lady Derringer sighed. "Well, there is only one thing to do."

He glared at her. He would not ask. Even though he secretly hoped she would tell him, since he didn't trust his own judgment, nor did he have any ideas.

"You must court her."

"Court her?" What hope did he have now of ever winning her heart? She must hate him. She was so angry with him, and rightly so.

"Yes. That is, if you want a woman who is full of Christian charity and compassion for the poor, a lady who has refused the marriage proposals of gentlemen simply because she didn't love them and they weren't in love with her. She hasn't squandered her fortune—your fortune—and if you don't want to lose her, you had better show her that you can give her what she wants."

"And what does she want?" It was irritating to hear Lady Derringer sounding so certain of what he wasn't certain of at all.

"Isn't it obvious?"

"No."

"She wants love, William."

He thought about her face just minutes ago. Her voice, how distraught she had been. Her tears. What a despicable man he was to cause her such pain. He thought he was giving her choices, but what she wanted was love.

"Can you give her that?" Lady Derringer asked.

Could he? He could give her money and status, but . . . he'd thought he was incapable of loving anyone again after Letitia had run off with the marquess. He'd been in so much pain. And he felt such humiliation, his pride injured for all to see. How could he have been so mistaken in her character, in her love for him? She hadn't loved him at all, but he'd been convinced she did. He was sure she was the pure, guileless, worthy girl she seemed to be. And though he couldn't admit it, he was afraid of being fooled again. He could not, would not be fooled again.

But how foolish would he look now, for people would surely hear of his elaborate ruse to give Miss Robbins fifty thousand pounds?

Lady Derringer had warned him.

"Well? Can you?" Lady Derringer was waiting for an answer.

He was glad he hadn't confided in anyone else but his aunt, and he might as well continue to be honest with her. "I don't know if I can love her as she deserves, but I do love her. I just don't think . . ." He fell silent.

"What will you do now?" Lady Derringer asked.

"I'll write her a letter."

She raised her brows. "I hope you make it a good one."

"I don't know if she will ever forgive me for deceiving her."

"I suppose this just proves that it wasn't money she wanted." Lady Derringer tilted her head, a cocky tone in her voice.

He went to his room, took out paper, pen, and ink, and started to write.

Before he could get more than a sentence written on his letter, a note arrived from Charlotte Robbins.

Lord Brookhaven,

Please advise me on how I can transfer the balance from my account to yours, as I do not trust my 'solicitor' Mr. Sullivan.

Miss Robbins

His heart sank. For some reason, the fact that she didn't sign her first name to the note made his heart feel as heavy as a stone.

Lady Derringer was right. This proved that it hadn't been money that she wanted, and it proved she had enough integrity to not accept his money.

Charlotte Robbins was not like other young ladies, the ones he'd known his whole life. She'd listened to him and said things he hadn't even known he'd been longing to hear. She'd been intelligent, intuitive, and thoughtful. She was a competent and capable teacher when she was with Samuel and Annabelle, but also was kind and enabled them to play and be children in a way he hadn't fully understood they needed.

He'd enjoyed her companionship, looking forward to talking with her every day on his walks. He felt compelled to understand her, but he also wanted his friends and the rest of society to accept her, which was why he decided to have a house party and invite her. Perhaps he also wanted to see how she would conduct herself, but what he'd found was that his friends had conducted themselves very poorly, while Charlotte Robbins had been everything he could have wanted.

Why hadn't he just told her he loved her and wanted to marry her? But he was afraid of being that vulnerable, especially now when she was so angry with him.

But he needed to write the letter quickly, as he had to go and deal with Mr. Sullivan before much more time had passed, so he wrote the letter and took it to her house on the way. Mr. Sullivan was no doubt packing as many of his belongings as he could carry to take with him to France or Italy or wherever he was fleeing to.

Twenty-Eight

My hand shook a bit as I opened the letter that the servant said Lord Brookhaven had just delivered himself.

Dear Miss Robbins,

You must think it very odd that I gifted you fifty thousand pounds and equally odd that I invented a dead relative to disguise the fact that the fortune was from me. Perhaps it was ill-conceived, and perhaps I should not have done so. I certainly did not do it to upset you in any way, nor did I do it to trap or manipulate you. But it was unfair of me to deceive you. I did, however, give you the fortune for your benefit, not intending for anyone to discover what I did, and the fortune is and always was for you to do with whatever you wish, and therefore I ask that you do not return it to me.

Also, it could not have been easy to have such a sudden gain in fortune but allow me to say that you have acquitted yourself very well.

Yours respectfully,
Brookhaven

What was I to make of it? This was no explanation at all!

I threw the letter on the floor, lay across my bed, and made a sound like a wild animal into my pillow.

The man was impossible!

What was it he had said? That it was unfair of him to deceive me? Well, at least he was right about that.

I got up and grabbed the letter off the floor and reread it.

It was intolerable. How could I endure his meddling in my life to such a degree, and for what? Why did he do it?

I sat at my little desk, grabbed a pen and paper, and started writing.

I am glad you realize that deceiving me was unfair. I hope you also realize it was demeaning, confusing, and cowardly.

I stared at the words. It was somewhat satisfying to write them, but it made my hand shake at the thought of him reading such words.

I tore that paper into pieces and took up another.

Dear Lord Brookhaven,

I am bewildered by your actions. I do not know what they mean. But I shall be returning your fortune to you forthwith, with or without your consent or cooperation, and I thank you for the enlightening experience.

Perhaps it was wrong to use sarcasm. I sighed, ripped that paper in half, threw it in the bin, and took up another sheet.

I realize I have you and Lady Derringer to thank for introducing me to your social set in London. But what I appreciated most was your friendship. I had thought you and I were good friends when I was your siblings' governess in Berkshire. I very much enjoyed our talks, and I've missed them since I left Lowndesbury House. I am sad that things have turned out this way between us, sorry that you didn't cherish our friendship as I did. I have wanted to know your thoughts during these last weeks while I've been in London, but you were distant and didn't talk with me as you had before. But now I realize I didn't know you at all. You were someone who would invent an elaborate ruse to observe me as if I were an exotic animal to be studied. It is intolerable.

I was going in a direction I didn't want to go in accusing him, and what would that accomplish other than venting my anger?

I took a deep breath and thought about what I wanted to say before continuing—and my tears dripped onto the paper as I wrote.

I thought perhaps there was some affection between us, something tender and beautiful, but obviously I was wrong. I admired your mind, the way you thought and felt about the world and God and people. You were honest and kind and seemed capable of great feeling, openly sharing your thoughts with me. But I am not sure if that was the true person I was seeing, or if the true person is the one who would deceive me into thinking I had an uncle who loved me enough to leave me his fortune. My heart is broken to think that they are one and the same person.

However, I am most sorry for what will happen to my servants, who were depending on me, and to Joshua and Sarah, who didn't deserve to lose their only security in life. You owe it to me and to them to make sure they are taken care of. I hope you will make a plan to do so, since I will no longer be able to.

Yours sincerely,
Charlotte Robbins

Perhaps I shouldn't have spoken so freely, but there was something satisfying in airing my feelings, in seeking to be understood. At least as long as I could believe that he understood.

I sent the letter by a servant. Only a minute later, before he could have even received and read my letter, I received a note from Lord Brookhaven.

If you choose not to keep the fortune as you have asserted, Joshua and Sarah will be taken care of. Lady Derringer will convey the plan and some particulars to you before the day is over.

The brevity of the note sent a pain through my heart. But of course, he hadn't yet seen the way I'd poured out my heart and spoke of my feelings for him. It was difficult, but I had to push those thoughts away and concentrate on the very happy fact that he had promised to take care of Joshua and Sarah.

It was time to tell Millicent, Hattie, and Mrs. Drake that the fortune was no longer mine and that we must vacate the premises as soon as possible.

I found Millicent and Hattie alone in the sitting room. Thankfully Mrs. Drake was elsewhere, and I told them a shortened version of everything that had happened. I might regret it later, but I felt I needed to be completely honest with them.

They were both shocked but said very little.

"Please do not tell Mrs. Drake the truth about where the fortune originated. She is not likely to be discreet, and I'd rather people not imagine evil things about Lord Brookhaven and me. I will tell her about Mr. Sullivan and the woman coming and saying that the daughter of my uncle is alive and is demanding the fortune be given to her, as the rightful heir. All of which did happen."

They both nodded, and I went to find Mrs. Drake. I told her as quickly as possible and took my leave before she could express thoughts and opinions that would only make me feel worse.

William rode his horse the fastest way to get to Sullivan's home. He still wasn't sure what he would do. He couldn't take him by the neck and choke him, which was what he'd imagined doing, but he also didn't want to wait for the constable. He'd confront the man himself.

It was a poor plan. He realized this before he even reached his address. If he confronted the man, told him he knew what he'd done, Sullivan would be on the next ship to the Continent, or even to America. He would escape justice.

William turned his horse around and went to find the constable, Beckwith. He told him only that Sullivan had tried to trick Miss Robbins out of her fortune.

He could have told Beckwith that Sullivan owed him two thousand pounds and that he wanted the man thrown in jail for swindling him. But if Sullivan went to trial, he would no doubt make it known that William had blackmailed him into deceiving Miss Robbins.

Beckwith immediately rounded up two of his stoutest men.

Together, the four men went to Mr. Sullivan's address and knocked on the door. No one answered. They knocked again. When Beckwith tried the door, it was unlocked. They went inside, the constable's two men going around to the back door.

They called out, "Anyone here?" but there was no sound.

William and Beckwith rummaged around, opening cupboards and drawers, closets and cabinets. Sullivan's clothing had been cleared out, the silver was gone, and the servants appeared to have cleaned out their spaces as well.

"He's hiding out somewhere," William said. "And he's probably got someone watching the house right now. Let's go. Come. Now." He waved at the other men, and they quickly left the house.

When they were back at Beckwith's home, the constable said, "Our only hope is that he didn't see us raid his house. We'll wait at Miss Robbins's home tomorrow morning for him, and if he keeps his appointment, we'll apprehend him there."

Which is what he should have done. This had been a mistake, all because he wanted to confront the man himself.

William nodded grimly. He thanked the men for their time, then went to speak to the Bow Street Runners. If Sullivan was still in England, perhaps they could find him.

When he returned home, he found Miss Robbins's letter.

His heart sank lower with every paragraph. It lifted a bit when he saw the words, *I thought perhaps there was some affection between us, something tender and beautiful*, but it sank lower than ever as he read, *but obviously I was wrong.*

He'd ruined everything. How could he hope that she would ever trust him again?

The servants were busy packing up everyone's belongings. Millicent and Hattie were also rushing around making sure they had everything for their trips home, while Mrs. Drake was always underfoot, clicking her tongue against her teeth and saying things like, "I suppose now you wish you had accepted one of the perfectly good marriage proposals. Perhaps Mr. Welton will still have you." Or, "I wonder that Mr. Sullivan made such a mistake as to not find the rightful heir before giving you the fortune." And, "Far be it from me to give advice, but you should return half of the young woman's fortune and tell her you will keep the other half for your trouble."

"Mrs. Drake, don't you have your own packing to do?"

"Already done. I had an idea that I wouldn't be here long, so most of my things were still in my trunks."

In the midst of this slightly chaotic activity, a servant announced that Mr. Welton was asking to speak to me.

I sighed and was about to say I didn't have time to see him, but Mrs. Drake, who was behind me, said, "Show him into the sitting room. She'll be down in a moment."

When the servant was gone, I gave Mrs. Drake a severe look.

"You need to hear what he has to say, now that you have no fortune."

"Did you send for him?"

"I may have sent him a note, but he came on his own. See how much in love he is with you?"

I huffed out a breath and marched down to the sitting room, leaving the door open for propriety's sake.

Mr. Welton was smiling as he slid to the floor on his knees. "Miss

Robbins, won't you please reconsider my proposal to adore you all the days of your life? Please say you will marry me."

I stared hard at him. "What is going on with you and Mrs. Drake?"

A look flitted across his face as he averted his eyes, his smile all but gone. "Wha—what? She is my mother's friend, nothing more."

"Tell me, or so help me, I shall—"

"Very well. I was so in love with you that I asked for her help in seeking your hand. But that is all. I swear, there was nothing more than that between us. You must believe me."

"Did you promise her something for her help?" That would make sense, as she'd been so bent on me marrying him. "Did you give her money?"

"No, no."

I put my hands on my hips and glared down at him, feeling almost like a mother scolding a child.

He made my mental image seem even more real as he looked sheepish and said, "Very well. You are much too clever, Miss Robbins. You have found me out." He paused a moment to take a deep breath and let it out. "I did offer her money if she was able to help me secure your acceptance of my proposal, and I told her she could have the cottage at my estate, as my mother's friend, when I came into my inheritance. But it was only because I loved you so dearly, Miss Robbins."

Or at least loved my money dearly.

"Won't you please say yes, Miss Robbins, and make me the happiest man in England?"

I pressed my hand to my forehead and took a few deep breaths, praying silently, *Lord God, help me.*

"You do know that I no longer have a fortune, do you not? Did Mrs. Drake tell you that?"

"She told me you were planning to give it to your uncle's daughter, but you don't need to do that. Marry me and I will have my solicitors take her to court. I am sure that you will get to keep most, if not all, of the money." He leaned forward, an earnest look on his face. "Let me guide you in this, Miss Robbins. I can help."

I made a mighty effort not to roll my eyes heavenward and said, "I am flattered by your attentions, Mr. Welton, and I thank you for your offer, but I must decline. Please do not ask me again. Good day."

And with that, I left the room to his sputtering behind me, "B-but, w-wait. Miss Robbins?"

I tried to go back to packing but ended up in my room, my forehead against the closed door, whispering, "God, please help me. Give me peace and wisdom. Please."

A gentle knock came at my door. I was just able to take a step back before a servant opened the door.

"Miss Robbins, forgive me." She looked startled, either because I was standing so close to the door, or because of the look on my face. "Lady Derringer is here to see you."

I didn't want to talk to Lady Derringer. I wanted to go to bed and hide my face. I would go back to Mrs. Southey and beg for my old teaching position and realize that adventures and experiences in the big world were not the pleasant things I had imagined them to be. I needed to be content in Milford with the lot God had given me.

But first I needed to ensure that Joshua and Sarah were taken care of.

I walked as regally as I could down the stairs to the sitting room.

"My dear." Lady Derringer looked at me with so much sympathy that tears sprung to my eyes.

I forced myself to think only about the most polite words of greeting, and soon the tears stopped threatening.

"I'm so sorry all this has happened this way," Lady Derringer said. "My nephew wished to come himself and talk with you, but . . . well, I could offer excuses, but that is for him to—"

"Let us not speak of him, if you don't mind. Please, won't you tell me what you have planned for Joshua and Sarah's care?"

"Yes, of course." She paused a moment. "Do you remember you spoke to me of an orphans' home where street children could go to school and be cared for? Well, why don't you remain in London and help start that very home? You can use part of the fifty thousand pounds. You could be the home's director."

She waited expectantly.

"I would like to help start a home for orphans," I said slowly, "but I intend to return the money to Lord Brookhaven, its rightful owner."

Lady Derringer smiled. "I am so glad to hear you say that you will help with the orphans' home."

I sighed. "I believe that some orphanages require children like Sarah and Joshua to have wealthy sponsors and to go through an application process. I would not want our home to require the children to have sponsors. I don't want to turn anyone away who needs a home."

"I also would not want to turn anyone away. But there is something I've been thinking about." She frowned a little before continuing. "I'm not sure we'll be able to house boys and girls together. Most homes separate them. And if we don't wish to turn anyone away, we will need a large place."

"I hadn't thought about that." I sighed again. This was to be a bigger undertaking than I'd originally thought.

"No need to worry. We will work out such details. But in the meantime, keep all your servants, and your guests are very welcome to stay as long as they'd like. It will take time to set everything up for the children, but we will certainly need servants."

She talked some more about possible donors for us to call on, some information we would need to provide for a permit, and I listened, but painful thoughts arose.

What would become of me? What would happen to my dream of being loved, of having a husband and children, a family of my own? Would I go my whole life without someone to love me?

I couldn't think like that. I'd immerse myself in this work of helping orphaned children, and that would be my joy and purpose. I'd forget about Lord Brookhaven.

I'd been so wrong about my fortune. In the beginning I'd thought it was supposed to help me feel powerful, in control of my future.

I'd thought the dancing and the socializing would bring me what I wanted most, a chance at happiness, an opportunity to find love and have a family.

But I'd been wrong, for the best thing it had brought me was a chance to make a difference in Joshua and Sarah's lives. I couldn't think about the fact that what I really wanted was to be a family with them, to take care of them myself, in my home.

And what was Lord Brookhaven's role to be in all of this? But I wouldn't think about him.

For now, I would follow Lady Derringer's advice, keep the money, keep my servants, and focus on starting a home for orphans. I would pour out my love on the children. It was enough. I could have a purpose in helping children grow up strong because they knew someone loved them. But eventually I'd have to return to Mrs. Southey's school.

Hattie decided to stay an extra day, but Millicent seemed eager to go.

The next morning, she said very little as I walked with her to the waiting carriage.

"I'm so sorry for how things turned out," I said.

Millicent only looked grave and said nothing. She'd barely said a word to me since I told her that the fortune had not come from an uncle but from Lord Brookhaven. I'd since regretted telling her that. I wanted to believe the best about her, but something told me that she wouldn't be discreet and would tell people what Lord Brookhaven had done. It was the sort of thing that would ruin my reputation, but that hardly mattered now, since I'd no longer be available for balls and assemblies and parties, and I'd eventually return to Milford.

"Have a safe trip home," I said. "Thank you for accepting my invitation. I very much enjoyed your company."

Millicent finally looked back at me as she climbed into the

carriage and sat down. "Thank you for your hospitality." She shut the door herself, and I lost sight of her face as the carriage rolled away.

My heart sank, my worst fears confirmed.

Hattie came to stand beside me, and she squeezed my arm.

Thank you, God, for Hattie. She'd been sympathetic, but I could see the horror in her eyes, the same horror and confusion I felt. But I set aside my own feelings and said, "I am truly sorry, Hattie, that you're having to cut your visit to London short."

"You don't need to keep apologizing. Besides, it is not your fault. But perhaps you can stay and run the orphanage."

"Yes, perhaps."

Dear, sweet Hattie. If only I could be as unencumbered with desires and selfish ambitions as Hattie seemed to be. If only I could have been content to teach at Mrs. Southey's school and not have advertised to be a governess, I wouldn't be feeling this pain in my heart right now.

It only took a moment to realize that I wasn't sorry I'd accepted the offer to become a governess for Lord Brookhaven. Though it had led to this pain and confusion, I wasn't sorry I'd met him. I'd seen a glimpse of his soul during our talks. I'd seen true feeling and warmth and sincerity, and it had meant more to me than almost anything else.

Now I would focus on helping others, Joshua and Sarah and all the other children whom God would allow me to help. Just as that verse in Scripture said, "For we are His workmanship, created in Christ Jesus for good works, which God prepared beforehand that we should walk in them."

Was this the work God had prepared for me? Or was I only grasping for something to make myself feel better?

Twenty-Nine

Since Mrs. Drake had gone, Gretchen and the footman accompanied the children and me on a walk, and we were setting out when we found Lord Brookhaven waiting on the sidewalk outside the door.

"May I walk with you?" He bowed.

"Of course."

The children greeted him with wide smiles.

So we set out, Sarah and Joshua, Gretchen, the footman, and Lord Brookhaven.

A group of men stood just across the street, one of whom was Henson. It occurred to me that they were probably waiting for Mr. Sullivan to show up and try to collect the fortune from me.

Lord Brookhaven was tall and well-built, with wide shoulders and a thick chest. A lady wasn't supposed to notice such things, but of course, ladies weren't blind just because they were ladies.

But I was still angry with him, angry and confused, and my mind kept going back to our last conversation when I'd cried tears of frustration and hurt over how he'd deceived me. And then there were the two letters—unacceptably brief letters—he'd sent. And now he thought he could simply take our morning walk with us?

Gretchen, probably realizing that Lord Brookhaven wished to speak to me, prodded the children along until they were several yards ahead of us and chattering excitedly about a group of geese that were pecking at the grass.

"I am aggrieved," Lord Brookhaven began without preface, "that what I intended to be a gift has caused you so much pain."

"It was the deception more than the actual gift that caused me pain."

"Yes. Quite right. It was very ill conceived, and I am sorry. I only hope that one day you can forgive me."

I said nothing. The contrary part of me hoped he sincerely meant the words, that he was very sorry, and that he was worried I might not forgive him.

"I also came to tell you that I had some men investigating Gilbert White. They were able to find evidence and witnesses to some of his thievery. He was apprehended early this morning, and the constable and barrister I spoke to say he will probably be sentenced to fourteen years and transported to Australia. It is the usual sentence for thefts of this kind."

Fourteen years was a long time, and very often, criminals sentenced to transportation to Australia never returned to England. And in fourteen years, Joshua and Sarah would be adults.

I should probably thank him for caring enough to make sure the man who threatened Joshua and Sarah would no longer be able to harm them—or me, for I was the person he had been threatening.

"And I hired some men who found that Mr. Sullivan has fled the country and gone to France, they believe. He will probably never be caught, unless he returns to Great Britain."

"And if he is caught and brought to trial," I said, thinking aloud, "I suppose it will become public knowledge that you gave me fifty thousand pounds of your own money. Perhaps it would be better if he was not caught." I said this with a touch of bitterness.

"Perhaps." He sighed. "I am very sorry, Miss Robbins. I realize my actions may possibly expose you to gossip, and you don't deserve that. I only hope that one day you can forgive me."

He was so contrite, I felt a pang of guilt for wanting to torment him.

After a few moments of silence, I said, "I do forgive you. And if you and Lady Derringer want to set up an orphanage with what is left of the fifty thousand pounds, then I am glad. I will not keep the money."

I wanted to ask if they would place Sarah and Joshua in the orphanage, if that was how they intended to make sure they were taken care of, but I knew it was.

"For now, as we are making plans and you are helping us set up the new orphanage, please continue on as you are."

What else could I do? I wasn't ready to leave Sarah and Joshua.

We walked along, listening to the children's chatter, and Joshua said, "Can Samuel and Annabelle come too?"

We doubled back to Lord Brookhaven's house to collect them. Suspiciously, they were already dressed and ready to go to the park.

They greeted me, with Annabelle embracing me, and we continued on our way.

When the children were all distracted and talking with one another, I asked Lord Brookhaven, "Were you planning to take Samuel and Annabelle to the park?"

"I was hoping you and Joshua and Sarah would ask for them to accompany us, but if you didn't, I was planning to take them myself."

I glanced at him from the corner of my eye. How I wished he loved me.

But the very next moment, anger replaced the longing. Why had he given me fifty thousand pounds, making me believe it was an inheritance? And why encourage me to come to London and establish myself in society? It was so confounding. *He* was so confounding.

Sarah stopped. "This is where I first saw you, when you went with me to help Joshua."

It was the very spot.

Two big tears spilled from her eyes.

"What's the matter?" I carefully knelt in front of her.

Sarah's chin trembled, then her lip. She shook her head.

I held out my arms to her and she relaxed into me. We stood there embracing each other, and I had to make a huge effort to keep my own tears from falling. Being able to comfort her seemed to heal something inside *me*.

The other children came near. Annabelle put an arm around Sarah, and Joshua and Samuel patted her on the back.

Sarah pushed herself out of my arms as she took a deep breath, which seemed to dry up the tears. Lord Brookhaven was watching us.

"All will be well," he said. "You will never be alone again. Miss Robbins, Lady Derringer, and I will make sure of that."

Sarah nodded. Then she took Joshua's hand, and we continued walking toward the park.

The children played blindman's buff and hide-and-seek, and Lord Brookhaven and I watched.

After half an hour, I asked, "Why did you do it?" I tried to keep an even tone, without accusation. "I just want to know."

"I wanted to give you choices. I wanted you to know what it was like to be able to do what you wanted in life."

I sat and pondered his words, directing my gaze to the children and their game, but not really seeing them. Why would he want to give me choices?

I was about to ask him, but just then, Joshua fell and Sarah cried out, "Joshua, you need to be more careful" in her best older-sister tone. "Do you want your arm to grow back crooked?"

As they raised their voices at each other, I wondered if I should intervene, but Gretchen began talking quietly to them, and soon they stopped arguing and started playing again.

Annabelle came over and looked pleadingly at Lord Brookhaven. "Can Joshua and Sarah come home with us?"

"It is all right with me," Lord Brookhaven said, "but you'll have to ask Miss Robbins."

The other children came running up to ask the same thing.

"Yes, it's all right, but you can't be arguing."

"We won't," they all chorused.

"I think they're ready for their tea," Gretchen said with a matronly smile. I couldn't help wondering if she'd be willing to share her mothering ways with a whole orphanage full of children.

We started on our way home, and I noticed Joshua's eyelids were heavy and his feet were starting to drag. He wasn't used to walking and running so much.

A minute later, Joshua stumbled. Without a word, Lord Brookhaven scooped him up, carrying him in his arms.

Sarah and Annabelle held hands and talked to Samuel as we went, the footman and Gretchen trailing the children.

The next week was a whirlwind of activity, accompanying Lady Derringer and Lord Brookhaven to call on various wealthy Londoners who might be interested in helping to start an orphanage and school.

One day, Lord Brookhaven, Lady Derringer, and I were having tea and discussing what we needed to do to secure a second building to house boys. I was secretly thinking that I couldn't bear to separate Sarah and Joshua. It felt cruel to do so.

"There is a building close to the docks," Lord Brookhaven was saying, "that might be suitable for the boys. But Lady Derringer knows a clergyman who has started an orphanage in his parish, not too far from here. He has a rather dilapidated building. It needs work, but it's large. The only problem is funds."

"We were thinking," Lady Derringer said, setting down her teacup, "that we might be able to work with him, fundraising and otherwise. He already has the necessary permits. His name is Gabriel Johnson, and he's agreed to meet with us tomorrow."

"Very good." It would save us some time and effort if we could join with him. But I had a nagging feeling that kept me from expressing enthusiasm.

As I was leaving, Lord Brookhaven helped me with my jacket. It was a simple service, something a brother might do for his sister. But when I looked up to thank him, his face was so close I could see the flecks in his blue eyes.

He didn't turn away, didn't even blink, for a long moment. I wanted him to speak. I wanted it so badly my heart seemed to stop beating.

"I will see you tomorrow," he said softly.

I took a step toward the door and looked away before hurrying out the door.

"William? The servant has just shown Mr. Johnson into the sitting room."

"He's early." William straightened his coat and turned to follow Lady Derringer.

From down the hall, he could see Charlotte entering the sitting room. Lady Derringer was probably introducing them.

William came in just in time to see Mr. Johnson looking smitten as he stared at Charlotte with a slack jaw.

William cleared his throat. It obviously startled him.

His aunt introduced them, and they sat. He eyed Mr. Johnson, then realized he hadn't smiled at Charlotte yet.

"Lord Brookhaven." She gave him an intense look. Had she read his thoughts?

Mr. Johnson shared the history of his involvement in rescuing orphans from the streets of London. He sounded quite noble—too noble. Indeed, he was so proud of what he had accomplished, it bordered on arrogance. Surely Charlotte would see through his braggadocious speech.

And surely she wouldn't think him handsome, though he did have the blond hair, small nose, and fair skin that women often liked.

Mr. Johnson looked almost exclusively at Charlotte as he talked. She was especially pretty today, wearing a pink and blue frock that set off her blue eyes and the color of her skin, the pink of her cheeks. For her part, she seemed to hang on his every word.

William was sunk.

Would she break his heart just like Letitia did?

But Charlotte was nothing like Letitia. Charlotte was good and kind and compassionate, and she would never marry someone just for their name or title or fortune—which meant she might marry this Mr. Johnson. She was truly too good for William, for he had deceived her, given her a fortune under false pretenses, and then left her alone and refused to tell her he loved her, letting her be preyed upon by every fortune-seeking blackguard in London. He'd ruined everything with his hesitation and with thinking she needed a fortune for society to accept her.

Perhaps he did have a mother who had scarred his heart in ways that had shaped him into this morose, melancholy half-monster, half-man. Perhaps his first love had betrayed and rejected him. But that did not mean he needed to punish Charlotte—or himself, for that matter.

No, she deserved someone like this Johnson, if he was sincere in his sentiments and desire to help poor orphan children.

But what if she had loved him? She'd told him of her feelings in her letter, but she'd since been quite cold to him.

How could he blame her? He'd been too afraid to express his own feelings for her, to reciprocate her expressions of affection. And now . . . he wasn't sure he could bear it if she rejected him.

The pain of being rejected by Letitia was still so fresh. He could still feel the desire to erase his own existence, even though he realized he was better for having lost her. But Charlotte Robbins . . . she was a true woman of virtue, and to lose her would hurt so much more than losing Letitia. Morose, melancholy creature that he was, he wasn't sure he'd survive it.

"Lord Brookhaven?" Everyone was looking at him.

Lady Derringer spoke up. "Will you be able to accompany us to

Mr. Johnson's Home for Orphan Boys in Cheapside tomorrow at two o'clock?"

"Yes, of course."

"Good, it is all settled. We shall meet you there tomorrow, Mr. Johnson," Lady Derringer said.

Mr. Johnson bowed to her and then he took Charlotte's hand and bent over it, looking her in the eyes.

The blighter didn't miss a trick.

As soon as he was gone, Charlotte said, "I must go as well. I promised to take the children to the park and teach them to play pall mall." She turned and looked at William. "Would you like to accompany us?"

"That sounds . . . pleasant."

Charlotte turned to his aunt. "Lady Derringer? Would you like to come?"

"No thank you, my dear. I believe I have a headache coming on."

When Charlotte turned to go, his aunt gave him a stern look, then a wink.

Lady Derringer was incorrigible. But at least she was discreet.

"We shall come by in half an hour." Charlotte gazed up at him.

"I shall be ready."

Just like the day before, William ended up carrying little Joshua most of the way home from the park.

He was hard-pressed not to laugh as he watched Charlotte Robbins fending off the many questions the children asked her and making sure they stayed close to her and Gretchen. Joshua had his splint taken off that morning, now that his arm was declared healed, which had seemed to give him more energy, more daring, and made him express himself more loudly. In short, he ran around as if he'd just been released from prison.

Not much instruction in the art of pall mall was given, but the children seemed to enjoy hitting the ball for a while, then started running around in circles, chasing one another and laughing. He occupied himself with watching them—and watching Miss Robbins.

And when Joshua especially had exhausted himself, William picked him up and carried him home, the other three children walking much slower than before.

Perhaps it was due to the presence of the children, but no one seemed to recognize him. He actually made it to and from the park without anyone trying to speak to him.

He helped Charlotte get the children into the house, and when Samuel, Annabelle, and Sarah all ran up to the playroom and when Joshua still didn't move, William realized he had fallen asleep on his shoulder.

Charlotte smiled. "I'll take him."

"I can put him to bed if you show me the way."

Charlotte nodded and led him to a bedroom upstairs with two little beds side by side. He laid Joshua in the first one, surprised he didn't wake up, and Charlotte covered him with the blanket. Before they could leave the room, Sarah came in and kissed her brother on the cheek.

Charlotte closed the door quietly and whispered, "They each have their own bed, but they sleep curled up together like kittens." She smiled, and he thought she'd never looked more beautiful.

As they walked down the stairs, she said, "Thank you. I'm sorry you ended up having to carry Joshua."

"I didn't mind. It reminds me of when Annabelle and Samuel were younger."

Charlotte had such a sweet look. He wanted to pull her into his arms and—

"Miss Robbins!" Sarah ran down the stairs toward them.

She pressed her finger to her lips. "What is it?"

Sarah began chattering about how the footman had promised to make Joshua a slingshot, if Miss Robbins allowed it. "But isn't that dangerous?"

"We shall talk about it later. We must not be rude to our guest, Lord Brookhaven."

Sarah looked at William, and he winked at her. "Not to worry. I'll see Miss Robbins tomorrow."

"Yes, tomorrow." She smiled, but her eyes looked rather tired as well.

If she was his wife, he would kiss her cheek and tell her he'd attend to everything while she went to rest.

"Miss Robbins." The housekeeper hurried toward them. "The landlord's steward is here to see you. He says it's urgent."

"Oh." She looked at him.

"Shall I stay and see what he wants?"

"You don't mind?"

"Not at all."

They went to meet him in her drawing room. He was a tall man with thin lips and a solemn face.

"I am the solicitor for the owner of this townhouse, Mr. Cunningham, and he has heard that you intend to turn this home into a school for orphans. He wishes me to convey to you that he will never allow an orphanage on his property. He will oppose any plan of the sort, and he wishes you to know so that you can vacate the premises and find a suitable building elsewhere."

"Who told you such a thing?" William demanded.

The man didn't reply immediately, his mouth opening and closing. Then he said, "It is the rumor on the street, sir."

Charlotte's face had gone pale, and she stared at the man, unblinking. A moment later, she straightened her shoulders and said, "You may tell Mr. Cunningham that I will stay here as long as I like, according to our agreement as written in my lease, and that I have no intention of turning this house into an orphanage."

The man was silent for a moment before replying, "Very good, Miss Robbins. I shall tell him." He stood and said, "Good day."

When the solicitor was gone, William waited for her to speak.

She let out a long breath, folded her arms in front of her, and said, "Well, I suppose I should have foreseen that, taking in two children off the street."

"How could you have known?"

She rubbed her forehead, looking more exhausted than ever.

"Are you all right?"

"Only a bit tired." She sighed again. "I shall see you tomorrow, then?"

"Yes, tomorrow."

Thirty

The next day, as the three of us rode in Lord Brookhaven's carriage, I thought about the need, the many children with no home, no safe place or safe people on whom they could depend. It was overwhelming.

I was a girl who daydreamed and created stories in my head, and I loved teaching. I wasn't a director of an orphanage, an organizer, or political figure. I never imagined being in charge of a dozen adults or a hundred children. I didn't want to disappoint anyone, but I wasn't sure I could be what they all seemed to expect me to be. But wasn't this all my idea?

The truth was, I'd rather be at home playing games with Joshua and Sarah, Samuel and Annabelle, making sure they were happy and well taken care of. After all they'd been through in their young lives, I just wanted to see them joyful and healthy.

But wasn't it good and right to save as many children from the street as I could? Lady Derringer and Lord Brookhaven were helping me, so I wasn't all on my own.

Mr. Johnson met us at the entrance of his home for boys, greeting us warmly and taking us on a tour of his facility.

"As you can see," Mr. Johnson said, "we have space that is not being used. We just need more funds to make the south and east wings of the building livable—repairing the roof and the windows, mostly. And then we will need the additional funds to hire more staff and provide food and necessities for the new boys."

"Do you use an application system for admitting the children?"

"No." Mr. Johnson looked even more serious. "We do have a waiting list, since we don't have the availability because of lack of funds to admit every boy who comes to us, but they are admitted on a first-come basis. No one is excluded because he couldn't get enough votes." By the expression on his face, he disapproved of the practice.

"If you don't mind my asking," I said, "what made you get involved in starting a home for orphaned boys?"

"You might well wonder, as I grew up a younger son of the Baron of Glenwood—spoiled and rather unruly, if I'm honest. I always intended to make the church my profession, but I was put off by the hypocritical clergy I met. I saw them as not particularly pious, too lazy for good deeds, and seeking an easy life. Forgive me, but this was my observation. I decided to go to London and seek out the greatest need, and I found it when I saw all the children begging. If there was ever a plight that needed to be addressed, it was that of the children living on the streets. I have no very good opinion of any so-called man of God who could ignore orphans in need."

I did agree, but there was something rote about the way he told the story, as if he'd written it down and memorized it.

But far be it from me to judge Mr. Johnson. He was certainly doing good work, housing these boys, some as young as three years old, who would otherwise have nowhere to go. And with winter coming in a few months, I imagined the gusty, cold winds and the first snowstorm.

Thank you, God, I prayed silently, *that I was able to bring Sarah and Joshua safely into my home.* In my mind I saw them shivering in the cold, with no one to care for them or feed them or give them warm clothes. No fire to sit beside when the snow began to fall, their little cheeks red and chapped, their toes turning dark with frostbite.

Tears pricked my eyes, and I shook myself mentally to drive those thoughts away as Lady Derringer spoke to Mr. Johnson about his patrons and donors and the monetary amount it would take to get the rest of the building equipped to house children.

Lady Derringer also asked about buildings he might know of that we might consider in our search for a home for girls. And before I knew it, we had a tentative agreement with Mr. Johnson to partner with him. He'd be in charge of the boys' home, and we would work toward getting a girls' home prepared.

We observed the boys going through their day, groups of them being instructed in various trades. The younger ones were led to the dining hall, one woman leading ten little ones, around four years old. One of them was crying but no one seemed to take any notice. Again, tears welled in my eyes. Was I to put Joshua here? And was Sarah to be housed in a similar place? How could I bear it?

Oh, I knew they were better off here than on the street. But this . . . this wasn't what I wanted. I wanted them with me, in my home, where I could watch over them and be sure they were well and happy, where I could wipe away their tears and make sure they didn't feel lonely or left out or ignored.

But I was no longer an heiress, a woman of fortune who could do what she wished, including taking in and providing for orphan children. I'd have no choice but to put my sweet little Joshua and Sarah in an orphanage.

I thought of how my heart ached when I caught sight of Lord Brookhaven carrying little Joshua in his arms and how tenderly he'd carried him to his bed and laid him there, cradling his head until it rested on the pillow. My mind had flown to thoughts of him as my husband, and the children as our children, along with Samuel and Annabelle.

Sometimes, the way he looked at me, I was sure he felt as I did, that he wanted me as much as I wanted him. Then why didn't he ask me to marry him? No, I must be mistaken. Besides, even if he did wish to marry me, he probably wouldn't wish to adopt orphans who were wholly unrelated to him. He was an earl, after all.

Lady Derringer seemed to have a new person for us to meet every day, and often we went with Mr. Johnson to speak to various wealthy donors and influential people. One evening we went to a dinner party with Mr. Johnson, where one of his largest donors, Lady Creekmore, had gathered some of her friends to hear a presentation.

"And you may be asked to say a few words about the girls' home," Lady Derringer had said.

"Me? I wouldn't know what to say." Surely they wouldn't want me to speak to a roomful of strangers when we did not even have a building yet.

"Who better to do it than you? You have already taken in two children. There is no one as passionate as you are about helping the orphan children of London."

"But . . . you should do it, Lady Derringer. You have more experience speaking in front of ladies and gentlemen."

"Never mind about that. You will do very well. You are young and pretty." She smiled in a conspiratorial way.

Lord Brookhaven, who was standing nearby but who I hoped wasn't listening, turned and glared at Lady Derringer. She paid no attention to him at all.

Mr. Johnson was sober and serious, as usual, and I began to wonder if he ever laughed. He seemed to pay quite a lot of attention to me. And when we gave him a ride in our carriage back to the boys' home where he lived in a single room on the topmost floor, he asked me quite a few questions about where I grew up and what I had done since coming to London.

Meanwhile, Lord Brookhaven sat in the corner of the carriage with a scowl on his face.

Well, he couldn't object. He didn't want me. He might as well let someone else ask me enough questions to decide whether or not he wished to marry me. For that was just what I suspected Mr. Johnson was doing.

Sure enough, the next day, Mr. Johnson came during calling hours. I was surprised, as no one ever called on me now that it was known that I was no longer in possession of a fortune.

I had tea with him in the sitting room, asking my poor housekeeper, Mrs. Bingham, to keep us company, since I no longer had a chaperone. We talked of the children, mostly, and I asked him about his childhood. It could hardly have been more different from mine, since he'd had a mother who constantly worried about him and followed him around.

"And how does she feel about your work here in London with the children?" I asked.

"She thinks it is something I will tire of and will leave London and find some country parish to settle down in. But of course you understand, Miss Robbins, that this is the work that I have chosen to do for my entire life. I don't intend to ever do anything else."

I nodded as if I did indeed understand, but for the last few weeks, I'd realized more and more that I truly did not wish to spend my life in an orphanage, overseeing scores or even hundreds of children, never feeling as if I was giving any one of them enough attention or love.

"Miss Robbins, I know that you will make a wonderful wife," Mr. Johnson was saying. "And because of your charitable heart and work, I know that you shall make me, in particular, an excellent wife. And that is why I ask you to marry me, to join with me in doing God's work here in London, so that we may encourage each other in this good work that God has planned for us to do."

It was the Bible verse that I had quoted to myself when I decided I was meant to help the orphaned children of London. Was it a sign that indeed I was meant to marry the clergyman Gabriel Johnson?

"I think . . . I need to think about it."

Mrs. Bingham was bent over the mending in her lap, pretending to work, her face bright red.

"You would have your own home," he went on. "I'd find a place—not as grand as this but adequate—for ourselves and the children

God would bless us with in the future. But you don't have to give me an answer now. Consider it carefully, but more importantly, pray for God to show you his will. You will come to the same conclusion I have come to, which is that God has brought you here for such a time as this, so that we might serve him together."

When he left, I went up to my room and knelt beside my bed to pray. But every time I tried to imagine being married to Mr. Johnson, a pervasive sadness washed over me. I imagined spending every day among a sea of children being herded here and there. I imagined my husband coming home late and leaving early, telling me that we were doing God's will and must ignore our own desires. I imagined feeling as if I mattered very little to my husband, that his work would always be more important to him than I was.

God, is that what you want from me? Do you want me to lay down my life for London's orphans?

But how could I bear to see them needing comfort and love and receiving instead only food and clothing and shelter? Wanting to save them all just made me feel overwhelmed and despondent. Worse, the thought of leaving my Sarah and Joshua in a large group home made my heart feel as if it was breaking in two. But perhaps Mr. Johnson would agree to allow them to live in our home and I could still be their mother.

Lord Brookhaven's face rose unbidden in my thoughts, and I imagined us at Lowndesbury House, the children around us, running and playing and laughing.

If God wanted me to marry Gabriel Johnson and dedicate my life to housing the orphans of London, then that was what I must do. But would I be able to forget Lord Brookhaven?

William was on his way from his tailors' when a lady stepped out of a shop just in front of him.

"Oh. Lord Brookhaven." Letitia—Lady Wexford—stood grinning at him. She was so close he couldn't avoid her.

"Good morning," he said, tipping his hat to her. He made as if to walk around her, but she placed her hand on his arm. He pulled his arm away and took a step back.

"Cannot we speak for a moment?" She sounded innocent, but he knew not to trust her.

"What do you want?"

People were walking all around them, one or two of them turning to look. He would need to get this over with as quickly as possible.

"Don't be uncivil," she said, poking out her bottom lip as if she were a child. "I merely wanted to put you on your guard. I have heard the gossips saying that you have made Miss Charlotte Robbins your paramour—that the fifty-thousand-pound fortune she inherited was not inherited at all, but that you gave her that exorbitant sum. Of course I told them they were mistaken, for if you had made her your paramour, then one of your own closest friends would not have asked the woman to marry them. There. You are welcome for my kind assistance."

He glared at her. Words bubbled to the surface. It took all his willpower to hold them in check. But his brief silence seemed to give her permission to continue.

"I do hope we can be friends. Surely you have forgiven me by now. In fact, you are most welcome to come to see me in Mayfair. Lord Wexford is away in the country for a few days, and I've been a bit . . . lonely." She leaned toward him.

He shouldn't have been surprised by her words. Perhaps he should even have expected her to say something of the kind. Nevertheless, speech failed him, and he only mumbled, "Good day."

He walked briskly away, feeling as though he had just escaped being trampled by a runaway horse and carriage.

As he walked, it was as if a thick London fog had lifted and what had been obscured for years was suddenly clear. He'd been so bitter about how Letitia had treated him, her betrayal and deception when she'd professed undying love for him, her utter disregard for his feelings, that he'd let it cloud his judgment and keep him from happiness.

How could he have even compared Letitia to Charlotte? There was no comparison. One was cold and cruel and the other was everything good and kind and empathetic.

He nearly laughed as he quickened his pace. He had to plan what he would say, how to beg Charlotte to forgive him for exposing her to gossip. And how to beg her to forgive him for not making her his wife months ago, when he first fell in love with her.

Thirty-One

"William." Lady Derringer accosted him as soon as he returned home. "Mr. Johnson was just here, and he said he wanted to know if you and Miss Robbins had some kind of understanding, as he'd heard a rumor that you'd given her a fortune and that was how she was able to live in London."

"He had no right to ask you that." Heat rose into his forehead.

"Apparently he has asked Charlotte to marry him, and he felt it was too indelicate a question to ask a lady."

He hated the way his aunt toggled her eyebrows at him. But even more, he hated that Johnson had asked Charlotte to marry him. How did he dare ask such a woman to be his wife? She was too gentle and kind-hearted and empathetic. The weight of the responsibility for caring for so many children, of pushing herself the way Johnson did and being in charge of an entire orphanage, would be too much for her gentle, sweet spirit.

"What did you tell him?"

"I told him no, that you two do not have an understanding or an arrangement or anything of the kind, and that he should not believe every rumor he hears."

His heart was beating in his ears.

"When was he here?"

"Less than a half hour ago."

He turned and strode out the door. As he did, he saw Johnson leaving Charlotte's townhouse, putting on his hat, and walking the other way.

He saw Charlotte's face, how she'd looked the first few days after she came to Lowndesbury House, a schoolgirl-turned-teacher, a poor orphan who didn't seem to realize she was poor. Her very presence in the world made life more bearable.

He couldn't lose her.

It was like a lightning bolt to his soul—he'd been a fool not to ask her to marry him. Now it might be too late.

Mr. Johnson left, and I sank back against the sofa. I was alone, having allowed Gabriel Johnson a private meeting with me, knowing it would be relatively short.

How many marriage proposals had I refused?

I hadn't expected to get another one after I lost my fortune. My days of flirtation and proposals seemed over.

I'd seriously considered marrying Gabriel Johnson. He was handsome, moral, and decent, but the thought of being his wife felt . . . oppressive somehow. Perhaps I was being ridiculous, overly sensitive, selfish even, to refuse Gabriel Johnson's proposal. Would I regret it?

I wasn't sure how I could financially care for Joshua and Sarah or how I'd be allowed to adopt them on my own, without a husband. But if there was a way, I'd find it.

The servant announced Lord Brookhaven.

I stood up quickly, just in time to see Lord Brookhaven enter looking slightly disheveled. His cravat was askew, and his hair was sticking up as though he'd been raking his hand through it.

We greeted each other, then he paced to one side of the room. I'd never seen that expression on his face before. Then he paced toward the other side but stopped in front of me—and fell to one knee.

"Miss Robbins, I've been a fool. Can you forgive me?"

I wasn't sure how to reply, but he only paused a moment before continuing.

"Please tell me you still feel as you did when we were at Lowndesbury House. You said in your letter that you cherished our friendship and missed our talks, that you thought there was something tender and beautiful between us—and there was. I was just too much of a fool to tell you. Instead I invited people to my home who were your inferiors, people who didn't appreciate you for who you are."

My head was spinning. I forced myself to keep listening, my eyes locked intently on his face.

"I know I don't deserve you. I've deceived you and turned your life upside down, exposed you to criticism and gossip. I never should have done any of it. I was wrong to do it, but please tell me you're not marrying Mr. Johnson. Oh, I know he appears to be the perfect husband for you, but please say you did not engage yourself to him. I don't believe he could ever love and cherish you as much as I do or as you deserve."

His face was so very dear, so intense and contrite. I could hardly believe what he was saying. Was I dreaming?

"You love me?" I asked.

"I've been in love with you since you stood on the roof that first night and coaxed me to come inside with you. You said you were lost and couldn't find your way back to your room. Do you remember?"

"I do remember." My hands were clasped in my lap, but I moved one toward him. I'm not sure what I planned to do. I certainly couldn't touch his face or smooth his hair back, as I wanted to do.

"But it was I who was lost, I who needed help finding my way."

He grabbed my hand and held it between his, then kissed my knuckles.

The feel of his lips on my skin sent shivers across my shoulders and stole my breath. If this was a dream, I didn't want to wake up.

My voice sounded breathy and strange as I said, "I . . . I told Mr. Johnson that I couldn't marry him. I refused him."

Lord Brookhaven closed his eyes, his shoulders visibly relaxing.

When he opened them, he said, "I know I'm not a good man, not like Johnson. He has dedicated himself to caring for orphans."

I opened my mouth, trying to think how to express what I'd been thinking and feeling.

"You don't have to explain. I know I'm not worthy of you, and I know I should have spoken sooner, should have asked you to marry me a hundred times before now, but if you will have me, if you think you could love me, please say you will marry me."

The look in his eyes, intense and vulnerable, made my stomach flip. He was still holding my hand, but I lifted my other hand and pressed my palm to his cheek.

His gaze never left mine.

I realized he was waiting for an answer. I drew in a quick breath.

"I will marry you. And yes, I love you. I love you so very much."

I barely got the words out before he leaned forward and covered my mouth with his.

I'd never been kissed before. The sensation was strange, intimate, warm, exciting.

My heart soared. He loved me. And he was kissing me.

When he pulled away and I opened my eyes, he was gazing down at me with such a tender expression, his arms holding me close. I felt as though I'd been captured, mesmerized by his dear face. I didn't want to move or do anything that would break the spell.

He said in a gruff voice, "I promise I'll always love you and care for you. You shall never be lonely or alone again. You may have whatever your heart desires, if it is in my power to give it to you."

"Your love, your conversation, that is all I want. And to adopt the children."

"Joshua and Sarah?"

"Yes."

"Of course we will adopt them. That is easy."

I pulled him closer, and he kissed me again.

His lips on mine made every other thought leave my head, except for the hazy idea that it was good that he was holding me so tight, because his kiss made my knees weak.

When the kiss ended, I suddenly couldn't meet his eye. I pressed my face against his shoulder. Our arms were already around each other, but his tightened, and I could feel his breath in my hair and his chin brushing my ear.

"Forgive me for my unorthodox ways," he said in a deep voice. "I know I'm not worthy of you, especially after all that I've put you through, but I promise to endeavor to be a better man, to treat you as you deserve. Will you be patient with me?"

I didn't have enough breath to laugh, but I lifted my head to look into his eyes. "All is forgiven, and you are already the best man I know."

"You truly do love me, then."

I reached up and touched his face. It was breathtaking to be able to do that small thing, to know that he was to be my very own husband, forever. I'd nearly given up hope. And we would adopt Sarah and Joshua. They would be cared for and would not have to grow up in an orphanage.

Oh, how I loved him.

"People will talk, you know," I said. "I am just a poor orphan, a governess, a nobody. You are an earl."

"When have I ever cared what people say?" He sighed and ran his finger over my lips and across my chin, sending a thrill through me. "I cared only that you wouldn't be hurt by the jealous, gossiping society ladies. I didn't want them to say unkind things about you or make you feel inferior, as you certainly are not inferior in any way. But I should have trusted you not to care about that. That is what I regret."

"We will forget all of that now." I stared at his lips until he kissed me again.

If his kisses continued to get better each time, I would not be able to prevent my knees from buckling.

After the kiss, he cradled my head on his shoulder and said, "But why did you not marry Johnson? He wanted the same things as you—to rescue orphans."

"Yes, but he . . . it is difficult to explain. I suppose the most important reason was—"

He'd leaned back to look at me.

"I was in love with you." I couldn't meet his eye as I bared my soul. "I wanted someone to love me, and he couldn't love me, not in the way . . ." Not in the passionate way I somehow knew Lord Brookhaven would love whomever he chose to love.

I buried my face in his shoulder again. He stroked my hair.

Marrying him was all I needed to be completely happy.

Epilogue

One Year Later
Lowndesbury House

"Mama! Come play with us. Papa is teaching us a new card game." Joshua ran to me and gave baby Colin a quick kiss on the cheek.

"I'll just watch you from here and cheer you on. I have to feed the baby again soon." Colin was only two weeks old, and I'd opted to feed him myself instead of hiring a wet nurse.

Joshua stared at the baby a moment longer, then ran back to the table as William began to deal the cards.

"Remember, don't show your cards to anyone else." My handsome husband winked at me before picking up his own cards and studying them.

I watched them—William, Samuel, Annabelle, Sarah, and Joshua—playing cards, laughing, and talking. And tomorrow, if it stopped raining, they would go out on the lawn and play pall mall. Sarah was becoming quite good and had beaten the rest of her siblings more times than anyone else. William wanted the children to know how it felt to win, so he rarely tried hard. I could play, but the children made the rule that I wasn't allowed to win.

William and I laughed about this in private.

How sweet life was now, surrounded by people who loved me. It wasn't always easy—the children fought and cried and had nightmares, and there were the usual vexations and trials of life, but to no longer be the orphan with no family was better than anything I could imagine.

How wonderful it was to be loved by William. His love healed my heart in ways I hadn't known was possible. His gentleness and goodness toward the children and me gave me a new confidence, instilled me with a profound peace, and even made God's love feel more real than it ever had before. I could literally *feel* God's love now, because I knew what it felt like to be loved deeply and well.

And I saw this effect in William also. He seemed more relaxed, more joyful, and he admitted that he felt a newly invigorated faith that he hadn't felt since he was very young—if ever. There was a quiet joy every Sunday walking home from church with our little brood.

There hadn't seemed to be any repercussions to our marriage, contrary to my fears of bringing shame to him. We had Lady Derringer to champion us, and the fact that my husband was an earl seemed to mostly smooth everything over. But if we ever lived in London again, I suppose we would discover how welcome—or unwelcome—we were in the uppermost social circles.

The orphanage for boys was getting its new roof, funded by the new donors we'd helped secure. And the home for orphaned girls was newly opened in a building not far from the boys' home, funded by the fifty-thousand pounds I had received. So far I had not been directly involved, besides that William and I had overseen the hiring of the director and the other caregivers, including Gretchen, with a handsome increase in pay.

Perhaps someday I would become more involved, but for now I felt God leading me to give as much love and care as I could to the children I already loved so profoundly. And it was enough. It was more than enough.

Discussion Questions

1. What were Charlotte's expectations when she set out for Berkshire and for her position as a governess for the Earl of Brookhaven?
2. What did Charlotte learn about her employer after her first meeting with him? What was her first impression of him?
3. Why were the other servants at Lowndesbury House not very friendly with Charlotte? Why might they have resented her?
4. Why might Samuel and Annabelle have been reluctant to get too close to Charlotte emotionally? What had their experiences with other adults been, including their parents and former governesses?
5. Why do you think Lord Brookhaven decided to have a house party and invite Charlotte, his governess? Why did he need his aunt Lady Derringer's help?
6. What were the reasons behind Lord Brookhaven creating the rather elaborate ruse of Charlotte's inheritance of fifty thousand pounds? Do you think this was a good idea? Why or why not?

7. How were William's and Charlotte's childhoods and circumstances in life different? How were they similar? Did this contribute to them falling in love, or was it more about how well their personalities and values complemented each other?
8. In Regency England, many wealthy people were opposed to helping children who asked for money on the streets, leading to the Vagrancy Act of 1824, which was used to prosecute anyone who begged or slept on the streets. How does the prevailing opinion of our culture and the people around us influence our values? Why do you think Charlotte and William went against what everyone else was telling them about giving Sarah and Joshua up to their "uncle" Gilbert White?
9. Why did Charlotte choose not to be directly involved with running the orphanage so that she could be home with Sarah, Joshua, Samuel, and Annabelle? Have you ever felt torn when you had to choose between two good things?
10. Why do you think it took William so long to admit his feelings for Charlotte? In what ways did his childhood trauma, and the way his fiancée betrayed him, affect how he reacted to falling in love with Charlotte?
11. If you have read *Jane Eyre*, discuss the differences and similarities between the two stories and their characters.

Acknowledgments

I want to thank the wonderful team at Bethany House Publishers for their skill and professionalism, for this opportunity, and for welcoming me so warmly to the team. It has been a true pleasure working with editors Jessica Sharpe and Jennifer Veilleux, as well as Rachael Betz, Emily Vest, Jennifer Parker, and Anna Dwyer. I don't know all the names of all the people who have made the publishing of this book possible and have accomplished each step of the publishing process with such excellence, but I appreciate each and every one of you. Thank you so much!

I want to thank my wonderful family members, Aaron and Faith, who have helped me brainstorm from time to time. You guys are so supportive, and I love you both so much!

I also want to thank my beautiful friend Kathleen Freeman for her friendship, for writing with me, checking in with me, and offering advice and brainstorming help. You are such a great friend and a great writer. Keep writing and believing and inspiring others!

For more from Melanie Dickerson,
read on for a sneak peek from

A Mismatch Made in London

Available Summer 2026 wherever books are sold.

One

I concentrated on putting the finishing touch of red paint on the paper soldier I was making for Matthew. I'd already pasted on the paper hat and jacket, and I waved it in the air to dry.

Matthew ran into the bedroom I shared with two of my sisters. He held up the little sword and the horse I'd made for him earlier. He grabbed the finished soldier out of my hand. "Now my soldier can cut his enemies to ribbons!"

Nathaniel, who was ten, ran into the room holding up a similar horse and rider. "No, you won't! I shall cut *you* to ribbons!"

"Attack!" Matthew cried.

They crashed their paper soldiers into each other, with many battle noises supplied verbally as they each claimed victory over the other.

"'Melia." Diana, who was two years old and always left off the first syllable of my name, toddled into my room with tears on her cheeks.

"What is it, darling?"

I could barely hear myself speak with the ruckus our brothers were making. I picked Diana up and carried her outside. "What's the matter?"

But before she could say another word, little Diana laid her blond head on my shoulder and closed her eyes.

My heart melted at the warm body lying so trustingly against my chest. I lightly kissed her forehead and sank down in the hammock that Father had strung between two trees. I settled my little sister more comfortably in the crook of my arm, then I gazed up through the leaves of the trees, enjoying the way the sunlight filtered and flickered its way through.

Our newborn baby brother had kept me awake for what seemed like hours the night before. I must have been tired, because when I heard someone calling, "Amelia!" I opened my eyes and realized I'd fallen asleep.

Diana was heavy on my arm, sleeping peacefully and drooling, creating a wet spot on my dress.

I raised my available arm and waved to my sister, Lavinia.

"Amelia, there you are. Mama wants you inside," she said, stopping and putting her hands on her hips.

I carefully stood up, trying not to jostle Diana too much, then handed her off to Lavinia, who accepted her very casually, letting her head loll around as if she didn't care if she woke up. But Diana slept on.

"A letter arrived from Aunt Kendall, and Mama wants you inside."

Eight years younger, Lavie was the sister closest in age to me, but our personalities were very different. Sometimes I envied my sister's ability to always seem so sure of herself and never get upset. I was the oldest, and I should be the self-assured one. But I seemed to possess all of Mama's feeling and sensitivity and very little of my sister's calm reason.

It was a bit demoralizing.

"There you are, Amelia." Mother's wide eyes and smile told me it was good news as she shook the letter at me. "Your aunt and uncle have invited you to London for the Season! What do you think of that? I had begun to think that they never would, as you are two-and-twenty now, but thankfully you are still as pretty as you were at sixteen." Her eyes seemed happy and wistful.

She began to speak of new dresses once I reached London while I read the letter, the principle point of which was

We will be at Woodbank on the sixth of March, as Mr. Kendall

must be back for the continuing session of Parliament, and shall take dear Amelia with us, if you can spare her.

Mrs. Kendall was my mother's sister, who had married very well indeed, outdoing both of her sisters when she wed a landed gentleman who'd won a seat in the House of Commons.

I had to admit, my uncle frightened me a bit. When I was a child, it was because he was always so serious and gruff. As I grew older, I understood more about what it meant to be a member of Parliament. I also realized that I was only a country girl from Buckinghamshire, and though my father was a gentleman, he had twelve children to provide for, and therefore my dowry would be quite small.

"You are a lovely girl, and there are many young men who will fall in love with you," Mother was saying, interrupting my reading of the letter, which did not mention me again anyway.

"Are you sure you can spare me? I am needed here. Who will help with the children?"

"Oh, don't worry about that. I can hire another servant. And Lavinia can help more. We shall do very well, though you are my best helper."

I hated to think of baby Diana crying and wondering where I was, for I knew Lavinia would not pay as much attention to her as I did; she would not hold her when she was fretful nor rock her to sleep.

Mother clasped her hands, her eyes darting about the room as she seemed to be thinking about several things at once. "You must flirt, but do it discreetly, and never offend anyone. Protect your reputation at all costs; don't go anywhere alone with a man."

"Of course, Mother. I would never—"

"And take your aunt's advice about who to flirt with and the gentlemen who would be the best catches."

"Very well." I smiled to myself at the thought of flirting with someone just because my aunt told me I should.

I wanted to ask her if it was all right to marry someone who was not so wealthy, and whether I could marry for love, but I stopped myself. After all, I cared about my siblings too much not to at least consider the fact that they would have a much better chance of marrying well if I first married well myself.

Nevertheless, it remained to be seen whether I would sacrifice love in favor of a large fortune. I wasn't sure I could sell myself in that way. Oh, I knew my mother would be horrified, as would every other member of Good Society, if I were to characterize marriage in terms of "selling myself." After all, a lady was expected to marry as well as she could manage, to make the best match in terms of fortune and rank. But I wanted a marriage of love and mutual respect, of romantic attachment and affection. *That* was what I dreamed of, and I wasn't sure I could pretend to love and respect someone who didn't love and respect me.

Certainly I didn't wish to saddle myself with someone who would cause me shame and embarrassment, such as a man who would keep a paramour, or who would say unkind things about me in public, or worst of all, ignore me.

I wasn't supposed to even know about paramours and the immoral behavior of gentlemen, but I read the newspapers, including the gossip columns that I'm sure Mother wouldn't approve of me reading. In truth, sometimes I'd feel a little sick after I read about the goings-on in London among what were supposed to be the best families. But if being knowledgeable about such things kept me from being ignorant and therefore prevented me from making a poor choice, then how could it be wrong? Leastways, I didn't wish to be naïve. Even the Bible told the truth about people's wicked behavior.

And now I was about to be in London, where so many wicked things happened. But I would be under the protection of my aunt and uncle, so I needn't fear anything worse than a broken heart. I hoped.

"Algernon returned to town a week ago, so you will see him right away," Mrs. Kendall said as we traveled in their carriage toward London.

I smiled to show I was listening.

"You two were good friends as children, were you not?"

Mr. Kendall looked up from his paper. The way he kept his head down and let his eyes look over his spectacles made him appear skeptical, although I wasn't sure if that was his intention.

"We were very close in age," I said.

"Yes, close as a brother and sister."

I didn't contradict her, but Algie had been often cross as a child. We did play together sometimes, but more often we quarreled, and Algie ended up sulking and demanding to go home, while I preferred to play with my siblings. As we grew older, we saw each other less frequently, and we became the better friends for it.

I secretly pitied him, as he was an only child, his mother having had several stillbirths, which seemed to put the burden of the family name—and his mother's happiness—squarely on his shoulders.

We arrived in London exhausted but happy—or my aunt and I were. I rarely could sense what Mr. Kendall was thinking or feeling, as he said very little and his expression rarely changed.

I was to have my own room at their London townhouse. I was thrilled at the thought of so much privacy and freedom, but whether from loneliness or the noises in the streets outside my window, I hardly slept at all that first night. How strange to be alone in a room without the heavy breathing of my sisters to lull me to sleep. I'd been to London twice before, but I'd forgotten just how noisy the nights could be.

As I lay awake, I wondered if Diana had been able to fall asleep without me there to rub her back. Would she cry and wonder why I'd abandoned her? Was my baby brother sleeping better tonight, or had he kept everyone awake again with his crying?

These next three or four months were supposed to be filled with pleasant parties, dancing, flirting, and meeting new people. Instead of enjoying it, was I destined to be sad, missing my family and my home?

"This dress will do until the seamstress can finish your new one."

Mrs. Kendall drew out my best dress and held it up to my chin. "Yes, you'll look very well in this if I lend you my cross necklace. I'll send the servant to dress your hair in an hour. In the meantime, I want you to memorize these names—young gentlemen to whom you should pay special attention if you are introduced to them. I will do my best to arrange a meeting."

"Yes, Aunt."

She was looking at me with a mixture of sober intensity and gleeful imagination, as if she were picturing each person as she mentioned them.

"First is Thomas Trowbridge. His family has an enormous estate in Westchester, and he seems eager to find a bride. He'd be an excellent catch, as he is the oldest and only son and so will inherit everything, including his father's title of viscount."

Mrs. Kendall rummaged through my ribbons as she talked, holding up various colors against my hair and the dress.

"And there is the Duke of Pennington, who is not the most handsome, but what of it? He is a duke and has multiple estates, and if you can distract him from the gaming tables, he might be able to keep all of them. In truth, he's already lost a small fortune and can't seem to help himself, but some of the other lords have been trying to prevent him from losing any more of his inheritance. After all, his is a very old family, and one needs to preserve the stability of the lands and inheritances. Mr. Kendall and I both feel that if he had a wife—both his parents are dead, you see—then he'd stop spending all his time at the club."

Thank you, Aunt Kendall, for thinking I might save a man from his gambling habit and therefore do my part to save England's nobility. But being foisted off on a man who couldn't control himself was not an ambition of mine. I *was* thankful she told me about his character flaw.

I smiled and nodded, encouraging her to go on.

"There is Lord Ogden's son, Cornelius Fortescue. He is the oldest and is quite charming. He only has one sister, who is married, and his mother has already passed away and so you'd have no competition, if you know what I mean. I like him very much for you, and I've heard he will be at the ball tonight."

Cornelius Fortescue. I'd try to remember him as a favorable possibility.

"There are a few others—Walter Barnstable, Lord Sandringham, and Morgan Elkins. But the one that everyone will be after is Jeremy Beaumont. Remember that name, Beaumont."

"What is so special about Jeremy Beaumont?"

"You will see." Aunt Kendall had a knowing smirk as she closed my box of ribbons and jewelry, having chosen what she wanted out of it.

"Is he handsome?"

"Young and very handsome, good manners, and a charming smile. He is as wealthy as the Duke of Pennington, and best of all, he is not fond of the gaming clubs or of drinking and carousing. Rather, he is known for his high morals and his fondness for his sisters. He has no parents—they have both passed on—so he has no one to interfere and may marry as he pleases. He seems to have become the favorite not only of all the marriageable young ladies, but also of their mothers. He will be difficult to catch, but . . ."

Mrs. Kendall lifted my chin with her finger and stared at my face, as if taking in each of my features one at a time. It was all I could do not to squirm.

"You could catch Jeremy Beaumont, I think, with your sweet, innocent looks and pretty features." She dropped her hand and stepped away from me, saying cheerfully, "It doesn't hurt to try. Someone will get him, and it may as well be you."

New York Times bestselling and two-time Christy Award–winning author **Melanie Dickerson** writes happily-ever-after romance. With over one million books sold, her readers trust her books to inspire hope, faith, and love—especially the kind with a fairy-tale-worthy end. When she's not writing, Melanie can be found watching *Pride and Prejudice* for the hundredth time, going on hikes to see caves and waterfalls with her handsome hero husband, and shaking her head at her slightly unhinged Jack Russell Terrier. She lives in the beautiful foothills of the Appalachians near Huntsville, Alabama.

Sign Up for Melanie's Newsletter

Keep up to date with Melanie's latest news on book releases and events by signing up for her email list at the website below.

MelanieDickerson.com

FOLLOW MELANIE ON SOCIAL MEDIA

Melanie Dickerson

@MelanieDickerson123